The S
We Cast

Sarah Tinsley

SRL Publishing Ltd

SRL Publishing Ltd
Office 47396, PO Box 6945
London
W1A 6US

First published worldwide by SRL Publishing in 2022

Copyright © SARAH TINSLEY 2022

The author has reserved their right to be identified as the author of
this work which has been asserted by them in accordance with the
Copyright, Designs and Patents Act 1988.

ISBN: 978-18382798-7-5

1 3 5 7 9 10 8 6 4 2

This book is sold subject to the condition that it shall not, by way of
trade or otherwise, be reproduced or transmitted in any form or by
any means electronic, mechanical, photocopying, or otherwise,
without the prior permission of the publishers.

This book is a work of fiction. Names, characters, places and
incidents are either a product of the author's imagination or are used
fictitiously. Any resemblance to actual people, living or dead, events
or locales, is entirely coincidental.

A CIP catalogue record for this book is available from the British
Library.

SRL Publishing is a Climate Positive publisher, removing more
carbon emissions than it emits.

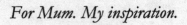

For Mum. My inspiration.

Nina

Now

Nina is deep in the sofa when the doorbell rings. Hitting pause on her laptop, she stills. It makes her feel like an intruder. An entire day spent in his flat while he's at work. Is he expecting someone?

When he left this morning, he hadn't let her get out of bed. Insisted she stayed there, brought tea and her phone. There was breakfast waiting when she finally got up. How long has it been since she slept a whole night without shadowed dreams? Since the first thing she felt on waking wasn't sharp panic? "Too independent for your own good," mum always said. Now she has help. Support. Someone on her side.

The bell goes again. If they see the glow of the laptop through the window, they might not go away. She clicks it shut, paused on the opening credits of *Queer Eye*. It has kept her buoyed up all day. She hasn't even got dressed yet. There were a pair of scrappy pyjama bottoms lying on the floor next to his bed and she's still got her hoodie. She was going to head back to her place, get a change of clothes, tidy up, think about what might come next. It felt like too much after everything that happened at the weekend. Better to rest. It's not like she had anywhere to go on a Monday morning.

It rings again. This time a hand rattles the letter box. Maybe it's his sister? He said something about her when they were lying in bed chatting last night. Some career type. She'd hardly be banging the door down at 3:30pm if she were like that.

Nina sits up, letting the blanket fall away. There's a cluster of crumbs where she's been slumped and snacking. Some of the old anxiety creeps in. Her skin prickles from the cold, away from the safety of the blanket. This time yesterday she was still in the police station. All those questions. What if she let something slip? She was so tired. Maybe they've found out what she's been doing all this time. But how would they know she was here?

She pulls her feet up underneath her. Unless he was in on it too. They were friends, after all. This could all be a ploy, something to get her to relax, confess.

Her name this time, shouted through the letterbox. She sags with relief. Teachers are slackers, everyone knows that. He must have come home early and forgotten his keys. Shaking her head to dislodge the paranoia, she walks down the hall. A ruffle of her hair is all she has time for – he's seen her in worse states.

'Did you get out early?' She sweeps the door wide. Too late, she realises the wrong face is waiting on the other side.

The sight of him is physical. Nina steps back, the last bit of Hobnob bouncing up her throat.

'He's not here.' She shields herself with the door.

'I know.' That face. So much of her energy absorbed by this man. 'I want to talk to you.'

'Go away.' She tries to sound forceful.

'The things you've said about me. It has to stop.' He steps closer. She remembers ginger beer, rum, his mouth.

'Leave me alone.' She pushes the door. It hits against

2

something soft – his foot, wedging it open.

'You still think I did it, don't you?' His face was so close. She looks around the unfamiliar hallway. There must be keys, something she can use as a weapon.

'If you don't leave, I'll call the police.' She makes the words loud. Maybe a neighbour will hear.

'Because that worked so well before, didn't it?' So self-satisfied.

'He'll be home soon,' she says. Horrible to admit she needs help.

'Oh yes, I can just see him putting me in my place.' He shakes his head.

'You're a bully.' If she can't shut him out she can tell him what she thinks. No violence this time.

'People think I'm a monster.' He almost looks convincing. If you don't know what he's done.

'It's what you deserve.'

His head tips, gaze travelling down her body.

'I just don't see the appeal. Smart woman like you.' What a prick.

'He's kind.' That's what she needs. Someone to help her out of this mess.

'Perhaps you deserve each other.' He moves his foot. Now's her chance. 'If you can stomach being with someone like that.' Something like disgust in his voice.

'What do you mean?' Her hand is on the door, ready to shut it in his face.

'Appearances. Not what they seem, all that crap,' he shrugs.

'We're not all shallow like you.' She leans forward, her voice a whisper. 'You will pay for what you did to me.' She hisses the last word out between a chink of the closing door. He's too fast. The door lurches out of her hand, bangs against the wall.

'Now listen here-' He steps forward, grabbing her

wrist.

She needs to fight back. Kick him, run away, anything. But it comes back. That awful paralysis. Like that night, five weeks ago, when she cowered in the dark, waiting for it to be over.

'Leave me alone.' It comes out as a pathetic whisper.

'I've had enough of this.' He barges in, slamming the door behind him. Pushes her up against the wall. 'We're going to sort this out.'

Trapped between his hands, she's taken back to the rumpled bed of a stranger, her throat closing in panic.

4

Eric

After

He sits on the bed, worrying his hands. The recent exertion has left him breathless, a heavy ache between his legs. That flush when you know your cheeks are pink. His pulse is a train-click.

On the back of the door is a calendar; a dog wearing a Santa hat, the front legs dressed up so it looks like a short fat Father Christmas with a massive canine face. He tucks his shirt back in, pulls the cuffs down. The stretched darkness of winter has always grated on him. That blank, white-skied space before spring arrives. It's been January for over three weeks. Depressing to be reminded of Christmas. Unless this date will become important. A first, even if it's not the way he's used to starting.

The hum of the party downstairs reasserts itself. Anyone could have walked in. He didn't check for a lock, put a chair behind the door. He looks around the room – like the spare one at Nan's house, none of the furniture matching. Some fake pine shelves and a white desk with a partitioned mirror on it. A strange place for something like this.

A glimpse of her, behind him in the angled glass. It's always awkward, afterwards. But usually there's at least some conversation. It looks like she's gone straight to sleep. Understandable, it was pretty full-on.

Imagine if someone had walked in. He could have at least tied his belt around the shelves and the handle. He pats down the tuft of hair at the back of his head, trying to dislodge the problem of locking the door. What is he supposed to do now? Nothing was said, it just happened. Maybe there were people that did things like this all the time.

It will look suspicious, how long he's been missing. Someone might have seen him loping up here, intentions so sound. He'd just come up to check she was ok, that was all. There was shouting after she'd gone upstairs with Will. He'd gone to Mojos, to find a "less mental one," he'd said. She never came back down. He checks his watch. Only 2:15. How can such a small number of minutes have passed? The back of his neck prickles, there's sweat on the short hairs.

He scrubs a hand over the skin, trying to remember how it escalated. One moment there was silence and darkness, his hands unsure. The way she was lying, so open and available to him. Then this heat and pressure, a need he didn't know he had in him. Had she felt it too? Somewhere in it all he got muddled. She'd made a noise, over and over. That was a good sign, it had to be. He's never been left trembling like this before. Not even with Bea. Could he ask for her number? He can't imagine how you'd assemble that sentence once you'd already shared so much.

The others will be settled in, those who've decided, or been forced through lack of success, to stay. Slouching around sodden ashtrays, concocting drinks with sour dregs. It's not the place for him, usually. Scuttling out before the drinking dares start, or his friends abandon him. Whichever comes first. Certainly not the one left with the girl. That was always Will.

He makes himself turn around, acknowledge the prone shape behind him. A heap of clothes and hair slumped under a stray coat. It seemed important that she wasn't cold. Her handbag sits on the floor. Of course, he could ask Will her name, if he had her number. But that would seem weird. She'd been kissing Will earlier in the kitchen, and now this. Maybe she's pretending to be asleep. It might be embarrassing, that she let those things happen with a stranger. Hopefully, that won't get in the way of seeing her again. He rummages in the bag and finds a driving licence tucked in a side pocket. He takes a photo. Just so he can find her again, maybe talk to her when it's less immediate.

He still feels slick in his pants. The sensation wets his mouth – stale beer, something metallic in his throat. It could be the taste of her.

A movement underneath the green fabric; twitching fingers. His hands had been pressed down on them, just a few minutes ago. It made him think of Bea – how angry he'd been when Will told him that she'd cheated on him. All those heartfelt tears a few weeks ago and she'd been carrying on behind his back. With his best mate. How unoriginal. The wind flutters at the curtains – a white shape at the window. So quiet. He'd made noises too, he was sure of it. People might have heard.

He has to leave, be normal, resume his hollow conversation with the sofa accountants. Somehow his legs don't move, and he sits there far longer than he should, staring at the door handle, trying to think of the best way he could have locked it.

Nina

It's important to make it across the office without talking to anyone. On the cusp of the swishing doors, she maps out a route. Too far into sales and Harris will berate her with his weekend, but too far the other way and Tom will find a sarcastic way of flirting. A weaving motion through the middle is the only option. Risky, as Dev would sulk for the rest of the day without a greeting, but it's still pretty early, odds are he hasn't made it in yet.

Head down, she begins her assault on the carpet. Too quick for the HR lot, wallowing around the kitchen like it's a watering hole. Mondays never start quickly for them.

There's a clear gap between the partitions at this end of Sales. But then, the looming size of Brian. The gap behind his chair is small, but he seems safely amused by something on his phone, either that or he's checking up his nostrils.

Speed is the only way. Nina turns her body at the approach, slips through the gap and is away, taking a sharp left towards the comfort of the other engineers, a missed comment falling to the floor behind her.

Last bit. Dev's space is thankfully empty, a few other milling bodies – they've been avoiding her more in the last couple of weeks. Her presence makes them think of deadlines now. That should dissuade conversation. The haven of her glass door is just a few steps away.

There's a smudge on the gilt of her name plaque, but she can't bring herself to raise a hand to wipe it smooth. Nina slips through the door, wearied by the smallest part of her day.

Secreted behind her desk, she is safe. Unreachable. Coming here should have made it better, a distraction from the dreams that left her blunt and smudged. She feels like an echo.

She writes the phrase on a post-it, a three-word sentence, then tucks it away in the bottom tray, the place for things that don't need attention. The desk is unchanged – her gold cat perched on the far corner, waving through the glass wall. The movement through it is detached, like events on a screen.

There must be something different. Being here usually brings relief. Nothing of that lightness this morning. She checks the filing cabinet. Everything is alphabetical, colour-coded, her emergency stash of cola bottles in the bottom drawer. In her rush to get out of the door, she forgot to bring anything for lunch. Another social hurdle – the sandwich van. The smell of coffee and disinfectant wipes from the previous inhabitant is gradually succumbing to her Juicy Fruit chewing gum and Tippex. She touches each item, turning the stapler to the left, unable to find the thing that is out of place.

"Should have gone straight to the police," that's what Holly would say. Not something she could face yesterday; a grey Sunday morning, skin prickling with alcohol residue and something else that crawled in her stomach. It's pointless to go there until she's sure what happened. Can present a clear and detailed account. Otherwise, why would they take her seriously?

9

Her reflection is an unwanted ghost behind the screen display. She peels off another slip of paper, adds a detail:

The window was open, two half-empty drinks on the shelves.

It is buried with the other. Now to work.

She usually leaves the door open. It gives the illusion that she wants to listen to others, doesn't think she's better. Of course, it also means putting up with the endless clicking of retractable pencils from Tom's desk and the "actioning" that Sai blurts into his phone, despite her polite reminder that, as a verb, it should only be used in the passive voice.

She pulls up her schematics, looks over the test results. Her creation. That's the best bit – the mini version in the test area that she puts under a range of pressures, temperatures. This project is deliciously hers, a unique prototype vessel heading out to the arctic. This is different to their commercial stuff. She's doing something worthwhile. The congratulations card from Dad is still on the desk. She's a part of something big. Something more than how alone she felt yesterday.

She scribbles a few numbers, a sketch of the boat the way she imagines it – not the functional thing it will be. Her version is a funnelled steam ship, a small figure leaning out over the edge.

Another note, another detail:

My shoes were stacked in a corner, one toe slipped inside the other.

The pile grows. It's impossible to concentrate.

'You ready?' Dev is clearly in meeting mode – a shirt, even if it is creased, his trusty pad in one hand.

'Of course.' They were supposed to be in the

conference room at 9, how could she have forgotten? She grabs the project folder, a notebook, a blue and red pen.

'Let's do it.' He leaves, all efficiency in his shoulders. That's usually her. It's odd to feel flustered. On the way out, she snatches the post-it pad, just in case.

'Right, gang, time to get to it.' Clive isn't wearing a tie today. His collar is open – he must have read somewhere that it made him look more approachable. He nods and smiles at each of them as they go in, like the dog in the Churchill adverts.

'First, I want updates.' He perches on the side of the table rather than sitting down. 'Let me know how it's going, before we move onto the Challenge of the Week.' You can hear the capitalisation in his intonation, the movement of his eyebrows.

Dev turns to a new page, starts to scribble. Last week was a goldfish bowl, Clive the Carp bigger and grumpier than the other fish. It could be taken as enthusiasm, if you didn't look too closely.

It's always Sales and Marketing first. Their ability to stretch out two points over twenty minutes means there's plenty of time before it's her turn.

Her fingers feel restless. She usually plans the tasks for the day, sorts out what to have for dinner, her whole week organised behind a facade of interest. Today she can't sit still. She can feel the pull of it; Saturday night, the party, yesterday morning. It can't be allowed to intrude here.

Hole in my tights, the ladder went all the way down to the left knee.

She hides the post-it, lets her pen wander on a clean page. Nina wastes her concentration on assigning a geometric shape to each person. Dev is a tetrahedron – his warmth reflecting out at all angles. Clive is a parallelogram –

unaware he is bent at an angle. Nina is a trapezium – the lines unequal, meeting in points. She makes the corners thicker, sharp arrows. The drone to her left stops. That was quick.

'So now it's on to the technical stuff – try to stay awake everyone.' The same joke, every time.

The words drop out of her mouth, even and measured. She's always been able to absorb and recite specifications – exams more of an exercise in repetition than a chore. Her need to be the most informed person in the room is an asset today. Systematic, that's how her PhD supervisor described her in the report. There's just one thing she needs to justify.

'The most sensitive part is the coupling. No point in putting all these fiddly measuring devices on board if they're going to wobble around.' She doesn't look over at Tom from Finance. He's bound to start making noise. 'Our testing has shown that we need a slightly different mechanism.' Keep it evidence-based, make it easy to understand. 'For example, when we measured wind speed in the test area, the rattling from the cheaper attachments meant that it could have been anything from 10-12 knots. Obviously, if we're going to help our investors save those polar bears, we're going to need to provide something a little more accurate.' Clive obliges her with a laugh. 'This will be more expensive, but I'm happy to cover that part in my presentation.' Agree to take the fallout in advance, nothing they can say then.

'We've never had a problem before. Didn't our last vessel have the standard ones?' Trust Tom to have actually paid attention.

'As I just said, this project is different, so it needs something more delicate.' She tries to keep the irritation out of her voice.

'We're already way over budget. Dev, what do you

think? Is this somewhere we could make savings?' Clive always asks Dev, he can't just take her word for it. She grinds the pen into the dents made by her lines.

'Don't ask me. Nina knows what she's talking about.' Dev smiles at her.

'Fine.' Tom taps away on the tablet in front of him. So now she has male support, he'll actually listen.

Her fingers worry at the paper on the notepad, rolling shreds into little balls. There's a twinge at the base of her spine. Maybe it's the seat – if she's hunched over it will hurt her back. She fiddles with the plastic tab underneath, enjoying the bounce as she gets the height right, the gulp of vertigo before it falls.

Her stomach, yesterday morning. That room. She'd woken up there around four. A slippery green coat thrown over her. All that rum, her head was throbbing with it. Then the pieces of the night, clicking together. How she'd become aware of unwanted hands, through the fog of alcohol. She flips through, finds a pink slip.

Round bruise at the top of my left arm.

The murmuring around her has stopped. Faces are turned to her, expectant.

'Would February the 25th work for you?' Clive's expression is taut.

'That isn't what we agreed.' Her voice sounds too loud. That cuts all the testing back by two weeks.

'Yes, that's why we're discussing it now.' She doesn't need to give him an excuse to berate her.

'The engine isn't nearly as complex as Nina's instruments, and I'm not sure we can float the presentation that soon.' Dev grins. 'We need to keep fishing for errors, it would be terrible if this company didn't take the bait.' He draws three ticks on his pad.

13

Fishing references, that's what they were supposed to squeeze in today.

'I would have thought the person with a First from Cambridge could make it work.' Clive's false smile doesn't reach his eyes.

'It's a matter of stringent tests and adjustments. That takes time.' She will not be pulled into his goading. Engineering wasn't mentioned at her comprehensive on Careers Day. She knew people must build and design things, but didn't know the word for it. The man with the clipboard simpered when she'd mentioned Cambridge. She tried to convince herself that it wasn't because she was a girl with a northern accent who couldn't afford the best trainers. Her recommendation came back with "Office Work." She'd taped it to her wall as motivation during revision.

'I'd hate to go back to them with a negative at this point.' Clive leaves it dangling, looking round for someone who won't disappoint him.

'It's all in the report. They can read it if they like.' Nina flicks through the pages she's assembled so far. These lines are hers. The numbers, the calculations. Something that was there on Friday is still here today.

'Seems like you've thought of everything.' Clive looks back at his desk. She's won, for now.

'Don't worry,' she says, turning to Dev, 'we can tackle it together.' She allows herself a smile. Dev ticks his pad next to her. Nothing has changed. She can leave what happened behind her and move on.

Bodies are cluttered around the van, the wash of faint sunshine drawing out more people than usual. After buying a sandwich, she hides at the edge, looking out over the grey car park.

'You not hungry?' She turns, bracing herself.

'Miles away.' It's just Dev.

'How's your end going?' he says.

'Perky. You?'

'There's no man alive that better understands the noisy things underneath boats.' He smiles around his falafel.

'Yeah, but without all the wobbly bits I'm sticking on top, it's useless.' She picks the lettuce out, biting the ends.

'Strong words as ever, Franklin. At least I'm able to climb aboard the thing we're designing.'

'These feet weren't made for floating.' She remembers herself a little.

'What about the Carp this morning?' He squeezes out the sides of his cheeks with his hands. 'We can't spend money making things work. What are you thinking, Nina?'

'You were such a suck-up,' she says. 'Smiling and making 'oh-yes-very-interesting' noises. I saw what you were drawing.'

'My best yet.' It was Clive the Carp at the end of a fishing line, a hook caught in one cheek. 'Good weekend?'

'Yes. Great. Brilliant.' Far too enthusiastic. She takes a big bite, nods at him, willing him to take over, start telling her about welding or archery or whatever weird thing him and Amy got up to over the weekend, while she was piecing herself back together.

'What did you do?' He's expectant, no chance of getting out of it.

'Holly organised a thing, a belated celebration for the promotion, being in charge of the project.' Holly went all out. Balloons around the table, a Nina-at-work quiz, cocktails. Then that group of lads that invited them to the party. Trust Holly to be distracted by male attention.

15

The tall guy with sandy hair who made her drinks in the kitchen. Took her upstairs. She digs her nails into her palm.

'Sore head yesterday?' Such a simple question.

'Right.' It comes out as a gasp. She'd yelled at the him when he'd made his intentions clear, told him to bugger off. That should have been the end of it.

Dev is looking at her strangely. Something has shifted. She feels stuck outside herself.

'You ok?' It must show, then. She must be tainted by it.

'Think I'm old enough to handle my drink. Not all of us think pissing in plant pots at the Christmas do is funny.' She didn't mean to snap. Anything to take his concern away from her.

'Alright, grandma.' He shrugs. This is who she is now, someone who can't respond to innocuous questions.

'You?' It must be possible to avoid talking about yourself.

'We made sushi.' He laughs. 'Well, attempted it. Not sure tinned tuna and risotto rice counts but it tasted ok.'

'I think Sakura is looking for a new chef.' That was the first time they'd spent time together outside the confines of the office. Dev and Amy had just moved in together, Nina had invited Holly but she'd been embroiled in the start of another fated romance. They'd drank too much sake and made equations out of the sushi.

'You're representing us at this gallery thing?' he says. 'I don't see why you need to go along to some modern art exhibition to suck up to our investors. Where does Clive get these ideas?'

'I think it's some kind of penance.' Two tickets, of course, on her desk this morning. At least Holly will make it more interesting. With any luck she'll pretend to be Australian for the whole night, like she did at the last funding event.

'We'll be in Morocco.' He grins.

'That is completely unfair,' she says. Their delayed honeymoon, after spending way more than expected on the wedding.

'Amy's so excited.' He gets an extra eye crinkle in his smile whenever he says her name. 'You sure you're ok?' Her face must look wrong.

'Oh absolutely. You get to have sweaty sex and cocktails while I have to stare at an installation put together by some nutter.' Her chest contracts, it feels harder to smile. She keeps chatting between bites, pulling out conversation threads to breaking point. Laughing, nodding, like you're supposed to.

'My dream team!' Clive wades awkwardly through the collected staff. His arms are spread wide, so he has to turn and slide, clenching his shoulders to get through them. As he gets closer, it's clear his outburst came a little early. He advances, puppet-like, the sustained smile straining at the edges. Finally he arrives, segments himself between them, a damp hand on her shoulder. 'This is the biggest project we've ever had, gang.' He nods, keeps nodding. A response is expected.

'Right behind you, chief,' says Dev.

'Absolutely.' She tries not to spray him with mayonnaise.

'They're still pushing for a presentation on the 25th.' Totally unfair of him to bring it up now.

'I don't think we'll be ready.' Dev doesn't fit under his arm.

'Nina won't be phased by a little thing like that, will you?' Flat out, getting it in the right condition to present to the investors is going to be tough. But if not, she'll be the one that couldn't handle it. She can't face that image of herself.

'Absolutely not.' Extra hours, working weekends, it can be done. Anything but admit she can't do it.

'Keep it up, gang.' Clive pats Dev several times on the back, then hurries off as if he's forgotten something.

'Chief? Jesus, I couldn't keep a straight face,' she says.

For the rest of lunch, the image of his hand lingering on Dev's shoulder refuses to fade, like sun spots.

*

The office feels hotter than usual. She runs a finger around the collar of her shirt, pulls the bunched-up material out of her armpits. Just one more, so she can focus:

A clump of my hair on the bed, next to the pillow.

This is ridiculous, she won't get anything done. She takes the pile of post-its through to the cupboard in the back. There's a whiteboard in there, the stuff she'll need to present in a few weeks. Nina puts the first one at the top, then lines the others up underneath. More than fifteen, little snippets of her confession.

The white curtains were open – someone could've seen.
My handbag was open, not sure if I left it like that.

Testing, that might help. The weight of things in her hands, controlled by her. She could go down to the test area, run a few simulations. But that would mean the risk of someone talking to her, asking how her weekend was.

For Christmas, when she was seven, she got her first set of Technic Lego. She lined up the nubs of grey plastic, the levers, wheels, and wires. That comforting snap when you put the pieces together. They all watched as the truck made its way around the plastic Christmas tree that had one branch sellotaped back on where the cat broke it. That was back when Kelly was obsessed with those creepy animals with clothes on. Her little sister enthused over a tiny set of shelves, a miniature porcelain toilet.

The flush on Sunday morning. The first time she saw the angry splash of her blood on the tissue as it broke apart in the water. Nina looks over her notes. The board is barely visible, papered with her confessions. She traces her fingers over them, adjusting, trying to assemble them into time order.

Woke up without my pants on.

Her hands move faster, it's important that everything is here. It should be documented. Nina shuffles the neon slips, placing them right next to each other, erasing all the white gaps. At the top, like a heading, is the first one she wrote this morning:

You were raped.

19

Eric

His attention slips halfway down the register: Franklin, Lisa, the girl with the snotty nose and butterflies on her shoes. The drone of 'Good Morning' stops. A couple of faces turn to him. They're spaced out, their red jumpers speckling the carpet. Knees are jutted out at angles, bouncing with start-of-day enthusiasm.

Lisa blinks at him, scrubbing a sleeve under her nose. Nina Franklin. Lisa has brown hair. They could be related. Was she someone's mum? Her house was only fifteen minutes away from his in the car.

He'd spent most of yesterday Googling her name, trying to find out more about her. There were over thirty on LinkedIn, most without pictures. Twitter wasn't much help either. Another late night, the red eyes couldn't be hidden today. He gave up when he realised it was one in the morning and he was scrolling through pictures of the fifteenth Facebook match, trying to see if he could recognise her.

The bell will go soon. He rushes through the rest of the list, cutting them off before they can greet him with their thin voices. At least with the Greek project underway it's okay to get the clay out first thing on a Monday morning. Aprons and splattering water will make a mess, but far easier than their usual plod through the numeracy syllabus. He won't have to sit under their gaze. It doesn't feel right with scrolling images of this girl in his head.

He drags out the tables, leaves the children huddled around their misshapen attempts from last time. The template they'd used was a standard amphora, curved neck and matching teapot handles. Some are lumpy and squat, some stretched out and thin. The bulges are disturbing. Everything looks obscene.

Sophie wails. He hurries over. Lester is poking her with the wooden stick they have for shaping the clay.

'Lester. That's not how we communicate.' Eric sits him in the quiet corner and tends to Sophie's despair with a sticker. There's something animal that they tried to educate out of them. It clearly hasn't worked on him.

'Sir?' A waving hand.

'Yes, Jason?'

'My dad says there's a way you can kill someone using only a pen.'

'Let's remember to keep our words suitable for the classroom.'

There are sniggers. It was better when Jason kept showing him pictures of the rabbits they bred in the garden. Heads are bowed, he decides to ignore the splattering of water on plastic from the Acorns table. It will wipe clean.

Even once he went to bed, his eyes were aching from all the screen staring. It had taken ages to get to sleep. He could see her legs, bent at right angles like a doll. The hidden strength his fingers held. He'd never understood when people said it was animalistic. For him, he'd always wanted it to be special, a communication of something. Especially with Bea. He'd get annoyed with her when she told him it was 'fun' afterwards. Something so intense had to mean something. He had to think of a way to see her again.

Leaning over a particularly wilted vase, voices arrive in the hall. They rise to a babble, moving towards his door. He sneaks his head out to see what's going on.

A bunch of people grouped around the door to the kitchen area, most of the staff from the Keystage 2 group. He glances back at 3B. It's non-toxic, they'll be fine. Walking over, bodies part. He stands in the doorway next to the dark-haired teacher that doesn't speak to anyone.

In the kitchen, Kirsty sits in the corner, one hand clasped over her eye.

'So there was a bit of an accident?' Foggert is here, it must be serious. She's fussing round Kirsty, sitting her down.

'I was leaning over to pick up the flashcards. He came right at me.' Kirsty's voice is muffled.

'Maybe he was running and didn't see you.'

'He said, "fuck you" and swung his fist in my face.' There's muttering behind him. Foggert goes to the sink and douses a paper towel, leaving slaps of water on the floor as she returns. Kirsty looks at it. 'What are you going to do?' It drips front of her.

'Well.' Foggert looks round, stopping at him. He should have waited at the back, overheard this news somewhere else. Now he's going to be involved. 'Eric can watch your lot, can't you Eric? We'll put a TA in with 3B.' Too late. He nods, there's nothing else he can do. 'Then you take the whole afternoon off.' Foggert smiles as if bestowing a gift.

'What are you doing with Perry?' Kirsty grabs the tissue and wedges it against her eye. It's already ballooning out, the skin taut.

'Well, he's having a Time Out with Dean at the

moment.' Foggert is using her assembly voice.

'This is grounds for expulsion.' Kirsty spits the word out.

'Well, it's tricky. First there need to be statements, then there are the governors—'

'The little shit punched me in the face,' Kirsty says.

'He's only six. He probably doesn't understand. You know there are issues at home, it's been a very difficult time for him.'

Such a simple excuse. Tracing things back to a mistake, a lack of something that wasn't provided. Eric weighs this against himself. Is his weekend debauchery a sign that something is wrong with him?

'You're the Head Teacher. I expect support.' Kirsty always told him not to be intimidated by management. It's something he's tried to emulate.

'We'll have a chat about this when you're less emotional. I can even get supply in, give you the rest of the week to recover.' She pats the chair behind Kirsty's shoulder and hurries out. 'I'll pop in and let the TA know,' she says to Eric, nodding.

He's been assigned a sliver of responsibility. He looks longingly at the Clover door, the simplicity of watching over them while they mutilate clay.

Kirsty is stranded, her visible eye reddening. It feels uneven – she's the one that looked after him when he came here four years ago. Eric casts around for something he can do. People wander back to rooms. Surely he can think of something kind to say.

Gilly rushes in and rubs Kirsty's shoulder. Eric spots the kettle and goes to the sink. Some comfort he can provide.

'Hot drink?' The kettle is under the tap before she can answer.

'Problems at home, my arse,' Kirsty sounds better.

'Is he Child Protection?' Gilly asks.

'No idea. He must be totally screwed up.'

'Tea or coffee?' he says.

'Tea, thanks.'

He feels the women watching him as he swirls the teabag. The milk balloons up like a bruise. When he takes the cup over he stares at the sloshing liquid. She takes it, steam muddling into her face.

'Why would he do that to me?' She looks straight at him. The blank confusion in her face is like a rash.

'Can you get her stuff?' Gilly pushes past him. 'And maybe you can have a chat with him. A kid like that, a male face would help.' So now he's being called on to be a role model.

'I've got that meeting for progression straight after school.' He missed the last one, still trying to mop up the mess with Bea.

'Would you? That would be great.' It's like she didn't hear him.

'OK.' He can do this for her, there'll always be next year.

'If you could go and sit with them. They've probably gone feral by now.' She clamps the tissue back in place.

He hurries down the corridor, the walls punctuated with bursts of colour. His limbs feel gangly, like when he was a teenager and his body felt like an oversized costume. The Buttercup door trembles, something rebounding from within. He swings it open. Their faces turn in unison, a communal breath before he is bombarded with questions. He constructs his stern face.

'Sir, what are we doing?' A boy squints up at him.

'Well, right now, we all need to be quiet.' He pushes the air down in his lungs, prepares the voice. 'Ok, let's see fingers!' He stretches his hands up and wiggles, staring meaningfully at the scattered faces that have failed

24

to notice his signal. They mirror him, digits waving. As he drops his hands, theirs fall too, as if attached by strings. Pinned in place by solemn eyes, he can't speak. Their unwavering attention is uncomfortable.

'Sir?' A quiet hand touches his arm. The girl has plaited hair. 'We usually have literacy now, but we could work on our jungle drawings until lunchtime.' Her eyes are absurdly adult. He nods. She gives an accepted signal. The classroom whirs into organised motion. Bodies scurry, each adept at their allotted task. In a matter of seconds, the sound of furious scribbling spreads out. Kirsty is good. He circulates, trying to find something to say about each picture. The girl with the sombre eyes has a bright patchwork of leaves covering most of the paper, intricate veins drawn in contrasting colours. Behind a large blue leaf with orange lines are the eyes of a lurking tiger.

Her house is wedged at the end of a terraced street. He imagined it would be a poky flat, a shared house at the rougher end of the estate. That dress she was wearing – lace on it, barely reached past her bum. Dark hair down her back, bright red lipstick. He thought she must work in a shop, be like those mothers that came to the school gates with too much makeup on and disappointment clutched in their cigarette fingers.

This place looks expensive. Tall bay windows, doors set inside a porch with a tiled archway. Hedges and Audis line the road. She could be married, be someone who went out at the weekend looking for something to liven things up.

Light floods out under the blinds of the downstairs window. He steps back, as if scalded. Of course she's home. It's a Monday evening. She seemed too fun for somewhere like this.

The girl in the kitchen held herself a certain way, a stillness that spoke of comfort in her own skin. He'd never felt like that. To think she'd seen something exciting in him too. That he could be spontaneous and sexy. Maybe she wanted to see him again, enjoyed that sort of thing. Then again, maybe she did it every weekend. He'd be just another conquest.

If she opened the blinds now she would see him, laid bare. He takes one step closer, willing her. Maybe she's having dreams too – tangled darkness drawing him back to that illicit place. Is she thinking about him?

Darkness. He's so close he can hear the snap of the switch. Glancing around, he steps onto the path up to her door. He fishes in his pocket, pulls out the small package. The last present he gave to Bea – a tangle of green stones on a silver bracelet. It's been sat on his window ledge like a memento for too long. He can't just go and talk to her, it would be too awkward. This can be a gesture, something to show how he feels. An encounter in a darkened room, a secret gift. It all feels like some clandestine romance. When he figures out how to talk to her, he can tell her who it's from.

This is ridiculous. They're both adults. There's nothing shameful about wanting to see her again. He reaches up and smacks the knocker twice. His breath catches at his own boldness. If he could be so free with her then, he can do it again.

Footsteps in the hall. He looks down at the package in his hand, up at the blink of light behind the door and runs back into the street. He crouches down behind the first parked car, breathing hard.

The click of the door. He waits for a voice, a question to reach him. Headlights appear at the end of the road. With the hum of the car, he can't hear if she's gone back inside. The lights move closer. He can't stay in the road, the car will hit him, or have to swerve into the line parked down either side. When the lights are almost on him he jumps up, squeezes himself against the front of the nearest car. The door swings closed, a glimpse of a shadow shutting it.

Nina

Nina

Nina lolls over the metal fence, speckles of spray catching her cheek. The pebble-spread beach lies below, sucked by the waves. Despite the chill, a few insulated bodies sweep over the humps with metal detectors, searching for treasures. The wind scours her face with salt, the smell of seaweed sieving her hair. It's a vigorous sort of cleansing. She pulls the sturdy fabric of her leather jacket close, zips it up past her chin so she's cocooned inside.

She couldn't go into work this morning. Once the map of her violation had been spread out on the board she couldn't face sitting back at the desk, tapping at the keys inanely. After gathering them into an envelope, she'd gone to see Clive, faked an illness. Texted that she wasn't feeling any better today. Her first sickie since starting there seven years ago.

Action is needed. Surely that will help her sleep properly, stop the distracted doodling when she's supposed to be working. Only something had called her here. The wash of grey sea was usually a backdrop to her journey home, nothing more. Today she wanted to feel its breath on her, be allowed to feel small.

Stretching away to her right, the line of metal protects bodies from the sea. She walks towards the pier – a bright smudge hovering over the waves, the breaking surf beneath like a skirt of lace.

Mum and Dad brought them here all the time in summer, a special treat for bright weekends and birthdays. The man in the cubicle – you had to tiptoe to give him the money – would present you with plastic tokens, shinier than coins, the indentations bumpy under your fingers when you rubbed them in your pocket. The roller coaster was her favourite. She'd miss out on the teacups, the rocket ride that shot you high in the air, to save up the six tokens needed to climb aboard the carriages in the shape of pirate ships. Kelly never had enough left by then. They called in Nina's Nemesis, her personal thrill. After the rides they went to the seafood stall to get cockles, the chewy blobs drowned in vinegar. Their acidity curdled in her stomach with the sensation of falling.

There are no chattering families here today. Past the windsock straining at its leash in the gusts, the coffee place they'd shelter in for a hot drink when it was too cold. The rides are round the other side, past the arcade, the endless clank of the 2p machines.

It's almost the same. There's a carousel with a fire engine, the wind catching the rope and clanging the bell. She sits on a bench, looks out over the abandoned fairground. The placement of her handbag on her knees makes her feel like Aunty Jean – the pose she'd take on long journeys, refusing to take her coat off on the coach. The roller coaster hasn't changed much; the painting of the ship is updated, the pirate a younger man without a beard. She can see how the structure fits together, bolted in sections, almost dangling over the edge. It looks so precarious. She can't imagine her tiny frame lurching around that reckless metal.

The first part goes round and round, getting higher each time. The view would cut between the clamorous rides and the empty sea. The quivering in her feels like that. Nina holds her breath, picturing the carriage slowing even more. The clanks and creaks at the top, the last moment of inertia. She always felt juddery for hours after getting off. The first drop was enormous, levitating her feet so she felt like an astronaut.

Her favourite bit was near the end, when you roll up and down like a ship on the waves, six times. At the beginning of each rise she started with her hands waving, but at the first jolt they rushed back to the bar, unable to resist the pull of safety.

This time will be different. On the bench, Nina braces her legs and raises her hands in the air. She imagines each drop, her muscles clench instinctively, trying to pull her hands back down. She counts down – six, five, four, three, two, one.

As an entangled couple walk past, Nina's cheeks ache with smiling. Perhaps action will be possible. She pats the riot of her hair, buoyed up back past the beach, deserted now, as if the wind has blown everyone out to sea, lost in the anonymous sky.

At home, Nina types the word into Google. So small. The second hit has it in quotation marks, uses the word 'alleged.' She looks at drugs, symptoms, causes, as if it's a virus to be prevented. Phone numbers, crisis centres, the police.

Cases may not be pursued because of insufficient evidence.

She pulls out the post-its, clears the fruit bowl from the dining table and lays the squares of paper out, one by one.

The clump of hair next to the bed.
Dress still rucked up around your waist.

30

The smell of condom rubber between your legs.
Your face pressed into the pillow.
One of his hands on your neck.
Crescents on your thighs from his nails.
Red marks on your bum.

It looks like a stranger's confession.

This list is helpful – a series of facts, as if they haven't happened to her. They shouldn't be in the order she remembers; it needs to be chronological. She swaps a couple around. He must have pulled her hair out after he smothered her face in the pillow.

Nina goes into the kitchen, mixes the vodka with bananas and spinach in the blender, so it's more like lunch. It masks the taste. The green colour almost makes it healthy.

Nina finds a marker pen in the messy drawer, writes a 'P' on all the elements she can prove. Over all of the scattered pieces, two dark scrawls are all she can come up with – the coat, and his number. The missed call he gave her, while they were flirting in the kitchen. He made the drinks; rum and ginger beer in neon green plastic cups. He must have made them strong, for her to pass out like that. Stupid, to let him control what she put into her body. Had there been something else in there?

Frustration gnaws at her; she should have carried the stuff he touched in a bag – now it will be covered in her fingerprints. Especially the coat, she wore it on the way home. It was big enough to reach past her dress, hide her skin, worth it despite the slithery way it pressed against her back. She could have taken the glass he held, picked up the clump of hair.

In some cases proving lack of consent can be difficult.

Her lack of retaliation was disgusting. Why was it suffocating, why could she only crouch in the dark, screw her eyes shut and wait for it to be over? Because calling

31

out would have incriminated her in some way, revealed something shameful.

Before she went to University, Mum told her the story, about the man that grabbed her wrists in an underpass when she'd been walking home at night. How she shouted, thinking someone would come and help her. His face creased with threats, he reached inside his pocket. Something to silence her. With one hand free, Mum kicked him as hard as she could, twisted the other arm free and ran. The strange picture of her mother as a vulnerable girl.

Nina kept this tale like a beacon whenever she was alone in the dark. It was innate, something genetic that would protect her if she were in the same situation. But all she'd done was lie there. What a disappointment she would be if Mum ever found out.

If you think you have been a victim of sexual assault you should get medically examined as soon as possible.

It's time to take action. Nina gathers a range of Ziplock bags of different sizes to gather her evidence. She opens the bin. The coat is camouflage green with a furry hood, half covered in the meal she couldn't eat yesterday – sauce congealing on the egg noodles, a crescent of courgette stuck to one of the arms. She pulls it out by the foul lining. Her eyes grope for significance. Someone has written a scribbly letter 'E' on the tag at the back. In the pocket, a bus ticket to Fareham, some fluff, a paper clip. Nothing much. She rolls it up as much as it will go, squeezes it into one of the large bags and huffs the air out. It's encouraging to make it this small.

The dress and handbag are still in the corner of the bedroom where she chucked them when she came in. Her bed still looks odd – the duvet pulled to the top, flat without the hump of pillows. That first night she woke up sweating into them, the feel of that soft cushioning like suffocation. An imagined pressure on the back of her neck. She shoved the pillows under the bed, hidden there until she could stand to feel them against her face again.

She picks up the dress. The fabric looks like an invitation – the burgundy lace, the way it scooped down her back. That dress, she turned in the changing rooms when she bought it, admiring the pull of it against her bottom. If it hadn't been so short, would it have made a difference? Nina repeats the same process for the coat – rolls it up, in a bag, squashes it small – relieved to have it hidden.

Her bag is the small rigid one she always uses for nights out, easy to clean after she's sat on it or had it wedged under a table in the pub. It joins the other items on the table. A rattle as she puts it down. Her driving licence is loose in the main compartment. It's usually in the side pocket, for those rare occasions she still needs ID. Did he touch it?

She takes a big gulp of the green liquid, willing the vodka to numb her. She clicks the lamp on, the bag casting a shadow like a hook on the wood. A movement outside. She looks up, as if his face will be haunting her window. A man with an age-creased face and a grey beret walks past, a dog lead dangling from one arm. The light is seeping from the sky –that grey winter shadow that mutes everything. There's a van opposite, another man hauling boxes into it on a trolley. The view out of the window is stained. Everyone looks capable of terrible things.

If he picked up her licence, there could be traces of him on it. She gets the tweezers from the bathroom cabinet and tries to dig it out. The metal keeps slipping off the surface, she can't keep the pressure. Putting her other hand in a freezer bag, she inches it out, plopping it between the slippery sides. The handbag goes into one too. Just in case.

There's quite a collection. Sealed bags under the glare of a spotlight. It looks like an episode of CSI. The last thing she needs is pictures, evidence of what he did to her body. She gets another drink, perhaps orange juice is a better mixer.

The ambient spotlights in the bedroom are too dark to take decent photos and the bedside light isn't much better. The brightest part of the flat is by the sofa, the lamp has a metallic arm she usually angles down to see her book. She can do the same thing, illuminate the bits that are important to building her case. It's like a schematic, something you need to break down into disparate parts, before it can be quantified and understood.

She snaps down the dark wooden blinds. Her evidence collection is like an unwanted dinner party. The first thing off is her jumper. There's no one here, silly to be nervous. She reveals her skin, her eyes catching on the shadows, as if someone is watching. It doesn't need to take long.

Nina segments her body, using the big swing mirror from the bedroom. Each corner and crevice is examined for marks. Her neck first – the smudge of purple on the right. Then nothing until her side – another bruise, a scratch. Her eyes, travelling down, echo the movement of his hands, how he pinched the skin when he pushed her feet in so her knees would bend.

The biggest scratch is on the inside of her thigh, the sharp finger of metal, the rattling, he didn't even take his belt off before he crouched over her. She tried to make herself as small as possible, but it didn't help.

Each time she angles the light onto the piece of her that he damaged. She focuses on getting the best picture possible, to remove herself from the process. Her arms start to shake. There's still redness around the lips, one of them swollen. The angle is difficult. She pulls the skin of her thighs wide, spreading herself out. It's too familiar. She leans against the table, breathing heavily. Another drink, to numb herself.

The bruises on her bum are unreachable. She stretches her arm round, taps her finger against the screen and then brings it back into view. There are ten blurry pink squares. She deletes them all. Maybe in the reflection, that might work better. She pivots the mirror, angles the bulb so it won't be visible. Much better. The purple finger stains are clear. The hands that clenched and released, clenched and released, some shout that sounded more like fury than pleasure behind her. Nina catches her breath. In the top left, the smear of her face. She looks reduced.

She runs her fingers over the soft plastic. The headlight of a car sneaks under the line of the blinds, catching the vacant expression of her photo on the pink rectangle of her driving licence. Her face looks empty, simpler somehow. It must be getting dark outside. A sound, the thumping of a car door in the dark. Footsteps. She runs to the door, snaps the bump of the catch, leans down and works the bolt across, sawing it up and down to shut herself in.

Dressing quickly, she assembles her arsenal on the table. It looks official; something has been achieved. The angle of the paper slips flicking up looks personal, believable. She should go now, take this collection of proof. She swigs back the last of the drink. But that will lead to another type of exposure, another examination. Only this time, she won't be able to control it.

A few drips of rain fall onto the windscreen from the sodden branches overhead. She watches the line of water meander down the windscreen. Just an hour or so, then it will be over. Someone else will take this weight from her, carry it forward to a conclusion. There'll be someone she can talk to, spill out her distress.

Nina presses her hand amongst the plastic bags, skates over their contents. Solid things, linking them together, proof. Surely three days isn't too long to wait. She shoves three sugar-free Polos in her mouth to try and cover the vodka smell. Probably not a good idea to drive but it seemed urgent, once she'd done the rest. She pulls her hat down over her hair and wraps a scarf round her neck so it covers her chin.

The building is squat, ruddy bricks and sharp edges. The blue plastic sign makes it look more like a library than a police station. A sign for the law courts next door. That's where she'll end up, her reputation poked and prodded. They'll ask her about her sexual history, want to uncover even more of herself. Let them try, there's nothing to be ashamed of. It could end up on the news, one of those landmark cases. She could make a difference.

Looking in her bag, her confidence sags. It's so sparse. Maybe she shouldn't have researched so thoroughly. It was hardly comforting, each case and statistic pushing her further outside the realm of possible success. She squeezes the dress through its packaging.

No, it will be different for her. There are bruises, his fingerprints. The missed call on her phone. There were people at the party who saw them together. All it will take is to link everything, pull it all together and he'll be arrested. Put in jail so no other woman is subjected to that. She has to report it. It's her duty.

Inside is a bare floor, plastic chairs and posters about neighbourhood safety. She scans them; *BEWARE OF PICKPOCKETS, LOCK IT OR LOSE IT, BE SEEN, BE*

SAFE. A drunk girl being held up by her friends – *DO YOU KNOW HOW YOU'RE GETTING HOME?*

A queue straggles back from the main desk. The man behind it looks flustered. She joins the back, gripping the largest handbag she could find, all of her valuable items inside. The inebriated figure in the poster keeps poking into her line of sight. The girl is wearing a skimpy dress. Nina pushes her hand inside the bag again, tries to keep her breathing steady.

It's too polite, like they're all waiting to report a missing pet or a neighbour who trims their hedge too severely. She gets to the end of her rehearsed speech three times, nowhere near the front. The man behind the counter only has a few smudges of black left in his hair. It's scooped over to one side, slicked like Granddad's used to be. He'd tap his comb over the Brylcreem, draw it carefully through. Nina could see the lines in it when she sat next to his armchair, watching him fill in the football pools.

She can't say it to him. Maybe they'll put her into a room, let her talk to someone there. They might take her fingerprints, her pictures, get a doctor in. Things will start to escalate.

She looks up. Somehow there's just one person between her and the desk. Glancing back, the queue has filled up, people making a trail all the way to the door. She wipes her palms down the side of her trousers.

The man in front of her has a wadge of paper edged in black and yellow stripes. He's muttering, shaking his hand so the paper rustles.

'These parking tickets are a fucking joke, mate.' The man slams the pile down, leaving his meaty hand on top.

'You'll need to call the traffic office.' The policeman gestures at a sign on the desk. 'Please refrain from using threatening language.' His voice is flat.

'I have to park there, it's for work, they put this sign up last week, all of a sudden I'm up to my neck in these.' He thuds his hand down again. She looks at his fingers, the pent-up anger in them.

Maybe they'll arrest him immediately, or she might have to identify him, stare at his eyes through one of those two-way mirrors.

'I can give you the number.' The officer slides a card over the counter. His face looks more crumpled close up. 'Call them between nine and five.'

'How am I supposed to do that? Some of us work.'

If she waits any longer, she'll lose her nerve. She sighs, making sure it's loud enough for them both to hear.

'You got a problem?' His eyes travel over her.

'People are waiting.' She points at the line of bodies.

'Well, I'm sure you can flash your lovely smile in a minute, some of us have important things to do.' He puts his back between her and the policeman. 'I want to talk to someone, right now.'

'Excuse me.' She taps his shoulder.

'I thought I told you-'

'We're all really impressed with how tough you are, but clearly you've had your turn, and there are a lot of people waiting.' Firm but polite, that was the way. Men are all mouth, that's what Granddad used to say, comb in hand. Don't let them think they're better than you.

He looks down at her, back at the line, the man behind the counter.

In the pause, she steps past him.

'How can I help?' The policeman looks relieved. She feels the weight of people's attention on her. The man with the tickets walks away, leaving her exposed at the front of the queue.

'I'd like to report a crime.' Her voice sounds so quiet.

'Lovely. I'll just take a few details.' He reaches for a pen.

'Is there a form I can fill in?' So feeble.

He studies her – she can feel his gaze. She can't meet his eyes. After a beat, a clipboard is handed over the counter. She grabs it and hurries to the corner, pulling a chair closer to the wall. The metal legs scrape on the floor like a gasp.

She gets as far as the date. There are spaces for all the things about her. Name, address, date of birth. It shouldn't be her that's made to give up all this information. There'll be a file, somewhere they keep these things. Her name coupled to a crime. Once it's there, she'll be marked with it. A percentage point in a statistic.

They'll look into her history, people she's slept with, things she's done. That time at college where she groped some guy on a patio bench at the end of year party. When her and Holly had a snogging contest in The Academy. Nina had got to nineteen. Her mind ticks through the men she's had sex with. A brief flash of skin and lips. Probably more than twenty, but surely not up to thirty yet. Each admittance into her bed feels like a stain against her, proof of the kind of woman she is.

The clatter of a throat clearing opposite her. Nina looks up. An anonymous face, wreathed in understanding.

'Can I help you?' The woman tips her head to the side. Her hair is pulled back tight, the black collar soft around her neck. Her expression is firm, but open. She wants to help. Nina reaches down to the bag, fondles the soft things in there. Time to pull them out, expose the truth. She looks back at the form.

They'd been to a few pubs, even had cocktails, full of a sense of occasion. In the club they'd had shots, maybe a bottle of that horrible fruity vodka stuff. The dress, her makeup. There were photos, already on Facebook. She would have to convince them that she didn't want it, after all those people saw her kissing him.

She looks back at the policewoman. Once the words are out, they'll lead into a chain, carry a weight, pull all of those around her into it. They'll think she's weak. Breathing out, she gathers the start of her speech. It's too important, never mind what they think of her. He can't be allowed to get away with it.

A buzzing in her pocket. She pulls the phone out. Holly. No word from her since the weekend.

'Hang on.' She stands, turns her back to the wall. 'Hey.'

'How's it going?' Muffled busyness in the background. She must have just finished her shift.

'Not bad.' A quick glance around – the woman still waiting, the signs on the walls.

'You sure? Only, I didn't hear from you after Saturday, you just disappeared. Which, I know, is normal for you, drunken homing beacon, but we were worried.'

'Right.' Not worried enough to try and find her, help her.

'Look, I know you're at work, and Clive the Cunt is probably waiting to give you an earful. I feel stupid asking really, I don't think you'll mind, but I wanted to make sure, and I felt bad because it was me who got the shots, and then I suggested going to that party in the first place, even though you said you were getting tired-'

'Holly.' This could go on for a while.

'Right. It's just, after all that crap with Scott, and moving house, you can still help out, right? I was just feeling really crappy, and he added me on Facebook, and we've been chatting, so I wondered if you'd mind that Will asked me out for a drink this weekend?'

40

'Who?'

'Bloody hell, you were more drunk than I thought.' She giggles. 'I'm sorry, it was your big night, I'm not surprised you don't remember his name.'

'I know this guy?'

'Nin, you were snogging him in the kitchen.'

'What?' It's him. She's talking about *him*.

'That tall guy you spent ages chatting to? Then you got all cross with him for some reason, had a go at him. I figured you'd gone off him, it was only a bit of drunk fun, right? And I'm not saying it's anything serious, but it's just nice to have attention, with Scott being such a shit, and he seems like a laugh. But I didn't want to actually meet up with him until I check with you.'

Nina concentrates on breathing, pulling air in and out.

'So, is it ok?'

'How bad was I?' She needs to know what it looked like; what other people might say.

'I dunno, you got all slurry, definitely more drunk than you usually get but I figured you were letting go because it was your night.'

'Right.' The woman is still there. A white word stitched into her T-shirt. Police. A symbol of everything that could help her.

'So... is it ok? I've got to get back on the ward.'

Everyone saw her with him. How drunk she was. That she was irrational, pissed. And now Holly wants to spend time with the man that did this to her.

'Nin?'

'Yes, it's ok.' What else can she say?

'You sure?'

'I've got to go.' She drops the phone back in her pocket, keeps her face to the wall.

No-one would believe her. If Holly wanted to go out

with him, he can't have been that bad. Was she just *that* pissed? Had she wanted to do it, after all? It wasn't like she fought back. Why would they believe her?

'Everything ok?' The policewoman is still there. Her face will shift into judgement once Nina tells her story. Just another slut who was asking for it, got so drunk she wasn't able to look after herself. Her parents would find out. Holly. She'd think it was ridiculous, crying rape, after all those people saw her with him.

'Sorry,' she says, gathering her arms around her body and standing. The chair clatters over. Nina dodges to the end of the row, aiming for the door.

'Wait.' The step of sensible shoes behind her. To think this would help, that she could make a difference.

The queue is stretched over her escape route. Nina glances behind. The policewoman is still following. If she makes her sit down, asks her questions, it will all come out. Then what will happen?

Barging through the nearest gap, she accelerates through the door – let them stare. Escape is the only option. There can be no resolutions here.

It's raining harder. No time for the umbrella, she dashes across the road, drips finding their way down her neck, stroking her skin on their way inside her clothes. There's a soft patter as it hits the plastic bags. A wasted attempt at evidence. Nothing like real proof.

Over the road, three cars down and she's safe. In the car, useless bag slopped on the other side, a moment to breathe as she clicks the seatbelt on. The weight of it sits on her chest – this failure to take action. Traffic is starting to accumulate on the roundabout. Each car moves with purpose, getting home on time, catching the shops before they shut. The prospect of her empty flat and no resolution looms.

As she drives away, the figure of the policewoman

waits outside the doorway, peering into the early evening gloom.

Eric

It looks like Mum's been at the garden again. A new border carved into the mat of green, clusters of colour laid in the earth. Soon there won't be any lawn in front of the house. He didn't bother to call, knew that Tuesday Family Dinner rolled around at the same time every week, even if he hadn't been a part of it for a while. A cat lolls in what's left of the grass. Not Monty, this one has a patch of white over one eye. It regards him sullenly, as if he's the intruder.

He pushes the door; she always leaves it unlocked. His shoes go in the rack by the door, stacked on top of each other with the toes tucked into one another – the space saving method.

The scent of cabbage hangs around Mum in the kitchen – focused on the metronome of the chopping board. All so homely. Where had that lewd part of him come from on Saturday night? People who liked that kind of thing grew up in houses with loose curfews and parents that let them watch unsuitable films, surely.

'This is a treat,' she says, gathering up slabs of potatoes. 'Everything ok?' She must know he hates this question; she busies herself in the cupboards, her head lost behind the doors.

'Thought it would be good to pop round,' he says.

'Lil's upstairs. Lovely to have you both here.' She turns and gives him a quick hug.

'Great.' That's his real reason for coming here. She's the only one he can talk to about the weekend.

'So, everything at work ok?' He's not going to be able to escape that quickly. 'I hear you're going for a promotion.' Lil's been flapping her mouth again.

'It's a Phase Leader job. The headteacher mentioned it to me, but I'm not qualified enough.' They probably wanted a decent number of applicants. It was obvious that Olivia would get it.

'She asked you to apply, didn't she?' A little squeeze on his arm.

'Well, I suppose I have been getting some attention.' It's good to be able to boast. It wouldn't hurt to come here more. After the weekend he'd been feeling more confident. As if a secret, powerful side of him had come out.

'Of course. All the effort you put in.' She retreats to the kettle. Not that she knows exactly what his day entails, but it doesn't stop her from enthusing to others about it. Nothing like the image of the caring son to spread liberally around your elderly friends. Especially when you compared it to Dad.

'I'll just pop up and see Lil.' She'd help him figure some of this out. His next possible move.

'I saw Bea in town. She was with some tall man. Must be hard you for you, love.' Typical. So much for lifting his confidence.

'We broke up ages ago.' Just like her, to poke at his weak spots. 'Stop going on about it.'

'Only a month or so. I know these things take time. She was a lovely girl. Seemed a shame.' She'd never asked. The implication that it was his fault.

'Hardly.' Now at least he can tell her something to take him out of the light of failure. He wasn't sure what else he could have done to make it work. All that trying, all those gestures, for months. Clearly it had been pointless. 'You know she cheated on me?'

'Oh dear.' She scoops the orange rounds into a bubbling pan. He can't believe that's it. There should be some shared sense of betrayal. 'Anyone nice at work, is there?' And that's it, back to the same old crap. He can't give her a funny response, this time.

'Finding a girlfriend so you can have grandkids isn't my life's work, you know.' Eric sees the impact fall in the droop of her shoulders. It's not his fault, she always pushes him into being unkind.

He wanders along the neatly clipped borders in the back garden, the stone hedgehog regarding him from a tree stump. Red geraniums nestle in the border, weeds tangling between the velvet petals.

'What did you say to Mum?' Lilly grabs his arm.

'She was hassling me about Bea again.' He's on safe territory here.

'God, why can't she leave it alone? She was mental.' Lil smiles.

'How are you, little sis?'

'You know me. Non-stop as usual.' She was always so calm. He couldn't fathom her place in the loud world of HR. His quiet sister in severe jackets. Dad would have been proud, at least. She stoops down and grapples the thin tangles out of the ground, clumps of soil falling onto the neat grass. There's always been something reassuring about her presence.

'What did you get up to at the weekend?' He brushes one foot over the loose soil, unable to look up.

'Clearly nothing compared to you. Big brother, you've

gone all red.' She shoves him.

'It's not a big deal, there was just this girl.' He shrugs.

'Tell me more! I do hope Mr. Fake was there to witness your glory.' She's the only person who's ever seen through Will's bravado.

'He'd left by then.' By which time Eric had made his own move. So much for safe, boring Eric.

'You'll never guess what I found out about Bea at the weekend.'

'Don't you start. You're as bad as Mum.'

'No, seriously, she was way worse than you thought. Well, him too. Turns out they had sex just before we broke up.' Will had painted it in such a pathetic light – that she had been a state, needed comfort. That she'd told him they'd already broken up. What a hell of a way to mourn.

'How classy. The best mate and the girlfriend. It is beyond me why you still hang out with him.'

'Well, yeah, only you haven't heard the best bit. I totally got my own back.' His dirty encounter with Will's failed conquest. There had to be a way to bring it up next time he saw him.

'You need to stop scoring points with him. Just forget it.' Lil hooks her arm through his. 'He's not a decent guy.'

The ground tilts a little – Eric find himself uneven in his own back garden.

'Maybe I'm not decent.' Lil would be shocked at his daring, how adventurous he'd become.

Lilly pokes his ribs, the bit just under the armpit where it jars. He smacks her hand away.

'What are you on about?' She prods the other side. He grabs both her hands. She squirms, stands on his foot.

'Come on, Lil. Stop. I need to tell you-'

'Dinner's ready.' Mum appears in the doorway.

At the table he concentrates on eating. The reassuring stodge of a lamb roast. Cutlery clangs. A smack of lips, the schluck of the mint sauce jar.

'Did he tell you about that promotion?' Mum pats the arm of her cardigan to find her tissue.

'You'll be great.' Lil squeezes his arm.

'Come on. I'm not experienced enough,' Eric says.

'People trust a man in charge more than a woman.' Mum nods, blows her nose.

'That's ridiculous. You can't say that,' Lil says.

'It's a fact,' Mum says. 'The one time we had a female in charge of our office it was absolute chaos. Wore the most dreadful outfits and bright pink lipstick. Never seen someone so bolshy.' The Age of Lynn was always referred to as a dark time. Eric scoops up a forkful of peas, eyes darting between them. Lil isn't going to let that go.

'Come on, you wouldn't comment on what a man was wearing.' She stabs at a carrot.

'Actually, Jeffery always has an interesting tie.'

'Even if she was more bossy, which I doubt, you probably only thought that because she was a woman. Honestly, mum, you should be sticking up for women in power in the workplace.' Lil's fork clatters onto the plate.

'Men are just better at being in charge.' She shakes her head at Lil's exasperated expression. 'You can look like that all you want but it's true. We're better at looking after things, managing a lot at once. That's why we're so good at being in charge of a household. Nothing wrong with that.'

'Dad forced you to stay at home and now you act like it was your idea,' Lil mutters into her plate.

'That's enough,' Mum says, her fork on the table a

full stop. That tone is familiar. Insulting him is still not allowed, after all these years.

There was shouting, in the garage. Eric would press his ear to the door that led off from the utility room, flaked with red paint. He was careful not to knock the doorknob that rattled in its casing. They shouted much louder in the concrete space, emotions bouncing off the walls. He was able to piece together fragments from the few words that rose above the others. Something about disappointment. That's why he'd always wanted to be different. Why he'd fought so long for what he had with Bea.

He tries to catch Lil's eye, she never knows when to leave it. The sounds of eating take over again. He drops a white square of bread into the gravy, little flecks of broccoli still floating in it. He swooshes and swipes, then flips it over. The first corner will be moist and gooey. The two of them, bookending him, get to the last of their meal, then sit quietly. He keeps his head down, unsure if they're about to start again.

'He left years ago,' Lilly says. 'You should be pleased we're old enough to sympathise, now we know what happened between you. He treated you like crap.'

'You wouldn't understand.' He glances up. Mum's face is stiff and pale. Something obscene has been said.

'After the way he walked all over you, made you give up your career,' Lil says. Eric chokes on his bread. There were hints that Mum had loved working in the art gallery, before they were born. Before they moved. Now she was stuck in some boring admin role after years of not working. But no-one ever actually mentioned it.

'He is your father.' Mum's voice is low and quiet. 'Wearing a suit and heels to work doesn't give you the right to talk down to me.' Lil snorts, opens her mouth. Mum stops her with a look. 'If this is the way I'm going to be spoken to in my own home then I'd rather you didn't come here.'

It's not usually this bad. Lil's face stiffens. He needs to bring them back together.

'Mum, Lilly comes every week. You do your shopping together.'

'Doesn't mean she can say what she likes,' Mum says.

'That's right, discuss me like I'm not here.' Lil stands.

'You always take it too far.' Eric didn't like to talk about him. It was too worrying to think that it was genetic.

'So, you're defending Dad? He was hardly your biggest fan.' Lil starts stacking the plates. 'She'll listen to the prodigal son, even though he hasn't been here for months.'

Mum stands up. The women look down at him.

'Don't help or anything,' Lil says. She throws her fork at him. It rebounds off his arm and leaves a brown smear on the pale flowers of the carpet. 'Jesus. It's like the fucking 1950s.'

'I will *not* have that language.' Mum folds her arms.

'I'd better fuck off then.' Lilly flounces out of the room. Her thudding footsteps up the stairs are followed by the slam of her old bedroom door. There's a chip in the frame from the repetition of this action. He searches for a remedy, something to calm Mum down. Maybe he can distract her with work stories, she always likes to hear about his students, as if they're surrogate grandchildren. He reaches for her arm.

She's smiling. Her head shaking, mouth stretched wide.

'Just like old times,' she says, picking up the fork.

'Are you ok?'

'She gets grumpy about helping me out. Don't take it personally.'

He tries not to let it register; how much older she looks these days. The pouches under her eyes, the permanent crinkles under her chin. The way her body has flowed out, a loose mass rather than a defined shape.

It brings back an unwelcome memory. That time he arrived here, unannounced. The shape of her disappointment, how he was useless in her defence. She's never mentioned it, in all this time. Her hands reach for the abandoned dishes.

'I'll do that.' He steers mum into a chair and clears the rest of the table. By the time his hands are submerged in bubbles, Lilly has come back down and made tea for everyone; a sideways apology.

'This your way of sucking up, then?' she says, digging her fingers into his sides. He's trapped, hands deep in the bowl.

'Piss off, runt.' He shoves her away with his hip.

'Rather that than a gangly coat hanger.' She grabs a handful of bubbles and rubs them into his hair.

'Are you getting Dad anything for his birthday?' he asks. It's next week. Her hands drop. She hasn't been to see him in years.

'You know I'm not.' She turns and picks up a tea towel, starts worrying at the cutlery.

'But he's your dad.' Eric's monthly visits had dwindled to every now and then in the face of extreme indifference. But it was important. A parent should be a part of your life.

'The fact that he provided half my genetic material does not mean he gets to make me feel small. I don't need someone like that in my life.' She thunks the drawer open, dropping the knives in. 'His shit behaviour moved us all down here and lost mum her independence. You know why he lost his job, right?'

'Enlighten me,' he says.

51

Mum appears in the doorway. She hovers, glancing between the two of them.

'Rich tea?' Lilly herds her out with the biscuit barrel. She comes back and starts on the bowls.

'So, what happened?' Eric asks.

'Let's not talk about him. What were you going on about before?' She nudges him. 'You manage to get some at last?'

'Will got these girls to come to a party at Chris' house. There was this girl Will was flirting with. I mean, she was kissing him and everything in the kitchen. But she looked at me. Our eyes met and she smiled.' It was only later he'd realised what the smile must have meant. 'Then they went upstairs and I thought that was it, but we could all hear her screaming at him, telling him to fuck off. So, I went upstairs and it's like she was waiting for me.' It feels weird, saying it out loud.

'So this is how you got your revenge.' She slaps him with the tea towel.

'Lil.' He pulls his hands out of the water and grips her shoulders. 'I think I might be a sexual deviant.' The water seeps into her shirt, dark stains spreading down her arms.

Lil shrugs his hands away. 'What are you talking about?'

'There's a dark side to me I didn't realise. I had this crazy night with a total stranger.' Eric turns away from her. She laughs.

His research has been comforting. There were certainly a lot of people out there that liked that sort of thing. The men getting a rush from the power. But women too, wanting to be dominated. Wanting to be hit, strangled even. She must have been one of those. Not wanted to say it out loud, but the way she'd been lying there, dress all rucked up. Clearly asking for something like that. He was desperate to see her again. Was it too late, to try the romantic approach? That was the only thing he knew how to do.

'The last time you had an online date you bottled it and watched her from a different table until she left.'

'That was a practice run.' The woman looked so different in person. There was no way she'd like him. She kept glancing over, she must have recognised him. The longer he left it, the more it became impossible. His drink untouched, he sat for twenty minutes, turned away from her. When he looked back he wasn't sure when she'd left. There was an empty glass with a chewed straw in it.

'You should give up on this online thing.' Lil returns to the draining board.

'Are you saying people don't like me?'

'You're a grower.' She shrugs. He passes her a plate.

'Didn't you hear me?' His attempt at confiding isn't going very well.

'I think our ideas of deviance might be a little different.' She has her worldly look on. 'You'd be amazed what I hear about in my job.'

'This isn't about some weirdo asking for a woman with a 25-inch waist and black bra to be their assistant,' he says. There were all manner of pervs in her line of work.

'You had some one-night fun with a stranger. I don't think we're on weird territory here.' She makes it sound so basic. It wasn't like that. Also, the thought that it was just for one night makes his stomach bounce.

'I mean, we did it and everything.' He feels like a teenager. 'Only, it wasn't like it usually happens. It was all, silent, and quite rough, sort of dirty.' When he touched her leg, she'd barely responded. Just shuffled it towards him. So he could see up her dress more. That's how he'd known. His hands slid up and she'd gone so still. There was something like a sigh, or a gasp. She must

53

have looked at him through that mass of hair, realised it was him. He picks up a plate and it sloshes the water against his tummy.

'So? Doesn't sound that bad to me.' She doesn't sound shocked. Is it normal? Has she done something like that?

'I didn't even know her name.' When he looked around the room he saw she'd left a condom on the shelf. It had shocked him, that she'd been so blatant about what she wanted. When he got up to get it she hadn't moved. It was so exciting, the way she lay there and let him pull her up onto all fours, it was so quick he hadn't had time to take his trousers off. She'd been so wet it hadn't mattered that he was rough. He wasn't usually like that but that dark silence had brought something out of him. She'd let him do anything he wanted. 'Only, I think I'd like to see her again. We had a connection.' That's the bit he keeps getting stuck on. The way it felt. He wants that again.

'You let yourself go, now you feel like you owe her or something. It's not a big deal. It's just sex.' She picks up a bowl, turns away. Maybe he was being a prude.

'Right. I just, didn't think I was like that.' He'd always thought of himself as a romantic. The opposite of Dad.

'Nothing wrong with a revenge fuck.'

'How are you two getting on in here?' Eric turns, startled. The shuffling of Mum's feet didn't register.

'I thought you were watching TV.' He looks for signs that she's been listening.

'Feel bad, leaving you two with all the work.' She pats his shoulder.

'It's the least I can do.' She'd be disappointed if she knew what he'd done. She told him to always be a gentleman. He wants to curl in her lap, lay his head on her leg like when he used to get terrible earaches. She'd rest one cheek on a tea towel and fill the ear with warm cod liver oil. The sound of the TV in the background came to him like he was under warm bathwater. 'I should come here more often, I'm sorry,' he says.

'You've got enough on your plate.' She rubs his back, her hand is so small.

'This is what he gets for washing up? I wish I got this level of guilt.' Lilly interjects. 'Come on, don't forget Deal or No Deal.'

'Oh, yes.' She leaves a warm imprint in the hollow of his back.

'What is wrong with you?' Lil closes the door.

'I just want to understand.' It feels like he's swimming around, unable to recognise himself.

'For god's sake leave Mum out of it.'

'It was nothing.' It was hard to admit that something like that got him so excited. 'Just not like me, I guess.'

'About time you got daring.' Lil almost looks proud.

He stacks the last of the trays, the crusted bits from years of use never quite coming off. He tries to recreate an image of her, smiling in the kitchen. All he can picture is her crumpled on the bed afterwards. A flurry of skin and sweat. There was definitely something there. Things like that didn't just happen, Lilly didn't understand. There had to be a way of talking to her. He could go back to her house, get to know the rhythm of her day, make it seem accidental when he bumped into her again. That would make it less awkward.

He adjusts his route home so he can see the light seeping out from under her blinds. Just knowing she's there, what they shared. It's enough. For now.

Nina

The door has been left on the catch. It's a predictable jumble – boxes half packed, a clutter of dishes in the sink, the cat stalking through it all. Holly scurries around the flat, shoving books in with cutlery and old birthday cards in with her fruit bowl.

Clive keeps emailing, demanding updates. This favour gave her a legitimate reason for scooting out early on a Monday, the day she usually stays late. The rest of last week was lost to bouts of panic over meeting the deadline and depressing online searches. When she got home she shoved her stash of evidence at the back of the cupboard under the sink, where it wouldn't taunt her. The weekend wasn't much better. Knowing that Holly was out, with him. The only thing that had been sent from Holly was a Buzzfeed list about engineers and a picture of a tiny pig with red boots on. Nina didn't have the courage to ask her how it had gone. She spent most of the weekend wallowing in a fog of vodka and takeaways, watching lame comedies on Netflix to avoid the circling motion of her thoughts.

Nina hasn't seen her since the party. Surely Holly will notice something.

'You're a lifesaver.' Holly bundles her into a hug.

'Sorry for getting you out on a work night.' This isn't what she should be apologising for. What happened with him at the weekend?

'I said I'd help.' Nina pulls back. 'How's it going?' Holly looks tired. It can't be great, to have to move house because your boyfriend kicked you out.

'Yeah, it's ok.' Why doesn't she ask Nina how she is? She's sure she looks different. 'The new place is actually a lot nicer, I'll have more space, you know what Scott was like, leaving all his computer crap everywhere, couldn't move for bloody wires.'

'And a whole bed to yourself,' Nina says. Holly is renowned for sleeping diagonally.

'I'm looking forward to leaving my clothes everywhere and not being moaned at.' She leans back, sags her shoulders down. 'Not that it isn't bloody depressing.' She shrugs. 'Another one I couldn't convince to stay.'

'Come on. You're too good for that guy.' Holly always managed to land herself with losers and somehow convince herself it was her fault when it didn't work out.

Nina makes a start on the already assembled boxes. Keeping busy has helped so far, especially now she's worried someone is following her. That strange knock on the door last week, the feeling she keeps getting that eyes are on her when she walks.

Nina tests the first box. Heavier than she thought.

'How many ramekins do you own?' She hefts it, the label contrary to the straining of her arm muscles. Impossible to concentrate, knowing where Holly was. Had they kissed? Had his hands been on her, too? She needed to warn her, or at least try to tell Holly what he was like.

'That's random glassware, too,' Holly says, assembling bags behind her. 'Like carafes and decanters.'

'Surely you're not allowed those until you're at least fifty. They stop you at the counter at John Lewis and ask for ID.' Nina heads to the door.

'Doesn't badminton build up arm muscles?' Holly retreats to the kitchen. 'The van keys are by the door,' she says, hidden under the sink. 'There's wine later.'

'Of course.' Nina's voice echoes in the stairwell. The door snags on the bristles of the brown mat. She wedges some post underneath, returns, repeats. Enthusiasm dwindles with each mounting of the stairs.

'Where's Scott?' He was usually cramped in a corner, hunched over a screen.

'Said he didn't want to see me leave.' For a moment she looks sad.

'Come on, he's the one that started with all that nonsense about not being ready for anything serious. Despite the fact he agreed to move in together.'

'I know, but he's been through a lot at work.' She shrugs. 'I don't know, I'm going to miss him.'

Nina could never fathom how forgiving Holly was. A few months after they'd met at a Zumba class (which they'd then skipped to go to the pub), Holly had disappeared. Almost a month with no replies to Nina's messages. She'd been hurt, but figured they didn't know each other that well. Only afterwards did she discover she'd spent all of that time with a random guy who'd made lewd comments to both of them at the bar. Apparently, he'd apologised while Nina was in the toilet and Holly had felt so flattered at the attention she'd given him her number.

Maybe that's the way in, try to get her to talk about it in relation to Scott.

'You feeling guilty about Saturday?' Nina pretends to look like she cares what Scott thinks.

'No way. I hope he finds out, the little shit.' She

smiles.

'Just a one-off, right?' It won't seem as bad, telling her what he did, if it's just one drink.

'Who knows?' Holly squeezes her arm and goes back to the clutter.

She hasn't asked her what happened, why she disappeared at the party. Even in the middle of moving house, she must see something different. Nina's been avoiding mirrors, the sheen of windows. Her reflection reminds her of her weakness. It's no good, she's going to have to tell her, whether she likes this guy or not. But not now. Let them get this over with first.

The next half hour is gratifying repetition. Packing, bagging, carrying. Maybe tonight she'll be able to sleep. A few items remain scattered around, the size of the flat inexplicably shrinking as they take things out. They take the last big bits down, a clothes airer wedged in next to a lamp and a shoe rack.

When forced to sit, Nina gets an itch in her head after five minutes.

'So, how's your weekend been?' Holly leans over to fill her glass up, too close.

'The usual.' She shrugs, flops her hands in her lap.

'How's work? Clive carping on as usual?' She sniggers. It used to be infectious. 'Carping.' She puts her glass down and flaps her hands at the sides of her cheeks, blowing them out. Nina laughs. The sound lacks humour.

The wine tastes sour but she drains it anyway.

'Let's do the cleaning.'

'Honestly, you don't have to.' Holly leans back on the sofa, rubbing her dirty shoes on the fabric.

Keep moving. In the kitchen, she sprays the tiles, swipes at them with a cloth. Her concentration begins to sag, her attention swirling, mirroring the circles of her hand.

'At least he was better than Jake,' Holly says, calling through the door.

Nina turns her attention to the sink, following the grooves of stainless steel up and down.

'He was better than Jake, right?' Holly walks in, a bag of rubbish in each hand.

'Anyone would be better than him.' This constant need for reassurance is a drain. Holly hasn't even asked how she is, why she disappeared. They left her there.

'I'm such a nightmare, aren't I?' Holly clatters the stuff to the floor and levers herself onto the work surface, heels clumping against the doors.

'You have a choice.' There's a ridge of something next to the plughole. Nina scrubs at it.

'Every time I say the same thing, then before you know it-'

'What time did you leave the party the other week?' She keeps her hand moving. Her voice level.

'Not that late, way too drunk. Shots are never a good idea.' Holly refills their glasses. 'Half one, I reckon.' The last time Nina noticed was at one forty-five, on her phone, in that room. If they'd looked for her first, called her, done something.

'What happened on Saturday with, you know, that guy?' Nina asks.

'Just had a drink, went to The Bridge. It was fun, he's alright.' She nudges Nina with her foot. 'I thought you didn't like him.'

She can't turn around. It's like an accusation.

'You don't want to get involved with someone like that.'

'Oh who cares, it's just a bit of fun.' Holly takes a swig. 'Anyway, he can't be that bad. You liked him enough for a couple of hours at least.' She squeezes Nina's shoulder. It's hard not to flinch, push her away. 'I can't believe you pulled your disappearing act again.' Holly doesn't notice the lack of response. 'Me and Karen got a taxi, didn't even know you were ok until Sunday afternoon.' She had to send something. Just a text, saying she was home. Holly didn't even ask what happened, just kept moaning about the move, complaining about her hangover, the stuff she didn't want to lose in the divvying up of their household things.

'I don't think you should see him again.' He can't be allowed to intrude into their lives.

'I'm not going to do the same thing, not again. I just want some fun.'

'You don't understand.' Holly could never take things lightly. It would escalate and then it would be Nina's fault for not telling her. Saying it out loud would mean admitting that she hadn't done anything. She'd just let it happen.

'Look, he seems nice, he didn't try anything on, it made me feel better, ok?' She drains her glass. 'I thought you'd be happy.'

'Why do you think I was angry with him?' This can be the build up. Just explain what happened, get it out.

'You always get opinionated when you've had a drink.'

'This is different.'

'I'm seeing him again on Friday. For lunch. If you liked him, you should have said something. I did ask.'

Nina turns, catching her arm on the all-purpose cleaner. It clatters into the sink. Holly's already heading downstairs with the last of her things.

So he didn't touch Holly. That must mean he thought she was different. Had seen something in Nina, thought she was weak.

She rights the bottle, swirls the liquid away. The plughole stares up at her.

***

She feels it again, walking from the car to her house. That itch, like someone's watching. Coming back later than usual, all the spaces were taken, she had to park at the other end of the road. She quickens her steps, speeding up between the pools of light dropped from streetlights.

There's something moving, up ahead. It looks like a crouched figure, down between the cars. Right outside her house. If she ran, could she make it behind the door, before he moved? Or perhaps she should turn back, get in the car. Drive back to Holly's, bring her here. It would feel safer, with two.

She probably wouldn't come. They'd hardly parted on great terms. Nina needed time, to plan out what to say. Lay out the facts, not get hysterical. Try to make it sound ok, like she wasn't weak. What else could she have done? You wake up with someone doing things to you, it makes you panic. You freeze. It was natural. Yet she couldn't think of a way of saying it that didn't make her sound at fault.

A shift in the shadows. Probably just a cat, or a fox. They were at the bins last week. It was that woman at number 25, leaving bags out. They could smell it.

Almost there. Her boots tap out a sharp rhythm, echoing off the walls. She digs a hand into her bag, grabs her keys, wedging them between her fingers. Head up, like you're confident, can look after yourself.

Crossing the threshold, the outside light snaps on. She turns, ready to be relieved by something fluffy slinking under the car.

A scurry of limbs, someone running away. Hood up, but it's definitely a man. The scuff of footsteps retreats down the road. There was someone waiting for her in the dark. She squeezes her keys, feels the ridges dig into her fingers.

'Hey!' Two steps forward. She won't be intimidated, not this time.

Far down the road, a car door slams. She backs away, keeping her face to the road as she fumbles the key in the lock behind her. Shadows from the bushes creep towards her feet.

Eric

That was too close. He sits in the car, his lungs aching from the sprint down the road. Did she see him? He'd expected her to be home, had just wanted to sit near the house, hear the hum of her TV, be close to her. He was still trying to think of a way to talk to her, make contact.

He waits until his breathing slows to turn the lights on, then heads out, keeping to the back roads. Squares of lights in houses show that everything's fine. Dinners are being eaten, TV watched, homework being done. All he's trying to do is see this girl again. Tell her he's thinking about her. Why is he finding it so hard? It's pathetic, all this sneaking around.

A takeaway is needed. The food coma caused by a big curry might mean he can sleep properly, without the dreams. They end at different times. The first one was darkness and heat, a muffled whimper somewhere that he couldn't see the source of. One took place in school, the parents and children standing around the bed, solemn and wide eyed. It was when Foggert walked over, business-like, telling him she hadn't done his data entry yet, that he woke, clamouring for breath. But there's always one presence, hovering over him. He doesn't have to hear them speak to know who it is.

As he pulls past the entrance gates, his phone buzzes. A missed call from Lil. She was hardly helpful. Dismissing it all like it wasn't a big deal. That's not how he wanted to do it. When you'd slept with someone, you had a responsibility. You had to follow it up, honour the experience. If she didn't want to see him again after that, fine, but he had to reach out to her first. Of course, that would be easier if he didn't keep running away every time he got close to her.

He shuffles the car around the stupid Honda that takes up two spaces and turns it off, sitting there while the engine pings and cools. Why is it so hard to talk to her? Of course it's embarrassing, but it has to be more than that. The box from the other night is still sat on the passenger seat. Of course. That's what it is. He has to move on, emotionally, from the last person he got tangled up with. And there is one way to do that.

He reverses back out and drives to Bea's house. It's so automatic he barely registers which way he flicks the indicators. That was another thing that grated. Five years together and she refused to move in with him. Went on about how people lived next door to each other or had separate rooms even though they were married. Maintaining independence in love, something like that. He was desperate to become completely enmeshed in someone. Couldn't imagine why you wouldn't want to jumble it all together. He should have known she wasn't right for him.

He walks up to the door and rings the bell, the box in his hand. Hopefully one of her annoying housemates won't answer.

'Eric.' She's recognised him before the door's fully open. 'What is it this time?' She leans on the doorframe, doesn't invite him in.

'I've been thinking.' He holds the box out. 'About the

best way to move on. I think you should take this back.'

'Look, that's very sweet and everything, but we'd already broken up by the time you bought it. I know it was expensive. You should keep it.' Her hair's never been so short.

'We hadn't broken up. That's when we were trying to be apart but together. Seeing how it felt.' Each time he'd tried to make it work, re-ignite the thing she said was missing.

'That's basically the same thing.' She sighs. 'Look, Eric, I think you should know. I'm seeing someone else now.' She sounds like she's trying to be kind.

'Right.' Must be the tall guy Mum saw her with. He can't show her that it hurts.

'I just don't think we've got anything to say to each other. Take care, ok?' She nods at him, that little half-smile she used to use on strangers. It's not fair to be discarded so easily. Doesn't she feel anything?

'You don't think we should talk about you and Will?' That's got her. She pauses, undeniable guilt in the way she looks at him.

'He told you then. That wasn't kind.'

'Pretty sure you're the unkind one. Don't I even get an explanation?'

'Fine.' She walks away, leaves the door open behind her.

He follows her through to the kitchen where she's sat, waiting for him, a packet of digestives placed in front of her like an offering. He can hear the TV humming from the living room.

'Tea?' She stands up, not waiting for a response.

'So when did you two start shagging?' Once they've hashed this all out he can properly move on.

'Let me just say that I don't think this is very helpful.' She slops the teabags out of the mugs. 'But actually it only happened once.'

'Right, because girls never go back for more with him.' The constant stream that passed through their shared house while he clung to Bea. She was supposed to be safe.

'You asked.' She sipped her tea, snapping a biscuit in half before dunking it in. He used to hate washing up her sludgy mugs.

'Why did you cheat on me?' It sounds pathetic but he has to know. He can't figure out why she would hurt him when he tried so hard to be a good boyfriend.

'I don't know.' She leans her chin in her hand. 'Everything was just so full-on. I think we'd talked about breaking up for like the fourth time.' It had been so embarrassing, coming down to his friend's stares after she'd been shouting at him upstairs. He didn't get it.

'Why did it have to be him?' She knew how intimidating he found him.

'I guess, in a way, I wanted to get at you?' She shrugged. 'Every time I thought we were done, and somehow we'd come back to trying again. I think I'd just had enough.'

'Right. Enough of the presents, the trips away, the notes in your lunch.' He thought he'd done everything right.

'I just felt smothered, ok? You never stuck up for yourself, said what you wanted. I wanted you to be more, I don't know, forceful.' That's what she used to scream at him for. How she didn't want to be responsible for his happiness. But it hadn't mattered to him. You were there for the other person, not yourself.

'I'm not talking about this again.' Well, he'd certainly shown he had a forceful side. She wouldn't recognise the man he'd been that night. He doesn't need her anymore.

'You're the one who came into my house on a

Monday evening and asked to talk.' She shakes her head.

'Maybe you're right.' They've had this same conversation, many times. 'And you know what, I've met someone, too.' He allows himself a smile.

'Seriously?' She shouldn't sound so surprised.

'Well, I mean, it's nothing much yet. We had a thing, so now I'm just trying to figure out what to do next.' He can feel his face redden. He should have made it sound cooler.

'Just don't be too full on, ok? You can be a little,' she sips her tea, 'intense.'

'What's that supposed to mean?'

'Come on.' She laughs. '"You must have "bumped into me" about five times before you asked me out.'

'You said that was romantic.' He'd just got back from Uni and spotted her on a mate's Facebook picture, a big group of them in a club. He'd hung around the places she'd put on her Instagram – smiled at her as she walked past him in her favourite coffee shop, been shelf-browsing in the place she bought the wool for her charity knitting projects.

'I guess.' She drains her mug, stands up. 'She's lucky to have such a thoughtful guy after her.'

'I hope so.' He leaves his mug half empty. 'Thanks, Bea.' All of a sudden it doesn't seem so hard to leave this house. He's done it enough times. Maybe now he can finally move on.

'Take care,' she waves at him and he doesn't even mind that she won't be walking him to the door. He picks the box up and turns away. For the first time, he doesn't look back at her when he leaves.

The following morning, she rushes out of the door as if something is behind her. A dark coat today, flapping all the way to her ankles. Something drops on the pavement behind her. Tuesday has brought him a sign. She thrusts herself into the car and drives off. He's just opposite, can make out the expression on her face before the interior light clicks off. Determined, some sense of purpose.

She leaves at 6:30. So early, he can get here and watch her before heading to school. There's something comforting in seeing her, knowing everything is the same. It's been hard to find a way of seeing her, all she seems to do is work. If she still hasn't gone somewhere else by the end of the week, he's going to have to take a more direct approach.

He leaves the shelter of the car and ventures towards the fallen object. It's a glove, the black fingers folded underneath. She has small hands. He picks it up, turns it over. A bit of fluff, some warmth from her body. She might need it, the temperature's not supposed to rise much above two degrees today.

He rushes back to his car. When he gets to the junction she's two cars ahead, indicating left. That's out towards the ring road. He has assembly today, hardly the most private way of being late. Everyone else goes right.

The slide behind her brake lights is exhilarating. They shuffle out of town, edging through traffic up to the roundabout. Behind him, a couple gesture and yell at each other in the front seat. He has a sudden realisation. His face will be similarly displayed in her rear-view mirror. Eric passes a hand over his face, scrabbling for the glove box. Luckily his sunglasses are there. He jams them on his face, wondering if it's already too late.

She heads out towards the motorway. If she has a long commute, he'll be stuck. His initial enthusiasm frays; he hasn't done his photocopying yet, there's a card sort to cut up, the supporting statement he keeps starting then deleting. He shouldn't have told Mum about the promotion. He could always pretend he didn't get it.

Olivia is far more experienced. She's done external training, data analysis, delivered that whole-school training on progress. There aren't any men in the management team, though. It could work in his favour.

Nina has disappeared. The bright blue of her car has been replaced by murky silver. He might make the bell if he goes straight to school now. Turning onto a side street, the grey of the city to his left, a flash of blue catches his eye. She's in the queue to go out to the motorway. To get there he has to cross two lanes of traffic, right across the carriageway. He accelerates, a flare of horns accompanying his dash.

He cuts in ahead of her, forced out onto the motorway. Braking, he lets cars stream past him on the outside lane.

There she is. The first glow of morning, the passing headlights, light up her face. Directly behind him, her eyes flicking between the road and the dashboard. She fiddles with something, maybe the stereo. Her face looks softer, more tired. He wonders what music is filling the metal space around her.

Nina. Like a refrain, a siren. There's intent behind her appearance – eyebrows forceful, hair pulled back. No suit though, he can't picture what she does. She seems to grow and shed different skins, that must mean she's clever. A sudden smile, maybe a joke on the radio, her whole face stretches wide with it. She indicates and pulls round him. He cups the side of his face, the distance between them feeling too intimate.

Ten minutes later she pulls into a large industrial car park. She's one of the first here. He crawls along, following the arrows, feeling exposed. He takes another loop. She's already out of the car and heading straight towards him. She knows. This will be where she confronts him, tells him to stop following her around.

The gap between them diminishes. He stops the car. When she's a few feet away, she turns left, away from him, towards the entrance of an imposing glass building. She didn't even look at him. The building bears the logo of a swirling wave. Nautical Solutions. She is swallowed up and he is stranded outside. He parks next to her car.

It's an Audi, much more expensive than his silver Punto. There's a smear of bird poo on the right wing. Pulling his shirt sleeve out, he rubs at it, the brown and white smudge fastening itself to the fabric. It's satisfying. One more thing he can do. He pulls the glove out and tucks it under the wiper.

Nina

She's in way too early again and can't get to the office; Kevin's desk is empty. The inner door keeps whooshing open and letting the cold air in. She edges closer to the desk – surely if she stands still the stupid thing won't open. Reaching into her pocket, the door slides open again. The car will be less draughty. She turns back, pulling her coat around her.

There's someone by her car. Leaning over the windscreen, as if they're giving her a ticket. Hard to see in this light, but they've got a dark coat on, a hood flapping at the back. A tightening in her chest. The hood. That man, crouched down outside her house.

Ever since then, she's seen danger everywhere. People looking at her. The idiot wearing sunglasses behind her this morning in his boxy car. Everyone was a threat. She's been double locking the door, walking as quickly as possible, keeping a kitchen knife in her bag ever since.

The figure turns. He might come and find her here, trapped. She squats down on the floor, makes herself small. Arms around shins, she lets her breaths go inside her coat, warming her up. One hand reaches out for the bag, the safety of the knife handle.

A rush of air hits her as the door opens. She stands, turns, ready to face him.

There's no-one there. It must have been the movement of her hand, setting off the motion sensor. The car park is empty. She hurries over to the car, sees a dark shape under the wiper.

Her glove. What an idiot. Some random person must have spotted that she dropped her glove on the way from the car and put it under her windscreen. Probably one of the people from the energy company next door. She gets in, turns the heater on and concentrates on slowing her heart rate.

There are birds nearby, chattering in the dead morning air. She sits in her car, trapped, the radio spewing news into the enclosed space. Terror, slumps, disasters, conflicts, journalists claw and rip, purporting blame, accusations and solutions flying. The race and hate of the species gnaws at her until Kevin opens the doors at 7:45.

Her desk is a mess. Scrawled sketches and measurements are scattered, growing like mould onto the floor, not quite in the bin. Her usual system has crumbled, these lapses visible to anyone. The first part of the morning is lost to tidying.

'Hey player, how's it hanging?' Sai appears at the door, his tie around his head. This is probably his attempt at flirting.

'Those numbers weren't right,' she says.

'Steady on, bitches.' He leans to one side and flicks his fingers out.

'What did you call me?' She doesn't have time for this.

'You know, like, Warren G.' He gestures to the limp tie.

'I think you're about ten years out. Those

calculations. They weren't right.' She doesn't have the energy to be polite.

'I double checked them with Dev.' He pulls the thing off his head.

'Why? You could have asked me.' Now her incompetence is being spread.

'You looked a bit stressed.'

'Great. Don't do me any favours, ok?'

'You're welcome.' He slinks off.

Nina watches Dev arrive. There's a swing to his gait, an entitlement in his gestures to those around him. Why hasn't she noticed that before? He didn't use to look like that. Not long after he started to work there he was struggling. He'd managed to sell himself a little too well, fluffed his skills in the interview. She'd taken him on, like a private tutor. They'd spent hours reviewing stuff, she pulled out her Uni notes, coached him on how to apply them to what they were doing on the job, run models, they produced a fake prototype for a vessel, called it "Sharky." It had teeth painted on it in the virtual drawings.

She hides in the toilet to avoid his usual morning greeting. Another exuberant account of his life is not needed today. The buzz of the office grates more than usual, each email appears sarcastic. All week it's been like that, people talking to her in the same way, her responses either muted or exaggerated. She doesn't know how to be normal.

Communication with Holly has been strangled, the odd message here and there but nothing like the usual. It's hard to maintain this version of herself. Once the visit to the police station failed, she thought that would be it. She could move on, forget it ever happened. Anyway, what can she do? Accuse the guy who's going out with Holly on Friday? There must be some way to vent her anger, her sense of injustice. It's affecting her work.

'Alright, stranger?' Dev leans round the door.

'I've just been so busy,' she says.

'I'm thinking his name is Kyle.' He smiles, walks in.

'Right, because that's the only thing that could be taking up my attention.'

'Well, a messy desk, looking guilty. These are possible signs.' He plops a bag of jam doughnuts on her desk.

'Signs of a paranoid mind,' she says.

'I find a healthy dose of fried goods is all the mental health provision I need.' Dev sits opposite her.

'Some of us take a holistic view of health.' She gestures to the doughnuts.

'Look,' he says, glancing over his shoulder. 'I'm not just here for bakery-related reasons.' He pulls one out and bites it, the sugar crusting in his beard. 'Just wanted to give you a heads up.' He looks awkward. 'I had to cover for you last week, check over some stuff for Sai, put in some approvals, do some of the paperwork that was missing.'

It's weird, having the conversation this way round. He takes another bite, looks at her. A blob of jam falls on her desk. She needs to speak.

'Thanks, sorry about that.' Nina fiddles with a pencil.

'Hey, you did it enough for me when we were planning the wedding,' he says.

'I know I've been out of it. I didn't mean for it to fall on you.' She needs to do better, find a way to balance this all out.

'No problem.' He shifts, there's something he's not telling her. 'It's just, on the days you missed, when you were ill.' He grabs a post-it from her desk, uses it to mop up the jam. 'Clive made a few comments, nothing huge,

75

but you might want to make sure he doesn't have a reason to be disappointed with you.'

'He's trying to get rid of me?' She smiles. Clive has never liked her, not since she told him she'd take his job within five years of her interview. That wasn't far off now. No wonder he was getting twitchy. It's not as if she can't catch up.

'I'd like to see him try.' Dev shakes his head, gets up. He pauses by the door. 'Just look out for yourself, ok?' There's concern in his voice.

Nina could tell him the real reason, it might be good to have at least one person to confide in. But that would lead to everything since, her failure at the police station, the situation with Holly.

'All good.' Nina smiles. She can feel it stretch her face a little too wide. There must be a way to make things better.

Her phone lurches on her desk.

'Excuse me,' she says, lifting it and turning away. She hears the click of the door behind her. It's Holly.

Want to go shopping at the weekend? Need new shoes.

That's what she can do. Tell Holly, even if it doesn't go anywhere. She'll have to find another guy to use for a rebound. He might be dangerous, it would be doing her a favour, really.

Nina gets more coffee to go with the doughnut and readjusts her brain. She can work through lunch. It's a relief, to realign herself with the mechanisms of the day. A sense of purpose swells as she piles through figures, charts, designs, adjustments. Disgruntled replies come back from the multitude of requests she sends out. They wanted an easy start to the week.

The office is a flickering space, full of twilight, by the

time she looks up. Everyone's gone, the cleaners scouring the floors over the other side.

It's too late. Working flat out, there's no way she'll be able to match Dev and meet the deadline. There's too much to be tested and certified before it can go on the prototype. The presentation is in three weeks. Impotence tugs at her; the last few hours were pointless.

The fluorescent lights scrape at her eyes, the whine of the vacuum gnawing. There are three ibuprofen packets in her bag – all empty. She's gone over the same equation three times in the last ten minutes, and each time she gets a different solution. Defeat is tangible. This is not who she is. She's never got anything lower than a B, and that was her Geography GCSE because the teacher was useless. There must be a way to get things back on track.

She shuts everything down and walks through the deserted space, the ghosts of shadows falling from each chair in the gloom.

Dev's desk is the epitome of organisation. She taught him how to get himself together. Stacked files, an in-tray labelled, colour-coded notes. A picture of him and Amy on holiday. Both of them stained with sun and happiness. His screensaver is a word of the day. "Juggernaut" shifts colours as it bobs around the screen. That means he hasn't logged out.

Nina ruffles the mouse. Stacked numbers in spreadsheets, all the files he must have been working on today. His chair still has remnants of heat. She scrolls through the ordered rows. The sum of his engine, the code to his success, all laid out. She could break his efficiency, skew his numbers, inflict some problems that would give her time to breathe. It can easily be undone, later. Checking for witnesses, she sits in his chair and pulls herself up to the screen.

Eric

He manages to get on the 5:23 to Brighton just as the whistle goes. Thursday is his blank time, it's always easier to get out early. His rucksack clangs with the four pack and bottle of whisky he picked up in Tesco Express on the way to the station. The train is stuffed with commuter cattle at this time of day. He wedges himself between two suit-clad business types. Opposite is a woman with a pram. God knows why she got on this train. The baby is cramming raisins into its mouth, staring at him.

Now to write on the card. He manages to lever his bag off his back and wedge it between his feet. There were only two "Dad" cards in the shop. The one he picked had a man with a hat on and a fishing rod. He's probably never gone fishing in his life, but maybe it can be ironic. No way he can hand over a card with "Best Dad Ever!" when they barely speak.

He takes a pen out of his pocket – there's also a wadge of snotty tissue covered in glitter – and pulls the plastic packaging off the card. There must be lots of meaningful things he could write. All he can think of is the time they almost made a go-kart together when he was seven but after sawing up wood and bolting wheels on his dad had lost interest. Even the word "Dad" seems a stretch. He writes "from Eric" at the bottom of it and seals it before he starts drinking and gets emotional.

It's always necessary to have at least one drink before visiting. If possible, two. After glancing at the mum behind the pram he gets a can out and snaps it open. The baby, seemingly in protest, throws the rest of the raisins on the floor and starts to wail. Eric pretends not to notice and takes a big swig, nodding at his nearest be-suited neighbour as if they have something in common.

The last time he visited was back in November. He'd decided to do a surprise visit, had the idea that he might be invited to stay with them over Christmas for once. Instead, he'd waited outside in the cold for an hour and a half. They'd been on a walk on the Downs and had come back fresh-faced and smiling, his girlfriend and her two young boys the image of the family Eric always wanted. After two cups of tea and stilted conversation he'd given up, sent them a card for Christmas even though he knew he wouldn't get one back.

At least he was expected. He sucked down the last of the first can and scrolled back to find the message. *Come over if you like. Cake is at seven.* Hardly an enthusiastic reception but better than nothing. He pictures Gail, her frizzy hair and that look she always shoots over to his dad when he visits. As if Eric is the one out of place. Her little boys, leaping onto the two of them as if they belong to him. Definitely time for another can before they get there. Almost a whole hour to get to Worthing. He could have driven but then he would have had to face them sober and the A27 is a nightmare at this time. He's sure the mum gives him a disappointed glance as she levers the pram off at the next stop. Eric squats down in the space she leaves and spends the rest of the journey scrolling through his phone, trying to find Nina on social media.

The dream comes back. The silent figure standing over him – it's always Dad. Something in the way he breathed, the way he cleared his throat. It was from the last time he saw him at home. After his first week in his new job at the school.

*

He can't remember why he decided to go home. Or why he still called it that. Usually he waited for an invite, something that came when Dad wouldn't be there. After a few awkward visits when he returned from university some unspoken agreement had emerged, and he only ever saw Mum. Sometimes he could hear him, shuffling about in the garage, or out in the garden, but they never spoke.

To go over unannounced was unusual. Perhaps it was that first experience of utter exhaustion after a week of work, that would become commonplace, that urged him to seek company and comfort.

Buoyed up with hope of congratulations, he headed for the familiar road. He sifted through the day, considering which bits would make Mum laugh, or impress her. Dad would make himself scarce, it wouldn't matter.

The house was dark. The brown Allegro sat in the driveway – maybe they were in the kitchen. He went in, unnerved by the silence of the place. He always assumed they were here, a constant presence until he arrived. No lights. They couldn't have gone out. The annual dinner at the end of the football season wasn't until September.

He realised he was placing his feet carefully, holding his breath. While he was here, he could at least scope out the kitchen. There were always interesting biscuits; maybe the fancy snacks she got when her book club people came over.

It felt like he was being watched. He glanced around, the bulk of the Welsh dresser looking ominous in the gloom, the glint of the spoon collection catching in passing headlights.

The shock of the kitchen light was loud, the fluorescent tube buzzing. He closed the door, not sure why. If he'd known what was happening upstairs, maybe he could have helped her.

He rummaged through the cupboards, assembling a selection. A cookbook lay open on the side, a recipe for Chicken Madras marked with a neon tab. He resolved to add spices to his weekly shop. Bea would like a curry made from scratch.

There was shuffling overhead. He looked up, squinting at the ceiling, waiting for the source of the sound to register. It stopped. Maybe they had mice again. Dad had mocked him for crying when they used traps. The broken bodies were so small.

He flicked the pages over to the puddings and opened a packet of crisps. More scuffling. Louder this time. Possibly voices, a deeper bass. His first thought was that they'd already gone to bed. It was nine, but it wouldn't be impossible.

There was a shout, cut off. Unless there were intruders. Heart thumping, he grabbed the frying pan and crept towards the stairs.

It was coming from the bedroom. He stepped carefully, avoiding the creaky board that used to catch him out when he was trying to sneak into Lil's room and sleep there.

A thud this time, like something had been dropped. He swung open the door, arm raised.

They'd been there the whole time. He wasn't sure what to make of it at first. Mum was leaning over the bed, like she was doing the sheets. Dad was turned towards the window, his shoulders rising and falling quickly.

'Oh love, no.' Mum flapped her hands at him, trying to shoo him away.

'Your face.' There was a red mark on her cheek, her hair rucked up.

'I'm fine.' She patted her dress and smoothed it down. He saw her tights, shuffled in a heap around her ankles. He could hear Dad breathing.

'Are you OK?' He walked over and put his arm around her, could feel her shivering.

'Oh, piss off.' Dad didn't turn around.

'It was a bit much this time.' Her voice was small against his chest.

'Cry to your little boy then.' He turned. The smell slapped him – whisky. His face was red and splotchy, breath ragged. He clattered his belt, doing up his trousers, sliding the leather through the loops. He didn't bother to hide anything. The pieces of the scene came together.

'You wouldn't understand.' Dad pushed past them, into the bathroom. The shower started running.

'Maybe you should go.' She disentangled herself.

'Mum, are you OK?' His construction of his father slipped.

'It's fine.' She reached down. There was a red mark on her leg, her wide pants were peach trimmed with little flowers. How had she let him do this to her?

'Does he hurt you?'

'Some things you learn to live with.' She laughed, almost a choke. Her mask slipped a little, he saw the disappointed woman underneath. 'Now come on, off you go.' It had been a relief, to be instructed like that.

He'd abandoned her. He could have confronted Dad, been the man he thought he should be. After he'd driven away from the dark house, Mum in a forlorn pool of light on the porch, he hadn't heard from her for over a month. It didn't occur to him that he should have gone back, offered support. When she finally rang all she would say was that he'd left. He wondered if she blamed him. He never told Lilly what he saw that night, the dismay of seeing an older version of his own face creased with such an expression.

*

There are balloons on the door. A big "Happy Birthday Dad" banner is taped to the inside of the front window. Eric wants to walk up and correct it with the pink pen he uses for school. Stepdad at best, borrowed dad at least. Stuffing chewing gum in his mouth to mask the train beer he rings the bell and stands back, securing his smile.

'Oh. Hello, Eric.' She sounds as if his presence is a surprise.

'Good evening, Gail. Lovely to see you.' He leans in to hug her at the same time she puts her hand out. They clash somewhere in the middle.

'He's just through here.' She backs away quickly, walks to the living room. 'Eric's here,' she says to the room.

'Hello.' Eric crosses the threshold and does a little wave. The room is full. There are several kids sitting on the floor, extra chairs brought in for the adults. There are a couple of familiar faces – the men who sat in the football stands with them on the days he convinced Eric to go. The bubble of chatter dies down and everyone looks at him.

'Eric.' Dad smiles. 'Thanks for coming.' He stands and walks over, moving close to him in the doorway. 'Want to chat in the kitchen?' Eric follows him, disappointed. It would have been good to join in the fun.

'Happy birthday.' Eric pulls out the card and puts it on the kitchen table. The glittery tissue is stuck to it.

'Still teaching then?' he says. At least he's attempting an interest.

'It's going really well. I'm hoping to get a promotion. Management. The sort of thing that would lead to me being a Headteacher.'

'Very nice.' He nods. Perhaps even a twitch at the corner of his mouth.

'You always used to say, the way to get ahead was to run the place.' It could lead to new links between them, he could be one of those people that visits their father at half term, goes out for beers.

'That's not what I meant.' He picks up the card and opens it. 'Watching a bunch of kids draw pictures is hardly work.' He reads what's inside, looks up. 'It's funny, I can be much more of a dad to Jonas and Kai.' He smiles, like he's being wise, not cruel.

'Why did you lose your job? You never told me why we had to move.' Maybe he can inflict his own damage in return.

'That what you're here for, is it?' Dad rests his chin in his hand. 'Thought your mum would have told you years ago.' He shrugs. 'Had a thing with a woman at work. Next thing you know, she cries rape.'

'What do you mean?' He's even worse than he thought.

'She was married. I guess he found out and she needed an excuse. Hounded me out of my bloody job when she was the one who came onto me.'

'People don't lie about things like that.' Lil was furious when some celebrity wife complained about her footballer husband beating her up and all the tabloids claimed she'd made it up.

84

'You've got a lot to learn about people. They're basically selfish and will do whatever it takes for an easy life.' He shakes his head. 'Didn't your dad teach you anything?' It's the first time he's referred to Eric like that in a long time. He wants to hold onto it, keep the moment going.

'I got you a present.' Eric takes the bottle out and puts it on the table between them.

'I don't drink that stuff anymore.' He picks it up. 'I'm sure one of the lads will take it off my hands.'

'Since when?' There was always a whisky bottle on the worktop when they were little. Sometimes more than one.

'Not for years now.' He shakes his head. 'Didn't bring out the best in me.'

'Is that why you did those things to Mum?' It's out of his mouth before he can stop it. Must be the cans on the train.

'Now.' He thunks the bottle down. 'That was a long time ago. I won't have you insulting me in my own house.'

'It's not an insult. It's a fact. I saw you.' He looks up, meets his eyes. This wasn't what he wanted to say but the anger rises quick and hot. 'You hurt her.'

'What happened between me and your mother is none of your business.' His voice lowers. That tone he used before everything exploded. 'I didn't ask you to come.'

'Everything all right in here?' Gail's cheerful face breaks something between them. Eric sags.

'But you're my dad.' He slumps into one of the kitchen chairs.

'I'll leave you to it,' she says, grabbing some napkins off the table and leaving.

'Look.' His dad sits down opposite. 'You're grown up

85

now. What do you need a dad for? And anyway, I've got my boys now.' He smiles. 'They're a handful and a half. And they need someone to keep them in line.'

'Family is important.' He sounds like a sulky kid. These arguments sound so reasonable in his head.

'I think you can choose who's important. They need my help. You wouldn't believe the amount of grief I get around town. They see a white man with a black woman and two kids and anyone would think we lived in South Africa.' He shakes his head. 'What do you need me for?'

'I've only got one dad.' So he can have someone to look up to. So he can figure out what kind of man he wants to be. So he can stop dreaming about this darkness in him that he worries might be genetic.

'Dads are for football games and Match of the Day.' He shrugs. 'You were never really into all that.' There it is. His failure to be a proper son.

'Can I come and visit again?' He stands too quickly and makes the chair fall over.

'If you like.' He leans in. 'Only I'd rather you didn't drink before you came.' He stands up, turns towards the door.

'Happy birthday, Dad.' Eric says it quietly but there's no-one left in the room to hear him. He stuffs the card and the whisky back in his bag and rushes to the door before his anger spills out.

On the street, he screws open the cap and chugs back a big swallow, making him cough and gasp. He ignores the old couple walking past. Of all the places to live. Worthing was where people came to die, everybody knew that. He strides in the direction of the train station. The fucking cheek. Telling him off for drinking after all the years of shit he had to put up with. It wasn't fair that those two got the dad he'd been denied. That being a father came with a list of requirements on his part. It wasn't his fault he thought football was boring. That he thought a trip to the West End was far more exciting than a draughty stadium. Why had he wasted all this time trying to impress someone that was clearly so uninterested in him? Especially when he'd seen the worst of him and had persisted in trying to find some good, thinking that it was somehow important to maintain a relationship with a pissed bully.

By the time he gets to the train station almost a third of the bottle is gone. He slumps onto a bench and watches people walk around him, glancing at him as if he's a tramp or something. What a state. Not even 7:30 and he's sitting on a bench with a bottle of whisky in his hand. Perhaps there's more of his dad in him than he realises.

He puts the bottle back in his bag, sits back and tries to clear his head before the next train arrives.

Friday morning – the last day he can hand in the application. The shower has hardly managed to hide the ravages of yesterday. Beer, whisky, and disappointment don't make for a fresh start. He scrubs a hand over his chin. It's itchy, like there are spots festering under the stubble.

The razor scrapes his cheek, the skin pink underneath. It feels cleansing, to cut it all away. Might make him look more presentable, more like management potential.

Better. He smears moisturiser on, enjoys the clammy feel of the new-shaven skin. No excuses anymore. He can give up trying following this sexually deviant woman around, impress Foggert and actually have a career. Maybe even meet someone new. He rubs a bit of wax through his hair, tries to flatten down the bit at the back that always sticks up.

Fresh shirt, jumper, shoes, it might rain today, best to put on the blue coat with the hood. He tips it up so the fluffy white bit is around his ears, then heads to the car.

At the end of the road, he stops, hand hovering over the indicator. Right will take him straight to school, left to her house. It's already seven, she won't still be there. Besides, he promised himself he'd stop. What is he going to do, ask for her number? He clicks right, sees a blue car approaching behind him. Similar colour to hers.

At the last moment he flicks the indicator down, makes a quick turn. It won't hurt, just to see if her car is still there. Not massively out of his way.

It's finally starting to get lighter in the mornings. Soon he won't even need the sidelights. An early-morning jogger heads past him, clad in stretchy neon.

Turning onto her road, he can see a group of people huddled at the far end. Something's wrong.

He slows, getting closer, trying to see what the issue is. There's a black car skewed at an angle, blocking the way. Looks like there's been an accident. Pulling into the next available space, he gets out, knocking his hood back. Maybe he can help.

It's her. The back of her car is jutting out at an angle, knocked into the car in front. She's leaning on the wing, holding her wrist out in front of her. Before he can step back into the shadows she looks up, straight at him.

Nina

The jolt of impact rattles up Nina's body. A thick metallic crunch. Her head snaps forward, right arm braced against the steering wheel. A sharp pain in her wrist.

Stillness. The seatbelt is a hard pressure against her chest, pinning her down. Her hands reach for the button, scrabbling. A force of memory overtakes her, strapped and rigid. Dark and muffled heat, that hand on her spine. The vicious pressure of him against her. She gasps air, unable to take enough in, weakening with each breath.

'You OK? That was quite a bump.' A fleshy face hovers outside, cutting out the light. In the rear-view mirror, a solid black car.

'Fine.' She appraises her surroundings. The ornaments of the day are on the back seat – stuff for the gym, folded up bags for shopping, scarf she doesn't need to cover the marks anymore, but wears anyway.

Nina was ahead of herself, feeling capable, she'd administered enough coffee to keep her going despite the lack of sleep, even managed some breakfast for once. She was going to end the week more positively than she started it. Now this.

She squeezes out of the door in the segment of air left between him and the car. A smell catches her nose –

shower gel undercut with sweat.

'In a rush, were you?' he asks. She barely reaches his shoulder.

'Well if I couldn't see you, it was clearly because you were going too fast.'

Points of attention niggle at her – a clump of people gathered on the pavement, all eyes trained on the spectacle she's become.

'Steady on there, love.' His hand pats her shoulder, the dampness from his palm creeping through her shirt. 'All get flustered in the morning, don't we? Work local, do you?'

'Porchester.'

'Quite a commute.'

'Like to get going early. The ring road.'

'Hell on earth. Get on it at the wrong time and it's more bunged up than my toilet after a curry.' He laughs, seeking approval from the onlookers.

A response is impossible. She grabs the pen and paper from the front of her laptop bag in the car. A twinge in her wrist. Offering them, another smile. Hopefully this will be over soon.

'Can you write your details down?' There are fewer witnesses now, they must have lost interest.

'I don't want to lose my no claims.' He looks at the pen like it's a foreign object.

'Let's just do it the normal way.' Keep the tone light. Nina leans on the top of the car. 'Name?'

'Just take it down the garage and let me know.' He gestures towards the people still gawking, waiting for a show. 'Five years of no claims.' He's making her look ridiculous.

'I have protection on mine,' she says. 'Who are you insured with?'

'Knows it all, she does.' He laughs. One of those

guys, he calls women "darling" and equates breasts with a lack of common sense. He reaches around and pulls out one of the big wallets like Dad used to have. Her wrist is really throbbing now. She leans her weight against the wing of the car, holds it up with her other hand.

'Blank cheque. No problem.' He taps it against the roof of her car, twice, like he's telling it off.

She tries again. 'If I can just have your name-'

'Am I saying it right?' His words are aimed at the man standing closest to them – blue coat, wind-ruffled hair. He's staring at her.

'What are you talking to him for? It's my car.' She rubs her wrist.

His wide hand reaches for her again. 'Come on,' he says, that look still in place. 'All you need to do is-'

'You come charging down the road in your stupid shiny car, clearly not paying attention to what you're doing. I know what I need to do. I need to get your sodding details so I can get a move on.' Her muscles tense again. Maybe she's sprained it.

'Like that, is it?' His face changes. At least this gives her something to rail against. 'If you think you're getting a penny from me, well.' He tucks the wallet away, like it's a precious gift gone to waste.

'Come on mate, she's got a point.' The man in the blue coat hovers closer. He keeps glancing over, like he knows her.

'I don't need you to defend me,' she says.

'There are witnesses.' He gestures back at the stragglers. 'You were clearly going too fast.'

The stocky man bounces his gaze between the two of them.

'Fine.' The pen and paper is snatched from her hands, he leans his head down and scribbles. Nina looks at the new arrival, smiles, keen to show appreciation without disrupting this progress. There's a tuft of hair sticking up at the back of his head.

Without a word, the details are handed over and the interloper stalks back to his car. The guy with the ruffled hair shrugs, squeezes his lips in a half smile. She nods, as if he's answered a question.

The car. She gets in and pulls up, the black hulk roaring past the moment she's up against the kerb. Scooping the fallen items on the seat, she has a quick glance in the mirror, clears a dot of black by her eye. A little tired, but OK. Time to check the damage.

The lights aren't even broken. A slight scratch on the boot, a small dent. She feels absurd. The car is her reflection, a dented carapace with a faulty mechanism inside. She'll just be late, that's all. If only her wrist would stop throbbing.

'Are you OK?' He looks nervous. 'I probably should have asked you that before, I mean after, but I didn't know what to say.'

'It's just my wrist, it feels sore.' If she's hurt herself then this stuttering guy doesn't seem like he'll be very helpful.

'I didn't even know your name,' he says. 'When it happened.'

'I'm Nina.' She slides up the arm of her coat. Her arm is red and swollen. 'Shit.' She touches the skin. It feels hot. 'Why would you need to know my name?' She looks at him. What is he talking about?

'It's just, I mean-' He puts his hands in his pockets, why does he looks so confused? 'Just, you know, so I could help you out with that guy, with the insurance.' He takes a step back. God this guy is weird.

'Thanks for that. Having a penis is an unfortunate necessity for dealing with that particular breed of male.' He doesn't even smile.

'You'll need to go to the hospital.' He glances up the road. Maybe he's just late for work or something.

'You think?' She turns her hand. Sharp darts of pain shoot up her arm. 'Yup, that really hurts. Last thing I needed this morning.' She sits on the wall outside the flat, tries to get the phone out with her left hand.

'Well, good luck.' He gives a little wave and walks off. So much for the helpful stranger.

If she can get to the hospital, get her wrist sorted, then hopefully she'll be back in work before getting even more behind.

Working the phone with her left hand is difficult. She gets as far as unlocking it before it clatters to the floor.

'Shit.'

Pick it up again, try resting it on one knee. Now to call a taxi. After three digits it crashes to the floor again. This is going to take a while.

'Hey.' It's the jumpy guy in his car, leaning over the passenger side, clicking the door open. 'You want a lift to the hospital?'

'Don't you have work?' One minute he can't wait to leave, now he's trying to help her. He might be a weirdo.

'I can get someone to cover for me.' He smiles. It's unfair to judge this guy because of what happened to her. He's probably perfectly normal. Nothing wrong with wanting to be nice. Besides, he hardly looks threatening.

'If you don't mind.' It would be so much easier this way.

'Course not.' He gets out, scoops up her stuff and puts it on his back seat.

'Thanks.' She gets in, holding her right arm up, across her body. It would be that side. Work is not going to be easy with this.

'The Alexandra has an A and E, right?' He leans over and pulls the seatbelt over her front. Very light eyes, pale

93

blue slipping to green.

'What's your name?' She settles back, OK to let yourself be looked after, for once.

'Rick.' He pats the back of his head. It makes even more tufty bits stand up.

'Thanks.'

He nods, glances over at her. They pull out into the morning traffic, her eyes catching on a break of blue in the clouds as she breathes through the throbbing in her bones.

Eric

She's sat right next to him. What is he supposed to say to her? The moment she looked at him, on the pavement, he was expecting something. A gasp, like a woman in a horror film, or a knowing wink with a blush, to acknowledge their dirty secret. Anything but what actually happened – nothing at all. She didn't seem to recognise him. How was that possible? Surely there was only so much a shaved chin could do.

'Where do you work?'

'Meadow Wood.' Unless this was all pretend. 'It's a primary school.' She was embarrassed, didn't want to admit to what happened.

'Teacher? Don't know how you cope. All those little sticky hands.'

'It has its moments.'

They'd be coming in from the playground now. He was going to get such stick. And on the day of the application hand-in. But he couldn't have just left her there. Also, it had seemed like, finally, the perfect excuse to talk to her. It was unfathomable that she hadn't recognised him. So much for the hero move.

She keeps looking out the window, uncomfortable. He should have asked her what she did. He wasn't supposed to know where she worked.

'What about you?' That gap was way too big.

'Engineer. We make prototype vessels. Working on one to go out to the Arctic, measure ice thickness and stuff.'

'Impressive.' That's what *Nautical Solutions* did.

'Beats finger painting.' Ah yes, the usual. Next will be something about all the holidays. He lets the silence draw out, wondering how he can make some sideways reference to the party.

The hospital is up on Portsdown Hill, just off London Road. Once they get past this roundabout it should be quicker.

'That was harsh, sorry. You are doing me a favour.' She touches her arm, sighs. 'This hasn't exactly put me in a good mood.'

'That's OK, I'm only educating the next generation.' Smile, to show her he's joking.

'Well, I'm saving the planet.'

'You win.'

She's so pretty. And an engineer. He can't help it, there's a little bit of pride. No way this woman would even look at him under normal circumstances.

'Here we are.' He pulls into the drop-off point, unclicks the seatbelt. 'You going to be OK? Need to get back to the small people.'

'Actually.' She's half out. Turns back, looks at him, really serious. This is it. It's been a pretence, all this time. 'They're going to get me to fill out forms, and I'm not sure I can write. Do you think the kids could cope without you for a bit longer?' She looks pale.

'Of course. Let me find somewhere to park.' She pushes the door shut, walks in through the sliding doors. Maybe she does want to talk to him after all.

'Well this is embarrassing.' She's sat there with a ticket in one hand, like the ones you get at the deli counter in Sainsbury's. 'There aren't any forms.'

'That's OK.'

'I think I've been watching too much ER.'

'You still want some company? You look pale.' Now he's called in, made the decision, it seems rude to just leave.

'Could you get me some water?' She pulls a pack of pills from her bag.

'Not sure you're supposed to take anything if you're waiting.'

'You've clearly never cut ahead in the bar queue.'

'You like living dangerously?' That was too close. Does she really not know him?

As the liquid dribbles into the paper cone, he looks at her, swiping her phone with her left hand. The things of her he's seen, what she let him do.

She's so together, so tough. Not the damaged thing Bea was. Maybe that's what women like that did. Sexually daring, didn't mind about the consequences. Have there been others?

Just give her the water. He walks past a pair of lads – one of them with a tea towel round his hand, pink with blood. A father with his kid, leaning back behind his head, looking towards the reception, the kid tapping furiously at an iPad, beeping noises and flashes.

She's glaring at the screen. Something's wrong.

'You have to be fucking kidding me.'

'What's up?' On her phone is a picture of a smiling girl, blonde, slight roundness to her cheeks. Leaning over her is the last person he'd expect to see on Nina's phone. Will.

'This is too much.' Her knuckles are white around the phone.

97

'Not Will's biggest fan?' Maybe this was the one he met at the club he went to. Eric can never keep track of them all.

'You know this guy?' That's not right. She saw them together in the kitchen. When she smiled at him.

'Kind of. We're not close.' She was angry with Will. Not a good idea to let her know they're mates.

'I wish I'd never met him.' Her head drops. Something like shame in her face. 'It was at this party.' This doesn't make any sense. She'd been there, waiting for him. Why else had she been lying there like that?

'The curse of alcohol.' Unless she'd been too drunk to remember.

'He's going to pay for what he did.' She says it quietly but he can still hear it. Almost a growl.

'Sorry?' She must still be angry at him for whatever happened upstairs.

'Thanks for your help.' Her face clears, shoulders drop. She looks normal again.

'No problem.' How embarrassing. She doesn't even remember everything that happened between them. He's been following a woman around when he is nothing but a drunken blur to her. 'Look, I've told them I'm ill, I can't go in now. I can hang around.' He hovers on the brink of leaving. On the other hand, this could give him a blank slate. He already knows they have chemistry.

'It's OK.' A painted-on smile. He's not important. 'Unless you know this guy's email address or something? Do you know him well?' Now she looks more interested.

'Not very well, he went to my school, thought he was a big deal. Bit of a dick to be honest.' Well, that bit was true.

'Do you know where he lives?' She leans closer. 'His phone number? Anything.'

'I guess. I mean, what do you want to do?' He lowers

his voice. It feels cosy, conspiratorial.

'I don't know.' She looks embarrassed. 'Just something, to hurt him.'

'He must have really pissed you off.' What on earth did he say to her?

'You have no idea.' There it is again. That look. Like she wants to cause him pain.

'I could help.'

'Nina Franklin.' A patient voice calls across the room.

She stands, winces as she puts her bag over one arm. Steps away from him, like he's forgotten already.

Then stops, turns.

'Wait here?' A question, not an order. Something pleading in her eyes.

'Of course.' Now he can start again. Get to know her properly.

The door clicks behind her, leaving him stranded on the plastic chairs. What will she do if he tells her Will's address? Smash up his house? She looked furious. If she sees them together, knows they're really mates, she won't want to know him. He opens Facebook, goes through all the photos of him and Will, takes the tags off. Defriends him. It's not surprising, after what he found out about Bea. If anything, Will deserves it. Sneaking around behind his back, sleeping with his girlfriend. Helping Nina out can help him get his own revenge.

The kid with the iPad starts moaning about being hungry. The pair of lads are still there, laughing about something. His eyes hurt. Must be the fluorescent lights. Horrible places, hospitals. That dark ward he'd lain awake in when he had his tonsils out, the scratch of the sheets, hiding the bulk of Bumblelion under his pillow so the nurses wouldn't think he was a baby.

His phone buzzes.

Birthday bowling on Saturday. Time to get shitfaced.

Will. He never asks if he's busy, just assumes he has nothing better to do. He is an arrogant prick. If you see him through the eyes of someone else, like her. He hadn't noticed it, not really. Just thought he was confident, sure of himself. He'd envied that, if anything. That had been why she'd liked him at the party, surely?

He can't believe she doesn't remember. It was so intense, how could something like that not stay with you? Of course, he'd had nights where he'd forgotten getting a kebab, or the taxi ride home, but surely this was more important than that. If she doesn't know who he is, then there's no way she'll be interested in a guy like him. Might as well slip off home, write this one off as a one-night failure. He stands up, turns towards the door.

'All done.' She's there, one arm pulled against her front with an off-white bandage.

'Are you OK?' Too late.

'Will be when the codeine kicks in.' She smiles.

'Do you want to go to his house?' It's the only thing he can offer her.

'Yes, I suppose. I don't know. Will he be there?' She looks scared. Of Will. That can't be right.

'Doubt it. Most responsible people are at work right now, not skiving.'

'Right.' She still looks unsure.

'Come on, what else have you got to do?'

Now they're back in the car, she feels too close. He can't stop picturing her from that night. There must be something he can say. Will always manages to get girls to like him.

'So, what's the plan?' She clicks the seatbelt in.

'No idea.' Maybe they can bond over their shared annoyance with Will. 'What do you think would piss him off?'

100

'He likes the way things look.' She wraps one arm around herself.

'I guess.' He'd never thought about it like that before. His car, the women he flirted with. Why he'd liked her, probably.

'Smash his windows.' Her voice has an edge.

'How about something less illegal?'

'We used to egg and flour the houses at Hallowe'en.' She grins.

'You were one of those.' Dad would have given him hell for something like that. Or would he? Maybe he'd have been proud.

'Not in my neighbourhood, I had a mate who lived in Leigh Park.'

'Sounds risky.' He was never allowed to hang around there.

'That's how I roll.' A snort of laughter.

'Let's do it.' Eric gets a fizzy feeling in his throat when he says it.

'What, really?'

'It'll give him a surprise when he gets home from work.' He'd get that squint in his eye, like he could smell something bad.

'OK.' She smiles. 'It's a start.' One of her legs is jiggling, thumb between her teeth, looking out of the window.

'There's a Co-op here.' He pulls in, gets out.

It's one of those local ones, random items piled high next to each other so they can squeeze everything in. The flour is stacked above suet, next to tubs of hundreds and thousands. Eggs in the next bit.

Impossible to take just these two things to the till. It will look suspicious. If he gets milk, butter, it will look like he's baking. At the counter he grabs a Twix. To calm the nerves.

By the time they get there he's managed to stuff his mouth full of caramel and biscuit the whole way, avoiding questions about how he knows his address, or why he agreed to this.

'Is that it?' She looks out the window.

'Yes, I think so.' He has to remember they're not supposed to be good friends.

'Don't park out the front. People will see!'

'Right.' He pulls around the stilled cars, waits further up. He was only here a couple of weeks ago. They'd watched a film and eaten pizza, filling themselves up with beer until he had to get a taxi home.

'This is crazy.' She's smiling. 'We're like a couple of kids.'

'I don't know how you do it.'

'You're in charge of eggs, I'll do the flour.' She puts the box in his hands.

'Isn't this criminal damage?'

'Please.' She rolls her eyes at him, grabs the flour, and gets out.

'You can do this.' He weighs the carton in his hand, imagining Will's hands all over Bea. He deserves something bad to happen to him.

Nina is standing by the closest hedge to Will's house, looking at her phone with the hand in the sling. Her other hand behind her.

'What are you doing?'

'Being inconspicuous. Until we're sure no-one's watching.' She looks up and down the street.

There might be CCTV cameras. If it gets back to the school, that would be it. Criminals don't get to teach. Mum would find out, Lil. All so disappointed.

'Ready?' She slides the phone in her pocket, hefts the flour. 'You need to go first, get it wet so this has something to stick to.'

She'd think he was pathetic. Running away from something like this.

'Right.' A little squeak in his voice.

He steps in front of the house. The green paint Will put on the front door, changing the name to "The Grove" so it would sell for more.

The first one splats at the bottom of the step, yellow splodges going up the artichoke paintwork. He spent hours choosing the right shade. Not enough force. The next is hefted right back, whacks into the window with an alarming noise, the mess spreading down the glass.

'Hurry up!' Her voice is urgent behind him.

Two, three, four, five, a pattern across the front – snot-white mixing with yellow and oozing over his precious exterior. The last one needs to be good. He takes aim, lands it right on the door knocker that Will found in some antique shop.

She hurries up behind him. Upturns the bag over the door, a huge puff of white falling over it. She gathers up the paper, creating a ball at the top, then hefts it into the wall, walking quickly over to the left. Each time she squeezes another lump to the top, one handed, before flinging it at the house. This is practised. There are clouds of it, whooshing up the walls, surrounding her in a cloud. It hovers in the air like smoke, tumbling down and dusting his shoes with a fine powder.

'Don't just stand there.' She catches his arm on the way past. His feet trip, he almost falls into her and then they're away, dashing up the street, not stopping to check for witnesses.

He gets in, starts the car, the other door slams. He didn't even lock it. Pulling out, he hears a beep. There's a car behind, someone waving their hands at him. No time to be polite. He accelerates away, quick turn at the end of the road, head towards the main road, get lost in the traffic.

A strange noise beside him. He glances over. Her shoulders are shaking, liquid lines in the fine coating of white powder on her face.

'That was fucking brilliant.' The words come between gasps of air. She's laughing.

The sight of her tugs at the corners of his mouth. What a mess they are. There's egg on the steering wheel, shell on his sleeve. He finds a side street, pulls in, lets the laughter blurt out of him.

She looks over. There's flour on her eyelashes, matted into her hair. His cheeks ache, belly hurting from it.

'You look a right state.' Just a few gasps now, the laughter running out.

'You can talk.' She rubs a floury hand in his hair.

'That was fun.' Something liberating about chucking stuff like that.

'Yes.' She looks down at her hands. Now's his chance.

'Do you want my number?' Her head snaps up. 'I mean, if you need any more help with this guy.' This can be his way in.

'Why would you do that?' Not exactly an enthusiastic response.

'Let's just say he didn't just call me names when we were at school.'

'OK.' He hands over his phone, she gives him a missed call. Now he has a reason to see her. And who knows, maybe eventually he can tell her what happened between them. For now he needs to rush back to work and get this application handed in. The brave reason he's late might even help his case with Foggert.

After he's dropped her off, her floury outline is left on the seat.

Nina

She wakes up the following morning disorientated, tangled in the laptop wire. A twinge in her wrist, it's stuck up at an angle next to her face. So much for looking after the fracture. When the text from Holly arrives at 11:30 she's barely halfway down the first pot of coffee.

Trip to town? Need shoes.

That sounds like a peace offering. Just the person to start off the weekend. All the gory details about her with that idiot. Although, maybe he'll have told her about the state of his front door. Find out how annoyed he is about it.

Such an odd day. The crash, the hospital, that strange bloke, sitting about waiting at A and E, having a cast fitted, that bloody Facebook post, no work done at all, spending ages on the phone to the insurance company. And between all that, the simple moment of joy, when she'd hurled flour at his door. She'd managed to hurt him, a little. The drain in the bath was still edged with a white paste.

It galvanised something. Ever since the police station almost two weeks ago, she's been moping about, letting things get on top of her. That won't happen anymore. This Will was clearly good. Had fooled her, Holly, was brazen enough to start on her mate after what he did. Well, that was about to change. He'll soon realise he shouldn't have messed with her.

Managing Holly will be tricky. A confession won't work, she'll just tell her to go to the police. That won't lead anywhere. But she could provide some information. As long as she keeps an eye on her, they've only been out for a drink, she can find out his weak spots. The places she can hurt him.

Cadbury's at 12?

Their usual meeting spot.

Dealing with Bella, make it 1.

Holly's cat has run up hundreds in vet's bills. First the weepy eyes, then a seed in its paw. Nina gave up a trip to Edinburgh to sit with the pathetic little thing; an enormous bandage at the end of one leg and a large plastic collar that drooped her neck, giving it the appearance of a sullen teenager.

That gives her a couple of hours. She can review her ideas, try to formulate them into something more concrete. There are scribbles and lists all over the table. It's hard to know what to start with. She needs to discredit him, make him suffer. It shouldn't be her who gets stuck late at work, fiddling the numbers of colleagues in order to give herself a break.

There's a lot to do. Fake accounts, gathering of information. Any contacts, addresses, they can all be used to her advantage. She will find a way to make him cower in the dark. She leaves the house buoyed with a sense of purpose, her weakness like a shed skin, still slumped on the sofa.

The first half hour is lost in a search for suitable work shoes and an update on the latest feline developments. Plodding through the sale selection in L K Bennet, Nina is subjected to every nuance – the goo that started coming out of her ears, the fraught visit to the vet's with the terrier that kept scratching at the front of the carrying box, the resultant misdiagnosis and drops, which caused trauma each time they were administered, and didn't work anyway. The loafers are a little too clumpy, but the ones without laces won't be sturdy enough for all the walking she does up and down the ward on a twelve-hour shift.

They graduate to Clarks, the return trip to the waiting room – a frightened budgie and an incontinent rabbit – this time oral antibiotics, but even when she put them in her food chopped up the bowl was clean apart from the specks of chalky white pill that the gravy had been licked off. The brown ones are too tight on the toes, but the navy blue look black they're so dark, and even though they cost more than she was hoping for, they're leather so it's a good investment, and she found a video on YouTube on holding the head and stroking the throat so a pill would go down.

Objectives achieved, they go for coffee and lunch, settle in the far corner so they can see the bobbing masts out of the window. Holly makes her contented noise – a little flurry of air accompanied by a sigh – settling her hands in front of her. Now attention will turn to Nina. She tries not to flinch.

'So how's things?' Holly says.

'Apart from this, you mean?' She waves one hand at the cast. Eating with her left hand is definitely tricky. 'Lost a whole day at work, and been dropping stuff all over the flat.'

'That guy sounded like such a prick. Will you get it back on the insurance?'

'I think so.' She can't mention Rick, it will lead back to what they did to Will's house. 'He took some convincing to give over his details, that's for sure.'

'No match for you.' Holly sits back. That look, as if Nina is something impressive.

'Just didn't give up.' Except she nearly had. If Rick hadn't been there, she might be stuck without any money. 'Anyway, I'm sorry I was off last week.' Best to change the subject.

'What's up?'

Work will sound the most plausible. 'I'm just so tired from work. This project is a monster.'

'How long is left on the Project of Doom?'

'The presentation's happening in just over a week.' The time has gone so quickly.

'Desperate Dev much of a help?' Holly came up with this after she met him, said he had bovine eyes.

'He's at the other end of things. We're almost in competition.' He's come a long way.

'The student has become the master,' Holly says.

'Something like that.' Nina hadn't thought of that. Maybe she should keep an eye on Dev, he'd be after her job next. 'How's all the prancing about going?' She maintained sarcasm in relation to Holly's evening pursuits.

'Auditions coming up. It's for a concert this time, lots of songs from different shows.' She fidgets. Why spend time doing something that made you so self-conscious?

'I see.' Nina had always found musicals artificial. You couldn't believe in a story when people kept bursting into song.

'I thought I might audition this time.' Holly shifts in her chair. 'For a solo.' She's always done chorus stuff before.

'Go for it. You've got a great voice,' Nina says.

'You really think I should?' It must be great to have a natural talent. Nina doesn't understand why it doesn't lead to more confidence.

'Of course.'

Asking her questions soon is important. It's making her distracted. Holly might suspect something is wrong. Their sandwiches arrive, this could be a useful point to shift to a new topic. As Holly picks off her onions, Nina gathers an opening.

'And what about this guy?' She can't say his name out loud.

'Not much to tell.' Holly looks noncommittal.

'Enough for a Facebook post.'

'That was his idea. A joke really, something about his mate knowing the guy that owns the bar.' A shrug.

'You wanted Scott to see it.' She tries to cut her food with her left hand.

'Well, he's tall, got that sort of football cute thing about him. The kind of guy Scott would think was a prick.' Holly reaches over and takes the knife, does it for her.

'And that's what you're looking for in your rebound?'

'Oh, come on, it was just fun.' She takes a bite from the edge. She always eats around, saves the middle bit until last.

'You don't know anything about this guy.' But if she does, that would be helpful.

'Yes, I do. He works in PR. Has a nice car. He even showed me pictures of it.' Eyes down, a little giggle. Oh god, she likes him. 'He calls it Kat, after the car in Knight Rider.' The car. That needs to be a target.

'Where does he work?' That's some help. If she could just get more.

'Not sure. One of those horrible shiny office blocks out by Cosham. I thought you didn't approve?'

'Last name?'

'What is this, an interrogation?' She scoops the foam off the top of her coffee.

'I was trying to take an interest.' Nina leans back, swallowing down the sour coffee that threatened to come up again.

'He'll never be short of kitchen goods.' She raises her eyebrows, waits.

'Argos? No, hang on, William Habitat. That would be sofas.'

'Think crappy TV adverts.'

'Lakeland! You can buy a super mop from him that doubles as a clothes hanger.'

'Or a clothes hanger with an attachment for brushing the cat.'

Her smile isn't forced now. It's a moment of easy silence.

'It's weird, isn't it?' Holly fiddles with her cup. 'We did talk about it, how he'd had a thing with you. He said he'd almost forgotten about it, went to a club after you guys fought.'

'Right.' So that's the story he's telling.

'I'm sorry, it was just nice to have someone pay me attention, buy me drinks, tell me I look pretty. I know that's pathetic.'

'It's OK.' Nina touches Holly's hand. 'I understand why you'd want that.'

'Are you feeling alright?' Holly smiles. Nina pulls her hand away. Is she acting differently?

'Just be careful, OK?'

'It's nothing.' Holly dips the last of her chips in the sauce pot.

'So, you're not seeing him again?'

'Well, he said he wanted to take me out for dinner.'

'Holly!'

'It's just some food. I thought it might be a laugh. And I'm sorry if it's weird for you, but you've always been good at separating this stuff. I know you wouldn't

110

go for someone like that, not really.'

'He's not what he seems.' She's an awful friend. Letting her spend time with someone like that.

'This isn't like you.' Holly leans in. 'I don't know what you mean, Hun.'

'You can't tell just by looking at someone, what they're like.' But the alternative, telling her, it just isn't possible.

'I'm not marrying the guy,' Holly says.

'Just be careful.' She can feel heat creeping up her neck. This is too close.

'Is everything ok?'

Nina's hands start to judder in her lap. She can't handle this level of concern.

'You know I don't like losing control, getting drunk. I wasn't that bad, was I?' Usually, she only had a couple of drinks when they went out. It's only since it happened she's been ending almost every day in a drink haze.

'I love drunk Ninnie.' Holly smiles.

Nina puts one hand over the other, presses it down.

'Nin?'

If she tells Holly, she'll tell her to go to the police. It will be oversimplified. And she'll have to put it into words, admit that she let it happen, didn't fight back. She can't stand pity.

'Jesus, aren't I allowed to be pissed off? You could have found your own guy.' It comes out more biting than she intended.

'Alright, Jeremy Kyle.' Holly sits back, shaking her head.

A truce has been reached. Nina asks a few questions about songs to deflect her further. Holly enthuses about lyrics and tone, waving her hands in an imitation of the actions she could do. It's hard to look supportive.

They resume their chat, dipping in and out of shop

111

doorways with no clear destination in mind. Nina picks up a pair of gloves and a hat, a long dark coat. She wants to hide herself.

Turning away from the counter, she's at eye level with the flushed cheeks of a baby, strapped against a man's chest, limbs wobbling. Outside, they're everywhere. Swollen women, heaving large balls of life under their dresses, toddlers yanking at sleeves, prams cluttering the walkways. Her monthly annoyance failed to arrive yesterday. She swiped the alarm off her phone, packed extra tampons for work. Nothing.

When Holly emerges from the changing rooms, Nina drags her to The Custom's House, the far end where families don't go. At the bottom of the first bottle of wine she adds a visit to the clinic to her new list. They talk about the holiday they went on when they first met, a week in a shitty apartment on a Greek island, gorging on yoghurt and sunshine.

At home, she Googles his name. The images are varied – a soft-eyed grandfather and a little boy in a red T-shirt, a square hole in the front of his smile. He's in the third row down, sandy hair gelled back, an exacting tie knot and a practised smile. His eyes are fierce blue.

It's a work profile. He's on Facebook too, and an Instagram account. A flurry of images – nights out, restaurants she's eaten in, that same grin sculpted in each one. The simple fact of his existence, infecting the same air as her. She goes to type something else, but her fingers are sweaty, sliding off the keys. She could have bumped into him in town today.

The sensation of suffocation creeps in. At first, little gasps, like something is in her throat. Then her lungs feel too small, the air thin. Weakness seeps up her legs, little black spots appearing at the edge of her vision. She sags to the floor, gasping, her chest hot. At the point where she's sure she'll choke, it recedes. The carpet keeps her company for another twenty minutes, until she can stand up again.

Eric

Eric

The sides of the two-tone shoes press on Eric's toes. He pushes his trainers over to the grumpy-looking teenager behind the counter and turns to find the others. Arriving late on purpose was the best idea, so he wouldn't have to do the awkward introduction thing when new people turned up.

They're in the bar area, spread out over several tables. At Eric's last birthday it had just been him and Will. Heading over to them, he fiddles with his shirt buttons. All the others are wearing T-shirts. Chris leaps up as he approaches and thuds his back. Eric tries not to flinch – he's never been able to trust his intentions.

'Walker! Haven't seen you for bloody ages.' A pint is thrust into his hand – the plastic bends under his grip. Afternoon drinking is something he tries to avoid. It makes him too honest about his emotions, like at the staff do last term when he told Kirsty she was the kind of woman he imagined himself with. At least her husband hadn't heard.

Eric finds a space near the edge. The others are lumped into rough social groups. Lots of denim and sportswear. Will doesn't even look up; he's telling a story to the office drones. Their attempts to look casual are a little too tailored; gel swooping their hair, like a wind has caught each one in a different direction. The Uni friends are over to one side, only a few this year. No Jason, they had a laugh at the last one, got into a debate about testing in schools. Eric recognises Ian, the one who was sick on the stairs. Over here are the lifers – college and school friends, they can sit quietly and let the others earn their spot. There's a familiar shift to inertia – Will's shadow has always spread wide. Eric fiddles with a beer mat.

He's looked at her number countless times. Not to use it, messaging her the following day is too keen, but good to know it's there. Saved under "Nina," more personal just to have her first name. She feels like an ally against Will. Or something separate, just his. And who knows what might develop over time.

The thud and slide of balls clunk at intervals behind them. Sharp lights flash in the arcade, the whirr of wasted money mingling with cheers from the lanes. He'd rather be there, getting lost in the scrolling images of racing games. There might be a way to sneak over. Eric isn't conspicuous.

Luke reaches over, grabs for the card in the front of Eric's shirt. It was so obvious, sticking out of his pocket like that. Now he'll become visible.

'You big softie,' he says, passing it over to Will. The story falters, attention turning to Eric. The card is bright and rude. Hopefully under group scrutiny no comments will be made. Will scans the words inside, his eyebrows lift, but he doesn't look over. The card is shoved behind him, presumably to avoid the hands that are already reaching for it.

'So, before I can explain, they all start clapping.' Will ends his story, an eruption of laughter from the office lot.

He should have left the card at home. The idea was to use it as a parting shot, leave his accusations behind him to sour Will's day. It's not often Eric can claim an upper hand. Now he's lost his element of surprise.

The first drink is almost empty, he can find a new way to ignore the others over on the shiny floors. After a few hours he can head home, there are some cans in the fridge and there's bound to be a mindless film on.

The noise of the group is growing, someone's telling a joke, the language loud and rude. There's a neat family eating a few tables away. The boy could be Kian, with frizzy hair and glasses. He always worries about bumping into them outside school.

'Time to bowl, gents,' Chris says, slapping his empty cup down. They all stand, moving like a herd towards the lanes.

Eric lingers over the dregs of his beer. 'I'll get a round in,' he calls to their backs, not waiting for a response. He didn't even count how many there were. 'Same again?' He gestures to the receding group. The barman nods and grabs a stack of cups.

'Nice card.' Will must have doubled back.

'No problem.' Eric concentrates on the filling liquid.

'You want to hear my side?' Will taps the edge of the bar.

'Not really.' He doesn't want the details of what they did, not from him.

'She started it, mate, I swear,' he says.

'Let's not do this.' Eric already knew. He'd felt like the consolation prize when he brought Bea home, introduced her to Will. He wondered what it was like to have women come up to you, to never need that awkward moment of exposition, the possibility of defeat. Will had always put her down so much, joked about her weight.

'This means you have something to say.' Will shakes the card in his face.

Happy Birthday. Thanks for fucking my girlfriend.

'It was supposed to be funny.' Eric can't admit how he feels. This is the closest he'll get.

'She wouldn't leave it alone.' Will sounds thoughtful, like there was something philosophical in his actions. 'I felt sorry for her, she said she was lonely. When you first started teaching, she hardly saw you.' A shrug.

'How very kind of you.' He would try and turn it around, make the failure Eric's.

'I told you, being all sensitive and spending hundreds on fancy emerald bracelets only goes so far.' He'd watch Eric's attempts at romance and make fun of it. At least when he had a serious girlfriend, he felt like he knew better.

'Yeah, I know. You're the one that ends up hooking up with people in the kitchen at parties.'

'She was a psycho.' He shakes his head.

'What happened with you two?' There has to be some reason she was so angry at him.

'She was all keen about going upstairs, then as soon as I got the condom out she started going on about how I was making assumptions. I mean, come on, why else do you take someone into a bedroom at a party? Bloody prick tease.'

Eric winces. It feels like she's his, somehow. He realises it must have been Will's condom on the shelf. Not a message to Eric, then. If she wasn't up for it with Will then why was she so keen with him? It doesn't make sense. He turns his attention to the cups lined up in front of them and gets his wallet out.

'I'll get these.' Will bats his hand away, pulls out his bank card. 'This night's going on the company expenses. Let's do a shot.'

'It's a bit early.'

'Least I can do.' Will looks uncomfortable. Perhaps he does have a conscience about it. 'Although I reckon I did you a favour, getting you away from that one.' He nods, like he's congratulating himself.

'Thought you'd have grown out of sleeping around by now,' Eric says. That's all it was, childish, not impressive. No mention of Nina's friend. He's exactly how she pictured him. How had he not seen it before?

'It's just a bit of fun.'

The shots are put down in front of them. They chug them straight down and Will turns away.

'You're going to have to get over Lori someday.' He winces, waiting for it to fall.

'Whatever.' He doesn't turn, there could be anything on his face. Maybe that's what made him this way. That was the only time Eric had glimpsed something like loss.

They squeak over to the lanes, the aniseed sweetness souring Eric's mouth. He finds himself in the middle when they get back to the group.

In Year 9, a rumour had circulated about Eric and Lizzie, the ugly girl from the estate with crooked eyes. For weeks, every classroom he walked into collapsed into silence, whispers accompanying him around the halls. He took to alternating between the library and the wall at the back of the science block with his lunch, to avoid the dinner hall. It coincided with Will ignoring him, even though they'd hung out every day before that. He knew he must have started it. After over a month there was a knock on his door on a Sunday afternoon. He overheard the familiar flutter enter Lilly's voice at the door. Screwing up his anger, he decided to slam the door in his face. Before he could speak, he knew it was useless. No apology or admission, just an assumption that Will was necessary to him.

118

This time he feels invulnerable.

'The Women's Institute called, they want their throwing style back,' he calls over the noise. Every time, no matter how lame the comments, Will laughs, and the others join in. This unfamiliar power is compelling. The game blurs, one ball thunking down after the other. Eric has to go and throw up before his last go. Once the game is finished, they can properly get going.

'What I want to know,' he says to Will, arm on his shoulder, 'is if she was such a fat boring cow, why did you want to fuck her?' He's sure his voice is quiet but most of the others look over.

'Two Anchors?' Will gestures to their new direction.

'I asked you a question.' Eric pulls on his arm.

'Fine.' Will stops, nearly causing a collision. 'I was jealous. You had this connection with her and yes, it did remind me of Lori. I didn't like it.'

'So, you took it from me.'

'Come on mate, you said it yourself, she was mental.' It's suddenly funny. She was a handful. They snigger, then a snort of drink comes out of Will's nose. They are in a haze of humour, together. It's bright outside.

The day meanders on, somehow it gets dark before they leave the next pub. They get chips, break the cycle with a can of Tango, then back into the fray. Between the wash of drinks and spattering in the toilet Eric remembers his other goal. He needs to find out what Will saw, if he knows.

It would be satisfying, in a way, telling him. Reverse the balance, be the successful one for a change. She was the one that pushed Will away, but hadn't done the same to Eric.

More drinks, more shots, the other people in the pub start to give them a wide berth. Eric still can't shake the fear of sleep. The nightmares haven't stopped. He can't understand why a night like that, something that probably happened to Will all the time, haunted him so much.

Yes, he will tell him, Have a moment of smugness for himself, that he succeeded where Will had failed. Then maybe ask him if it was normal for a one-night stand to give you dark dreams. He zips himself up and staggers out with such purpose that he bashes someone's arm and gets a slosh of lager down his left leg.

The doorbell buzzes. Eric is spread diagonally on his bed. He didn't even take his shoes off. Grumbling, he rolls over. The harsh grate of it goes off again, for longer this time.

It isn't going to go away. He levers himself upright; the thud of a headache arrives when he's vertical.

Lil's voice is impatient when he gets there. 'You were supposed to be helping me get a patio umbrella.'

'Sorry.' He leaves the door open and goes to get some water.

'You look like shit.' She's her usual riot of colour, even her hair makes his eyes hurt.

'Thanks.' He rinses the iron taste from his mouth. 'Will's birthday.' He slumps onto the sofa. Maybe food would help his stomach.

'Oh.' She looks disappointed. 'You made up then?''

'Something like that.' He remembers an arm around Will's shoulder, whispering things into his ear.

'You never learn.' She stands in the debris of the front room.

'What's that supposed to mean?' He can't remember what he told him.

'Never mind, brother dearest.' She flutters around, picking things up, tidying.

'Leave it.' He fishes his phone out of his trousers. Battery's dead. Lil moves to the kitchen. He can hear her dropping things in the sink, running the tap. 'Stop!' he yells through the door.

'What's up?' She stands in the doorway with a cluster of mugs in one hand.

'You're being a pain.'

'I never understand how someone who can organise a classroom lives in such a pit.'

'Please, stop.' He finds an open can of Coke on the table and drinks it. Even flat, it's wonderful.

'Look.' She reaches over and pats his hair down. 'You don't need friends like that.' She sits on the sofa with a bag of crisps and a glass of squash. Clearly, he won't be getting rid of her any time soon. Eric turns the TV on, so at least she'll stop talking to him.

There's a red smear oozing down the coffee table. Jam from the toast when he got home. He hates having to defend it, but the odds are he wouldn't have friends at all if it weren't for Will. He's been like this, sitting on the side-lines, ever since they first met.

*

Eric straightened the grey duvet in his bedroom and checked that his shirt was baggy around the back in the mirror. The carpet was still mottled purple. Mum promised she'd change it when they moved here. He flattened the back of his hair, regarded himself carefully. If he could make it out of the door without Mum asking any questions, he could invoke his right to secrecy. He crept down the stairs.

'See you later.' He threw the words behind him as he walked through the door.

'Are you going out?' The worried slant of her voice was muffled. A brief glimpse of her, distorted through the ridged glass panel. Almost there.

Dad's van was pulling in. The tyres scrunched on the gravel of the drive, the "Ray's Repairs" sign at a slight angle. Eric hated the plastic sheen of it, reducing Dad to this. When he asked Mum about this drastic shift in career, she enthused about the fantastic opportunities of having your own business. Lilly whined about the gluey own-brand jam and watery squares of frozen fish, until Eric kicked her under the table in an act of big brotherly censorship. Dad was oblivious, his lectures on decent employment unchanged. Eric collected speeches about failure in his head that he could never deliver.

Maybe he hadn't been spotted. He might be able to dodge around the back, make his escape through the cutaway behind Frances Street. He gave the shuddering metal a wide berth, swerving behind the bushes. The road was a few steps away.

'Where are you off to in such a hurry?' The voice carried past the foliage. Eric slumped back along his exit route to find it blocked by both of them; Dad solid and grubby, Mum fluttering a tea towel in her hands.

'He didn't even say where he was going.' She delivered the accusation and hung back. Typical.

'I didn't raise you to be a liar.' His failures always came out as an inherent flaw.

'It's just some mates,' Eric said.

'More of that online crap?' Dad never liked the amount of time he spent on the computer.

'I'm going to the park.'

'The hell you are.' His tone was final.

'I've heard there are all sorts down there.' Mum crept forward again, still not meeting Eric's eye. 'He's such a gentle soul.' She pressed her hand on the shoulder of his checked shirt. At least she didn't ruffle his hair anymore. Dad's eyes darted between them.

'It's about time you learned to handle yourself,' he

said.

'There might be drinking, Ray.' Mum's hand hovered over him.

'I was down the pub at his age.'

'That's not exactly-' she coughed, as if covering something up. 'I suppose it means he's settling in better.'

'Can I go now?' There was a window.

'Don't be late.' Dad turned, Mum trailing behind.

Eric hurried outside the confines of the garden. He had a penknife and a set of adventure cards in his pocket. Chris had been so casual about it earlier, asking what he should bring had been impossible. A few months ago, a rumour limped around his tutor group about Holly Matheson giving a blow job to Sam Everett in the bushes at the park. Hopefully this wouldn't be an initiation. His fleeting experience in a cupboard with Gemma Warren back in Hadlow hadn't lent him much confidence in that area. Luckily, she hadn't been able to negotiate her way past the knotted waist of his tracksuit bottoms to discover it was too late for any additional attention.

He shifted the can of lager he'd swiped from Dad's stash in his jeans. It dug into the bones at the bottom of his back. The stack in the corner of the kitchen wasn't vanishing as quickly as it had been in the old place, Mum was even talking about getting a dog to walk along the seafront. Lilly had found more giggling idiot friends quick enough. He had resisted, keeping connections with Jake and Harry through their intricate online worlds. Speaking to no-one at school at least meant they had no ammunition.

Scuffing through the rubbish behind Frances Street, the air hummed with possibility. Whispers of the sea cut through the chunks of air between houses; still an alien and disturbing sight. Being near the coast gave him the impression he was permanently at the edge of something, about to fall off. Down at Southsea Park he liked to stay back, the blue wash easily mistaken for the sky. The point near the aquarium where the land cut away gave him vertigo. There was something comforting about the long rolling fields of Kent. Solidity in land you could see all around you.

Today was different; being near the precarious edges felt dangerous, exciting. The waves were akin to restlessness and change, unchecked and volatile. He would become one with this watery beast, lose himself in the depths. Plunge into the heady atmosphere he was entering and emerge, dishevelled but rejuvenated; baptised by unholy waters.

An hour later he realised he was being set up.

'Honestly, they get you really high.' Chris waved a see-through bag of large blue pellets at him. They looked like horse pills. Luke had his back to them, his shoulders heaving.

'I'm fine, thanks.' Eric wondered what the plan was, how they were going to use this to ridicule him in school.

'That girl Lori is well impressed with people that take drugs,' said Chris. There it was. The only girl who had spoken to him; he'd commented on her book and she'd been kind, a silver dot on one side of her nose.

'She's coming over later.' Luke turned around; the humour gone from his face. 'We think she'd like to see you off your face.' He grabbed the pills and stepped towards Eric; he was at least a few inches taller. Chris put a hand on his shoulder. This could end badly. They were going to get their way, whether he joined in or not.

Glancing across to the road for an escape route, Eric saw a dark shadow accelerating across the grass.

'Hey, what's that?' If he could distract them, maybe he could get away.

'Must be Will, trying to spook us,' said Luke. Chris' hand was still on Eric's shoulder.

'You could hide, get him back?' Anything to delay his enforced drugging. A look passed between them. They grabbed his shoulders and forced him down behind the bench. Their fingers were tight on his bones.

The shadow detached itself from a bush and crept towards the bench. It hesitated. There was something lumpy clutched in its hand. Eric recalled a sandy-haired figure completing the group – his laughter always carried across the canteen.

'Guys?' The voice lacked its usual force. He became human in the pool of light next to the bench; baggy jeans and a Stussy hoodie, a cap casting dark shapes over his eyes. He was about six feet away now.

'Luke? This isn't funny.' He rested himself on the edge of the bench, inches away from them.

The two boys either side of Eric erupted with a hoot of calls and grabs. Eric hung back, poised to escape. They separated, scuffing their feet. The boy looked at him, suspicion shadowing his face. Will Lakeland, the most recognisable face in school.

'This is Eric, the new kid. You know why he's here.' Luke blocked Eric's escape.

'It was his idea to goose you,' said Chris.

'Is that right?' Will stepped towards Eric, examining him. 'Little fucker.' It was unclear if he was joking. Looking at the bag, Eric realised it was full of beer. He reached behind and pulled the can out, a desperate bid to make a connection.

'Already got mine.'

'You shit it out, did you?' Luke said.

'Export strength, nice.' Will met his eyes. There was a suggestion of a smile.

'Nicked it off my dad. I can get loads.'

'Thinks he can be useful.' Will stepped closer, the power of acceptance hanging around him. He brushed Luke's hand away, patted his back. 'You might be just what I need, Eric.' There wasn't time to assess what was needed, it was enough to have avoided a hospital trip.

'What you losers up to?' A brash voice in the dark. Lori Gillespie stood with another girl. Both had plaited bunches. The other was blonde, limp, hanging back. Lori gripped a glass bottle in one hand.

'Ladies.' Will swept his hat off, bowing low. They giggled.

'What you doing here?' She waved her bottle at Eric.

'You must mean Walker.' How did Will know his last name? 'He drinks the hard stuff.' Will chucked one arm around him. He fitted underneath his shoulder.

'Don't hang around with this guy,' she said, a smile in her voice.

'It's Rick,' he said. Eric was hoping a new nickname might change his popularity stakes at this school.

'Can we try some of yours, Walker?' Will grabbed his can before he could respond. 'You ever done a beer bong?' He pulled out a compass and jabbed it in the bottom of the can. Liquid spurted out. He jammed his mouth against it, then pulled Lori in, their lips so close until she took the can from him. She sucked out the last few drops.

'There's more where that came from.' Will steered her over to the bench. The blonde girl hovered closer to Eric.

'So, where are you from?' she said.

'Kent.'

'That's nice.'

'Not really.' He looked over at Lori, the snake of plaits down each side of her face.

'You're in my Maths class. You're good.' Her eyes

126

were dishwater grey.

'I'm going to be a mechanic. Like my dad.'

'That's nice.' Her mouth was thin. 'Rick.' She smiled.

'Not really.' He looked over at the bench. They were all laughing in the pool of light.

'You want some?' She held out a bottle.

'No, thanks.' He fumbled in his pockets, looked down until she lost interest and walked away. Eric inched into the shadows. He wasn't sure if he was still immune. The sea chafed at his ears. They wouldn't even notice if he left.

He slid the key into the lock. There was a catch about halfway; you had to wiggle it. At the click, he paused. Nothing. The living room door was shut. Bright colours and muted exclamations crawled under the space underneath onto the speckled carpet. Sounded like Parkinson. The gauntlet of the stairs lay before him; at least one squeaky tread and the banister had loose screws at the top which made it rattle. The haven of his bedroom stretched a few metres beyond. He put his foot on the first step, then retracted it and slipped off his Kickers. Placing each foot deliberately, he was about a third of the way up when he heard a deep voice advancing towards the door. His legs sprang into action, two steps at a time, surging upwards, hurtling round the corner, through his door, shutting it with more than a little force. Surely, they heard.

Footsteps ambled through to the kitchen, the fridge door opened and shut, and the feet returned. He may have imagined it, but he was sure they paused at the base of the stairs. He jumped into bed fully clothed, dreading the disappointment in his father's eyes when he realised he was sober and had come home forty-five minutes before his curfew.

*

Three episodes of *Come Dine With Me* and Lilly's still spreadeagled on the sofa. At least she's brought him some more toast.

'So why are you guys friends, anyway? I never got that.' She won't leave it alone.

'Better to have a friend like that than no friends at all.' Once Will had stepped in, seen some sort of potential in him, he'd found an entrance into a social life, girls talked to him.

'Not sure about that.' Easy for her to say. She didn't have to hide things from those around her, like enjoying musicals, or crying at episodes of TV shows. He had never felt secure in his expected mould.

'Just because you're happy being a complete loner.' He could never understand why she wasn't fussed about being in a relationship.

'Better to be alone than fit your whole life around someone who will probably just disappoint you.'

'Why are you still here?' he says.

'You know you love me really.' She pats him on the head, gets up and puts the kettle on.

'You might have a point, though.' He keeps his eyes on the TV. 'Always being overshadowed by a friend, that can have consequences. Make you do things, you know, that are out of character.'

'Just don't let his bullshit get into your head, big bro.' Lil pulls the fleece blanket over them. 'You don't want to be like that.'

The theme tune starts up again, scrolling images of food, that bit where the woman takes ages to put some chocolate mousse in her mouth. 'Looks like they're going to argue in this one. Always the best bit.'

128

What did he say to Will last night? All he can remember is a quiet chat, just the two of them, wandering towards the taxi rank. Will's horrified face.

Nina

Nina

On Monday morning she decides to put her plans into action before working on the stuff for the presentation. No news from Dev yet so hopefully he's still stuck on the problems she's created.

What she needs is information. Just some basics, to give her something to go on. An email address, links to his social network, something to target him with. There's White Pages, only a few pounds for a subscription and she has access to all his information from the electoral roll. She clicks and swipes, intent on the screen. It's getting easier, moving the mouse with her left hand.

Quite a list of different addresses. There are gaps in the dates, he can't have registered to vote at all of them. Some at the crap end of town, maybe he was a student in a shared house. Even one over fifteen years ago, out by Cosham. Surely this flash twat didn't come from round there? He's never left Portsmouth. That must mean he doesn't have a degree. It seems worse, that he's not intelligent.

She copies and pastes each one, puts it into the spreadsheet, with the dates. The first tab is for addresses, maybe the past stuff will come in handy. The next is for contact details. Work email is easy enough, Assistant

Personnel Manager. Bullshit title for smarming about in an office, no doubt. Then there's his phone number from the party, the landline number from his address. She could really do with a personal email, that would allow her far more access. There must be some way of finding it. If he's not that smart his security settings might not be that good.

The third tab is for ideas – various ways to bother him, distract him, anything to get that feeling back – when she stood in front of his house. In control, able to inflict something.

'Feeling better, then?' No doughnuts this time. 'Or should we be sad that Kyle didn't work out?' Dev doesn't come in, just leans against the open door.

'You should have seen me earlier.' It's good to see him – he'll be impressed with this. 'I need to leave early and I managed to use the words "glandular," "menstrual," and "orifice" into the explanation of my doctor's appointment. How many points does that get?'

'Right.' He looks down at his feet. 'At least a seven, I guess.'

'Oh come on. I know, nothing can beat the "fungal" meeting record. I hope you're keeping that Mario mushroom polished in honour of your accomplishment.'

'So you're leaving the office again?' He can wipe that judgemental look off his face. No-one here works harder than her, usually.

'It's just an hour early.' To get set up before Will gets home. 'I haven't been well.' She gestures at her arm.

'Not stopping you from typing away today.'

'It's a busy time.'

'Did Sai say anything to you?' He drops his voice, checks behind him.

'No.' Why is he being so weird?

'We've had some errors crop up. Can't figure out

131

where they've come from.'

'I told you, check your numbers, ten times if necessary.' He has noticed, then.

'I know the Franklin method.' He glances back out, into the office. What is he so jumpy about? 'I think I'll just have to go back through, track any changes that were made.'

'Sounds good.' So that's it. He knows, or at least suspects something. 'You can always ask Clive to extend the deadline. I'm sure he won't mind.' That would be perfect.

'I guess. Do you need more time as well? Clive is giving me so much grief.'

'All good this end.' No way she's going to admit how behind she is.

'Right.' He pushes the door, as if he's going to come in.

'I'd better get back to it.' She looks down, she hasn't got time for chat.

'Ok.'

On the screen is the same picture she found last Saturday. So smug with self-interest. This is what she needs to focus on now.

Dev's still there, one hand on the door, as if there's something unfinished. A brief flash of a smile, a nod, that will get rid of him.

He gets the hint, lets the door click behind him, something like sadness in the way he shuffles back across the office. What was she supposed to say? He can't help her. And keeping him off the trail of her sabotage is vital if she's going to be able to concentrate on this, not get too behind with work. No, it's for the best.

The next step is fake accounts. She's already thought of a name — Helen Clarke. Unobtrusive, and a combination of two of her engineering idols. There's a slew of pictures she got from a friend from primary school who moved to Australia. No worry about him recognising her.

Email account first, then she uses it to create an entire person with a job (shop assistant), music likes (rap, all the crap he'd probably like with misogynistic lyrics), and even a couple of pictures of a cat to add to the overall picture. In fifteen minutes there's a whole new person, who's made posts and comments on Twitter. She even shows up on Google. It's disturbing, how easy it is. She keeps expecting something to pop up, accuse her.

On Facebook, there's loads of stuff about him she can use. That's the fourth tab. Personal information. She can't see his date of birth on Facebook, they'll need to be friends. It will look suspicious if she invites him straight away. Instead, she likes something one of his friends has posted and comments on something else. If she builds it up slowly, he might add her.

His news feed is open though. He went to Los Angeles on holiday last year, had a weekend in York last month. He's unravelling, the pieces of him yielding so easily. Pictures of his car, him posing next to it. A black BMW with personalised number plates. W1L 1AM. Oh dear.

On his Instagram feed are links to nutrition and workouts, how to get the perfect abs. It's tempting to send something now, place a ripple in the pond, but it's best to be careful, build it slowly, so he isn't alerted too soon. It's strange to think that there are pieces of herself, or anybody, laid out like this, a digital skeleton.

There's an email from Clive marked urgent. Probably trying to get her attention, nothing she can't handle. It seems a waste to stop now, she'll have to go back over everything, re-open all the tabs.

No, it can wait. She's never been behind before, it's

hardly a big deal. They'll just have to wait for her, for once. She sits back, stretches the fingers on her right arm, rests the cast on the table.

Perhaps she can start with an online deluge, something to irritate him. She looks through magazines and mailing lists. That's safe, they could have got his information from anywhere. Ones with daily emails are best, that way it will be constant.

Start with a few things he'd like; weight training, newsletters about cars, usual stuff. Nina opens a few tabs, filtering the search results will take too long. She does it in the order they come up – *Home Business, Notion, 91, Creative HEAD, Vintage Life, Holdfast, Smashing, Crux, Flowerona, Nowhere, Ceiga, B+H, Impact, Film Eye, Science, McFarland, Heat.* By the time she gets to the bottom his details are instinctive to her fingers. All those emails, flooding into his inbox. The time it will take to undo her simple clicking. They always make you go to the website, double check you mean it, try to sell you something. Even if someone were to figure it out, there's no way he can trace her IP address.

Nina sits back, savouring his imagined rage. Perhaps he will lose some sleep, waste time writing complaint letters. He could start to get behind at work. She sighs. It's not exactly the same.

She clears her history and deletes the files and the backups. The spreadsheet goes onto a memory stick, to be kept in her bag. Everything is covered.

Other people must have done something similar to this. She Googles "legal revenge online." There are posts, links, ideas, comment threads. She never would have thought of this stuff on her own. There's one idea in particular that she likes. It fits with how she perceives him, invades his privacy.

Nina creates a Gumtree account with a different

email address, his mobile number, address. It was amazing what you could do with a few simple details about someone. She has to find similar photos. The hulk of his car is easy enough, she might have to make up the sofa. There are enough homely-looking photos online to make it believable.

This will need to be monitored, so she can set up appointments at times that will be most annoying. She creates adverts for his car, his furniture. Kittens would be good, that would get a lot of interest. Make them free, no, cheap, can't be too suspicious. Now to let the responses come.

She sits back, looks over her progress. Something is missing. When she used her housemate's toothbrush to clean the toilet after she was sick in the kitchen sink and didn't clean it up, she'd sat in her bedroom with Holly, giggling while they heard the sound of running water and brushing from the bathroom. It's not as satisfying on her own. She gets her phone out, looks at the last missed call. Rick. He'd been fairly jumpy and weird, but it was the first time she'd genuinely laughed since all of this started. Perhaps because he didn't know her before. There was no pressure to be the same person she'd always been. She composes a message. Maybe she doesn't have to do this completely on her own.

She's been hanging around for hours. He came home far later than expected, then left his lights on, poncing about in his living room. Eight times she's gone around the block, slowed and stopped, found a different parking spot. Finally, it's dark and the blinds are down, she should be safe. She crosses the road, up the path next to his car, and into the shadow of the door, imagined eyes watching each movement.

As she loitered around his road, the evening crawlers

thinned and morphed into commuters, families, escaping to warm destinations. She watched them being swallowed up by their homes.

Creeping forward, she weighs the object in her hand. It feels heavy, hopefully it will be big enough. As she reaches the border, by his wheelie bins, there's a muffled thump. She crouches down on one side of the car, one arm folded under her coat like she's a Bond villain. A cat screams in the dark, scuttling footsteps over the fence. The streetlight glints off the hubcaps. He must polish them.

Glancing up and down the road, she edges round to the back of the car, against the wall of his living room. The sound of the TV hums through the glass. Now to execute her plan.

She takes the potato and pushes it against the end of the exhaust pipe. There's a thunk as she hits it against the end. She stills, waiting for a reaction from the room behind. Her breathing sounds so loud.

It's too fat, it won't go in. Twisting it, pushing it, nothing works. Now she's got it stuck. Levering herself against the floor, it comes out with a faint sucking noise. Hardly stealthy.

Luckily, she's prepared for this. Nina takes out the peeler and shaves a little from each side, stuffing the peelings in her pocket. The earthy smell mixes with exhaust fumes. This time it goes in, leaving a milky trail behind it. She uses the blunt end of the peeler to jab at it, pushing it further. It suddenly pops, there must have been something pressing against it, and it rolls away, thudding inside. The clunk sounded loud. Nina flattens herself against the wall, hoping her woolly hat doesn't show through the window. There's a swish, the blinds going up. She stills – hopefully the dark will shield her.

A sharp bang on the window behind her. She nearly

falls over, manages to grip onto the wall with her good hand and stay pressed back. He mutters something about kids and drops the blinds down. They clack against the window ledge. So close.

As she waits for her heart to steady it's all she can do to stop herself from giggling. That felt good. There must be other ways she can find to torture him.

Eric

He sits in the bar, tugging the jumper down over his shirt cuffs. Should have got changed before coming to meet Will. It's the easiest thing to wear for teaching but somehow this combination always makes him feel like he's in school uniform. He taps his fingers on the edge of his drink. No doubt he'll be reprimanded for his wussy choice of orange juice and lemonade. Yesterday was a complete write-off thanks to bowling, so there's no way he's starting down that road again. It's always impossible to stop, even when it's a school night. Somehow the pull of another drink is too much, and he wakes with a fuzzy head which makes teaching impossible.

It's weird that Will asked him to come out for food. More than once a week is definitely a first. Maybe he wants to boast about his conquest with Nina's mate or has made some improvements to the flat. No doubt he paid someone in to clean the mess off his door.

She was late this morning. He was edging into the road when she hurried out, toast between her teeth and a travel mug in her good hand. The dark coat was slipped off one shoulder, revealing a slash of purple. Her car stopped behind his- he could see her anxious face, lines etched under the eyes.

His phone buzzes. Great, does that mean he's going to be late? Eric hasn't eaten since lunch, the lump of cheese and potato pie with lukewarm peas was hardly satisfying. One day he'll actually get organised enough to bring in lunch, cook enough the day before to take with him. Fat chance.

It's her. Nothing for days, and then this.

Fancy a stake out? This will be worth getting up for early on a Sunday, trust me. Meet at Shop Express, 6am sharp.

What's she up to? Surely not continuing her weird vendetta against Will. The flour thing was fun, but that had to count as payback for him trying to sleep with her. Still, a stake out. Like something you see in cop films, eating doughnuts and trying to look inconspicuous. She has weird ideas about how to have fun on a Sunday morning.

It's flattering, that she wants to see him again. This might be a premise, something to give her an excuse. He flushes at the thought of it, of her, of what they did. Does it count as a date? Best to wait, though. Don't want to reply straight away and look too keen.

A couple walk past him, the man shrugging off his jacket to reveal a yellow jumper. Maybe he could buy something new on Saturday to wear Sunday morning. Was he supposed to wear black? He swigs his drink, watches the couple at the bar. This is the same corner they've sat in for years. From the days when they had fake birthdays memorised and wore far too much Lynx, to the arrival of their eighteenth birthdays which led to first a swagger and then a drooping, as if it hadn't been worth the wait after all. Was that what made a friendship? Familiar words exchanged in familiar places, not some emotional connection. At work, Gilly and Kirsty get locked in over the kettle in the staff room, mirroring actions, heads nodding in the gaps, hurrying to finish each other's sentences. The way women get. Such exposure.

Conversations with Will shift around a few set topics – work, films, computer games, music – occasionally commenting on some recent news or sports results. Eric can't imagine the ripping up of intimacy that happens with other people. When Will's uncle died, they spent almost four solid days in the pub. Will's chat was interspersed with anecdotes, like the time Uncle Alec had taken them for a cycle ride and it had tipped it down, so they hid in a disused barn, or when they went to Devil's Dyke to look at the scenery but spent most of the time learning how to do Walk The Dog with a yoyo. These tales took the place of sentimental confession, the act of sharing replaced the need for discussing feelings.

Boring to shift it all back to daddy issues, but had he looked for someone like that? A surrogate, to give the same mix of superiority and disappointment. Someone to make him feel inadequate. And here he was, again, leaving him hanging. Like he was the expendable one.

'Typical.'

'Talking to yourself, Ricky boy?' Will pats him on the shoulder, dumps an expensive-looking laptop bag at his feet. 'What are you having?' He always does this, waves his wallet around, like he's so successful.

'I've got a drink.'

'Not some kiddy drink you can have at work.'

'What comes with the burger and a drink offer?' Eric picks up the menu.

'Don't worry about that.' Will shakes his head. 'Teachers.'

'I might be getting promoted, actually.' This isn't strictly true yet, but he can't help boasting.

140

'Nice one.' Eric can't tell if he's being sincere. 'I'm thinking the mixed grill. Need a protein injection to start the week off. Come on, my treat.' If he protests it will look even worse.

'The blue cheese burger and whatever lager comes with the deal,' Eric says.

Will ambles over to the bar, one hand still in his pocket. It would look cool, if you didn't know it was rehearsed. That evening they spent over at Will's house in Cosham when they were seventeen, walking up and down the landing next to the mirror, trying to tip the shoulders back, command respect. Eric always thought his looked like he was a bad actor. Thing is, you practised enough, it got natural. Just look at him. He's never had problems with success.

*

'Where did you get to?' Will slouched next to him on the bench outside the library, jerking the book out of his hand.

'I forgot the time. My parents make me babysit.' For over a year they'd been spending time at the park. Every time Eric snuck off, embarrassed to admit he had a curfew.

'You got a little brother?' Will peered at the book. *Jack*, by A.M. Holmes. Eric wondered if having a gay dad would make him more popular.

'Sister. She's twelve, a total pain.' His parents delighted in re-telling the story of how he'd cried at the age of six when his mum told him he couldn't marry Lilly.

'Your parents hit the town? Must be where you get your drinking habits.' Will nodded.

All the time, it felt like he was taking part in some

sort of test.

'I can't reveal my sources.' A shared grin.

He had to smile. Will kept those who thought he was a loser in check.

'So, what do you think of Lori?' Will asked.

'She seems alright.' Eric controlled his voice.

'Luke thinks I should ask her out. What do you reckon?' Of course. There was an implied answer here. In Eric's imaginings she drew him out of himself, they shared a secret world between the keys of his computer and the sheets of his bed. It never stuck, like a glitch in a background.

'What would she see in you?' Eric shook his head. It was the correct response, the thing boys said to each other. He was pleased to have read it right.

As if calling her into being, she wandered through the door; Converse and short school skirt, hair snaking around her shoulders. The passing of time had made her more appealing, fleshed her out. Eric took himself away, waving the pages at Will, fleeing the scene before he became complicit.

Outside, a breeze shivered the ornamental trees, trapped there like prisoners. A skater type in a beanie hat barrelled into his shoulder, splattering his book to the floor among the leaf mulch. He might not get his library deposit back. He turned, thinking he might say something this time, but he was already through the swinging doors, stepping around a couple, their hands entwined as a mark of status. When the glare of the sun shifted, he saw it was Lori and Will.

They meshed into an awkward group, the new couple at the centre. Chris and Luke were mostly huddled together, which left Eric trailing with Fiona, the blonde one. Occasionally she kissed him, although it was probably only to be kind.

As the days diminished, the other pair of boys were sucked into the skater crowd, hunched around illicit cigarettes behind the wall that led up to the playing fields. Fiona's presence dwindled, until she started to ignore Eric in Geography.

On a Friday in December, the three of them discovered themselves on a street corner and realised it was routine. The cliff edge of their futures lay ahead, the hurdle of exams a welcome distraction from what lay beyond. Once things shifted at home, after more frequent arguments with Dad, things changed. He had more freedom, saw them almost every day.

Scuffing along the streets the following spring, they found themselves drawn to the old parts of the town. They slouched around monuments dedicated to those who had left and created America, Australia, new worlds and spirited adventures. Eric felt like a ship with a broken hull, steering in circles, scudding into a sinking hole. They sat in the historic dockyard, among the lumps of rock used to tether the boats to the shore. He put his hand over the stone, the rain-thudded dents a place for fingers. That summer Eric steeped himself in alcohol, the welcome blurring it produced. It made the constant presence of his beautiful failure more bearable.

Lori had an older cousin with a flat in the city who was away a lot. When she knew it was safe, Lori sneaked the key from under the plant pot and let them all in. They found a drinks cabinet heaped with rum, vodka, far more potent than the cider they used to keep themselves afloat. They found a vibrator and a leather harness in her drawers and laughed too hard.

Eric was left stranded with a bottle of whisky in the front room, creaking the door of the old-fashioned drinks cabinet open and closed, open and closed, the squeak accompanying the giggles from the bedroom.

'What you doing?' Lori reached and took the bottle for a drink, their hands touching briefly.

'Nothing.' He could never find words when she was looking at him. Lori ruffled his hair and went into the toilet, the door not shutting completely. He stepped a little closer. The sound of pattering. He pictured her sat there, the whole bottom half of her exposed.

'Good view?' Will tapped his shoulder.

'Do you two have to keep sneaking up on me?' He swigged from the bottle to avoid the pinkness growing in his cheeks.

'Come here.' Will took the bottle out of his hand and led Eric into the bedroom. 'Get in.' Will opened the wardrobe door.

'No way.' He searched his friend's face for motive.

'She's coming back!' Will pushed him in and clunked the door shut. Eric held his breath in the dark space, fumbling around to try and get his bearings. He was mashed against what felt like coats and jackets. To the left there was a little more space, perhaps some shelves. He eased his body that way.

'Where's Ricky?' Lori's voice sounded close. She giggled. He hadn't realised how much of an amusement he was to her.

'Don't take the piss. He thinks it makes him sound cool.' Will was near the door, he couldn't see him. 'He went out for more booze.' He should open the door, reveal this idiotic joke and leave them to it.

'He drinks too much. I worry about him,' she said. He liked the idea of her concern. She was close, cut into strips through the slatted door. Her hair hung down like a curtain.

'You're too nice.' Eric saw a hand creep around her

waist.

'Come on. Let's go and talk to him. He's been so quiet since all that stuff with his dad.' So they talked about him, shared his failures together.

'I've got other plans.' Will swooped his hands up and pulled off her T-shirt. The bones of her shoulders jutted out under her hair. If the door wasn't there, he could have touched her.

'It's cold in here.'

'Not for long.' Will's head appeared over her left shoulder. He looked straight at Eric, holding his gaze while he flipped her bra open. Then her jeans, pants. In less than a minute she was naked. Eric couldn't move. Her bum was a soft white curve, little red lines from her jeans drawn on it. His trousers felt tight. Will turned her around, his head buried in her neck. Her back was arched.

She was glorious. A little mole perched above the triangle of fuzz, her nipples high and hard. He imagined taking the swell of them in his hands. It felt like the seams of his jeans were straining. Will pushed her down on the bed, shoving his hand between her legs. She let out a little sigh, like he'd told her something surprising.

A coat hanger was jabbing Eric in the neck.

She was writhing, grabbing at Will's back. Her hair looked so soft on the pillow.

Eric scraped the edge of his fingers along the bump between his legs. He watched her face – the eyes screwed up, wrinkles along the top of her nose. There was a little click as the top of his zip unlatched. Her motion continued, surely she hadn't heard. He dragged the tab down slowly, feeling the pull of each of the teeth on the way to the bottom. Peeling the damp fabric of his pants away, he pulled it out, stroked it, his eyes fixed on her.

Will's hand stopped moving. He stood up and took

his top off, started on his trousers. She had a desperate look on her face, high colour in her cheeks. Will stripped off his trousers and pants, his penis bouncing up after being released. Eric's hand stopped. Will got on top of her, most of her hidden by him.

'Hey!' Her voice sounded muffled.

'You know it doesn't feel good for me.'

'Tough.'

'I didn't bring one.' Will slid his hand up her leg. 'Just this once?'

'Like the last time.'

He leaned over her, holding himself, dipping up and down. Her legs slid a little wider. He stopped.

'You're right. We shouldn't.' He rolled off her, lying on his back.

'Now I want to.' She wriggled.

'Safety first.'

'Whatever.' She got up, slung one of her knees over Will. Eric could see it pushing into her. He resumed his motions. Her bottom squashed down and pulled up, the length of her spine reaching up, her hair flung forward. Her toes were bunched up. She moved more quickly, breaths escaping each time. Eric closed his eyes, the image of her milky skin against the dark red wall pasted behind them. His hands, clutching at her, pulling her onto him, that warm dark place, his hands lost in her hair, arching her back, again and again. A sudden rush, moist warmth in his hand, then shuddering clarity.

The bed was creaking, the legs juddering. Eric's stomach was hollow. He shoved it back in his pants, damp, and zipped his trousers up. His left hand was cupped, the contents cooling and thinning out. He wiped it on one of the things behind him. It smelt musty.

A flurry of arms. Will tried to turn her over but she fell off, cracking her head on the wall. They reorganised their limbs again so she was lying on her back. He started off again. Eric thought he saw a wince in the movement of her legs. He wondered if it hurt. There was a crick in his neck, his left leg ached from being twisted round to the side. Still, they carried on.

Will started to mutter, his movements becoming jerky.

'Ohfuckyesohfuckyesohfuckyesohfuckyes.' Each time it got louder. Eric looked away. The last one was a shout of triumph.

*

Will comes back from the bar, a bag of crisps waggling between his teeth.

'So how's it going?' Eric nods a thank you.

'Not bad.' Will swigs his drink. 'Still haven't heard back from the police about them bloody vandals. And I thought I heard someone hanging around the car when I got home last night.' He shakes his head. 'Not going to help the house prices, if there's some dodgy kids causing trouble.'

Eric picks up his drink to hide the smile. What's she been up to now?

'Terrible,' he manages, swallowing to hide a laugh. The car is perfect, he's obsessed with it.

'What's the big promotion then?' Will asks. 'They putting you in charge of the crayons?'

'Phase Leader.' Just nod, bite back the sarky response. 'It basically means I'd be in charge of a big group of kids, checking their progress, monitoring them, that sort of thing.' The idea is growing on him. He could make a difference. Plus, it would mean less teaching hours. He's always so exhausted by the end of the day.

'Aren't they learning songs and how to tie their laces?'

Will shakes his head. 'I don't know how you manage it mate, all those little kids running about. Good on you.' He lifts up his glass in a salute, drinks. Almost half empty already.

Will leans back and looks over the room. He looks comfortable everywhere. 'Look, I wanted to say.' He's not even looking at Eric.

'You going to give me tips on classroom management?' Eric says.

'It was out of order.' Will puts his glass down. 'What happened, with Bea, you were totally right to be pissed off with me.' He fiddles with the edge of the table. This is unexpected. 'We've been mates for ages, and that's just, well, it's not what you do.' He picks his drink back up.

'Right.' That seems as close to an apology as he's getting. 'I appreciate that.' He's not sure what to say.

'So, we're ok, yeah?' Will says.

Eric looks at him. The space he takes up, so solid. That surety has never rested on his shoulders.

'I guess.' Maybe he wants something. 'You didn't seem fussed when you mentioned it. In front of the others.'

'Hey, she said she'd told you, that you were fine with it.'

'You talk to her?' Unbelievable.

'She messaged me on Facebook,' Will says.

'And you got a conscience all of a sudden.'

'I said I was sorry.' Now he expected him to be grateful for an apology.

'You think you're better than me.' Eric feels it bubbling up, all the stuff he's never said.

'Steady on.' Will shakes his head.

'You like being the popular one. I was always the one that made you look good.'

'It's good to have a mate from back in school. A real

148

one.' He puts his glass down. 'Is this about the weekend? That stuff you were telling me.' Oh god, what did he say?

'Look, I was drunk, and she was definitely up for it, I don't know why she doesn't remember.'

'You what?' Will's looking at him like he's mental, face all screwed up.

'Who was the burger?' The barman hovers over the table, plates weighed in each hand.

'Me.' He can't look at Will. What has he said?

'And the mixed grill. Feeling hungry then?' A smile. There's no reaction. Just the silence, spilling out between them. 'Can I get you guys some mayonnaise, or chilli sauce?' His head turns between them. Eric shakes his head, picking at the pile of chips. 'Right then.' Almost a sigh as he walks off.

He has to say something, break the tension. Picking up the vinegar, he concentrates on getting some on each chip. Then the salt, so it sticks. Still no movement.

'Salt?' Eric waves it in Will's direction.

He takes it, shakes it over his plate. 'You were going on about your dad, about how hard it was for you.' His voice is low, quiet. 'Then you started banging on about me, and Lori, and how you always felt like you weren't good enough. Something about how I'd ruined you.' He puts the salt down. 'I think. I mean you were rambling on for ages. You were hammered.'

'Right.' So much for bragging about his conquest.

'So, what are you talking about? Who was up for it? Don't tell me you've been getting some action without telling me.'

'Nothing really, nothing. It was just, you know, this girl, and we had a thing, and she was really drunk.' He's going red, he can feel it.

'You didn't have sex with her, did you? Pretty sure you want them to be conscious.' Will raises his eyebrows.

The Shadows We Cast

'Well, I mean, she wasn't that drunk.' She moved, and made noises, he's making it sound like something terrible happened.

'Right.' He picks up his cutlery, starts sawing through the steak. 'You OK?'

It was Will who was being odd, not him. He has to shift the attention back.

'You're the one giving the touchy-feely speech.' He forces a laugh, potato getting stuck in his throat.

'Well, you know what? I've met someone.' Will smiles down at his chicken breast. 'She seems pretty decent.'

'What, that girl you found at the club?'

'God no.' He crams in some peas. 'No, this one's a nurse.'

Eric splutters into his beer. He means Holly, Nina's friend.

'Steady on.'

'Come on. You, actually getting on with a woman? Having conversations, waiting to sleep with them?'

'Well I'm not a fucking saint.' He grins. 'Why do you think I liked her in the first place? She was well up for it.' So much for romance. 'Only, we got chatting and that. She's interesting, funny, gets this little crease over her top lip when she laughs.' He picks over his food, stabs a chip. Is he going red?

'Bloody hell.'

'We went out for dinner, she's coming over at the weekend.' He shuffles in his chair.

'That's great, good for you.' Why does it feel uncomfortable, to have him like this? As if he's peeled away a layer of himself.

'Steady on.' Will nods at Eric's glass. It's empty, how did that happen?

'Want another one?' Eric knocks the table when he slides over, clatters the cutlery to the floor.

'Sure.' Will's looking at him funny. There's something behind the eyes. Disbelief, or suspicion. What an idiot, to blurt that out. Now Will thinks he's some sexual weirdo.

Standing by the bar, he feels Will's gaze on his back. What does he know? He wasn't there. There's a niggle in his stomach. He keeps thinking back to that night, trying to remember whether she was moving before he took her pants off.

Nina

The sun hangs low, slung under the expanse of sky. It's peering into the bus, like it doesn't have the energy to climb any higher for the rest of the day. Nina's face is a full colour shadow every time they pass a lorry or house tall enough to reach higher than the side of the bus. Since she got on three stops ago it's filled up; three boys leaning around the orange pole in the centre, a glut of old ladies with their trolley hampers herded into the pram section. She places her right arm in her lap, protecting it from people walking past. Only another week before she can have this taken off, feel whole again.

She could have driven, but it's been ages since she's been on a bus. This seat was always her favourite when Mum took her into town. The tall ones towards the back which let you peer down at the world, the hump of the wheel underneath your feet, reminding you of the mechanisms moving you forward. They'd go to the library and she'd sit on the tiny chairs, taking her time to decide which eight books would be the ones to go in her book bag. Then they'd go to the cafe on the corner and she'd have an iced bun with watery squash in a polystyrene cup. Mum would call her a little rabbit when she left teeth marks on the rim.

Dev was peering at her over his monitor when she left. He's barely spoken to her in the last two days since their little chat. He can't have found the mistakes, she buried them so carefully. Even if he has, there's no way he can trace it back to her. Clive's annoyed with him now, the pressure's off, she can worry about more important things.

The purpose of her trip looms. An alien mechanism that could already be ticking inside her. Every other scare has been a false alarm, panicked calculations over calendars and sexual mishaps resulting in nothing. She's just late, it will be fine.

The Lego brick facade of the bus station swings into view, the bus juddering like a dog expelling fleas until they all get off and it coughs into silence. It's chilly, the wind scraping her skin.

The pharmacy is in the middle of the row, between a sullen cafe and a hardware shop, hula hoops and washing baskets scattered out the front. Nina walks in, goes to the fated pregnancy test boxes. Why are they all blue? Maybe she's supposed to be thinking about the sea, or the infinite sky of her uterus. There might be a day that she approaches this section with pleasure, even hope. It seems absurd.

The cheapest has two in it, all you get is one line or two. She's bought that one before, but she threw the instructions away with the first one and then couldn't remember what the lines meant when she got the second one out a year or so later.

She gets the digital one, a special display to show you how many weeks along you are. Joy. She grabs a foot file and a pack of throat lozenges, meeting the cashier's gaze steadily. Just a few normal bits, nothing to worry about. She pushes down the feeling of guilt, for once it's not her fault she's here. Can't blame an over-enthusiastic moment or a missed pill. So unfair, to have to go through this as well.

Outside, the wind buffets the carrier bag, dragging it around the shapes inside. She was going to retrace her steps, confine herself back home for the rest of this trial. The wind flaps the collar of her coat. She has to know.

Nina goes into the cafe next door – "Lucys" in drippy paint. There are trays of scones and flapjacks under taught cling film in a Perspex display. She orders a coffee, glancing at the sign for the loos. She takes the Styrofoam cup and sits in a rickety aluminium chair as close to the toilets as possible. A sip sends a sharp flash over her tongue, scalding her throat. She flips through the discarded paper on the table, holding down the flat page with her cast. It's all big headlines and scandal; celebrities and their vanity.

Another swig, a slap of heat. She swills, sips, winces, blows harder, spattering droplets onto the plastic table. After five minutes she puts the cup down, almost full, teeth marks gouged in the edge.

Perched on the edge of the seat, a sign in comic sans says, "Please wash hands!!!!" A pot of lurid pink soap sits on the edge of the sink, the toilet roller holder swinging off one screw. At least she'll only be here for two minutes. She pulls out the packet. She's stuck in this shithole about to pee on a stick while he's probably swanning about on some fancy lunch with a client. The balance must be redressed.

Her phone buzzes. Holly.

Hope you're ready for us! Should be there for 7. Hugs xxxx

Shit. She invited them over the other last month. Before all this.

Gathering everything together, she curses her bus decision. Now she'll have to carry everything with just one hand. And then there's the flat. Not much better than her desk at the moment, a complete state. And the bus will take ages. She shoves everything back in the bag and rushes out past the deserted cup.

They'll be here in twenty minutes. Nina scours the flat, looking for signs of abnormality. There are heaps of scribbled paper all over the table, post-its around her desk. She takes it all and heaps it in a bag, shoves it in the boiler cupboard. Pillows. They'll think she's weird. She puts a rubber gloves on and pulls them out from under the bed. The soft puff as they fall makes her neck shudder.

A charred smell on the edge of burning brings her back to the kitchen. Nina pops the toaster – the pitta bread is singed round the edges. It's fine, makes them more rustic. She cuts them into strips and adds it to the big plate – carrots, peppers, marinated anchovies, olives, stuffed peppers. There was dip somewhere.

Back to the scrunch of carrier bags on the side, she left the houmous in there. The pregnancy test is nestled smugly underneath. She wouldn't put it past some of them to snoop in her bathroom cabinets, but she can't take it now. The result will need to be absorbed, alone. Nina hides it in the bottom of the chest of drawers, a pair of tracksuit bottoms wrapped around it.

She preheats the oven – the two plates of paella will only take fifteen minutes. Fine, with a few bags of salad. Not exactly cooking but work is always a good excuse. At least there's plenty of wine.

Her bladder nags. It wouldn't hurt, just to get it out of the way. What if she is? The blue bra was a little tight today, and she's been so tired. Was it nausea, this morning, when she felt rough after her second coffee?

No, she needs to focus, they'll be here soon. Wine glasses. There are napkins somewhere, the ones from her parents when she bought the place. Bright and sunny they said, just like her. She places them diagonally against the plates. That looks good. They won't be able to see anything different, it's not like she's changed.

Of course she's tired, clacking away at the computer until the slump of night, drawing up locations and plans for lunchtime excursions. Constantly checking accounts, replying to Gumtree posts. It's exhausting.

Doorbell. Please let it be Holly. She rushes down, remembering on the way that she didn't even get changed, the smell of her leaching out of her clothes as she steels herself behind the door. It's Nicola, wrinkling her nose as she comes in.

'Is that meat? Did I tell you I'd gone veggie?' Nina does her best to smile. Another fad. Last time it was eating nothing but things she could forage, until it was pointed out that cheese didn't come under this category.

'Nope.' She can only handle Nicola in large groups. 'It's seafood paella.'

'Oh well, fish is fine.'

'Right, they like being eaten.' Nothing. This is going to be hard work.

They fumble over conversation in the kitchen. Nina gets the wine out; Nicola asks for a soft drink. She'll have to make do with water. No ice, she used it up last week, along with all the gin and vodka.

Nina nods, finishing half her glass of wine in the time it takes to hear about a crocheted hat and Mindfulness classes.

'You'd love it. Someone like you, so self-aware.' Nicola picks at the bowl of crisps, brings one up to her nose carefully before putting it in her mouth.

Nina wants to laugh. Her head is a blank, then random thoughts drop her to the floor, or pin her to the sofa, intent on alcohol, or send her out, searching for destruction, the thought of blood behind her teeth.

'Just a minute.' Nina goes into the bedroom, shuts the door behind her and stands there, looking at the lamp. When the doorbell releases her, she grabs a cardigan to excuse her absence. It's Holly. She holds her too tight, hugging her close.

'Nicola's here.' Hopefully it's enough of an excuse.

'She's always on time. Sorry.' Holly presses a bottle into her hand.

'She crocheted a hat,' Nina says.

'Bloody hell.' She knew Holly would understand.

Now she can relax. More wine, put the paella in, Gail arrives with another bottle, Michelle has chocolates, then Alice, a bottle and a pot plant.

'Thought you'd like this!' she says, clumping it down on the side, smattering crumbs of soil about.

'Lovely.' Nina puts it on a window ledge, faces away from them, closes her eyes, and breathes. In and out. This is supposed to be fun.

She keeps drinking steadily, using the excuse of cooking to take her out any time a response to a question is required. Once everything is on the table, there's no escape.

'I'll just get a white, shall I? To go with the prawns?'

'You're not going anywhere,' Gail says, 'after all your hard work.' Holly laughs, to confused response. Apparently, it wasn't meant as a joke. Nina doesn't taste anything but her plate clears gradually. Cut, chew, repeat. Michelle is talking about a guy she's seeing. Now's the time to nod, pay attention, maybe give one of her usual sardonic responses. It can't be that hard to play the role of herself.

'I just think, maybe, he has a different way of showing his affection than me.' There's nodding. 'Like, I'm quite physical, and I use words a lot, to express

157

myself.' She pauses, sips. 'Whereas I think he's more quiet, he doesn't feel the need to tell me how he feels all the time. So if I don't hear from him, even for a week, it's not that he doesn't care, he's just secure in himself, he doesn't need to express it all the time.' Heads bob dutifully.

'That's bollocks,' Nina says.

'You haven't even met him.' Michelle's mouth pulls together, thinning her lips.

'If he's not messaging you, clearly he's not that fussed.'

'Come on,' Nicola says. 'Remember Carl? He was like that.'

'Exactly. As soon as you stopped making an effort he buggered off.' She drains her glass. 'Don't waste your time.' Nina returns her attention to her dinner. She doesn't see why they're so quiet, it's up to her to point out the lies they tell themselves. That's always been her role. 'Pudding?'

They congregate on the sofa afterwards, nibbling at mints, chewing over the old and new. It's no good. Her words and actions are the same, but they feel forced. She's misshapen, can't press herself back into the mould they have for her.

Silence stretches out and the cardboard packet rolled up in her trousers is all she can think of. It's impossible to wait any longer, and they can all moan about her if she leaves the room anyway.

She digs it out from between the clothes, shoves all the packaging into the bin in the bedroom and sneaks to the toilet. Nice and quick, a little bit of the warm stream on her hand when it misses. Wipe it off, then the lid goes on she puts it on the back of the toilet. Now to wait two minutes. She hears a clatter from the room and decides to go back in. Big breath to prepare, then she's ready.

Catching her foot on the raised bit between rooms, she stumbles. Must be the slipper socks. They're talking about travel. Gail and her husband are planning a trip to South Africa.

'I might go to Tibet,' Nina says, her voice sounding loud. Gail stops, halfway through talking about safaris, something like that.

'That's interesting.' She doesn't have to look so pissed off.

'Since the promotion,' Nina says, picking up another glass of wine, pretty sure it's hers, 'I've got all this money I don't know what to do with.' They should be happy for her. She tries to remember why they're her friends, what tied them together in the first place.

'I'd better get going,' Nicola says, standing.

'Careful you don't trip and fall face first into a cow.' Nina laughs, it sounds loud and echoey. She looks around, waiting for a response. Nothing. The rest make their excuses and troop out, leaving her to clean up. She wanders into the kitchen. Holly's there, stacking the dishwasher.

'Everything ok, Hun?' Holly says, lining up the glasses.

'Thought that was a wash-out. Everyone was so quiet.' Nina shakes the bottles. There's some left in one of the reds. Doesn't matter if it's mixed with white.

'What's going on?' Holly's watching her.

'Let's stay up late, blow off work, watch films, hang out.' The nights they couldn't be bothered to go out not long after they met were brilliant – they'd watch DVDs of *Buffy the Vampire Slayer*, drink the cheapest red wine from Threshers with Tesco value chocolate. It can be simple again.

'I've got to work tomorrow.' Holly clacks plates into the dishwasher. She hasn't even drunk that much.

'Come on, let's have a Buffy marathon. We can-'

'I wouldn't hide something from you.' She pauses, a mug hovering above the washing rack. This is not the time for confessions. Nina wants to indulge, forget.

'If people don't like hearing the truth about themselves then they shouldn't come here. They know what I'm like.' Nina shrugs.

'It was a bit much,' Holly says.

'Clearly, seeing as they all fucked off.' She doesn't need them anyway.

'Except me.' Holly moves over, too close. 'I can stay. Let's watch some stuff, have a laugh.'

It would be so nice, to let herself be looked after. Sit down with Holly and let it all pour out. Only, she's not safe anymore. And it's Nina's fault. She's let her carry on spending time with the man who attacked her because she can't face admitting what happened.

'I'm a terrible friend.' She looks at the floor, grabs the kitchen counter for support when she wobbles.

'What are you talking about? You're the best.' Holly hugs her. 'I'm not going anywhere until you tell me what's going on.'

'I can't.' She shakes her head, pushes Holly away.

'Come on.' She smiles. 'It can't be that bad.'

'He's a monster. Please don't see him again.' Holly's face changes, she steps away.

'I don't know why you're so obsessed with this. He seems like a lad but he's actually really sweet. I might finally have found a good one. Can't you be happy for me?'

'Just trust me. Please.' She puts her hand on Holly's arm. If she can just get her to stop seeing him, it will be fine.

'You haven't even told me why. How am I supposed to trust you?'

'Because I'm your friend.' It should be enough.

'What do you even know about him? You met him for like an hour when you were pissed.' Such a tiny amount of time to have changed her so much.

'It doesn't matter.' She shakes her head, now isn't the time. Next time she sees her, then she'll tell her. 'You need to get home if you've got work.'

'Are you sure?' She's already looking around for her bag. So much for not leaving.

'It's fine.' Nina let's herself be hugged, goes through the pleasantries and it's a relief when the door closes and she's alone again.

She can't be what they want. Settling down with an emergency bottle she put in the freezer, she finds *Ghostbusters II* on Netflix and crunches on ice crystals. At the bit with the evil ghost nanny flying through the air, she remembers the test in the bathroom. Anyone could have gone in and seen it. She crams more half-frozen wine in her mouth and walks to the bathroom, her hand hovering at the door as if there might be an intruder in there.

It's on the back of the toilet. She forces herself to walk over, look at the tiny window. The digital words 'not pregnant' sit there smugly, they've known for longer than she has. It's not as reassuring as she thought it would be. Of course, it's a relief, but it's just another reminder of her violation, that she needs to do this at all. Nina returns to the sofa with the wine and the test, glancing over at it just to make sure.

Helen Clarke is proving popular. Likes and comments, people sharing her posts and tweets. It's exhilarating, this lack of reprisal or identity. She can say and do whatever she wants, safe in this cluttered space.

After all the wine last night, she couldn't face a whole day in the office. There were loads of people who went out for lunch, it just wasn't her usual pattern of behaviour. She'd taken the long route round to avoid Dev and picked up a Subway on the way to an internet cafe not far from the office.

She glances over at the counter. The woman is flicking through a magazine and sucking a can of drink through a straw. This way there's no link back to her, no trail. She swivels the rickety chair, drums her fingers on the side of the partition separating her from the others. The Lucozade Sport and painkillers seem to be keeping the worst of the hangover at bay so far. The flat was still a tip, but that could be cleared up later.

It's satisfying to see the results of her hard work. Taking a day off from her monitoring yesterday has allowed more of it to build. He's pissed off. Comments about taking the car to the garage, how junk emails are wasting his time. Chipping away at his smug exterior, finding ways to niggle him. It doesn't feel like enough, but it's a start. The weekend will be even better when she gets to witness his annoyance. At least she'll have some company for that. Seeing him again, it will bring it all back. Impossible to be alone for that.

Now she can think about the next phase. More risky, but with far more possible reward. To pull this off, she's going to have to imitate him, get people to accept an online version of himself that she's created. And believe in it. She's spent enough time reading his posts, hopefully she'll be able to mimic his words, his manners of speech. Some can be copied directly, with different bits put in between to incriminate him. Bit by bit, she'll expose him for what he really is. Then she can tell Holly, tell everyone, once she's got the weight of opinion behind her.

The first thing to do is to link him to dodgy sites, threads, other people like him. Start to make associations. She wipes her hands down the sides of her trousers, checks again to see if the woman is looking at her. She creates another fake account. This one will be him. She creates some social media profiles using the address, saves the passwords on the spreadsheet. He's not on Twitter much, she can use that to her advantage. Now she can really do some damage.

Why do men rape? A slew of results pop up. The usual crap about victims – not all are young and attractive, being drunk doesn't mean you're asking for it. Next is an article about a teenage girl who was told she 'groomed' her teacher into having sex with her.

An article written about a convicted rapist. How he had a bad childhood, was addicted to pornography. A list of risk factors – hatred towards women, feelings of powerlessness, difficulties in forming relationships. All kinds of men – pilots, doctors, accountants. More mixed than other types of offender.

A sense of entitlement, of punishment, boredom. Politicians tweeting about how they wouldn't even rape someone because they were too ugly. Another article – nothing to do with the inability to control their urges. It's because they can, because that's how society is set up. No wonder so many go unreported.

She's one of them. A statistic. One of the numbers on the screen that adds up to the 85%. Nothing special or different about her, just another unfortunate.

She sits back, pressing the skin of her thumb between her teeth. The rage is like a physical thing. A solid mass in her gut that needs this, has to see these things, so it can be chipped away, broken down into pieces of bile and released. She pulls the bottle out of her bag. It looks like squash, only a bit of vodka mixed in, just to numb her.

Help her get through this next part. Breathe deep, it will be worth it.

Back to the screen. There's a Reddit thread, boasting true confessions.

A guy in the US, says he "supposes" he must have raped something like twenty women.

I was really popular in college, knew I could choose who I wanted. I'd pick the quiet ones; they were always surprised when I asked them out. They seemed grateful. Maybe after one date, or two, we'd go back to mine to watch a movie. I had the attic room, nice and quiet, I used my bed as a sofa, a blanket shoved over it and a load of cushions. I had an air conditioner. It was always turned on when they came back, so it would get cold. That way they'd want to get under the covers. Cuddling, they liked that. There was always a lot of wine. I always filled their glass regularly. The film would be scary, or romantic, whichever fitted with that girl. To start with, I'd just kiss them. Every few minutes, get them worked up, then turn away again. At first nothing at all, no hands, nothing. Just kissing. Bit by bit, I'd start to let my hands wander. At first, they didn't mind, especially just putting a hand up their top, but once I moved further down they'd get bothered, push my hand away. I always reassured them, say I wasn't going to do anything they didn't want to, leave them alone for a full twenty minutes or so, before starting again. That way they'd get horny but then think I didn't want them. Each time, just a little bit more. It depended on the girl, how long that first bit would take. Once I actually got my fingers inside, they were usually too embarrassed to say no to anything else. It was pretty easy, just to roll onto them, carry on kissing. I'd make sure I had trousers on that I could just slip off, they didn't always realise that it was out until I was on top of them. A couple of them tried to push me away but I'm a pretty big guy, I was there on a football scholarship. By that time, it was usually too late. I usually managed to do it without a condom. Afterwards, some put their clothes on and left right away, or we'd just cuddle for a bit and then go back to watching the movie, as if nothing had happened. If I saw them around campus again, they never said anything.

Nina can feel her heartbeat in between her legs. All those girls. It's written so casually, as if he's confessed to not paying a parking fine. What's more disturbing are the comments. Some outraged, many congratulatory, saying that they'd have to use that one themselves.

There are lots more websites with threads like this. She adds a comment at the bottom, using the email address she created.

I raped this one girl, it was easy. Once she was off her face on drink I just went in there and fucked her. She was kissing me earlier that night so I knew there was no way I could get blamed for it. I made sure her face was pressed into a pillow so she couldn't see my face while I did it. The bitch was wet, she was wearing this tiny little dress, she was gagging for it.

Nina stops, reads back over this vile image of herself. The shame of it makes her cold. Because she had thought about it, at least for a while. Otherwise, she wouldn't have gone upstairs with him, even if she did change her mind.

She shakes her head, blinks, her eyes feel hot. This is about his shame, showing him for what he is to others. If she puts his name on it, that might be too much, no-one would do that. She adds one letter, *W*, for people to make that link if they want to. She copies the post and pastes it onto the bottom of ten different forums. Bit by bit, she'll allow those around him to see his true self.

Eric

It's bloody early for a Sunday. Usually, he likes to procrastinate. Shove on some tracky bottoms, take too long over Facebook, stretch breakfast out by taking it into the living room and picking at it for a couple of hours. Anything but get started on the weekend work he inevitably leaves until Sunday evening.

He only replied to say he was coming, didn't ask for details. God knows what she's got planned. He's parked three streets down, is wandering up and down the tiny aisles in Shop Express. The guy behind the counter looks suspicious – who comes shopping at this time on a Sunday? Unbelievable that stuff is open this early.

It took ages to decide what to wear. Based on last time, and whatever she was up to outside his house, it seemed like he should be wearing black. He dug out his old jeans – more grey than black – along with the bobbly sweater Mum got him for Christmas one year that he never wore. The combination wasn't great. More like a Milk Tray man that had fallen on hard times. Not the look he wanted for what might be a date.

In the end he'd settled for the slightly darker blue jeans and a grey jumper. Still hard to see but made him feel less like a mime. For the third time he picks up a tin of corned beef, the shelf furthest away from the counter. This used to be his favourite sandwich – sliced and spread with chunky pickle. He could buy some, while he's waiting.

There she is. Standing outside the shop. Wearing a hat, that was a good idea. She glances in, grins, waves a hand for him to come out. The man behind the counter watches him as he leaves, flicking over unread pages in a paperback.

'Thought you weren't coming.' She puts a hand on his arm, looks relieved.

'Just keeping a low profile.' It's good to feel needed.

'I have snacks. We don't have much time.' Her hand is still on his arm.

'Right. What are we doing?'

'Follow me.' She walks ahead, not waiting for him.

Just opposite Will's place is her car. Without speaking she opens the door, nods to the other side. He gets in, fitting his feet between carrier bags in the footwell. Two coffees are in the cup holders. It gives him a jolt, to see this preparation for him. He's expected, wanted even.

'Wasn't sure what you liked.' She picks up the cup closest to her, glances over briefly but shifts her attention to Will's door. 'A shame it's been raining. You can hardly see the marks anymore.'

'How's the arm?' She's holding it comfortably now, as if she's got used to the cast.

'I get this thing taken off tomorrow.' She doesn't turn around. 'Think I'll mostly be scratching it for the next week.'

'So what are we waiting for? Don't tell me, you've planted drugs and then called with an anonymous tip-off.'

'Not a bad idea.' She nods, as if considering it. Is she serious? 'We're going for maximum annoyance, not a prison sentence.' She laughs, but it sounds a little forced.

'I see. In that case, you've planted an ants' nest in his garden. No, a hornets' nest. We're just waiting until he runs out of his flat screaming, from where you put jam in his bed.'

That one does get a laugh. 'You're full of bright ideas.'

'Barely conscious at the moment. This is a very rude time on a Sunday.'

'I appreciate it.' She looks round, squeezes her lips together. 'Seriously.' There are circles under her eyes. Hair scraped back. Still pretty. 'You must think I'm a nut.' She looks away again.

'Not at all.' There must be something he can say, to make her feel better. 'Some people dress up in costumes and have fake battles at the weekend. This is bloody normal in comparison.'

Her shoulders drop a little. That's better.

'Oh, look, there's one.'

He looks up and down the street. There's a prim-looking woman holding a piece of paper. Looks like she's in her 40s. Is this what they're waiting for? It seems like an odd retribution.

She walks up to Will's door. Nina scrunches down in her seat, pulling her hat down. He copies her, placing a hand on one side of his face. What if Will saw him? She'll realise that he's been lying to her. He keeps thinking about what Will said, about being unconscious. Maybe he should just ask her about that night, see what she says.

The woman looks down at the paper, knocks on the door. A couple with a pram pass by on his left. At least they've got an excuse to be wandering about at this time.

She knocks again. Leans around, looks in the darkened window. Raps on the glass.

'Brilliant.' Nina laughs.

It takes another two knocks and a rattle of the letterbox before the door opens. Will is rubbing one eye, hair up in angles, knobbly feet sticking out under his dressing gown. A fluffy one from John Lewis, he'd sent Eric the link when he'd bought it. Ninety quid on something you wear out of the shower.

Inside the car, over the other side of the street, the words don't carry. The gestures are pretty clear. Will's waving hands, the woman stepping back, hand to her chest, all offended. Further arm waving, but she's not giving up. She pushes the piece of paper at him, tracing the line of something with her finger. He rubs a hand over his head, clearly exasperated. She folds her arms, looks like she's about as impressed as he is. One more flail of his arm and he goes back inside, slamming the door.

'Perfect.' Her shoulders are hunched down, eyes barely visible under the hat, but they're shining.

'What did you do?'

'I may have created a Gumtree account, set up a load of stuff for sale, arranged a few visits for Sunday morning.'

'That is brilliant.' And a little worrying. This must have taken a while to set up.

'Just you wait. There's going to be kids coming for kittens, blokes coming to buy his car.' She gets out a box of Jaffa Cakes, grabs two and passes them over. 'Nutritious breakfast.'

'All on the same day?'

'It's the kind of thing that only works once. He'll find the account and disable it, or complain to Gumtree. I figured my time to make him suffer was limited to one morning.'

'I'd hate to get on the wrong side of you.'

'Give me some credit. I've never done anything like

this before. What he did.' She looks away, 'well, trust me, he deserves it.'

The next one comes five minutes later. A mother, marshalling two small children who are fidgeting with excitement. They even have a pet carrier.

'This should be good.' She folds her arms over her body, sinks back down.

She's loving this. Imagine having the drive to go this far to piss someone off. Then sit there and take it all in. Look at the difference. Will and Bea sleep together, and he just moans at them. She's in a whole new category.

It takes longer for the door to open this time. The kids are bouncing, barely contained behind the legs of the woman. They must be around year three or four.

Will clocks the kids, checks himself, pulls the robe closer around his neck. Polite smiles this time. The same face he uses when one of those charity people accost you in the street. So nice they almost apologise to him for the bother. Shaking his head, smiling sadly, as if he just wished he had a kitten.

One of the kids starts wailing. The mum is clearly flustered. She drags them off, no doubt promising something to cheer them up.

This time Will stops, looks out of the door. As if he knows they're watching. Eric's heart thuds.

'That was close,' Eric says. The door snaps shut again. 'Did you see his face? I can't believe how angry he got at that woman. And pretending to be all nice to that last one, what a prick.'

'I guess.' She drinks her coffee, swirls her finger round the hole in the top.

'Come on, this is amazing.'

'So why are you enjoying this so much?'

'I don't know.' Now the attention's on him, not a good idea. 'He was really unkind, you know. Names in the corridor, that kind of thing.' It doesn't sound convincing, even to him. Something has to be given away. 'Actually, he slept with my girlfriend. She was my first…you know…love and all that.' He keeps his eyes pointed down. 'Then next thing I know, she's gone off with him.' It's true enough, hopefully.

'What a fuckwit.' She shakes her head. 'So what did you do about it?'

'Me? Nothing.' As if. 'Listened to a lot of REM.'

'Glad I could help you get your own back eventually. People like that, they don't deserve to be happy.' Her voice drops. So much anger bubbling back there. It seems like overkill, for what he did.

'Here's another one.'

A bloke this time, dark blue jeans and those trainers that look like shoes. He even goes over to the car, leans down to look inside, kicks at the tyres.

The door opens before he can even get there. Will's dressed now, a tight T-shirt that shows off his use of the weights next to the big mirror in his garage. Shouts before he can even speak. The other guy doesn't respond at first. One hand into his pocket, gets out his phone. Clicks through, not even looking at Will. That's going to piss him off so much, being ignored like that. Then he holds his phone up, points a finger to it.

That's it. Will's off. Gets right in the other guy's face, raising a hand but not touching, just getting close. He doesn't move. When he's run out of words, Will is standing there, shoulders heaving, his face all pink. The guy walks over to the car, tips his head back, lets off a gob of spit onto the rear window. Walks off, not looking back.

The door slams like the hinges are going to break.

'Well this is all very satisfactory.' She seems to have perked up.

'So is this what you often do with your spare time?'

'Of course.'

'You're an engineer. I thought you'd be building models or something.'

'Right. Just like you go to art classes and volunteer at youth clubs during the summer.'

'Fair enough.' Back to twiddling with the cup. 'I did go to a pottery class once, if that counts.' One of Bea's projects. The squat little vase he made that was too small for any type of flower was still in the back of one of the kitchen cupboards.

'Well, if it comes to that, I might have bought a robot arm kit.' She laughs. 'Not that it was massively useful. Couldn't get it to pick anything up. Ended up using it to hang jewellery on.'

'Knew it.'

'In fact, I'm going to a design show this week,' she says.

'Really?'

'It's a work thing. Networking, sucking up to the investors. Always a bore.'

'The trials of being a slave to the corporate world.'

'Holly will make it bearable.' She smiles. 'There was this really dull convention I got stuck at one year, up in Cardiff. Managed to get Holly in. She turns up with a litre of Jameson's and a hip flask. So we just spent the weekend going round smiling at everyone, being really chatty and friendly. My boss was very impressed by my networking skills.'

'She sounds like a laugh.'

'Yeah.' Something a little sad around her eyes. 'Usually.'

The realisation stabs at Eric. They're really good friends. Girls, they tell each other everything. Holly must know, about what happened at the party. Had they talked about him?

'Problems?'

'Oh, it's nothing. We've been mates for ages.' But then he'd have to reveal how close he really is to Will. Somehow the thought of not seeing her again is uncomfortable.

'Here we go again.'

The gauntlet of people gets repetitive. Sometimes the door opens, sometimes not. Nina passes over a packet of skittles. He picks out yellow and green, mushing them into a sticky paste. Glances over at her. Just like him, chewing, eyes fixated on the exasperation of one man.

He could ask her if she wanted to get a coffee afterwards. De-brief, talk over how it went. Or lunch, go to that place on Arthur Street that's got chunky wooden tables and cutlery in jam jars.

'You have to be fucking kidding me.' A real grate to her voice.

The door is open again. Only this time, it's to let someone out. Blonde hair, he recognises her from the Facebook picture. This must be Holly. All giggles and smiles, wrapping her hand around the back of Will's neck like he's property.

'I don't think so.' Nina clicks the door open.

'Wait.' They'll see him. Everything will come out. 'He'll know it was you.' The door is still open but she doesn't push it any further. 'He might call the police. Make the link, between this and the flour or whatever.'

'Right.' It might be the police that scare her, or the threat of uncovering whatever else she's done. She clicks the door shut again. 'I don't fucking believe this.'

They're still kissing, one of his hands exploring her back, reaching down towards her bum.

Without saying anything, Nina starts the car and drives off. Eric scrambles for his seat belt.

'Aren't there others coming?'

She pulls right out in front of an oncoming car. A horn blares at them. Round the roundabout at hurtling speed, over a pedestrian crossing without checking, stares and accusations falling.

They stop at the end of her road.

'Thanks.' Her voice is thick. She's trying not to cry.

'Are you OK? What's wrong?'

'I told her to stay away from him. He's sick.' Tears are falling down her face.

'I don't understand.' It was just an argument.

'He raped me.' She covers her face with her hands. 'I was in that room on my own and he came in and attacked me.'

'What?' He stares at her. Shoulders shaking, tears pouring between her fingers. She's talking about him. How can she think that's what happened?

'Oh god, I'm sorry.' She wipes her face, leans over him and reaches into the glove box. He shrinks back, remembering when he touched her. If she didn't want it why didn't she say no, try to stop him? 'I barely know you and honestly, I haven't told anyone.' She gets a packet of tissues out, blows her nose. 'This sounds crazy but it actually feels so good just to say it out loud.' She laughs. 'He raped me. Will raped me.'

'I...I don't know what to say.' Maybe she hadn't moved at all at first. Oh god, what has he done?

'I'm sorry, this is really not your problem.' She smiles at him, rubs his arm. 'Thank you, so much. Just for being here, and for being so nice. I've been such a fucking state for the last three weeks.'

'No problem.' He can barely get the words out.

'Look, I've just realised I've driven home and I didn't ask where you lived. Or do you want to come in? Another coffee?' Her eyes are still splotchy from crying.

174

'No, no it's fine.' He unclips the seatbelt, reaches for the handle. He has to get out of there. It's obscene now, sitting so close to her.

'Are you sure?' If anything she looks disappointed.

'I have to go.' He opens the door and walks away, not even shutting it behind him. He concentrates on putting one foot in front of the other, his head full of images of that night, what he did, how he didn't wait for her to respond but just carried on anyway. How could he have thought it was dirty fun? He attacked a defenceless woman and now she's losing it, creating a vendetta against his best mate who didn't even touch her.

Wind gusts around his jacket, the sky shaded grey, that stern colour that tells you the sun won't be out for the rest of the day. He's a terrible person. The knowledge of it weights his steps all the way home.

Nina

The workout studio is dark and sweaty. Nina's near the back, she slipped in late so Holly wouldn't see her. She always comes to this class on a Monday evening. It's full, people crammed in lines, jerking and pulsating to the music.

She holds her arm in front of her. It feels withered, thinned out from the time pent up in the cast. They took it off at the hospital this afternoon. This is hardly the rest the doctor advised. At least she can reduce her thoughts to where her arms and legs have to go next.

Holly is near the front, blonde ponytail flicking around. Once she'd finally blurted her confession to Rick, she felt free. Now she could tell Holly, get this man out of their lives. It might not be too late to go to the police. She must have totally freaked him out, the way he left like that. She's sent a couple of apologetic messages but no reply yet. It feels important to show her gratitude. Maybe it's because he was a stranger, but she felt so relaxed around him. If it hadn't been for him she might not have found the courage to speak to Holly.

The music stops. People shake and stretch, the scent of sweaty bodies filling the air. Nina places a hand on Holly's slippery arm as she leaves for the changing rooms.

'Hi.'

'Hello.' She turns away, doesn't look very pleased to see her.

'Look, you were right, OK?' Nina takes big steps to keep up – she's a lot taller than her. 'I've been hiding stuff, and I've been a dick, and I'm sorry.'

Holly stops, turns.

'Finally something we can agree on.' She's smiling.

'Can we talk?'

'Of course. We can head back to mine.'

They chat and change, Holly asking about her withered arm. It feels like it used to. Why didn't she just tell her from the beginning?

Alone in the car, she feels the weight of what she has to say. Holly will be furious, that she's let her sleep with this guy.

'That was tough.' Nina offers this first.

'Yeah.' Holly taps the steering wheel. 'So are you going to tell me?'

'I think I need to build up to it.' Where can she start? The unravelling at work, Dev looking at her suspiciously. Sunday morning, cocooned in that car. With Rick there it had felt safer. The nausea at seeing Holly's hands all over that man, knowing what he'd done, they'd done. Bitter coffee vomit in the sink, she hadn't made it to the toilet after Rick rushed out of the car.

'Come on, Nin.' She reaches over and squeezes her knee. 'It's me.' Holly glares into the mirror. 'Get out of my arse, you prick.'

'I've got myself in such a mess.' Nina looks away, at the blurred procession of people on their way to pubs, restaurants. Her morning had been spent creating a fake account on Twitter. @BigWillLakeland. She hadn't followed him directly, so hopefully he wouldn't notice

177

until she'd been able to do some damage. He seemed to be more of an Instagrammer anyway. She'd kept the tweets safe, for now. Just to up her followers, get him an audience. She couldn't reveal this paranoid tapping to Holly.

'I know this version of you. All silent and snarly. In a couple of weeks you're going to crack and tell me everything anyway, so let's get it over with now.' She grins. It's true. Just like when she got passed over for promotion, and the time Aunty Becks had a brain tumour. Holly won't let it rest.

'I think it's your turn. You're tapping the steering wheel.' She wasn't the only one who could spot behaviour.

'Fine.' Holly lets out a huff of air. 'I stayed over at Will's.' Surprising that she'd confess so quickly.

'I see.' Keep the voice level, don't let on that she saw her there.

'It might be weird for you, but, well-' Holly sounds guarded. 'I actually really like this guy.'

'Oh, Holly.' It's worse than she thought. 'This is getting beyond a rebound.'

'That's not fair. Maybe at first it was, but now, I don't know.' That same smile she saw on her face on Sunday morning. 'He's a laugh.'

'You don't know him. I should have told you before. What he's like.' She's a terrible friend, not to have told her.

'Let's not do this again.' She sounds irritated. They pull up outside the flat before she can say anything else.

Inside, Holly busies herself with gathering up glasses, food. They slouch around the coffee table with wine and snacks.

'Right.' Nina thinks of a way to start it. Should she just blurt it out? No, maybe build up, set the scene.

'Look, seeing as you're here,' Holly says, 'I wondered if you could give me your opinion on my audition piece?' Immediately her cheeks bloom with colour. This is unexpected. Nina always troops along to the shows, on the last night so she can get in on the after-show party, but Holly is a face in the crowd. She had one line in the last show, delivered it in a high-pitched voice wearing a ridiculous yellow bonnet. Not her idea of a good night.

'Of course.' She can't refuse. This is something important to Holly, she's always going on about doing more in the shows, but has never had the confidence to do it. Her time to be the supportive friend.

Holly rushes out, comes back in with a trilby style hat and a jacket.

'Don't look.'

Nina dips her eyes, peeking up as the song starts. Holly has obviously practised this a lot. The timing of her leg swings, the hat rolls down one arm, is plonked back on her head. Something about Broadway, being a baby. It all sounds fairly misogynistic. There's a lovely tone to her voice, but it lacks something.

'What do you think?' She stops, gasping for breath. The last note was long, accompanied by a flourish with the head and arms. It was pretty impressive.

'Wow,' Nina says. 'That's so good, I didn't know you could sing like that.' This will be such a boost for her, if she gets the part. That group of oddballs is her entire social life apart from Nina.

'Thanks.' Holly flops down. 'Ok, so that's my humiliation dealt with. Are you going to talk, or what?' Holly nudges her, takes the piece of chocolate out of her hand on the way to her mouth. 'Come on.'

'OK, I think I'm ready,' Nina says. If she can say it to a stranger, surely she can say it to Holly.

'That's more like it.' Holly curls one foot up

underneath herself, leans in.

'That creep you're sleeping with. He…well…he attacked me. At that party.' It's out. 'I had all that rum, and then went upstairs, with him, but I told him to fuck off because he got a condom out without asking me, was all cocky.' One leg starts to judder. 'And then, I went for a lie down. I don't know, too drunk. But when I woke up.' Her face is hot. She can't look at Holly. 'He was behind me. My face was all squashed into the pillow. I felt it. I could feel him. He raped me.'

'What?' The piece of chocolate is still in Holly's hand, wavering in front of her mouth.

'That's where I was, on Sunday morning. I woke up there.' Her skin crawls at the memory. She gulps the wine, lets out a long breath. 'And I'm so sorry, I should have told you what he did as soon as you said about meeting up with him. But I just couldn't say it. I felt, weak, like I should have done something more to stop him. And I didn't want you to think that of me. You always say how strong I am.' She sighs. 'I'm sorry, it's been so horrible.' She lets the weight of her head fall. It's done. Holly will tell her to go to the police, or they could go and confront him together. Either way, it's over.

'Hun, are you sure?' Holly's voice is small. 'I mean, of course, if it happened like that, I'm here for you, it's just-' she takes a big breath. 'We've talked about that party, a few times, and Will went off to a club. He said he took a girl home, he's been really honest with me. Look, if something happened, you don't have to be embarrassed about it.'

'What?' Her leg stills. 'You think I'm making it up?' She grips her hands together.

'No, I don't mean that.' Holly shuffles closer. 'It's just that, if you were really drunk, and something happened, that maybe you were ashamed about

180

afterwards or something. Hey, we've all been there.'

'I don't believe this.' Pressing her nails into her palms. There's a blob of chocolate and marshmallow that's fallen onto the table, sinking into a puddle of goo.

'But if that's what you really think happened, then of course, we can talk about that.' A hand on her arm.

'Don't touch me.' She cringes away from the warm palm. This was the person that was supposed to help.

'Come on, talk to me, what actually happened, what do you remember? We can work it out.' That simpering voice. She thinks she's lying. 'You don't have to bring him into it. Let's just try to figure out what happened.'

'I see.' And there it is. She'd rather protect her new rapist boyfriend than admit to herself she's been duped by someone like that.

'Shall I get another bottle of wine? Or maybe some tea.' She stands up, awkward.

'Don't bother.' The marshmallow is sitting in a pool of brown now.

'Oh come on, I'm sorry.' She sits back down again. Puts an arm around her. 'Talk to me, please. I just wasn't expecting that, and it's not like you're the kind of person that wouldn't, I don't know, fight back? I'm just talking rubbish. Please.'

'I said don't touch me.' The creep of her skin allows her to stand, anything to get away from it. This false pleading. 'You're disgusting.' The air feels so hot. It's like in the flat when she looked at his face. Everything's going to shut down soon, she has to get out.

'Give me a break. You drop this thing on me, without any warning.' Her voice sounds injured. She has no idea.

'You are disgusting.' Nina can look at her now. This so-called friend. For what she is. 'I saw you, outside his house, slobbering all over him. That vicious, horrible-' there isn't a word for what he is. 'I tried to tell you what

181

he was like. But you wouldn't listen. So desperate not to be alone, after the last one dumped you for being too needy.' Spit comes out with the words. 'You're pathetic.' She wants to hurt her, rip at her in the same way. 'You can't sing for shit. You bounce from one guy to the next, desperate for someone to love you.'

If she stops talking, the blanket will fall over her lungs again. 'You deserve each other. Someone like that, who would force himself on a passed-out woman at a party. Looks like you're about the same level of challenge. Fuck him on the first date, did you?' It's there, in her eyes. Of course she did. 'Opening your legs and giving it up to whoever pays you some attention.' She can make it, to the door. Her anger can get her out. 'I always thought you were a slut.'

The door is there. Turn the handle, down the stairs, the keys must be there somewhere. Where did she park the car? Further down, there wasn't space, she was late, and Holly was driving them to the class. There it is.

She heaves her body inside, legs feeling rubbery. The car jerks into life. Rain streaks down the windscreen, she fumbles for the wipers. For a minute she can't understand the source of the wetness on her face, thinks she must have left the window open for the rain to soak her cheeks.

Eric

There's a crash from round the back of the house. Eric clanks open the side gate and walks past the herb garden.

'Lil, what are you doing?'

The light from the living room through the patio doors illuminates the scene in the dark garden. She's sprawled in the middle of the decking, a large striped patio umbrella laying diagonally across her. He dumps his bag and hurries over.

'You were supposed to be here ages ago,' she says. He takes the weight of it so she can get up. 'Look what you've made me do.'

'You should have waited.' He sets it back down. The base is skewed at an angle, half off the decking.

'Don't break it.' She waits behind him.

'Where are the instructions?' He doesn't want to turn around, is worried he looks different after what Nina told him yesterday.

'Thought you wouldn't need them.' She indicates the piece of paper on the table. 'Drink?'

'Go on then.' He picks up the page. The words look like a scrawl.

Lil disappears through the sliding doors.

He'd tried to think of an excuse for leaving Lil to deal

with this on her own. His day passed in a blur, the slightest gap between lining them up for beanbag races taking him back to the car, her crumpled face, that horrible word. Eric looks down at his hands. Slight fingers, nails flaking from all the washing up after painting, red patchy bits from where he used to get eczema. Not the sort of hands that would do – that thing.

He looked it up yesterday, wondering if he'd somehow been confused about what it meant. Men waiting in bushes, women held at knifepoint, sobbing slaves forced to do their master's bidding. They were all the things he pictured when he thought about it, which he hardly ever did. One dictionary website said it has to involve force. That would be a struggle, a fight. But it hadn't been anything like that. On another one it said that consent can't just be given, that it needed to be ongoing. He couldn't figure that out. It's not like you ever stopped and asked, in the middle of it. That would be weird. Oh, by the way, is it OK if I put my hand there? Not very sexy. And there were the games Bea liked, where she'd pretend not to want it, go all shy, shake her head at him, drop her head, eyes glinting up at him from under her fringe. That had been great. Nothing like a "yes" given there.

Nina had been drunk, clearly. But there had been plenty of times when he'd woken up with only a vague memory of sex. If anything, it was a prerequisite. Gave him the confidence to get naked and not be embarrassed about all of that stuff. And she hadn't stopped him. Hadn't said no. Her shuffling consent had been implied, sure, but you don't let someone do stuff like that to you unless you want it. In the car, she'd been so certain, so upset.

He remembers himself, reads the instructions. There's water in the bottom, so hopefully she's just knocked it out of whack, rather than bending the pole. Down on all fours, he realigns the bottom – she hasn't screwed it tight enough. Just put the top bit on, then it's sorted. He grabs the pole, lifts it. The end sways away, the canvas dipping and drooping, the weight of it pivoting in his hand.

'Harder than it looks!' Lil sounds triumphant. She puts two beers on the table and grabs the pole. They manoeuvre round, get one end in, then walk the rest of it up. It thunks in, juddering the table and knocking one of the bottles over.

'Shit.' She grabs it, the liquid frothing over her hand.

'Don't worry.' He takes it from her. They stand back, get a sense of the overall effect.

'Isn't it a bit big?' he says. The space looks swamped.

'Whatever, I'm not taking it back now.' She sits at the table, leans back, as if basking in tropical sunshine. Eric looks up through it, the flicker of airplane lights just visible behind the fabric.

'It's February.'

'Yeah well, it was reduced.' She swigs her beer, looks at the sky. 'Anyway, there's going to be an early warm spell this year. I read something about migratory birds, and how they've arrived early. I want to get the most out of the garden this year.'

'You said that last year.' She'd hosted three "summer" events, each of them ending with Eric turning sausages under an umbrella.

'The house martens were probably late.' She leans over and picks at a plant in one of her pots. He couldn't believe it when she told them she was buying her own place. He'd felt cheated – he was the older one, he was supposed to do that stuff first. She was so positive, independent. Why couldn't he be more like that?

A buzz in his pocket. Probably Will, demanding his

presence at some event or other. Since their dinner last week he was best avoided. Too many awkward questions, too much suspicion. Especially now he was sleeping with that girl Holly.

It's from Nina. He swipes, what does she want?

Are you free on Friday? Got that gallery thing and Holly's bailed on me.

There've been two messages already, apologising for what she said in the car, thanking him for his help. Now she wants to see him again. She wants him to go with her, to a work thing. This is big.

'Who's that?' Lil is still in her imaginary summer.

'Oh, just Will. Asking about Friday night.' He puts his phone in his pocket.

'Can't you find someone else to hang out with?'

'Yeah, right.' He has found someone else. Only she thinks he attacked her.

'I think you're fibbing.' Lil pokes him in the ribs. 'You've met someone, haven't you?'

'What?' He swigs his drink. Were his cheeks pink? It had been exciting, to see her name on his phone.

'Come on, is it that woman at work you have a crush on?'

'There isn't anyone.' He sits down, lets the shadow of the umbrella fall over his face.

'You know, she was your mentor.' She enjoys teasing him.

'Kirsty? She's married. And anyway, we're friends.'

'You were bordering on hero worship when you started working with her. Honestly, we thought you'd be engaged before the first year was out.' Lil and Mum, their special little chats.

'It wasn't like that.' She'd impressed him, that's all.

He liked women like that, who knew what they wanted.

'So who's the new one?' She's not going to let it go. Something to distract her, that's what's needed.

'I went to see Dad.' That should shock her.

'Mum told me. I don't know why you bothered.'

'You didn't say anything.' The two of them, talking about him. They must do it all the time.

'She thinks you have to do it. That you haven't dealt with it, him leaving I mean.'

'Nice to know you've got me all figured out.'

'You seem a lot calmer than when you came over for dinner. The mystery lady is clearly having a good impact on you.'

'I told you-'

'I know. You just grin at your phone all the time when a mate texts you.'

'You're unbelievable.' He leaves his beer, goes inside.

He sits on the toilet, head in hands. What a mess. There he was, imagining she wanted to go on a date with him, and all the while it was about Will, or actually Eric, and getting her own back. All of the plotting she's been doing, how much time it must have taken. She's completely obsessed with it. Why would something that lasted such a short time affect her so much? Clearly she's unstable. Probably best to use this as an excuse to bow out, let someone else deal with her.

He flushes the toilet, for authenticity. Checking his face in the mirror, he smoothes down the back of his hair. He'll just say sorry, he's busy. Not like he owes her anything. Besides, it's not too clever, spending more time with her. It's possible she'll recognise him, or he'll let something slip. Safer to stay away.

'Find out about the Phase Leader job next week.' Start talking before she gets a chance to question him. Find a new line of conversation.

187

'What do you reckon your chances are?' Her bare feet are up on the table. Isn't she cold?

'Think it's good to show I'm keen, but I'm probably the least qualified.' It has to be Olivia that gets it.

'You're forgetting the Penis Factor.'

'Excuse me?'

'Apparently men often go for jobs they're not qualified for, and get them, while women will wait until they're sure they're good enough.'

'That doesn't mean I'll get the job.'

'People prefer men to be in charge.'

'Come on. You're just pissed off you didn't get that job in Head Office.'

'Because some neophyte with an oversized tie got it.' Jerry and his posturing had been the subject of many a phone rant. If he got the job, he must have been the best person for it. Not that he'd admitted that thinking to Lilly, of course.

'The next one is definitely yours.' It made him uncomfortable, seeing Lil in all her work getup. She looked masculine. Probably better she stayed where she was.

Lil nods, makes agreeing noises. 'So what's her name?' This is ridiculous.

He bashes the top of her bottle with his. The beer gushes up and over the sides. Lil clamps her mouth over it, snorting a little.

'Very mature.' She shakes the drips off her hands. 'OK, you can keep her secret for now.'

'Aren't there any snacks?' She usually gives him something when he comes over.

'If you tell me her name,' she says.

'Nina.' He smiles.

'Fine.' She goes into the kitchen, comes back and plonks a plate of Jaffa Cakes on the table.

'Come on then, tell me the grand plans for the garden this year. Don't tell me, a pagoda down the bottom, an ornamental bamboo plantation with its own panda.'

'Bamboo would be a terrible idea in a garden this size.' She shakes her head, launches into her plan. Arms waving, she paints a picture of Mediterranean perfection over the dark scrubby grass in front of them. He munches, mixing the orange goo with his beer. Not entirely unpleasant.

In the car, she'd nibbled all the way round the edges, then peeled the jelly off the top and eaten the cake part. Then the orange circle was rolled up, slid between her lips and stayed there, her cheeks poking in as she sucked the chocolate off.

He gets his phone out, taps a quick message in reply.

I'm in.

It would be rude to let her down. She's clearly in a fragile state. Ignoring Lil's smirk at his phone, he sits back and grabs another cake. Maybe there is something there. He can't place the reason, but it's important to see her again.

Nina

The gallery is quiet, people milling around in pairs- muted words and gestures. Nina feels exposed. She shouldn't have worn heels, they're too loud on the hard floor. She tugs down the hem of her dress. Silence saturates the air, dulling the lights that hang around the paintings like haloes. It's like the grey day has penetrated. Why is she so nervous?

Nina positions herself in front of a landscape, a pack of hunting dogs lurking in the foreground. The door is right there, she'll see him as soon as he arrives. Nothing from Holly all week. Some sickening update on Facebook with a picture of some flowers. Doesn't look like she's about to apologise any time soon.

A man hurries in, thick drips following him. The hood of his waterproof hangs low over his face.

'Hi, Nina.' He stops, dripping, in front of her.

'I didn't recognise you.' She grips the plastic wine glass. Is it weird, that she asked him? Her friends have all run out and since she told him he feels safer, somehow.

He deposits his coat. His shirt is dark blue with white spots. It looks like he made an effort, some squishy stuff in his hair to make it stay in fixed lines. And he's given up his Friday night.

'How's the car?' he asks.

'He'll live. Got a scar now, which obviously makes him cooler.' She wonders what other people will think, seeing them together like this. He's not unattractive. Cute in a scrawny way.

'What's his name?'

'Perses.' She always pictures the car with a triangular beard strapped to the front grille. Concentrating on the conversation, she resists the urge to tug her skirt down. It's only above the knee, not too much of her is exposed.

'God of Destruction. Very suitable.' That one usually needed explaining. 'And the arm?'

'Still feels like I've been given some weakling's arm to carry around.' She waves the skinny wrist at him. 'You know mythology?' Nina's dad read them to her when she was little, adding in the gory bits that were missing from the bright animated versions. The Hydra always crept into her thoughts when the fence rattled in the wind.

'I was obsessed with this book about the Trojans when I was a kid. Plus there's this game called God of War.' His face scrunches up. 'I was going to leave it a while before mentioning computer games.'

'At least this one sounds educational.' He's been thinking about seeing her again.

'Well, in between killing stuff with fiery chains. Every day's a school day.'

They walk into the main gallery. The bit she's been avoiding – here's where all the suit types are. Hard to feel confident when the only other women are serving drinks. Clive's idea of a sophisticated setting to suck up to their investors – some modern artist that creates sculptures out of disused mechanical parts.

'So what do you think of this, Sophocles?' She gestures to a wire and wood piece, little nuts and bolts hanging from it like leaves.

'Classic lines.' He nods, rubs his chin in a parody of thought.

'How classic can a stump be?' she asks.

'You shouldn't be so restrictive in your views.' It's actually relaxing, having him here.

They stop in front of a huge slab of metal. Mottled colours linger in it – orange, red. It looks angry.

'How about you?' His tone is soft. It's hard to take someone else's concern. 'I mean, what's engineering like? It must be amazing. Like building toy models. But bigger.' Just a work question. She swallows down the bubble of her embarrassment.

'Sometimes. I have to defend myself a lot.' It was good to be different in lectures at first, she liked to be noticed. Until she realised that her ideas were rubbished on days she wore skirts.

'You must enjoy it,' he says.

'Mostly. When I'm not made to explain that I'm not a student, or an assistant.' She started avoiding conferences, it was so wearing to say the same things over and over.

'But, the important stuff.' He brings her to a stop next to a large wheel. 'Cheese or cake?' He holds an invisible microphone under her lips.

'Tricky. The best thing is to combine the two.' His eyes widen when he's messing around.

'Everyone's a winner that way.' He nods.

'I had this toffee cheesecake when I was in New York. With this really bitter raspberry sauce. It was amazing.' The trip she'd won for her project at University. That had shut them up.

'See, for me it's cheese every time. Stinkier the better.' He has a habit of patting the hair on the back of his head. The tuft is back, despite his efforts to stick it down.

Further into the room the stuff gets bigger, some of

the pieces towering over them, a construction of cardboard hanging off one wall. The bulk of the crowd are here, in reverent groups, talking quietly. She should circulate, go through the rigmarole of explaining who she is each time. This always happens, despite her name badge with the job title on it.

They stop in front of a giant nail. Little mirrors have been stuck in a spiral all the way round. The pair of them are fragmented, small details replicated in each of the tiny squares.

Clive has spotted her. He waddles over. His "meet the people" look always involves him undoing more buttons on his shirt than is advisable.

'Ah, Nina.' He always sounds surprised at her presence.

'Good turnout,' she says.

'And you are?' Clive extends a hand.

'Rick.' He sounds so polite.

'Lovely. She kept you quiet.' Clive nods between the two of them, keeps nodding.

'We've bonded over an interest in the possibilities of wire shaping,' Rick says. She tries not to laugh.

'Splendid.' Clive touches her arm. 'The people from George and Coombes are here. Best foot forward, dear.' He taps her again, as if she's faulty, and rushes off.

'Your boss?' Rick looks apologetic.

'Unfortunately. That was his signal to go and make enthusiastic noises at that lot.' She nods at the biggest group. Mostly men, balding, crisp suits. Some of the faces that will be staring at her on Monday, looking for justification for their investment.

'Ouch.' Eric takes two glasses from the nearest tray and hands her one.

'Best foot forward, dear.' Eric does an imitation eyebrow waggle. Clive's comments made her feel like an incompetent aunt.

She walks over to the group, repeating the mantra she learned from Michelle Obama in her head – "I'll show you."

'Good evening.' Turn up the smile, this must be George, or possibly Coombes. Interchangeable white faces turn to her.

'Lovely drop of fizz.' The one closest to her has a light sheen on his forehead. 'You work in the office?'

'Something like that.' Here we go again. 'I'm Nina Franklin, Chief Engineer on the project.' The usual raised eyebrows.

'You lot get everywhere these days.' What was that supposed to mean?

'I hope you're enjoying the exhibition.' Best to ignore it, get on with being pleasant.

'Bet you were one of those who was really good at Maths.' Another one weighs in, his cheeks wobbling as he nods his head. 'There was one at my school. You always get one.'

'The research team are very pleased with developments. It's a very technical specification but I think we're meeting their needs.' She should have brought a diagram, something to hold in her hands.

'No need to talk shop.' He squeezes her arm. His hands are damp. 'All here to enjoy ourselves.'

'Does your young man here like model building as well?' She can sense their relief when they turn their attention to Rick. Her presence always makes them uncomfortable.

An insistent buzz in her bag. Her phone.

'Excuse me.' This conversation can't get worse. She picks it up and turns away.

Ms Franklin?

'Yes.'

I'm calling with your results from the sexual health centre.

'Right.' She checks around her, that sounded so loud. She sneaks into a different gallery.

HIV - negative, chlamydia - negative, genital warts - negative, gonorrhoea - negative, herpes - negative.

'Right. Thanks.' Nina lets the nearest wall take her weight. This disruption into every part of her life. She feels tainted.

'Everything OK?' Rick peers round the doorway.

'I need some space.' She walks away from him, them, into the quieter parts of the gallery, past a stern man in uniform stationed at the door.

A canvas with a gape of blank space is on the left wall. She steps closer. A watercolour, the tiniest dabs and strokes leaving the impression of waves and movement, something beautiful in the way it looks unfinished. There's a tiny gap of white at the back. Is it a boat, or a building? It's like an imperfection with meaning. Footsteps behind her. She waits, absorbing the fading blues, preparing herself. Now is not the time for small talk.

He's sat on the leather bench. So still. She sits next to him, the cushion hardly giving.

'What do you see?' Her voice is hushed by his stillness. Perhaps he sees something else in the blanks.

He places a finger over his lips, glances behind him, dips a hand in his jacket. The man in uniform walks away, clearly he has a circuit.

A tinny slosh, the tang of alcohol. Reaching over, he places the cool flask in her hand, his fingers warm.

'I know I'm not Holly.' His voice is almost a whisper. 'But I can at least make this more interesting.'

Nina takes a big swig, the liquid intense in her throat.

'I'm sorry.' He says it so quietly. 'What happened, I mean.'

She doesn't know what to say. There hasn't been much time for sympathy. It's warming. They huddle, passing the swishing liquid between them. Each mouthful is tinged with rust – the amber of the whisky and the burnished metal inside. She pictures the tiny filaments of corrosion, carried down inside her.

'You must think I'm crazy.' The house, the car, the selling stuff. So much time and effort fixated on that horrible man.

'Look, Will is hardly a nice guy. That is not new information.' He leans back. 'I guess, I don't know, I just wouldn't want to give him the satisfaction of letting one night affect you so much.'

She tenses. So much for him understanding her.

'You think I want to?' She leans forward, away from him. 'It's like-' she searches for the feeling, a way to make him understand '-it's like my body isn't mine anymore. To do that, without permission. I don't know how to stop thinking about it.' She feels diseased. That night and the ensuing silence. It's a darkness, spreading through her. The tiniest light of confession cut out when Holly didn't believe her. At least Rick isn't calling her a liar.

'This might help.' He waves the flask at her. 'It's also artistic appreciation enhancement. Those mountains look so much more,' an artistic flick of his hand, 'bumpy.'

'We can't hide here all evening.' Michelle would be disappointed. 'Let's see if it really works.' They go back to the room of tortured metal.

She has a toilet emergency before they can test the effects. When she gets back, he's nodding, deep in conversation. She can't make out who he's talking to. It's impressive, that he'd make an effort with this lot, especially after almost emptying the flask. Nina feels wobbly, her lack of dinner increasing the problem. She gets closer.

'I see what you mean, that's fascinating,' he says. He's talking to the nail. A few people glance over, a wide space around him. He keeps nodding earnestly at it.

'What does it say?' she asks.

'He, my dear, given the proportions.' He sweeps his arm in a grand gesture.

'Let me give him a hug.' She wraps her arms around it, little glass squares digging into her skin.

Tightly clipped footsteps hurry across the floor. He passes the flask to her. She shoves it back at him. It's suspended between their hands when the guard comes into view.

'No touching the exhibits,' he says. 'Or bringing your own alcohol. I'll have to ask you to leave.'

'Art and alcohol have a very long history,' Rick says.

'Just a minute.' She reaches out and sweeps through the nuts and bolts, producing a dull jangle.

'I must ask you to leave.' He steps forward, clearly not wanting to touch her. Conversations have run out around them. They've become a point of display. Clive is watching her from the door. It's difficult not to laugh.

Nina walks briskly out, her heels getting in the way. She scoops them off her feet and rushes out into the dark grounds, hedge-cut shapes looming. There's a bench. She plops down, assembling her breaths.

'I've never been kicked out of a gallery before,' he says, flopping down beside her.

'Happened to me in a library once,' she says.

'For what?'

'It was a dare at Uni. I made a bet that I could make a construction two metres in height with the periodicals before someone stopped me.' Crouched in the dark, she'd made a perfect stack, integrated layers so it was stable, until the security guard found her.

'Did you win?'

197

'1 metre 75. So close. I had to steal a library card for a month so I didn't get behind.'

'Impressive.' He turns to her, the streetlights casting long yellow shadows on his face. There's a scent of something floral wafting in from the garden, undercut with the fumes of the nearby road. His hand reaches up, he's patting his hair again.

'Don't.' She grabs his hand.

He shuffles on the bench, hand still clasped in hers. The fingers are cold, with a nugget of warmth in the palm. His eyes are in shadow, it's hard to see. She could lean forward and kiss him, he's so close. Now the possibility has presented itself, she can't concentrate on anything else. Does he want that? He's not moving away. She moves closer, trying to see his expression. Serious, eyes wide. Is it permission or panic? She scrolls back – searching her thoughts for something like this, an attraction, wanting to be close to him. How will it feel now, is she different? The tickle of anticipation feels the same, the expectation hanging in her skin.

She leans in and presses her lips to his. The delicate weight of it, the metallic aftertaste. He doesn't move, hardly responding. She squeezes his hand, pushing more insistently against him. After a moment, his other hand comes up and cups her neck, the thumb brushing just under her ear. There it is, a warmth under her ribs, the skin of her neck flushed. It hasn't changed her, turned into something that can't feel.

She turns, rests her head on his shoulder. The smell of him seeps out from under his coat. She closes her eyes. Where did that come from? It must be the alcohol, or those awful men, and she was just grateful to have an ally in there. That's what he feels like – an accomplice. Someone to help her.

'Do you want to go home?' he asks.

'Not yet.' They sit under the light, cold creeping up her legs. She thinks of the box of broken things she kept under her bed when she was younger, the hours she spent tinkering until they were fixed.

Eric

Eric

The staff room is cluttered with bodies. It's not usually this busy. Eric skulks by his pigeonhole, examining each piece of paper closely in the hope that no-one will talk to him. Something about dyslexia training, in-house, after school tomorrow. He spent the weekend veering between excitement and despair. She kissed him. But she also didn't know she had a vendetta out on the wrong person.

'Morning.' Olivia is standing right in front of him. She's wearing a suit, not her usual long skirt.

'Hello.' He smiles, glances around him, feeling observed.

'I just wanted to say thanks.' He can't tell if she's joking. 'For not applying.'

'Right.' He never actually said he wouldn't, she'd just assumed. It wasn't his fault. She walks over to the rest of the Year 5 teachers, her smile thin.

A general clearing of throats and shushing, associated with the arrival of Foggert.

'Morning all.' An approving glance around the room, the scurrying figure of Alice, her diminutive PA, parking herself on an adjacent chair. She's already scribbling on her spiral bound notepad, head bowed. 'Just like to say a big thanks to the staff who helped to organise the dance extravaganza,' she waves vaguely at heads, 'last week, which was an absolute triumph. Parents were absolutely thrilled, and the kids, er, the pupils, were just wonderful. Particular thanks to Olivia Greenaway,' Eric can feel her preening from the other side of the room, 'for all the front of house work and the promotion, without which it couldn't have gone ahead.' She looks down at her notes, apparently ignoring the light grumble emanating from the PE staff who took up the bulk of the graft rehearsing and preparing a squabble of fifty children into some sort of artistic order.

'Also a big thank you to the Year 4 team for their fundraiser last week, great to see so many of the local community supporting us and, of course, for all the delicious cakes provided by staff and parents. I hear the "Guess the Number of Skittles" raised two hundred pounds on its own, so excellent work all round everyone.'

Her features drop, a shifting of the eyebrows to indicate a more serious note. 'Now, as we all know, the big "O" is expected this term.' An obedient ripple of laughter at this often-repeated joke. 'So we are shaking up the team, introducing some new roles. The first to be appointed is the Keystage 1 Phase Leader, a key role which will ensure we are solid at our very foundation.' She rocks back on her heels, scanning the room again. Maybe she used to be a drama teacher. 'So, the person taking on this vital position-' there's something of the gameshow host about her. Eric half expects Alice to strip off her dowdy outfit to reveal a sequinned bikini. Olivia straightens, her shoulders stiffening.

'-will be Eric Walker.' After a short pause, cues are read and the staff mutter enthusiastically, a flutter of applause. Eric stiffens under the heat of attention. Glancing over at Olivia, she glares at him, several hands patting at her shoulders like a massage.

'Have a great day.' Foggert strides out, Alice hovering behind.

Conversations erupt around him. Painting his face with some sort of urgency, he edges to the door, gripping his paperwork.

Through the door and he's safe. There are enough excuses to keep away from the staff room for the rest of the day.

'You kept that quiet.' How did Olivia get out so quickly?

'It was just to show an interest. Honestly, I didn't think I'd get it.' Eric tries to back away, but there's a wall behind him.

'Then you shouldn't have done it.' Dots of pink on her cheeks, eyes blinking furiously.

'Hang on, that's not fair. There's no harm in trying.' He addresses his responses to the left of her ear.

'You are under qualified. She just wants a male face to stride about and look important, to even the balance.'

'Hang on-' there are people coming out now, she's making a scene.

'Some of us have a plan, work bloody hard for what we want.' She steps forward. 'You just walk in and take it. People like you disgust me.' That's a bit much.

'It's just a TLR point, not even that much money.' She looks so upset.

'To you maybe. I'm going to have to move now. Leave the school I love because I want to progress. You selfish, horrible-' she looks around. The hall is busier now, '-man.' Her voice cracks at the end. What a lot of fuss over some extra money. He would have shown much more grace if she'd got it.

He hurries to the classroom. The door clatters as the early ones come in, sounds bursting from them like bubbles. Jason bears down on him.

'Sir, I read that elephants have see-through stomachs. And they can breathe underwater. So if you were inside one, and it was in the water, you'd still be able to breathe.'

'Right.' Eric allows himself to be lead away with a string of chatter, uncomfortably aware that he's now in charge of making sure hundreds of pupils actually make progress.

They sit around a large bag of Kettle Chips and the unopened grape fizz.

'You should have said you were coming.' Eric pulls at the frayed edge of his T-shirt – the old Mickey Mouse one he wears to bed. With that and his checked pyjama bottoms, it's hardly what you'd want to be seen in with these two around.

'Had to be a celebration.' Will looks his usual, comfortable self. Arms splayed over the sofa and one leg propped up.

'How did you know I got it?' He'd just settled down in front of The One Show after banishing imaginary conversations with Olivia where he sounded more confident from his brain.

'He reckoned you would have got in touch, moaning, if you hadn't.' Chris leans over the table, emptying the bag crunch by crunch.

'Silence meant success.' Will picks up the bottle, peeling off the gold foil.

'Well, thanks then.' Being around Will gives him the jitters these days.

The cork is popped, the bubbles shoot up the glasses – a present from Bea's mum – as Will pours it out.

'Waste of time.' Chris picks up the glass and peers at it.

'Just cutting back on the weekday drinking.' Will

sniffs it and takes a sip. 'Not bad.'

'Is this some health kick?' Not like him, usually jumps at the chance of a drink.

'Important to think about what you put into your body.' He swirls the glass like it's a fine champagne.

'That's your nursey girlfriend talking. Whipped much?' Chris drinks the lot down in one go. 'Tastes like piss.'

'Thanks for thinking of our livers.' This Holly is having a big influence.

'So what you going to do with all that extra cash?' Trust Will to think about the money.

'Haven't thought about it. Anyway, it's not much.' His first idea had been to buy a necklace of green stones, to go with the bracelet. What was she doing this evening? 'Nothing like what you're on.' Will was always buying new things, going on fancy holidays.

'I make sure I get what I'm owed.' Will smiles over his glass. 'Finally get a decent car, save up for your own place. Get some new clothes. About time you got out there again.'

'Still mooning over the chubby one? Give it a rest.' Chris slaps Eric's arm on his way past him, to the loo.

'Thanks for bringing him.' Eric looks back at the closed door, lowers his voice.

'He's alright.' Will pours more bubbles into his glass.

'It's a nice gesture.' He nods at the table. 'Can't be up late, got to get in early, make a start on all the new stuff.' Foggert's got him in with her first thing to look over data.

'I wanted to talk to you about Holly.' He leans forward, hands on knees, all serious.

'Why?' Stay calm.

'Well, it's her mate Nina, really. They had this big row about that party we were at. Apparently-' This is it. He's going to be found out. 'Apparently she was attacked by someone. And she thinks it was me.' He leans back, lets his big statement sink in.

'What?' Eric chokes on his drink. Who else has she told about it?

'Yeah. She's got it into her head that I sneaked back there and, well, shagged her while she was passed out.' He shudders.

'If she was passed out, how does she know?' There's nothing to link it back to him.

'Pretty sure you'd be suspicious if you woke up with a wet nob and your trousers down.' A snort of laughter.

'I don't see why you're so fussed.' They need to stop talking about this.

'You taking the piss? Some random says I took advantage of her and I'm supposed to just let it go?' Now he's getting angry.

'If you didn't do it, I wouldn't worry about it.' A shrug. Move on. No big deal.

'What the fuck do you mean, if?' His hands go all white around the glass.

'Steady on, lads.' Chris slumps back into the sofa, scooping up another handful of crisps.

'Ricky here doesn't think I should get worried about someone accusing me of rape.' At least Chris coming in has calmed him down.

'You what?' Chris sprays crumbs on the floor.

'At the party. It's all a misunderstanding.' That's all it is. It wasn't like that, not really.

'That's where you met this nurse, right?' Chris' grin is flecked with crisp bits. 'Or do you mean that crazy girl? She was proper mental, not surprised she's making shit up.' Back to this again.

'I don't see why you'd lie about something like that.' Now Will looks worried. So that's why Nina and Holly fell out. Because of him.

'Oh come on. Happens all the time.' Chris licks his finger and rubs it round the packet. 'Girl gets pissed and shags some bloke, wakes up and regrets it, next thing you know she drops the "r" bomb, trying to get some money out of you.'

'He's not a footballer, Eric says.

'You know what I mean.' He pulls the salty finger up to his face.

'Maybe some stupid little kid might do that. But not a grown woman.' Now Will is looking at him. Does he suspect?

'I don't know what you're talking to us for.' Eric needs to steer the conversation away somehow.

'You were there, too. Maybe you saw something. Someone coming on to her? Going upstairs after me? I don't know.' Will's still looking at him.

'No reason we would have seen anything. You didn't.' He's fiddling with his glass. Stop, that will look suspicious.

'I left, remember? Went on to Mojos.' Now Will puts his glass down.

'He wasn't there. You were looking for him, wanted someone to go with you.' Chris needs to shut up.

'That's right.' Will's eyes land on him again. Is that suspicion? 'What were you doing?'

'A guy can't go for a shit without getting grief about it?' That sounds too defensive. Like he's hiding something. 'I thought you were coming over to congratulate me.'

'I'd like to help her.' Holly has made him soft.

'Woman's Best Friend here.' A joke, that will help.

'Come on, can you imagine? It must have been terrifying.' He means it.

'Can't help you, mate.' Keep it light, turn attention

206

away. 'Must have been a dodgy Chinese or something, I was up there for ages.' Eric makes himself laugh, look at them, meet their eyes. There's no way they can know.

'Have a think, alright? I told Holly I'd let her know.' Will's still staring at him.

'I'll get us a proper drink, shall I?' He heads to the kitchen, leans against the counter for support. Did he really think he'd be safe? There were so many people there. Someone must have seen him going into that room. If Will is fishing about, it might not be long before he finds someone. He has to make him stop asking questions.

'Alright?' The voice makes him jump. His guilt must be obvious. Chris should be safe, at least.

'Give me a minute.' He opens the fridge, moves things around as if it's difficult to find the beers that are right at the front. Chris wanders back into the living room. Too much drinking recently.

Like Friday. The whisky. He had a banging head on Saturday. The way she'd sat, so quietly, and then just leaned in. He'd nearly jumped off the bench. It had been awkward after that, but he had no idea what to say. She'd smelled so good, the touch of her lips had jangled all the way down him. But it wasn't right, was it?

Still, she must be feeling rough. Her best mate had buggered off, she was there tapping away at her laptop all hours of the night. Would be good to offer something, at least.

Need me for any stake outs or museum drinking? Just let me know

x

Eric takes the beers through to the front room, just two, to wind Will up. They sit and sip and conversation turns to work. Should be on safer ground here. He tries not to wince each time Will looks over.

Settling down into the chair, he lets his mind wander back to Friday. The scratchy wood against his hand, the wind shivering up the leg of his trousers. The mix of shame and excitement when he'd pressed his hand into her neck and kissed her back.

Nina

As soon as Clive finishes his drone, she'll have to get up. Counting through her slides, Nina tries to keep her hands still in her lap. Coombes, or possibly George, looks bored. The other one is nodding, making notes already.

It will be fine. There's that one slide to flip through, just press the clicky thing twice, they'll never notice. She can't bring up the timescale, it probably came through on an email she didn't pay attention to. It was definitely eleven weeks, in the first schedule. Best not to mention it, so it doesn't draw attention to the fact that she's running behind. The entire weekend lost to developing her online profile, leaving incriminating evidence around the Internet.

The second she got in Clive scooped her out of her chair for a pre-briefing, ignoring her plea to make final adjustments to the presentation. Some of the numbers and specifics will have to be fluffed, but she's always been good at talking. Although that's usually because she's so well-informed, knows the detail of everything she's discussing. She glances over at Dev, seeking reassurance. They didn't have a chance to talk before it started. He keeps her gaze, looks pissed off. Before he can respond to the tilt of her head, the furrow of a question in her eyebrows, he turns away. That's odd.

The bored one sticks a finger in his ear, rotates it, his face adopts a squeezed, satisfied look.

How did this happen? She had lists, all the stuff she needed to do. The weekend wasn't enough, especially with a fuzzy head on Saturday after all that whisky. That's the last time they saw her – giggling and rushing out of the gallery with her shoes in one hand. And what had she been thinking, kissing Rick? He was sweet, and it was so nice to feel normal again. But this was hardly the time for anything like that.

Clive steps back. Expectance shifts. Nina gets up, fiddles with the computer display to get her slides up. Good font, professional colour scheme, no problem.

'The specification for prototype ZX52-' it all comes back. The initial designs, the problem factors, the calculations. She feels her shoulders relax, the designs she prepared all those weeks ago popping up, the decisions she made and why. In a couple of slides is the one she'll need to flip over quickly, all the numbers she was going to put in after the testing that hasn't happened yet. The ear poker leans forward, typical that he'd get interested now.

A double click on the pointer, just a brief flash, then she's through.

'Initial testing has been very positive-' She can fluff it, give a general overview, make up a couple of glitches so it seems more plausible.

There's a cough from the side. Dev, waving his hand, shaking his head. One of the visiting assistants is giggling. Clive, grinning at the visitors, turns to her. His face freezes. Her sentence stutters to a halt. She turns.

How could she have forgotten? An undulating fish, a stream of bubbles popping out of the open, red-faced fury of Clive the Carp. Dev took that photo in a meeting when he got angry about people stealing the milk. She clicks the button, it jumps to the last slide. "MAKE SOMETHING UP" is written in red, capital letters. She meant to change that one too. Yesterday, when she was tweaking the wording of her fake Twitter posts, creating a slew of images for his Instagram. She'd gone out to take pictures of women hanging around bars, to make him look disgusting.

Clive strides up and switches the projector off.

'Right, time for a break, then we'll move on.' He keeps a smile on while the men lever themselves out of chairs. Frantic under-volume chatter starts at the brink of the room. The temp looks delighted. Nina stands, horrified, rolling her finger over the buttons on the clicker in her hand. She doesn't look up.

A hand on her arm. Dev. The door clicks closed.

'What the fuck did you do?' That's hardly supportive.

'I forgot, I meant to change it-'

'Not that.' She looks up. 'What did you do to my computer?' He knows.

'I don't know what you're talking about.' She shakes her arm free.

'You didn't want to be the only one to look bad, was that it?' He's standing too close. 'Now when they come and look at the boat we've got to try and cover up why the engine exploded when we tested it.'

'That's your fault, you should have checked your numbers.' She taught him that, he should know better.

'Yes, ten times, the Franklin method.' He spits the words out. 'I did that the day before. I knew it was right. When we ran the programme the following day, it was different. I tracked the changes. Made at 9pm.'

'I couldn't let him know it was too much. He's looking for an excuse to make me look bad.' It sounds pathetic, out loud. Ruining Dev's work to protect her

211

ego.

'So it *was* you.' He looks hurt. There wasn't any time, she didn't know what else she could have done. She shakes her head, looks for something to say. 'Amy always said you were a manipulative bitch.' He steps away from her.

The door creaks.

'Nina, a word.' Clive pops his head in. Time for the fallout. Dev is almost at the door.

'Dev, wait.' She could tell him. It's not like there aren't reasons behind her actions. He might understand, help her make sense of this mess. His hand reaches for the door.

'Please don't tell Clive.' She's in a bad enough situation as it is. There's no time for confessions now.

'I countersigned your mortgage.' He doesn't look up, pulls the door gently closed.

Nina steadies herself, heads out across the office, towards Clive. The air feels full of furtive glances. She keeps checking, but eyes are trained on desks and screens when she looks around. She knocks on his door like a naughty student.

'Come in.' He's sat down, fingers twined together on the desk in that pose he stole from *The Apprentice*. 'An explanation, please.' He looks so smug.

'You didn't give me enough time.' If he hadn't moved it forward, everything would have been fine.

'I don't have any record of your objection.' He flips through pages on his desk. 'Nor do I have any emails, feedback, anything telling me there was a problem.'

There's a highlighted sheet in the pile, he pulls it out. 'And then I have this.' He flicks it with one finger. It's too far away to read. 'From Dev Healy.' It's too late, he already told him. 'Claiming that you made changes to his calculations, without informing him, that led to the damage of company property.' He actually smiles. How could Dev do that to her? 'Would you like to respond to these claims?' He clasps his hands together, leans in.

Heat flushes her face, emotion prickling at the corner of her eyes. She looks down, blinking. He won't have the satisfaction of seeing that. She shrugs.

'In that case, I have no alternative but to effect your immediate suspension for gross negligence.'

She's never been fired from anywhere, not even the crappy Saturday job in the fish and chip shop that saturated her skin with grease.

She breathes, tries to form a sharp response. This will all be temporary, there's paperwork to do, lots to prove, they can't make this stick. The rest can be negotiated, when they realise they need her.

'I'll get my things.' Her words sound dry. It's as much as she can do to turn, walk out of the room.

They're watching her openly now, the thudding from the workshop downstairs louder without the usual hum of keys and chatter.

In her office, she doesn't have a box, everything will need to be crammed into her handbag and the laptop case. She gathers up the scattered pieces of herself. The cat, the cola bottles, the Tippex mouse, the notebook covered in rockets, the postcards from Holly, the camel mug Dev brought her back from Morocco.

She keeps her movements mechanical; lift and put, sweep and drop. She puts the congratulations card in from her parents last – a polar bear saying "grrrreat job!"

There's nothing else to put in the bag. She looks at her empty hands.

Dev's face does it. She shouldn't have walked that way, but it was the fastest route out. He's angry, that's clear, but there's something else too. All those years they've spent working together.

He glances at her, briefly, but it's enough. The clenched control over her face is lost. Squeezing her lips together, she speeds up. Tears drip into her bag, slipping down the side of the bear card, collecting in the mug, bouncing off the camel ears that always threatened to go up her nose when she drank her tea.

Flanked by silence, she can't meet any of the curious stares that follow her progress. Quicker, just get out of the door and it will be over. Her face must be red. How they're going to talk about her, laugh, when she leaves. All those times she took the piss out of them, waved her first-class degree about. They'll have a bloody field day.

Kevin's head pops up as she goes through the swish of the doors.

'Leaving early again?' There's a smile in his voice.

This is her fault. All that time she's spent at home, in cafés, obsessing when she should have been focusing on her job. She will have to tell people, her family, after all her posturing about a good education and what it's done for her.

At least the car is close. She slings her stuff onto the passenger seat and there, behind the steering wheel, lets everything collapse. First Holly, now this. She is alone.

A low moan escapes her throat, the hiccup of more tears, rushing out now, a squelch as she pulls the arm of her best presentation work shirt underneath her nose. It all vibrates through her, a damp patch growing on the collar of her shirt.

Then, nothing but gasping air. Tiredness pulling at her arms. A strange calm. Traffic on the ring road hums in the distance, a van chugs past, probably headed for the industrial estate. The whir of everyone else's day is continuing around her, oblivious.

Her breaths steady, slow. Hands reach up, tighten

around the wheel. A solid force presses her head up, finds a smear of bird shit on the windscreen.

None of this is her fault. Her lateness due to not being able to sleep, her paranoid online searching, the accusations she threw at Holly. It all leads back to that room, that night, that man. He has taken these things from her. Has weakened her, turned her into this pathetic thing.

There's a way back. If she can destroy him, ruin him the same way he's ruined her, then she'll have balance. Knowing he's out there, defiant in his freedom. Who knows, maybe he's done it to other women. She has to make everyone see what he is, then she can get back to herself, re-order and repair. There'll be an appeal process, a chance to have her say. By then, she might be able to claw back some respectability.

Sleeves damp, she heads home, stopping on the way for supplies.

She can broaden her scope, now she has more time. The box sits on the floor, full of promise. That will be the final stage.

Gumtree first, for the pleasure of reviewing the feedback. The messages are hilarious.

No need to fucking shout at me, mate. Are you selling it or not?

I have never met anyone so rude in my life. Rest assured I will not be attempting to purchase anything from you again.

The interest in the kittens was huge. Her careful replies, she tried to imitate the way he wrote on Facebook, agreeing to times and places for them to come over.

It might have reached its end, she's not sure what else she can legitimately try to sell, and the feedback won't make him popular. The Twitter posts can be increased, that will give her something to focus on.

Or something more direct. Get the message into his workplace, start to irritate him more directly. It's risky, especially with the Holly connection, but she's been smart enough about keeping her IP address hidden, not using any of her real emails. There's no way he can trace it back to her, even if he makes the connection. Bloody Holly, ruining her element of surprise. She's probably told him about her mental friend by now.

At least she can enjoy his public profiles. His rage, rants against her, all the things she's thrown at him. It makes her feel powerful. She's lucky he's so vocal with his annoyances.

Will Lakeland Some prick waking me up after a night out, poking at my car. I told him I'd call the police.

Nina allows Helen to make a comment.

Helen Clarke Nightmare!

The first one felt so exposed, as if he'd know it was her. Now it feels like another way of leading him off.

A picture of him, eyes dragged down with sleep.

Will Lakeland This is how impressed I was with your little scam, mate.

He's tagged a friend in it. There are comments of denial underneath.

She scrolls through the most recent photos, mostly pubs, work mates, a stag do. He announces himself in each one, arms spread wide with entitlement.

The fake Twitter has nearly a thousand followers

now. That might be the best place to make the attack more personal. So far it's been light, neutral. Sharing articles and offering a few comments. Time to make him look worse. Nina searches for some articles on women "making up" rape claims in order to get revenge. They're depressingly easy to find. A survey saying that over a quarter of the public think a woman is to blame if she's drunk or wearing a short skirt. An article with the "top 4" reasons women cry rape, along with a slew of shuddering comments. She shares one of them, schedules another for later. No need to comment, the intention is clear. Just to up his misogyny points, she shares a comment made by some idiot about how we need International Man's Day. He needs to have a voice. Rapists are always woman-haters.

Big Will @BigWillLakeland
Typical bloody woman.

That should be enough to lay the foundations of something. Hopefully get him a following, so this voice is more public. Then she can share something really incriminating.

A buzz on the table. It's from Rick.

Need me for any stake outs or museum drinking? Just let me know
x

It's like he knows what's happened today. It would be comforting. Invite him over, share a bottle of wine. He's the only one that knows what happened, the only one that believes her. He even knows this guy, he could help her find far more than she's been able to.

Unless it's the kiss. Maybe he's looking for something more, thinks it will go somewhere. That cannot be encouraged. Also, he brings out the truthful side of her. If they spend more time together, she might tell him everything. He'll think she's crazy. Might even report her. It's one thing to throw flour on someone's house, quite another to imitate them on social media. Send the email she's about to. As comforting as he's been, and there's even a tingle of something, it's not fair to involve him anymore.

Thanks but I think you've done enough. Really appreciate it. Good luck with everything x

There. Enough of a goodbye without making it a big deal. Better to do this on her own.

The list of his work associates is long. One by one, she pastes the addresses into the "To" box. Her eyes get blurry, fingers cramping over the repeated tap of shortcut keys.

It's done. Over fifty, brilliant. She sets the text to large, inputs her simple message. Straightforward, but should be effective.

Pressing "Send", she leans back. Something has been achieved. Now to wait for the fallout.

Eric

Mum is buried in the flowerbeds, stooping and rising. With her knee cushion, it looks like prayer.

'Weeding?' Eric calls over the lawn.

'A constant battle.' He can hear pleasure in her voice.

'Looks like you're winning.' There are even, dark spaces between the plants. His favourite is in the corner – a spiked purple thing. It always looked like it could belong with the dinosaurs, or on an alien planet.

'Thought someone as important as you wouldn't be skiving,' she says.

'It's my blank time.' She always forgets his Thursday timetable. He stands over her, looking down at the top of her head. The hair is sparse.

'Help me, sweetheart.' She waves a hand for him to pull her up, stands next to him. It was a great moment, the first time he measured the two of them and found he was taller. Now it feels disappointing.

'Everything OK?' He squeezes her arm.

'I'll put the kettle on.' They walk to the kitchen. 'You went to see your dad, then?'

'I know, I'm stupid.' He hasn't seen her for over two weeks. Impossible, everything that's happened since then.

'I think it was brave.' Mum fills the kettle and

switches it on. It's between them, like a marshal.

'He'd rather be a dad to her kids.' He's been stirring it over since Nina told him what he did. Was it his dad, that made him like that?

'He always thought a son meant having a miniature version of yourself.' She takes the teabags from the canister on the side, a slash through the "E" from when Eric got a penknife for his seventh birthday.

'You're not like that with Lil,' he says.

They watch the side of the kettle glow from blue to red. The switch snaps off.

'She says you're seeing someone.' A little smile as she pours the water in.

'Do you guys have to talk about me all the time?' He gets the milk out of the fridge.

It's been hard to stop thinking about Nina. Two days since she dismissed him. Did the kiss mean nothing? He can't decide if it's a shame, cutting something off before it's begun, or if she's done him a favour.

'Did I ever do anything, I don't know, violent, when I was little?' He still can't figure out where it came from.

'You were always a gentle soul.' She pats his arm.

The smell from her cardigan – the yellow bottle with the sunflowers on. He buried his face into that scent with a split lip after tripping out of her high-heeled shoes, playing dress-up with Lilly, desperate Dad didn't find out how it had happened. There was still a rusty stain on the arm.

'Why did we move? What happened with Dad's job?' That might be the key to it, the thing that's odd about him. 'I mean, he told me, I just wondered if it was true.' Maybe he can find out if he pretends he already knows.

'He talked about that?' She won't look at him.

'Quite a bit.' He sips his tea, prepares himself.

'It ended up in the papers.' She sits in her chair by the

window. 'Probably because she was Asian.'

'Mum!' Please don't let her pull out another excuse about her generation.

She holds up a hand. 'If people think you're racist it's news. Especially then. With him being white, and her boss. Especially when she made up all that stuff about him attacking her.' At least she's looking out of the window so she can't see his face. Was that what happened? Was it genetic?

'You believe him?' He tries to keep the shock out of his voice.

'He lied about a lot of things. I'm sure there were other women. But that's something else entirely.' She gets up, rummages in the cupboard. 'I'm sure I've got some biscuits here.'

'He said it was hard on you.' That's not right, Dad wouldn't have said something like that.

'Well that's nice, finally.' She takes out a packet of gingernuts. 'Went on about his job, his reputation. That she was an attention seeker. Didn't deny it happened, though. More like he was proud of it.' Her eyes flick up, register his expression. 'It was all a long time ago, anyway.'

'You should have told me.' Hadn't he felt proud, at first? That sense of complete control, that he was capable of anything. Maybe this was why, he'd been trying too hard to be like his dad. Clearly Mum thought it was some affair, not the attack this woman claimed it was. Either was possible. He wished he knew. To understand what he was, or know why he had become like this.

'You didn't need to know.' Her hand flips, like it's inconsequential.

'That's not fair.' It could have made the difference, changed his reactions to his own anger. 'I deserved to know what he was like. Didn't you worry, that I would end up like him?'

She laughs. The fist of it buckles inside.

'It's not funny!' A shift in her expression. She thinks he's weak, useless. She's the one who stayed all that time, let him do those things to her. He steps closer. 'It might be hereditary, something I could have been warned about.' It could all have been prevented. 'It's your responsibility, to tell me what he is, even if you don't like it.' That expression, like the disappointment in the bedroom that time. He was scaring her. It was too late, he'd fulfilled some preordained sequence, his pattern of behaviour fixed, like his dad.

A warm hand on his. The skin a crinkled wrapper over her bones.

'You were desperate to impress him. I didn't want to ruin the way you saw him then.'

Eric looks at his feet.

'What sort of man am I?' he says, dropping the words by her slippers.

'A disappointed one.' She rubs her hand over his hair. Perhaps it wasn't fear he saw in her. They have both been betrayed. 'But you always made things right.' She gets a plate out, arranges the biscuits in a circle. 'Remember when you jammed a pen into Keiran's Nintendo? He wasn't even there but you told his mum what happened, said you'd save up for a new one.' He lets her hug him. That yellow flower smell. 'You're one of the good ones.'

That's what he needs to do. Maybe he made a mistake, but it's not too late to make up for it. Nina said it herself, she doesn't have anyone left. So he can help her, be a friend. Free them both from what happened in that dark room.

Her face is blotchy, hair scraped back. It took five minutes of knocking for her to answer the door.

'We're going out.' He waves a carrier bag at her, wafting hot chilli smell into the space between them.

'I don't want to go anywhere.' She leans on the doorframe. 'I told you I didn't need your help.' She rubs a hand over her eyes. It looks like she's been in her pyjamas all day.

'Yeah, it looks like it. When was the last time you had a proper meal?' He picked up supplies on the way over from Mum's, stopping at the burrito van. There's even a side salad from Co-op.

'I don't know what you expect after the museum but I'm just not up for anything like that.' She sounds tired.

'Who said I was? You're the one that came onto me.' He grins. 'Come on, I just want to help out. I don't have many friends who make tearful confessions in my car and then run away.'

'I don't know.' She's wavering, looking at the bag.

'You've got five minutes to get dressed then I'm eating these myself.' He turns around and sits on the wall at the end of her front garden.

'Fine.' The door clicks shut behind him. He swings his legs, turning his face to the sun. Finally some warmth. He can't stop smiling. This was it, all along. It feels good to be the saviour.

'You'd better have something good in that bag.' She stands beside him, her body lost in tracksuit bottoms and a big hoodie. 'Isn't it cold for a picnic?'

'Come on.'

They walk to the tiny park at the end of her street. Once they've found a graffiti-scrawled bench he hands her a paper plate, the burrito, a bowl of salad, a fork and a napkin. In a final flourish he takes out bottles of Corona and lime wedges wrapped in cling film.

'Someone's organised.' A weak smile. It's a start.

'I didn't know whether you liked spicy food or not.

223

Then I realised I asked for chilli sauce on both. Sorry.'
He watches her as she takes a bite, screws a lime wedge
into each bottle.

'Spicy is good.' There's a blob of sauce on her chin.

'You OK?' Probably not a good question to ask.

'I don't know.' She's drinking faster than she's eating.
'It's like those dreams, where you know something bad is
going to happen.'

He coughs, a jalapeño gets stuck.

'You know where it is, just out of sight, almost on
you.' She looks down, her knuckles whitening around the
bottle. 'So you try to scream, pour all the fear out, in case
someone can hear you. But you just make a pathetic
squeak, chased away by the wind. So you have to let it
come.'

Silence pools around her fingers. He has to think of
something to say.

'That doesn't sound great.' This is a glimpse of what
he's done.

'I got fired for gross negligence.'

'What?' A splodge of salsa falls in his lap.

'I tampered with someone else's project and blew it
up. And ridiculed my boss in front of our investors. It
happened on Monday.' She doesn't look at him, keeps
staring at the leaves. 'There'll be an appeal, I'll have to
give my side. But what am I supposed to say? It's true.
I've been distracted, got behind, I panicked, then turned
on one of my mates to try and cover up the fact that I
couldn't do my job anymore.' Breath leaves her in a huge
sigh. She glances over. 'I feel like I can tell you anything.'

'I'm sorry.' What has he done to this woman? 'I'm
sure it will be OK.'

She drinks. Almost at the end of the second beer
already. 'I've been hanging around the flat mostly,
messing about on my computer. I can't tell anyone. Not

like I've got Holly to talk to either.'

'I'm here. If there's anything I can do.' He lets his offer hang.

'Did you take drugs when you were younger?' She looks at him. Her eyes are so dark today. The brown in them mirrors the blackening of the sky. He's not sure what the right answer is.

'I suppose so.' He shrugs, goes back to his food.

'We used to take pills and go dancing.' She's stopped eating. 'The fizz of it, right under your skin.' Her smile looks wistful. 'I'd stand for ages, swaying, rubbing the tips of my fingers together, feeling numb and electric.' She finishes her drink. 'Any more?'

He passes another out of the bag, their fingers glancing.

'We learnt about explorers at school.' He rests his hand in his lap. 'I asked my teacher where I could go if I wanted to be the first to find something.' Her look had been pitiful. 'I was gutted when she said they'd discovered everything already.'

'There's always the Amazon rainforest.' She picks up her burrito.

'We should go there. Take an alpaca, roam the jungle and find ancient ruins.' That's the way he always saw his older self. A skinny Indiana Jones. 'Find treasures and use them to barter with the locals, they could teach us how to fish and stuff.' Escape all of this, forget that horrible night ever happened.

'Right.' She must think he's mental. 'Unless we keep the treasures, then we could set ourselves up as gods, sit on stone thrones and get everyone to do our bidding.' She's smiling. 'Think about it. Every night, a sky full of stars. In the day you could wander for miles and just get lost in the wild.'

'You'd have to watch out for the snakes. And pumas.

225

Is it pumas in the rainforest?' Maybe they could go away in the summer holidays. He's always fancied South America. All that time with each other, something was bound to happen. They'd come back, tanned and together.

'There's always something to look out for.' She sighs, leans back. He's ruined it.

'Are you still hassling Will?' It's a dangerous question.

'I don't want you getting involved.' She passes a hand over her face, smudging black on her eye. 'But he has to pay for what he did to me.' She finishes the beer, looks at him. He hands her the one he was saving for himself.

'Be careful.' At some point Will is going to make the connection, especially after what he said the other night. Now they'll both be in trouble.

'This is nice.' She squeezes his knee, goes back to the drink. His skin shivers at the touch.

'Nothing like some spicy food and a few square foot of greenery,' he says. Thank God he went over there today. Two days roaming around on your own wasn't healthy. 'Although we need some proper countryside for some real recovery time.'

'Tomorrow?' The question is quick, she turns to look at him. Something desperate in her eyes.

'I've got work.' She really does need him.

'Right.' Her head drops. 'Never mind.'

'What about Saturday? I can't promise Aztec treasures but I'm sure I can think of something.'

'Sounds good.' She leans back, reaches her hand over to his. He shifts his beer over, squashing the rest of his dinner. Her fingers brush over his and then loop over, twining between. 'Thank you.' Her eyes close.

She looks calmer. Just a short trip down the road and he's had this effect on her. It's the least he can do. She's lost her mate, her job, all because of him. He can replace

226

all that, be there for her. Give her whatever she needs.

Her hand is warm. He keeps still, not wanting to move unless it disturbs her. Not long until spring. The clawed branches around them will sprout green and the winter will be forgotten. It doesn't matter what the start was, they're good for each other.

Nina

Doorbell. He's early. Nina pulls the band out of her hair, it's better when it falls around her face. She squeezes her lips together, an attempt at making them pinker, then opens the door.

It's Dev.

'Expecting someone else?' he says.

'Sorry.' She must look disappointed. Dev is different somehow. It hasn't even been a week. Feels like an age, stuck outside her own routine.

'How's it going?' He looks reluctant to be here.

'Lady of leisure.' She shrugs, tries to look pleased.

Dev scratches his head, looks back at the car. Amy's sat in the driving seat. Probably making obscene gestures through the glass.

'The office is, well, you know,' he shrugs.

'Great.' She doesn't want to know. Things should unravel without her, or stop. The whirring of her prototype, she can't stand the idea of other people touching it.

'I thought,' he says, squinting. 'I thought you might say sorry.'

'I did.' Now she sounds defensive. 'I mean, I am.'

'Look.' He shifts his feet. 'There must be more to it.

Something you didn't tell me. I mean.' He rubs his nose. 'There must be something else. Come on, Nin, help me out here.'

'I've already been fired.' There's nothing to be remedied. 'Is this part of Clive's big investigation?'

'Hey, no.' He sounds offended.

It was a joke, but there was a flicker on his face. She used to tell him everything. Maybe they wouldn't have been friends, if it weren't for the office.

'I don't really know why you're here,' she says.

'You wouldn't do something like that. I know you.'

'Not that well.' She doesn't like this assertion of knowledge.

'I want to help,' he says. 'Come on. After everything you did for me when I started. It's the least I can do.'

If she gave him her reasons, the truth, he might not reveal it, but she might get her job back. This had to be extenuating circumstances. All sense of what she'd hoped to achieve was slipping. A spam account and abusive emails. It didn't affect him enough.

'There was something,' she says. How to begin? 'I mean. This thing. It happened to me, and then I couldn't concentrate.' She has to lean against the side of the door. 'I couldn't stop thinking about it. Wanting to get some sort of ending. I still do.' She needs to move beyond annoyance. Something to threaten him, make him feel weak.

'It's OK.' Dev places a hand on her arm. Nina glances to the car, tries to read Amy's expression. She can't do it here, under scrutiny.

'I want to talk about it, I do.' Just saying it, that might help.

'How about tomorrow? We can sit down, have a chat, see if we can't get The Carp to get the stick out of his arse.'

'Somewhere quiet.' To be able to say it all, out loud. 'That Portuguese place with the tarts? They have a little garden out the back.'

'Of course. About 11?' A real smile from him. There are people that care about her, she isn't alone.

'Thanks.' She watches Dev get back into the car then closes the door, leans against it. She feels lighter. It can't be healthy, the amount of time she's spent obsessing over this. Now she has a way back.

It's definitely going to rain. They've gone so far from the car, there's no way they'll make it back without getting wet. Doesn't look like the picnic is going to happen. Nina pauses to twist some of the tension out of her ankle. The distance between them stretches. Rick is a beige smudge on the flattened grass. His shoulders are squared with dedication.

They have been swallowed up in the grey-green stretch of hills. Only two miles out of town and it feels like the Cotswolds. The gym trainers haven't withstood this change of terrain – her toes are squashy. Her only raincoat isn't up to much either. Pitted against this wind it feels like a carrier bag, sweat gathering on her forearms. This sprawl of green is much better than the folds of her duvet, or another walk round the park. The clenched tension in her head is falling away, buffeted by gusts of wind. She leans into it, her weight balanced by this natural force.

It was only a joke, but maybe going away would be a good idea. With him, she wouldn't be bothered by past events. He's new. There's money in the bank, and after meeting up with Dev tomorrow the future might not look so bleak. A delayed return to work, caused by stress. Finding corners of the world to poke her toes into. This must be what healing feels like.

A shadow cuts over the grass. Overhead, a bank of seething cloud. Sunlight and blue smack up against the heavy lump, like an unnatural eclipse approaches.

A run will warm her up. He's stopped up ahead, next to a scrub of bushes and stunted trees. She rushes forward, the ground uneven, lifting her legs high so she doesn't trip and look like an idiot.

'What are you doing?' she asks. He's poking around, looping up brambles.

'It's supposed to be here.' Rick scuds his knees to the ground, peers under the tangle of twigs.

'I thought it would be easier to see.' She'd never heard of geocaching before. It was unbelievable, this network, all these hidden things all over the country.

'Part of the fun.' He smiles up at her.

She pokes at the bushes with her foot. Presumably it will be conspicuous, something bright and unnatural.

'That's clever,' he says. He's hunched over a dead branch. 'Look at this.' He reaches for her hand, pulls her down. There are small numbers carved into the bark. She leans in, feels around it for a seam. Her fingers find a split. She slides it – a sawn-off section that reveals a dark hole stuffed with leaves.

'That's amazing.' She wasn't expecting such ingenuity. It smells rotten. He sticks his hand into the darkness.

'This is the first one.' He holds out a small box.

'There's more?'

'Depends on the cache. This one has twelve. It's called the Dirty Dozen. This is one of the nanos.' He looks up. Nina doesn't manage to change her expression in time. 'Not that we have to do all of them.'

'It's fine.' She nudges him. 'We can go to a pub for lunch, right?'

'Not sure that was on the itinerary,' he says. 'You want to open it?' He places the box in her hands. It's slimy round the edges. It looks so military. The official stamp reminds her of ammunition and bombs.

'What's inside?' She rattles it.

'No way of knowing. Starts out as one thing, the person that planted it. After that, you get to swap it with stuff, or leave it as you found it.'

Nina clicks the catch open. It's delightful – trinkets carried in pockets and secreted here to please those that follow.

'Look!' It's all themed; a miniature toy gun, a red bandana, a Barbie cowboy boot. There's a yellow plastic ball from a Kinder egg. The satisfying pop – one of those grown-up skills that feels triumphant in light of childhood impossibility. It's a plastic horse, complete with saddle and wearing a Stetson. There's a stub of pencil and a notebook. She flops through the pages, scrawled names, words of encouragement, jokes.

'Do we have anything to put in?' she says.

He hands her a Lego man with cow-print trousers and a lasso. He's organised.

'Let's call him Clint,' Rick says.

'What should we take?' The little man has drawn-on stubble and a wink. She doesn't want to give him away.

'I think this would suit you.' He wraps the bandana around her neck, his fingers brushing her ear as he ties it. A clump of hair gets caught, pulling against her skull. He teases out the strands one by one, releasing her.

'Howdy.' He takes a picture and leans over to show her. The red brings out the pink pleasure in her cheeks.

'Send it to me.' She leaves the Lego man on top of the box and picks up the pencil.

Nina and Rick. Blazing the trail.

A slap of rain hits her words, smearing the first letter.

The grey has caught up with them. He stands and looks around.

'Doesn't look good.' Rick zips up his much sturdier looking waterproof and flips the hood up. He even has proper walking boots, smeared with overuse.

The drips are heavy and sparse – a promise of worse to come. She swings the lid down, then hesitates, grabs the little plastic man and shoves it into her pocket. She secretes it back in the hiding hole for the next finder. No-one will know of her little violation.

He grabs her hand and pulls her up and away. They run. Down the hill, slick pools of mud growing, feet sinking deeper. It's exhilarating. Her hood is lashed down behind her, flurries of rain whipped into her face. Her breaths are high and sharp. A quick glance over at him leaves a warm spot. Her hair ropes with moisture, whips against her face. Their feet splash, her screams high and loud. She lets go and runs, allowing her arms to flail as the slope gets steeper, whooping into the wind.

By the time they reach the car it's like they've jumped in the shower, fully clothed. Inside, the heater roars, the air a chilly blast, the engine a rumbling bass beneath. The wet material leaves her skin crawling with cold.

'You OK?' he says, rubbing her hand.

'Just a bit chilly.'

'Here.' He reaches round into the back and his jacket rides up, revealing a slice of pale skin. He tucks a fleecy blanket around her, strokes the hair away from her forehead.

'My nan has a blanket like this,' she says.

'Fine, don't have it.' He tugs at the red tartan material.

'I didn't say it wasn't warm.' She draws it around her shoulders.

His feet tap on the floor. He's always nervous when

they're alone, like he doesn't know what she expects of him. Unfurling the fabric, she drapes it over him, leans in, the handbrake a barrier between them. She nudges her head under his arm, the length of it falling down her back. He stills, the warmth of him seeping into her damp clothes. The rain thuds off the ground around them, a beat on the roof; a percussive cocoon.

Inch by inch, she slides her face closer. The heat of his cheek is against the side of her forehead. Her body is stretched over the gap between the seats. His breath touches her lips. The final movement is so small, to place them together. At first they rest there, weighing on each other. Then mouths, tongues and movement, a sticky patch on her top lip where his nose is running. A drip from his hair makes her flinch. She slips her hand under his jumper, the tight bump of his ribs, a fuzzy patch at the top of his chest. Around the side, the curve that disappears into his back. He doesn't move beneath her.

A small sound escapes when she slides her touch across the top of his trousers. What does he want? She dips down, searching for a response. A possibility wavers before her. Her lips thin in the kiss. This time one finger dips under the elastic. There is a brush of wiry hair, the skin pulsing and warm.

His hand reciprocates, pushing under her jumper. She stops. It's just a hand on her tummy. The fingers are squeezing, one catches the edge of her belly button. She concentrates on the thud inside her, huffing breath out of her nose to regulate it, stay unclenched. It's like the fingers are disembodied, crawling on her. They creep up to touch the edge of her bra, then moving up, cupping around the curve of her breast. It shudders down her skin, echoing the grip that tightened on her the last time she was touched.

The judders start in her legs. She pushes them

straight, tries to keep the muscles taut. He hasn't noticed. If anything, his movements are more urgent. She feels separated from herself. She opens her eyes – he's blurry and close. One squeeze more is too much. She pulls herself away, leaning her forehead against the cold glass.

'You don't have to.' His voice comes from far away. 'It's not right.' He sounds so nervous.

She nods against the door. There must be something wrong with her.

'We shouldn't.' There's something sad there.

Rick comes halfway between them.

'I'm here,' he says. He rests his hand on the edge of her seat. Nina's fingers sit next to it, feeling the comfort of its presence.

'You know, don't you?' she says. It's impossible, that he doesn't realise how she feels. On the edge of this teetering emotion, if allowed to slip forwards, the power it will give him over her. 'Be careful with me.'

She sits and waits for the air to get warm.

Eric

The cold is bone-deep by the time he gets in the shower. He droops his head, lets the water scald his back, clenching his fists to get the blood back into them. Twenty-three minutes, the sides of their fingers touching. He watched the time trip past on the dashboard clock, not daring to move.

They're on the edge of something. What's the best thing he can do? Keep being around, make sure she knows she's safe, comforted. Not pressure anything. After what he did, he needs to let her take what she needs. This is his atonement. Selfless, really, to put himself forward like this. Not the sort of thing Dad would have been capable of. He's the better man after all.

He's not sure what to plan next. Dropping her straight home was the only option seeing as they were both soaked, and she hadn't mentioned the pub again. It's probably important not to rush it.

She'll need to look for a new job, but she's so clever that's hardly going to be a problem. So different to Bea. That's been his issue, he's just been going after the wrong type of woman. He's always been drawn to the broken ones, the weak ones. Like Mum. He used to feel like he had to help someone to be useful, to let them use him.

Not like her. She's independent, strong. They can be equals.

Trailing his towel through to the bedroom, he looks out across the city. You can catch a glimpse of the sea from here – a dark mass behind all the buildings. Shapes cut out of it by the tower, the twitching masts in the docks. Moving here had proved to be worth something after all.

He lies down, letting the last of the moisture dry on his skin. Traces a line down his chest, following the route she touched earlier. So gentle. If he hadn't touched her back, would she have carried on? His lips open, breath escaping at the thought of her fingers on him.

The buzz of the phone. Insistent. He leans over, irritated at the intrusion. It's Will. Five missed calls and three messages, what the hell does he want? There's no way he's talking to him now. Let it run out and he can return to his pleasant daydream on the duvet.

It stops. He reaches over to put it on silent. His fingers catch in the movement. Nina's name is on his screen.

Scrambling up, he opens the messages.

My colleagues got the loveliest message about me. Can't trace who sent it but it has to be Nina. Seriously, what do you remember about the party? Do you know anything about her? This is getting out of hand. Call me.

The last one is the screenshot of the message. Bloody hell. She's not messing around. This must be what she's been up to in her evenings, tapping away at her computer.

This isn't good. Not for her, or him. If she carries on like this she could get into trouble, then it all comes out. There must be a way of stopping her, moving her away from this crazy campaign. Best to leave Will to his own devices for now, there's nothing he can do and it might make things worse if they talk.

He'll take stuff for dinner over to her place, tonight. They can talk about the future. Move her away from all this backward-looking vendetta stuff. It can't be healthy. Pulling some clothes on, he scrolls through his phone, searching for some good recipes. Moussaka, that was always popular with Bea. Takes time to prepare, but that might be good. Cooking together in the kitchen, working together. That's how bonds are created, shared experiences built.

Give her a nudge, this stuff with Will will blow over and everything can get back to normal.

238

Nina

There's nothing else to do this afternoon, might as well have a look over her progress. Each time she thinks it will give her a sense of closure, allow her to sleep. Maybe that moment with Rick would help. He was so sweet. Taking her places, trying to cheer her up. Maybe that's what she needed. Someone caring like that.

The Twitter reaction is encouraging, in a way. Far more people have liked the awful articles than she would have hoped. Thirty retweets for his comment about women. Awful to think how many others there are like him, out there. At least a few of the retweets and replies are outraged. One of them's a man. Words like bigot, misogynist, woman-hater. Perfect. Exactly the image she wanted to create for him.

As for the email, it couldn't have gone better. He's even shared a picture of it on Facebook, giving it more publicity than it had in the first place.

WILLIAM LAKELAND IS A FUCKING RAPIST.

So simple, yet so effective. Of course some of the comments made it a joke:

Kate Griffiths Been caught at last.
Luke Thomas Upset anyone recently?
Ollie Simms Might finally keep it in your pants now.

But some sensed his underlying violence. Maybe she wasn't the only one.

Fiona Samson Knew this day would come.
Caroline King Couldn't happen to a nicer person.

That's probably enough. She's pissed him off, placed doubt in the minds of his colleagues and friends. Too much further and she might incriminate herself. She shouldn't have told Holly. There's no way they can trace it back to her, but it might still look suspicious. Best to delete all the accounts, so no-one can find anything on her laptop. After tomorrow, with Dev, she can move her focus forward again. Make some plans with Rick, even. No need to rush, it feels good as it is for now.

The rest of his pictures come up, after the one of the email. She flicks through them, slurping coffee and trying not to get toast crumbs between the keys. He's not all that. No matter what happened, she couldn't let her life be dictated by this prick. Time to move on.

There's a picture of her. In that kitchen, his arm draped round her neck. Holly is in the background, just the side of her face, squeezed in at the edge.

She drops the piece of toast on the table, smacks the mug down. It's impossible, it can't be. Who took that photo? She pulls her dressing gown tight, scrubs at the bit of skin where his hand was, right there, for everyone to see.

Nina is almost in the centre of the picture, her eyes wandering, hair rucked on one side. There are drinks in hands, smiles, some unknown people leaning in, silly expressions, a hand waving behind her head. It's as though all these people are squeezing her, pushing her next to this man, with his painted smile. His fingers rest on her skin, just above the collar of that dress.

A draft catches her collar through the window. It's cold. Nina shifts on her seat, rubbing her neck. Her hand brushes the site of his bruise, the grip on her neck as he pushed her down. Little spots gather at the side of her vision.

Chris Richards has posted it, an anonymous face among the group. The rest of their night, the flashing lights behind them, drinks raised in salutes, all shirts, shouts and bravado. She circles back to the spectre of her own face. There are comments underneath.

Jake Knight Nice tits.
Lorraine Jones-Freeman Where did you find this one?
Jake Knight Heard she was a bit of a nightmare, mate.
Fiona Sampson Like them pissed, huh?
Chris Richards Great tits.
Luke Thomas Yeah Jake, she went mental at him.
Lorraine Jones Freeman You look like an idiot.
Will Lakeland Absolute mentalist.
Jake Knight Looks well up for it.
Fiona Samson Just another weekend, eh?

It feels like eyes are on her. She feels itchy in her skin, the glare of accusation angled back at her. It's a silent message of self-congratulation, a statement of his ability to do whatever he pleases with her and she is unable to retaliate.

Her hand is cramped around the mug. There must be something she can do. It can't be possible, that he flaunts her like this. What he did. It's unacceptable. She presses her palms together, focuses on breathing. There will be no falling to the floor, no panicking. This man has abused her and he has to pay.

A public comment. Something terrible, that can't be ignored. There are examples online, people who lost their jobs. If she puts out a few, mentions some names in there, it should work.

Big Will @BigWillLakeland
Some dumb bitch just asked me the time while looking on her phone. If I smack her round the head, is that abuse or just a restart?

Big Will @BigWillLakeland
Maybe if we didn't have a female monarch this country wouldn't be so stuffed full of shit.

Then a couple more, scheduled for later. Just to spread out the fun.

Big Will @BigWillLakeland
The way to a woman's heart is through anal.

Big Will @BigWillLakeland
Can you believe all this bullshit about women's rights? Put your pants back on and get me a beer.

That's bound to piss people off. There are crescents etched in her palms from her fingernails. People need to know, to see this man for what he is.

She copies an image from Facebook and opens a Word document. Time to use the printer that's been sat in its box for the last week. This has to end. Everyone will know what he has done, who he is.

Eric

Nina isn't home. The carrier bags sit at his feet —
aubergine, onions, lamb mince, a bottle of Shiraz that
was on special offer. A lemon cheesecake — hopefully it
didn't get too squashed on the way here. His enthusiasm
deflates as the sun sinks lower.

Eric sits on the low wall, flicking through Twitter
feeds. There are two more angry messages from Will.
He's going to have to talk to him sooner or later. But
only once he's got a safe version of the party straight in
his head. With any luck, he can steer Nina away from her
obsessive behaviour, that will calm everything down for
both of them.

'What are you doing here?' Nina looks flushed,
wearing a backpack, a baseball cap.

'Surprise,' he says. She doesn't look happy to see him.

'You didn't say.' She hurries inside, leaving the door
open wide behind her. He picks up the bags, the jar of
salad dressing clanks against the wine bottle. So much for
a pleasant dinner.

She's standing in the middle of the living room,
facing away from him, still wearing the bag.

'Everything OK?' he says.

She slides it down her arms. It looks new, something

you'd go hiking with. There's a papery scrunch as it hits the floor. She turns, doesn't even look at him, lumps the weight of herself at him, hands tight behind his back. He lets the carrier bags drop, hopefully nothing broken, takes the back of her head in his hands. She mumbles into his chest.

'What?'

She rolls her head to one side. 'I don't want to do it anymore.'

She's realised what he is. It had to happen, there's no way she could continue to see him like this.

'I'll go,' he says.

Her arms tighten, she looks up at him. She looks terrified.

'Please,' she says. Her head droops, she leans her nose against his chest. 'I need you.'

Eric pulls her close again, squashing her against him, feeling the heat of her breath against his chest.

After dinner he suggests a late-night walk by the sea. Once they started cooking it was better, she got absorbed in the repetitive movements, the slow stirring of the white sauce. Still distant though. Should he tell her that he knows about the email? That might be too far. But something about all this mess. Help her to get some perspective, step back from all this.

It's not the bright circle of light reflecting from lapping waters he had in mind, but the streaks of light from the city are still attractive over the churning waves. Best not to dwell on the scummy white stuff creeping up the stones nearest to them.

'You know, you're really important to me,' he says. Not very subtle.

'You're just saying that because I chopped the

244

onions.' She squeezes his hand.

'I mean it.' He rubs his thumb along the back of her hand.

'You know what,' she says, 'I fancy you.'

He laughs, he hasn't heard that phrase since school.

'I mean it. There's been loads of guys who are interesting, funny, intelligent, but I wasn't that fussed. With you, it's like—' She looks sideways at him, strands of hair tailing off her face in the wind. 'Like when I used to chase Graham Jennings around the playground in Year 6.'

'Loads of guys, huh?' He nudges her.

'Thanks.' Her head drops. It was supposed to be a joke.

'Well of course,' he says. 'Who wouldn't want to be with someone as beautiful as you?' That smile. It makes him giddy.

'Suck up.' She nudges against him.

'The thing is,' take it steady, 'I'm worried about you.'

'It was you that suggested the second bottle.' That was defensive. She did seem to be drinking a lot.

'All this stuff with Will.' She stops walking, drops his hand. 'You said you wanted me out of it, and that's fine, but it seems like it's still bothering you.' Her face is lost in shadows. 'I just think that it can't be good for you, all this obsessing over something. Some things you shouldn't hold on to.' That was too close to the mark. He sounds like he knows too much. 'As far as I can tell, anyway.'

'You don't know what it's like.' She wraps her arms over her body.

'Of course not. But it feels like you're giving him too much power over you.' Just a minute ago they were holding hands. How can he get back there?

'You think I haven't tried? I hate how polluted I am by all this.' She shakes her head. 'It's useless.'

'I'm trying to help.' He steps towards her, tries to catch her expression. 'I care about you, I think you're great. I just want you to be happy. This seems to be doing the opposite.' The thing is, that's actually true.

'I guess.' She looks over the waves. 'All that stuff with the flour. It was fun. It made me feel like I was in control.'

'I'm not sure it's fun now.' She has to stop this. It's the only way he can be safe. He risks it, touches her arm.

'I suppose.' She doesn't push him away.

'Maybe it's time to move on.' What a terrible cliché. And it's better for her too. This isn't just about protecting himself, he's sure of it.

'You're right. I'm done.' She leans her head against his chest. He looks down, the smell of her mingling with the sharp seaweed tang. 'I feel stronger with you,' she says.

Eric pulls her close and looks up at the moon, muddled through the clouds.

Nina

It's better than she could have hoped. Over three hundred likes, hundreds of retweets. The one about hitting the woman in the head is the most popular. She scrolls down the results, her face stretching wide with the pleasure of it. So many people, all saying what an idiot he is, asking how he can share something like that. A slew of names and abuse, all directed at him.

There's a few from people mentioning his job, they used the company name. An official response.

Portsmouth Financial Services @PFS
A claim has been made against the validity of this account. Employee suspended, pending investigation.

Portsmouth Financial Services @PFS
This company is an equal opportunities employer.

A sound escapes from her throat – joyful, cathartic. After all the plotting, a simple tweet carried the most weight.

She leans back, waits for the sense of fulfilment to arrive. He's out of a job. Just like her. Things have balanced out. He'll be snivelling in his shiny car, moaning to Holly about how unfair it all is. Now, of course, she'll see what an idiot he is, leave him, come crawling back to Nina with apologies held out in front of her. They can have a weekend away, or maybe a holiday, another Greek island with empty beaches and cheap local beer.

Things will be different now. She can fold up this corner of herself, find a route back to her quiet office through Dev, just a couple of hours before she meets him. Of course he'll understand, after what she's been through. If he doesn't hold his complaint up, there's nothing to stop her from coming back.

And there's Rick. He's been so patient with her moods, erratic behaviour, now she can direct her attention to him without worrying about this. He's invited her over for movie night tonight. What a lovely, normal thing to do with a Sunday evening. She can go back to being like everybody else.

Her right knee bounces on the chair. It doesn't feel like enough. She scrolls through her accounts, the spreadsheet that took so long to assemble. It will be strange, to stop this.

No, it's for the best. If Rick's noticed she's been off, it must be obvious. That moment under the streetlight last night, pressed against him. She's safe now. The first time in weeks she was able to sleep. That had to be a good sign. Plenty of time to shower and look normal before going to meet Dev.

She sits in the car, watching the cafe door. They're not supposed to meet for another twenty minutes. And, knowing Dev, that will be more like forty. Especially on a Sunday.

How is Will feeling, right now? Still slumped in bed, with no prospect of getting up tomorrow morning? He could be hanging out with the early-drinking losers in a Wetherspoons, commiserating with a flat pint and a bag of scampi fries.

It wouldn't hurt, just to have a look. She logs out of the Twitter app, back in as Helen Clarke. There are a load of comments on his feed, must be from mates. Some asking if he's ok, some calling him a prick. A few have shared the @BigWillLakeland tweets, that's not going to be helpful.

Something new pops up. She scrolls up, is confronted with a close up of his jubilant face.

@W_L_Pompey

HR proved it wasn't me. Back in the game!

It can't be. Not even a full day out of employment. After all that time – setting up accounts, tapping away at the computer. That's the reason she started messing up at work. She wouldn't have lost her job if she hadn't been concocting bullshit tweets to send to his fake account.

His leering face peers out of her screen. Behind him are railings, the angled brick of a building, topped with glass. Of all the places he could be. It's a way to get at her. Show her he doesn't care, that he won't be held responsible.

A tap on the window. Dev is actually early. Stepping back, he waves, raises an eyebrow expectantly. Here's where she should get out of the car, go and speak to him, continue with her day.

That face is still on her screen. He's never felt afraid, never felt weak and vulnerable. Always got what he wanted. Including her. It's not right.

She puts the car in reverse, waving an apology at a confused-looking Dev, before heading back to the place it all started.

The stairs are white, motivational posters in pink and lime green on the way up. When the club is open it must be possible to hear the thud of it through the walls. Nina's legs are heavy, her thighs complaining before she's even halfway up. Weeks since she last picked up a racquet. One of the other things that can resume, after. She has to face him. It's the only way.

Smiling people in all the posters, lifting weights, sweating cheerily. Were people so image obsessed that a twenty-four hour gym was necessary?

Will would choose this one. A gym right over a club. That was the beauty of Gunwharf. All the gratuitous pleasures squashed together on top of each other. If only they hadn't gone there. If only she hadn't talked to him.

He might have watched her, when they danced. Was she the kind of woman men targeted? Nina didn't imagine herself as weak. She can remove this warped connection she feels to him, shift the balance so he will be in her control. He needs to feel afraid.

There are bright spotlights pricking the surface of the shiny floors, a lime green column next to the reception desk. The woman behind it is lean and angular. It looks like a disco for healthy people. There aren't any chairs.

She gets a day pass and goes through to the changing rooms. All she has to do is look around, find where he is and talk to him. Make her threats, nothing he can do in a public place, then a quick exit. She could be home in half an hour. Her bag clanks as she puts it in the locker. The last-minute addition she got out of the boot. Just to help her feel safe.

Stretchy material covers thighs and backs, furious activity while staying in one place. It always seems like the thrashing of disappointments, the static exuberance of the gym. Nina looks out for wide shoulders and light hair, bracing herself as she walks into each room. The free weights, full of flexing men and mirrors, spotting and grunting. Surely he would be there. Then the one with all the machines – lines of people staring at walls. A yoga class in a darkened studio, the other one full of people on exercise bikes, a stumpy, defined man in the middle leaping onto pedals and shouting at them. He's not here.

She can't wait anymore. This has to end. Nothing has brought the release, the sense of justice she expected to feel.

There he is. He's outside, at the desk. Stooping over, using his smile on the receptionist. He picks up his bag, walks towards the exit. It must have been while she was changing. She's just missed him. Now he's outside, she won't be protected by the presence of others. But she's built it up, she can't string herself out any longer.

She rushes into the changing rooms, pulls her clothes on over the top of her gym stuff, puts the cap on, pulls it down low, throws the bag on and runs for the stairs.

'Hey!' Her voice echoes. 'Will!' Footsteps. She can't tell if he's moving away or towards her. 'Rapist.' The syllables bounce down the space between them. An echo of her message to him, what she papered his street with.

Nina doesn't wait for his response, concentrates on keeping a steady beat with her feet to get down as fast as possible. Her breaths are quick, lines of sweat running down her back. She's hardly a frightening sight.

There he is, outside the doors, walking towards the car park, on his phone.

'Stop!' she shouts. Control is slipping from her. He turns round. There's still a few feet between them. She doesn't want to close the gap.

'You?' he says. 'I thought so.'

He recognises her then. Nothing about him suggests fear.

'I've just called the police. Think they'd be interested in your little poster campaign.' He puts the phone in his pocket.

'You don't want the police involved. They'll be more interested in you than me.' She leans on her knees, breathing heavily. 'Trouble at work?' He needs to know she's in control.

'So I've got you to thank for that.' He steps towards her. 'You've made an impression, I'll give you that.' His eyes travel over her. 'You looked better in a dress.'

Nina looks around. There are some people at the far end of the car park, walking over. It's still public enough.

'You need to do exactly as I say. Otherwise there will be consequences.' It's hard to keep the quiver out of her voice.

'Right. You going to advertise something else on Gumtree? Scary.' He's too close.

'We both know what you did.' She needs to sound threatening. 'And so does your good mate Eric.' There it is, a flicker of something. He looks less sure of himself.

'I've had enough of this.' He grabs one of her wrists.

'I'll scream.'

'Go right ahead.' He pushes his face close to hers. It's too much, she might be sick. The taste of ginger beer, these hands.

'We got a call about a disturbance?' The people that were walking over. Two policemen. Will glances from them to her, drops her hand.

'This man raped me,' she says. That sentence, embedded in her like a stain.

'Stop saying that!' He shakes his head. 'This has to end here. I'm sick of your crazy shit, you little-' The larger policeman steps in front of him.

'I think we all need to calm down.' The young one puts a hand on her shoulder.

'You got me drunk so I couldn't fight you off,' she says, leaning round, trying to face him again. 'You sneaked in, when I was passed out.' She sounds hysterical. This isn't right, not what she wanted.

'This woman is totally mental.' He's so tall, full of his own entitlement. The police are going to believe him over her. In the gym she saw her reflection. Sweaty, in trampy sportswear. This is what he's reduced her to. It's all been a complete waste.

'I think we'll need to get statements from both of you,' the older one says.

There must be some way of hurting him, anything. She needs to separate herself from the police.

'I'd be happy to go to the police station to fulfil that request.' She shifts her voice. She's educated, rational. The police exchange a glance.

'I've got nothing to hide.' He looks so believable.

'Maybe one of you should come along with us.' The older one keeps looking between the two of them.

'I'd rather take my own car.' She looks at him, forces herself to smile. 'Otherwise I'd have to come and pick it up later, and I'm sure I'd get a ticket. That would make the start of my week a little difficult.' She takes off the cap, keeps her gaze level.

'Yeah, that's fine,' the young one says. She pulls her business card out of the rucksack, hands it to the other guy. At least she had that on her. Will does the same. He's wary, watching her closely.

There's a buzz on the shoulder of the young one.

'Honestly, couldn't tell it was a Sunday,' he mutters.

Will walks away, his car must be around the corner. Perfect. She leaves a big gap then walks in the same direction. They don't know where her car is. She doesn't check to see if they're watching her, that will look too suspicious.

Round the corner, she breaks into a run, ducks down so he won't see her. She grabs the weight of it out of her bag, crouches at the end of the row.

As he pulls out she steps in front of him. The brakes squeal, the bumper inches from her shins. She raises the wheel brace high over her head. The car's stalled, he can't start it again. Nina brings it down on one of the lights, shattering it. Then the second. She scrapes a deep groove down the centre of the car, the shiny paintwork peeling off, a bright scar left beneath. She won't have long.

Will sits there, gawping at her. She goes for the wing mirror, smashing the glass and yanking it off the side of the car, the electric mechanism whining under her hands. The wing, leaving thick dents in it, working her way down towards the back. Running feet approaching across the tarmac. She rushes to the back, takes out the lights, pries the BMW sign off, bashes a dent in the boot. Heavy arms take hers, knocking the weapon to the ground. She offers no resistance, watching him as she is taken away, the light of fear finally finding its way behind his eyes.

Eric

He slops the bags onto the table. Pizza, ice cream, popcorn, bottle of wine, he picked up some cheesy DVDs at the counter – a nervous purchase. What does she like to watch? She might think his Netflix history is ridiculous. Historical dramas and war films. The flat looks a state too. What's needed is a superficial tidy, something that makes him look more organised without appearing soulless.

Eric scoops the assorted paperwork off the table, that can go in his work box file, to be sorted at the end of term. There's a pile of marking – that can stay – remind her he's caring, looking after future generations, all that. He's dithering over whether to leave his PlayStation out when the phone rings. Unknown number. Probably just some sales call. Unless she's got held up somewhere.

'Hello?'

'It's me.' Her voice is muffled.

'Hey, I was just thinking about you,' he says. Was that too much?

'They said I could call someone.' Her voice is muffled. 'So I just wanted to talk to you. There's nothing to say, really.'

'Where are you?' It sounds like a hollow corridor.

Someone talking behind her.

'They arrested me. Because I smashed his car. I know I said I'd stop, but I couldn't help it. He was so smug,' she says.

'Are you in prison?' He tries to piece it together.

'Custody, holding, I don't know what they call it. The thing is, they said I could have someone here. When I tell them everything, what really happened. I want you to be here. Would that be OK?' This is far worse than some bothering emails.

'I don't understand.' He needs to stall for time.

'I'm going to tell them everything. What happened—' She swallows. This is it, what he's feared has arrived. 'I want to tell you, the police, even if it doesn't go anywhere, I need to say it.' He can't sit there with the police, hearing his crime told back to him.

'Look, maybe Holly should be there.' Great idea. They would prefer that to a man anyway.

'I want *you* here, please.' After everything he's done, he can't give her this.

'Anything you need. But I really think she'd be better.' There's a pause. 'Don't you think?'

He scribbles the number down. She sounds so lost. What a mess, that it's her that ends up getting arrested.

'I'm scared.' Her voice is so small.

'It's going to be OK. Is there anything I can do? I can pick Holly up if you like.' He needs to offer something.

There's silence. When her voice returns, it's more controlled. 'Holly has a key, you'll need to go and feed the cat. The food's in my backpack.' She doesn't have a cat. 'It needs to be put out.' He tries to piece it together. The gap is too long, he needs to be reassuring.

'I'm here. I won't let anything happen to you.'

'Rick–'

'I love you,' he says.

'Thank you.' A voice blurts behind her and the receiver is pressed down. Nothing but a beep. He can't fathom what she means, or what he should do.

He needs to talk to Holly, get her to go down there. Nina will thank him, it's better if she's there.

Phone again. He looks at the display. Surely not, this is ridiculous.

'You are not going to believe the fucking day I've had.' He sounds pissed off.

'Will?'

'Yeah, I know, you said you didn't remember anything, but you were the only person with half a brain that was at that party and I need your help.' This is too much.

'I have no idea what you're talking about.'

'Hang on.' There's clanking behind him, mechanical noises. 'Shit. I have to go. Get your arse down to Allen Motors. I need to talk to you,' Will says.

'No, I'm not running around after you.' He's already gone. Eric sits with his phone in his lap, muddling through the last few minutes, debating the next course of action.

Of course, it's inevitable. Silly to think he'd escaped. It was always going to lead back to the shadow of himself in that darkened room.

Nina

By the time they come to get her, panic has given way to boredom. Nina's read every word of the magazine, twice. She wasn't allowed a pen. It was only to make the faces ugly. A knock on the hollow door draws her out from wondering whether to buy a pair of boots this late in the year and what she can watch on TV later if they let her out today. Is it still Sunday?

She smells stale. Her hair feels brittle when she smooths it behind her ears. They go through another door, another lock, another corridor – the same bland colours, the same blank walls. She feels deadened. No panic or fear, just flat. She can't be bothered to talk to the person escorting her.

Nina is put inside a room, a woman follows her in and the door locks behind them. The table and chairs look like office furniture. The blank face of a camera lens is pointed towards her from the corner. They sit either side of the desk, like a job interview for Crimewatch. The chair has a fuzzy seat. Something about the combination of this with her trousers and the shorts she still has on underneath causes an insistent itch. She shifts around to minimise contact.

'Nina, my name is Lydia. I want to talk to you about

the incident with William Lakeland in the car park of Gunwharf Quays. This room is under surveillance and I will be taping the interview.' She pulls out a tape. How very archaic. 'If needed, we may use these tapes in evidence. Do you understand?'

'Yes.' It's time to wake herself from this stupor. Nina arches her back against the tight muscles from sitting on that bed for hours.

'This is Constable Lydia Symonds, interviewing the suspect Nina Franklin with regard to a charge of Criminal Damage to a black BMW on the morning of Sunday May 2nd. The time is sixteen hundred hours on Sunday the 2nd May. The interviewee has stated that she doesn't wish to have a legal representative present.' Nina thought it would look suspicious if she asked.

Lydia slips a strand of hair behind her ear and opens the file in front of her on the table. She nods a few times, flips some pages. Surely this woman will help her.

'Why don't you tell me what happened this morning?' she looks calm, friendly even. She hasn't lost a whole day then.

'Yes, but it's more than that, it relates to something that happened in January.' If she admits what happened, it will make her looks terrible.

'For now, we just need to deal with the incident today. Did you bring a wheel brace to Gunwarf Quays with the intention to damage property?' Still so passive.

No. That wasn't what I thought. It was about protection. I just picked it up, not thinking really. It's all about this thing that happened.' She needs to clarify the things that came before, show that it wasn't her fault.

'Did you damage the vehicle belonging to William Lakeland?' she asks.

'I'm not saying I didn't, but it isn't as simple as that.' There can't be a permanent record of what she did.

'Once this is out of the way, we've arranged for a specially trained officer to talk to you.'

'Why won't you let me talk?' This isn't fair.

'Nina. You're here to answer a charge. That's all we need you to do.' The camera regards her. If she gets a criminal record, there'll be no way back to her job.

'It was on the 23rd of January. If you don't know the context, how I got there, then it makes me look bad.' It sounds so childish. There'll be more to answer to, if Will has accused her of the rest. Hopefully, Rick has taken care of that, removed all of the traces back to her.

'If you are not prepared to discuss the charge, you will be returned to custody until you are willing to do so.' Lydia isn't as friendly as she seemed.

'But it makes a difference, doesn't it? Why it happened?' Nina lets panic enter her voice, rubs her face.

'There are various stages to this. Right now I need a statement from you, and a statement from him. The rest comes after. We need to deal with one claim at a time.' A slight improvement.

'Will I have a criminal record?' That's not the type of person she is.

'If he doesn't withdraw his statement it will probably be a conditional caution, based on the amount of damage caused to the car.' She looks down at her notes. It's all so official.

'I lost my job. If people know what I did. Without knowing why.' Excellent. Now she sounds desperate.

'You will have an opportunity to tell us everything. I'm sorry if it's making you uncomfortable, I need to know what your answer is. Did you—'

'Yes. But I wasn't intending to do it. I had the thing in my bag because I was scared. Then I got angry, I suppose. He'd called the police. I didn't know why.' She's got to keep her head. There's nothing to connect her to what's been done to him. She's been so careful. 'So yes, I damaged the car. I didn't mean to hurt him, I'm not a violent person. I lost my temper.'

'Thank you.' A small smile. 'I know this is difficult for you.' Lydia looks back down at her folder. The words are there, but she doesn't seem very sympathetic. 'This part is all very straightforward. It's an administrative issue now, really. As I said, it will probably be a conditional caution, but let's not worry about that now.'

'OK.' Nina sits back. If they find out all the things she's done, she'll be in trouble. Even if they do believe her story about the party, there's no proof. The bruises have faded. Somehow she is once again in a small room, powerless.

Eric

Holly is already there, waiting outside Nina's flat. He was sure he'd get here first. He's only seen her in pictures. In person she looks much taller, lighter hair. So different to Nina. She only reaches his shoulder.

'Is she OK?' It's strange, that they haven't met. Holly must know so much more about her.

'She didn't sound great on the phone,' he says. All this time he's spent with her, he should have noticed that she was at some crisis point.

'What happened?'

'I don't really know.' He can't make the connection, how she ended up with Will and his car. 'Something about criminal damage.'

'Never underestimate that woman.' Holly shakes her head. 'So she needs a change of clothes?'

'That's all she asked for.' Eric had to make up some reason for going into the flat. He needs to get in and have a look around, try and figure out what Nina wants him to do. Clearly Will hasn't told Holly what happened.

'And, hi.' She smiles, hugs him. It's awkward. 'Good to meet you.'

'Did she tell you about me?' He wonders if he meets expectations.

'Not really.' She shrugs. 'But then, you've probably seen her more than me. We had a slight falling out.' It wasn't mentioned when he called Holly earlier. As soon as he said she was in custody not much else was offered.

'Oh, she didn't say anything.' Best not to let her know too much. Her link with Will makes her a potential problem. 'I guess she's been keeping some secrets.' That sounded too harsh.

'Something like that,' she says. Holly doesn't know what to make of him. He's used to that reaction. 'Let's do this.' They go into the flat. It's a surprising mess. He's only been here a few times, but he was nervous of sitting, it was so tidy. The backpack is on the table.

'Could you get her clothes? I wouldn't know what she'd like.' He places a hand on it. The contents need to be reserved for him.

'Yeah, no problem.' Holly wades through the stuff on the floor. There's a pile of books, a pair of jeans, an open packet of crackers on the coffee table next to a half empty glass. She's almost out of sight. He turns his attention to the bag, he can't imagine what must be in it.

'Have you seen it like this before?' Holly pauses by the door. She looks uncertain, as if they're in the wrong place.

'Not at all. It was ridiculously neat,' he says. She nods, the frown persisting. With a shrug, she goes into the bedroom.

There's a folded piece of paper and a memory stick. Nothing else. He looks in all the pockets, maybe she meant a different bag. The message wasn't clear. Does she want him to take this stuff to the police station? He opens the page. There's a large photo and some writing.

'Is it serious?' Holly's back. She's standing by the door with a pair of trousers hung over one arm. He forces his eyes away from the page, the fragments of it all

263

assembling before him. 'With you two, I mean.'

'I don't know.'

That's why Will called him.

'Sorry, I don't mean to pry. It's just…' She tips her head. 'This is a bit of a shitty situation. So, are you going to hang around? I know we've just met…but…' If he doesn't give a good answer she might come over and see this.

'No, I understand.' He hasn't tried to put it into words before. 'She's wonderful. Really. I don't know what she sees in me.' It doesn't look like that's enough. 'When she called me today from the police station I told her I love her.'

'Nice.' Holly smiles, turns back to her clothing search.

There's a close-up picture of Will, grinning. Above it, in huge letters, the word "rapist."

What has she done? He looks at the printed page. There must be more copies, this was something intended for display. He doesn't have time now, he'll have to take this with him, get rid of it, hopefully that's where her clues were leading him. Eric folds the page back up and puts it in his coat pocket with the memory stick. Holly comes out and he hands her the bag. This should send the message – that it's empty, he's followed her instructions.

She puts a stack of clothes, pants. He looks away, it's too personal.

Holly goes into the kitchen. He trails after her, feeling useless. It doesn't feel like he knows her at all. Holly pulls out a box of cereal bars and looks inside. He'll have to deal with Will next. Make some excuse to Holly and try and get him off Nina's back. How can he do that?

'Knew it,' she says. She pours out the contents – a Wispa and a Boost. 'She might need these.'

Of course. This is someone Will actually cares about.

'You know what, she did talk about your fight. It was about some guy called Will, right?'

'Something like that.' She shuffles through the contents of the cupboards, not looking at him.

'What happened?'

'I don't really know.' She fiddles with the zip on the bag. 'We were out for her promotion, ended up at this house party. She reckons she was attacked, while she was passed out. She thinks Will did it.'

'That's awful.' So Holly doesn't believe her.

'When she told me, I wasn't very helpful. I just didn't think Will could do something like that. And now, well, she's been arrested.' She lets out a sigh. 'What a fucking mess.'

'I'd be careful, if I were you.'

'Nina talked to you, too?' Will has worked his charm on this one.

'No, not really. She didn't tell me about what happened, just that she didn't like him. But I've known him for years.' He can plant something, a way to help Nina. 'He doesn't exactly have a great reputation with women.'

'Oh, he told me all that.' She zips up the bag, ready to go.

'So he told you about the last time this happened, the other rape case?' She stops, looks at him. 'Not that it was reported, she didn't tell anyone. This was back in college.' After Lori left him. He was a mess. 'On a night out, he had sex with this girl, out behind Mojos. They were both wasted. Only she reckoned he forced himself on her. That she was scared by him, that's why she went along with it.'

'What happened?' Her voice is quiet, concerned.

'I don't really know. One minute she was really upset

265

and then she just stopped talking about it.' It's not a complete lie. Michelle was absolutely mortified that she'd let herself get that drunk, let him come onto her, but it was nothing like that. Enough to get Holly on Nina's side, perhaps, enough to put Will in a difficult position. Anything to take attention away from discovering what actually happened that night.

'Anyway, I just thought you should know.' He smiles, nods. Just a friendly bit of advice.

They go outside. He pauses by the gate.

'See you at the police station?' She tucks the bag over one shoulder.

'I don't know if I should go.' He can't sit there while she talks through the things that he did. 'Something like this...I think it's better if you're there.' He needs to go and sort things out with Will, cover his tracks. 'I meant what I said.'

Holly allows her displeasure to register before walking to her car.

Nina has been living in the shadow of Will all this time. It's something he can relate to. Perhaps he can do something useful for her, finish what she started.

Nina

Back through the dark corridors. It could be any time of day outside. After a short rest, the person that's specialised in sexual assault charges will arrive, then they put together her statement for the events of that night. She doesn't even have her post-its.

Nina feels blurred with solitude. Just a few steps more, then it will be over. It's important to keep her head, concentrate on not letting anything slip about her vendetta against Will. He could have said anything, to try and absolve himself, make her look bad. The door with metal-meshed glass is ahead. A familiar smudge of blonde hair through it.

Holly. Her figure is solid in the wavering room. Nina slumps against her, warm and soft. He was right, it's better that it's her.

'You're an idiot,' Holly says.

'Knew I could rely on you for the tough love.' Nina keeps her head buried.

'That's what you get for playing dodge.'

They sit, Nina's head resting on the cushion of blonde hair. Words simmer around her. She needs to find out where Rick is, if he took care of the stuff in the bag. But not yet. Her eyes droop and she lets it come – sleep pulls her down.

Her neck wakes her – a spike of heat wrenching her head from its awkward position. A whispered conversation is taking place overhead.

'Look who's up.' Holly squeezes her arm.

'I was just saying, it might be better if I come back tomorrow.' An unfamiliar face, blue shirt and trousers. 'They can get me over again if need be. I'm Louise.' The rape specialist. What a strange thing to choose – like becoming a zookeeper, then only looking after the snakes. 'You could go home, get some rest.' Her bed, the soft pressure of it. No pillows, she still can't use them.

'I'm here now.' It needs to be said. Already she's worried there are missing minutes in the scrolling of her memory.

'There's no rush.' Louise's face is calm and firm. It reminds Nina of the policewoman, the first time she came here.

'I want to.' If she leaves, there's no guarantee she'll come back. Nina stands, her head bubbling at the quick loss of blood. 'Can we do it now?'

'We'll get everything ready. Should be about ten minutes.' Louise retreats through the swing door.

Holly has her backpack. Please don't say he left it in there. It was the only way she could think of to get rid of it.

'Look what I've got.' Holly pulls out a can of deodorant and dry shampoo.

'You're a bloody lifesaver.' When they went to festivals Nina insisted on taking dry shampoo. Her thick hair smeared up with grease after a few hours without washing. Of course Holly would remember that.

Nina grabs the bag and goes to the toilet. She scrabbles around, searching for the page and the memory stick. They've gone. Hopefully, he's thought to dispose of them somehow. She can't imagine his reaction. That's one way to find out what's been bothering her. This image of her that he has, it must be shattered now.

Emerging from the metallic bathroom, she feels revitalised. Well, at least less scummy. Holly hasn't moved. Another person whose image of her will be warped. It will be enough to tell someone, she doesn't need witnesses.

'Maybe you should wait out here.' Nina doesn't sit down. 'What about your boyfriend?'

'I'm so sorry. I'm such a shit friend.' She stands, puts a hand on her arm. 'I shouldn't have doubted you over some bloody guy. I'm in if you need me there.' She shrugs. 'No judgement.'

Nina winces at the phrase. That bright day in Bournemouth when she took Holly to the clinic – Jake left when he found out she was pregnant. Outside – the clinic looked like a normal, terraced house– she'd waited in her car, looking out for the agreed halt code. They said they'd stop, at any point, if you changed your mind. It didn't come.

A few weeks later she got a text asking for her to come over, found Holly curled around herself on the floor, tears shuddering out of her. They talked until dawn, drinking enough vodka between them to cause a spate of vomiting at 4am. Holly had said the same thing, that she didn't want to seem like a different person.

It would be better to have her there.

The room reminds Nina of Aunt Gilly's lounge. Walls the same colour – that green that hovers somewhere between olive and mushy peas. There's even a sofa in the corner, lumped and brown. The table and chairs are an imitation dining room. It's constructed comfort. Apart from the cameras.

'Wherever you think you'll feel most comfortable,' Louise says.

Nina sits at the table, Holly next to her. Louise and another woman are opposite. There's a clutter of plastic cups around a jug of squash and a packet of Rich Teas. Nina half expects Aunt Gilly to come in, fuss around her with a plate of homemade scones and tell her she's looking thin.

'This is Karen Farley.' Louise introduces the older woman with a tight bun. 'She's a liaison officer working with Adult Services, specifically incidents related to sexual or domestic abuse.'

They do a little show, about how she can leave whenever she wants, take it at her own pace. Better to just get it over with, it's been drawn out too long.

The preamble is over quickly. Holly interjecting, guilty – it had been her idea to go to the party. The drinks, the location. As it gets closer, she feels more uncomfortable, hot, shifting on the chair. She can't keep her hands still. It's important to remember that nothing happened after that. No reference to his house, his job. These are things that need to be hidden.

'Did he kiss you?' Louise asks.

'I kissed him.' It looks worse, but she can't lie, not about this bit. 'It wasn't something serious, he was clearly cocky, but he was good looking, so I didn't think anything of it. Just a bit of fun.' It's something she did a lot. It didn't feel risky.

'Then what happened?' Her pen scribbles over the paper. This is official.

'He asked me to go upstairs. I said no. Then nothing, for a while. We were drinking.' It wasn't like her, to keep drinking like that. She was so buoyed up by the idea that she deserved it, that she'd achieved something she'd always been told she couldn't.

'Do you know how much you drank?' It's hard to admit it, this makes her look weak.

'Not really. We were drinking rum and ginger beer. I can't stand that smell anymore.' A small laugh. The women nod. Holly looks shaken. 'But he was mixing them. So it could have been a lot. I mean, it must have been.' She definitely missed a step on the way up.

They let the silences spill out between her words. It's hard not to fill them up.

'And then he was pulling my hand upstairs, and I went with him. But nothing happened. Not then, at least. He got a condom out and everything, was so sure of himself. So I walked out. He followed me, we argued.' His face changed. He called her a prick tease.

'Did other people see this?' More scribbling. Louise flips to the next page.

'They must have done, it was pretty loud. I screamed at him, swore, called him a cunt, I think.' Her face had felt red, she was so furious with his assumption that she would fuck him, just because they were kissing. If only she'd gone downstairs then, made her way home.

'Do you know what time this was?'

'Not exactly then, but I'd left my bag in the room. So I went to get it.' The fabric round her neck feels tight. She fidgets, pulls it down.

'Take your time.' It's the first time Karen has spoken. Nina looks up. She's safe here, it can all come out now.

'I got so tired all of a sudden. I thought it might be a drug, it was so quick.' She felt like she couldn't move her legs. 'So I got my bag, it was 1:45am. Then I lay down, I was so tired. It was only for a bit.'

A little noise next to her. Holly couldn't have known, it wasn't her fault. Nina had laboured too long over what might have happened.

'I sort of half woke up, and there was a hand on my leg. It slid up, and then took my pants off.' The moment her confusion had turned to panic. And she hadn't moved, or screamed. Just lain there, unable to stop what was about to happen.

272

Eric

The waiting area of Allen Motors is a shabby room with homemade laminated posters on the wall and two orange chairs in one corner. Will is in the workshop part, visible through a large window that doubles as a reception. The car is a mess. Both lights shattered, a huge gouge in the front of it. Eric feels a little swell in his chest. Something between pride and fear. Will's voice rises behind the glass partition. This is going to be tricky.

If it had just been the Gumtree stuff, the egg and flour, maybe a few hassling emails. She's been doing this for weeks. A calculated attack, searching for contacts and addresses, finding ways to make Will's life a misery. It's absurdly impressive. Eric isn't sure he would have thought of half of it. And so careful, the way she's covered her tracks. He opened the spreadsheet at home, after leaving Holly. The final bit, though. Creating a fake account, writing hateful things in his name. He's underestimated her. It's his fault. He unleashed this.

Will walks in with a guy in overalls.

'So that's without the labour?' Will does not look happy. Eric isn't sure where to start.

'Yes. We'll get all the numbers over to the insurance company. It shouldn't be a problem. You'll need your crime number, all that sort of thing.' The man ticks off things on his list.

'How long do you need it for?' he asks. Will loves that car.

'Over a week, I'm afraid. Our bodywork guy isn't in for a few days.' The standard man-in-garage head shake.

'I've got a conference tomorrow,' Will says.

'There's a courtesy car.' He glances back through the window. 'What happened?'

'Some psycho bitch who's been stalking me. Followed me to the gym and trashed my car.' It's unnerving, the amount of stuff she found out online.

'A girl did this to your car? Jesus.' The guy laughs, heads back to the workshop. A gasp of mechanical noises escapes with the opening of the door.

'Bad day?' He can't help it, there's something satisfying in all this.

'This Nina? She's mental. All this stuff, people at my house. I've been put under investigation at work.' Will looks pretty freaked out. 'I had to prove to my boss that this online bullshit had nothing to do with me. It's a fucking joke, mate.' She did well.

'What are you talking about?' He needs to let him reveal what he knows.

'I don't bloody know.' Will covers the ground between the chairs and back again. 'I get a call from my mum telling me there's pictures of my face all over her street with "rapist" on it, when I get home they're all over my street, too. I'm still getting nutters turning up at my house asking to buy my cat and some girl whose top I had my hand up at a party just trashed my car.' Eric doesn't like to think of that. He shouldn't have to share everyone with Will.

'You think they're connected?' He tries to sound disinterested.

274

'She's going to pay. I'm going to find out what that little bitch has done and she will find herself in prison. I told the police everything. She's not getting away with it.' Will sits on one of the chairs. This does not look good for Nina.

'It might not be that simple.' He needs to find a way to help her.

'I don't think you understand, mate,' Will says. 'Emails went out to all of these people, even my boss, calling me a rapist. I've been reported on websites I've never even been on for unsuitable content. I read it. There's someone who is apparently me, confessing to raping someone at that party.' This is new, how far did she go? 'This could ruin me. Who's going to want me to work on their accounts now?' He looks desperate. 'You were at that party. You know I left. I didn't touch her, not after she went psycho on me.' Will pats the chair next to him. 'You can help.' He is a required presence again.

'True.' Eric sits. It doesn't help him, if this all comes out. There's no way Will could have done it. Almost straight after the fight he left, he went on somewhere else. There must be someone who saw Eric walking into that room.

'So she's clearly nuts. I bet there are fingerprints on the posters. Then we've got her.' Will leans forward, keen on his plan. His use of "we," it only comes out when he wants something. It's always been one-sided.

'You might be underestimating her.' He says it quietly. He's not sure what he should reveal.

'Maybe. Like your thinking, we need to find out more,' Will says. He looks so pleased with himself.

'Right.' The arrogance of him. 'Like I'd want to help you out.'

'We're mates.' A shrug. Like that forgives it all. It's too much, he needs to be put in his place for once.

'When it suits you.' He can't allow him to talk about her like that. 'I thought you were all horrified that something happened to her?'

'Hey, it's hard to be sympathetic when I'm on the receiving end of all this shit.' So self-involved.

'Let's say it did happen. She was raped.' Eric hasn't said it out loud before. 'And it was someone else. You need to give her a break.' He never thinks about others.

'Why is she blaming me?' He stands. The profile fits — he's got that wide-set look, the square jaw. The cockiness.

'Wouldn't put it past you,' Eric says. After what he's discovered about himself, about her, anything's possible.

'That's not funny.' He walks up and down, agitated. 'I'd never do something like that. It's sick.' He stops, looks down.

'She's fine though, everything's OK.' Eric looks at his hands, folded over his knees. 'I'm taking care of her.'

'You know her?' That got his attention.

'We met last month.' Such a small span of weeks. 'We're together now.' It's nearly true.

'If she's pasting pictures of my face on walls and battering my car in, I don't think she's OK.' Will steps closer. 'You've talked about this? She's gone to the police?'

'She didn't tell me about that stuff.' Eric keeps examining his hands.

'We were at the party, we could help her, try and find the guy.' Will crouches down.

'After what she did to you?' Eric's palms are moist.

'Once she knows it isn't me, she can take all this stuff back. Tell everyone the truth.' He shrugs, like there's an easy solution.

He can't have Will digging away at all this.

'I want you to leave us alone.' He makes his voice

loud but can't hide the wobble.

'No way, I need my reputation back, she's got to help me out.' Will sits next to him.

'You're all compassion.' He's not kind, just wants to get something for himself. 'Look at what she's already done. The Gumtree adverts, the emails, the posters. This was planned. You have no proof that she has anything to do with it.' Eric keeps his voice very quiet. This can be the one time it's admitted.

Will looks around, unable to speak, for once.

'Take back what you said to the police or you will find your life is a fucking misery.' Eric's voice is shaking.

'Why?'

'Maybe you pissed off too many women, screwed too many girlfriends. It's about time you faced some consequences.' It sounds good, like the speech delivered in Reservoir Dogs. It gives him a little rush.

'I don't see why you have to do it like this.' Will leans forward. 'I said I'd help. We can help her get the guy who did it. She said something about being passed out in that room? I'm sure someone would have seen him, the guy, go in there.'

Eric stiffens. He has to make Will drop this.

'I saw your new girlfriend today.' Time to show his strength. 'She didn't seem too happy about your run-in with Michelle.'

'What did you tell her?'

'Just that things like this seem to keep happening to you. This isn't the first time you've attacked someone.' Eric sits back.

'You little shit.' That worked.

'Come on, you think she'll still want to see you after her best mate accuses you of this? They've been friends for years.'

'There's no proof. I can tell the police where I was. I

277

don't know why you don't want me to help sort it out.'
He sits back, his face changing. 'This isn't about her. It's
about you, isn't it?'

'Of course not.' Eric looks at him. He can't show his
guilt.

'You'd want to find out who did it, if you really cared
about her. Unless you already know.'

He puts his hands over his face. This is bad. There
must be some way of making it seem like it's for her.

'Look.' He has to think quickly. 'The last thing she
needs is another witch hunt. This whole thing has been
incredibly bad for her. I think she needs to move on.'
That sounds convincing.

'But if we find the guy, he'll get done for it, no
problem.'

'Of course.' Now he's got him. 'Because that's going
to happen. How many times have you heard of cases like
this leading to prosecution? It would be her word against
his.' Something he was relying on, if it came to that.

'I guess. But we've got to at least try.' That's better.
Less accusing.

'You said work had discredited the accounts anyway.
It could be some random nutter, for all we know.'

'There might be some DNA. On something from the
room.'

'I don't think that will help. That room was full of
coats, loads of people would have gone in there.'

'Right.' Will looks thoughtful again. The clanking
from next door reaches through to them. Almost there.
Just need to get him to drop the charges against her, and
they're safe.

'How do you know what was in the room?' Will says
it quietly.

'People put their coats in there, and you said it was
that one, or maybe she did, something like that.' What an

awful answer. He should have waited, thought about it.

'You sure this isn't about you?'

'Don't be ridiculous.' He looks away.

'I knew it.' Will leans forward. 'Always the quiet ones, right?'

'I didn't say that. I didn't say anything. I'm not capable of something like that. You, the way you strut around, fucking anything that moves.'

'At least I respect them.' Will looks so relaxed.

'Oh yes, taking a different girl home every night is very respectful.'

'I wouldn't do it if they didn't want me to.' He shakes his head. 'You're no better than your useless father.'

'That's enough!' He's up, out of his chair, fists clenched. People are watching through the window.

'Now that looks like a lot of pent-up violence to me.' Will leans back, a little smile on his face.

How does he manage it? He was supposed to be the accused one, defeated. Somehow he's sat there, smirking. It should be the other way round.

He turns, breathes, tries to clear his jumbled thoughts. It doesn't matter what he thinks he knows. There's no proof. There must be a way of getting the upper hand.

'I'll tell Holly other stuff.' He throws the words over his shoulder. 'About that time you took two girls home, or all those times you went to strip clubs.'

'That doesn't matter.' How can he sound so calm? 'If she trusts me, she'll believe me, no matter what her friend thinks. And she knows most of that stuff anyway.'

No good. His heart is racing now. There's proof, of everything, in his pockets. What if he gave it to Will, let him accuse Nina? She'd probably go to jail, it wouldn't be a problem anymore.

Breathe. No, it wouldn't be for that long, and she'd

know it was him. There has to be something. He ticks back through the things Will cares about. His car, his Mum, his holidays, his job. That's it. Something he can't wriggle out of. Eric's shoulders drop. He hadn't realised how tense he'd been.

'Just one thing left, then.'

'Give it up, Ricky boy. I think we're done. Perhaps it's time I had a chat with your little girlfriend.' He comes and stand next to Eric. Always so sure of himself.

'How much did you spend on your birthday night out?'

He just looks at him. No response. Is he worried?

'Must have been a lot, right? All your mates, all those drinks, the curry, the bowling tickets. Can't imagine your boss would be too pleased about that going on the company.'

'People always use their expenses for personal stuff.' He sounds blasé, but maybe a hint of uncertainty underneath.

'You get what you're owed, right? I'm sure that all those bonuses and extras are above board. You wouldn't take any bribes from investors, would you?' That expensive tie he was crowing about. The watch.

'You don't understand my job.' Will puts his hands in his pockets. That's a sign of nerves.

'I think I can figure out enough to know that accepting bribes would lead to you losing your job. Losing any future jobs, right? Can't be seen to be fiddling accounts. No-one would touch you after that.' He's definitely on to something.

'As lovely as your wild theories are, there's no proof.' That's basically an admission of guilt. Just a little push, and he's got him.

'Why would I need that? All it would take is some words in the right ear. They could look over your

280

accounts without your permission.' He's pretty sure that must be how it works. 'Especially after the recent shake-up, you're bound to be on the suspicion list. Easier for them to show you the back door.'

'Look-' The word catches in his throat. This is it. He's never managed to avoid a sarcastic comeback, a withering response, before.

'No, you look.' Eric steps closer, lowers his voice. 'I can fucking end you and you know it. So stop pretending to be all calm about this. She might have tried to trip you up, but I can push you flat on your face. The girls, the swagger, the money. You fit the profile. If I back her up, then it isn't just her word against yours. Or maybe I get on the phone to your boss. Write a nice anonymous letter. Either way, you lose.' Eric's hands are shaking. It feels wonderful. 'So, this is what's going to happen. You drop the charges, tell the police you retract your statement. Tell the insurance whatever you want, or don't tell them at all. I think you can cover the cost. If this blonde idiot really wants to keep seeing you, it's never mentioned. You don't support or deny it, you just change the subject. Those two are very close friends. She will tell Nina everything. I will know. I'm sure you'll find another one. It's never been hard for you.'

'That's what this is really about, isn't it?' Will shakes his head. 'Jealousy's a terrible thing. Look what it's done to you. You're a fucking disgrace.'

'Whatever. You just wanted me as a friend because I made you look good.' It can all come out now.

'I know you think that.' A shrug. 'I thought we were mates. We had a laugh.'

'So, we're agreed?' He just needs this, then he can leave.

'What a big mess you've got yourself into, Eric.' Something like pity in his face. He walks back to the orange chairs, sits down. 'Piss off then.' Will tucks his hands behind his head. 'You're disgusting.'

Trust him to act like the big guy when it's him who's been backed into a corner. It doesn't matter. None of it does. He's cleared up the mess, sorted it all out. He never needed Will in the first place.

Outside, the sun is fierce, his eyes filling up. Must be hay fever already. The pent-up aggression knots itself over and over in his gut, his hands clenching at each turn, burying it deep. He quickens his stride. The paper is still in his back pocket. He pulls it out and peers at the grinning face, dodging past clusters of tourists on their way to the castle.

He finds a spot near the shore, a bank of pebbles leaning down towards the sucking waves. The memory stick plops into the sea. Now the page. He crushes it into a ball and hurls it out, leaving it bobbing on the surface; the last debris of his failings.

Nina

She gulps at the squash, heat building in her chest. That was just the first part. The moment when she'd realised what he wanted to do. Dread had seeped in then. 'I didn't do anything. Not even open my eyes. How is that possible?' She wasn't sure if it was part of a dream at first, crawling up through the fog of sleep.

'You must have been afraid.' Karen again.

'Yes, but it didn't seem real. You think.' Another sip. 'It will be angry and scary but it was…sneaky.' So soft and gentle, like it wasn't a big deal. 'I wasn't expecting it to be like that. And everything was fuzzy.' All that rum, it had made her feel so detached, at first.

'But then he picked me up, pushed my feet in so my legs would bend. Then, I panicked. My dress was up, I wanted to pull it down, but he was there, and more than anything I felt so embarrassed. Everything up in the air, on display.' It felt as though she'd allowed it, that she couldn't say anything.

'Would there be marks on him?' Louise is all efficiency, she wants facts.

'I didn't do anything.' It's an awful thing to admit. 'There was a pause, I wasn't sure what was happening. It was frightening.' That sense that she was completely helpless. 'His hand was on my neck, pushing it into the pillow, my face. I couldn't breathe. And I thought.' Stay quiet and hidden and it will stop, squeeze your eyes and maybe this is the drink and you'll wake up and nothing will have happened. 'I thought that if I was still, if I let him. He'd let me go.' The anger that's gnawed at her. Like it was her fault.

'That's what happens when people are threatened. It's survival.' Karen's voice is soft.

'It's stupid.' If she'd tried to fight him off, done something. It wasn't her, that thing on the bed. 'I always thought I would. If it happened. That I'd scream, do anything, rather than let it happen.' The inertia, that was the worst thing. While he thumped behind her, smacking her head into the pillow, yanking her hair, those sweaty hands gripping and releasing her bum. Every part of her vibrated in time, slapping against him. It felt like such a long time.

Nina's fingers pick at the edge of the table. She can't look up.

'Do you know how long the attack lasted?' Louise sounds the same. That word, attack. It verifies her.

'He just stayed there.' He leant on her back, breathing hard. Started to throb, she could feel the pulse of pain between her legs. 'Until he'd caught his breath. Sometimes I wake up and it feels like he's still there.' Nina scrubs her hands over her face.

'Did he say anything to you?' There are too many questions, she wants it to stop.

'I don't know.' When he'd released her, she'd curled tight around herself, and shut off. 'I must have passed out, or gone to sleep, but that doesn't make sense.' Let this be over.

'It could be the body's way of dealing with the shock.' Karen, the voice of understanding. She must see that she

284

Sarah Tinsley

can't do anymore.

'Then when I woke up.' It was dark, and cold. 'I was alone, it was something like four in the morning.'

The images that come unbidden in the fog of sleep — her head pressed into the pillow, clawing hands, hot breath, the pounding, her desperation, inability to move, and the pressing, grasping hands.

'Thank you for telling me.' Louise's voice is soft. Nina can't look up at that kindness. It's good to know it's there.

Everyone leans back. Nina pours some squash, it brings moisture back to her mouth. Holly's hand is on hers, her breath coming in sniffles.

The women are discussing something, having a disagreement.

'Nina.' Louise leans over. 'I know this is difficult, but I hope you won't mind me asking you something related to the incident.'

'Of course.' She's told them everything. It doesn't feel like a search for justice anymore. Just a release.

Karen looks unhappy.

'William Lakeland made all sorts of claims, along with the car. He thinks you've staged some sort of vendetta against him. That you threatened him.' Of course he would do that.

'What?' Her reaction needs to be controlled, plausible. 'I don't know what to say. Not long ago I lost my job, everything's been so hard.' She looks up. Hardly any sleep, all that stuff she's said. It seems to have an effect. She must look awful. 'I've been drinking too much.' A little laugh. She sounds hysterical. 'I want the days to pass quicker until I don't have nightmares anymore.' No lies, and surely they won't notice she's sidestepped the question.

'Come on, this is ridiculous. I think she's had

285

enough.' Holly jumps in.

'We might have to call you back in for questioning.' Louise doesn't want to let it go. Karen leans over, murmurs something in her ear. 'But for now, I'm sure you could do with some rest.'

Holly takes her hand and leads her away. She feels drained.

In the waiting room, another welcome face. She rushes over, wraps her arms around his waist.

'Thank you.' Just knowing he was here, waiting for her.

'You asked.' Rick speaks into the top of her head, nudging his mouth against her temple. So warm, so safe.

'I want to go home.'

'Of course. Holly's going to take you straight there.'

'What about you?' She pulls back, looks up at him.

'I think I need to talk to them.' He pulls himself out of her arms. 'Sorry for not saying anything before, but I was at that party.'

'I don't understand.'

'I didn't think it was important. That was silly of me. I guess I was embarrassed because of what happened with you and Will. I know this is more important.' He takes her hand. 'I was on the sofa in the front room. I didn't see anything. But if they've got some questions, if it can help, it's the least I can do.' He squeezes her shoulder.

'OK.' Another revelation is too much. She turns to Holly. 'Can we go?'

'Here.' Holly hands her the Wispa. 'This is just for starters.' She puts an arm around her shoulders, steering her towards the door. Cold air wafts through, signalling escape.

Eric

Bringing coffee was a bad idea. The remainder of it is seeping through him, squeezing an ache into his temples and jiggling his legs. He's still holding the cup, the cardboard ridges soggy in his palms. There wasn't a bin in the waiting room, so now he's rolling it around between his hands. They said he had to wait here. It must be a trap, a way of wearing him down before they begin.

Eric snaps the cup onto the table, spurting brown specks onto his blue T-shirt. This is ridiculous. It was his idea. A way of heading them off – who would offer to talk about something when they were guilty? All they know is that he was at the party. There's absolutely nothing to link him to Nina. Apart from the fact that she just hugged him outside. And his ex-best friend is suspicious of him.

The only vaguely absorbent item in his pocket is a receipt. He's dabbing ineffectually at the dark spots with a scrap of ink-stained paper when the two men walk in. Probably not the sharpest start.

'Thanks for coming in,' the first one says. 'I'm Sergeant Peter Donahue and this is Constable Kyle Francis.' Kyle looks younger than him, his blonde hair spiked up. Eric's always suspicious of people with goatees.

'No problem.' He moves his arms, placing them in his lap.

'Can you tell us why you're here?' Peter raises his eyebrows, they have grey wiry hairs poking through the dark fuzz.

'Nina was just in here, about something that happened at a party. I was there.' That sounds OK. 'And, I just wondered if I could help.' He puts his hands back on the table.

'Did you speak to her at the party?' The same movement above his eyes.

'No, of course not.' That sounds too much like a panic answer. 'I mean, I didn't know her then. It was quite random, that I met her later. We didn't make the connection.' They leave the silence to open out. 'Sorry, it's weird, being here, I've never been in a police station before.' Nothing. 'And, you know, Portsmouth isn't very big, we're roughly the same age, so I guess it figures we might bump into each other. Strange coincidence.' He could tell the story of how they met. It's quite sweet, if you don't think about why he was there.

'If we can get back to the night in question.' Kyle leans in. Typical of someone like him. Eric was just getting going, about to make their meeting entirely plausible.

'Did you see William Lakeland and Nina together at the party?' he says, looking down at his notes.

'I know him, or I used to. We're not friends anymore.' It sounds like he's at school. 'That is, we fell out. It's not related.' Eyebrows again. He needs to stick to answering the question. 'I was mostly in the front room, chatting. But when I went to get a drink, yeah. Will was pouring rum, said something about the party getting better. The next time I went back he was in the corner, snogging this short, dark-haired girl.'

'Was it Nina Franklin?' Kyle writes something down.

'I'm pretty sure it was, they were chatting too, laughing, it was definitely her.' Eric needs to make his story plausible, make him seem disconnected from it all.

'And where were you at around 1:30 am?' Kyle asks.

'Was it that late?' What an idiot. They haven't noticed. 'I didn't realise it was so late. I'm a primary school teacher, so I have to get up really early most of the time so that means I don't stay out late. Not very often.' That will make him look more appealing. Gentle.

'Did you see anything unusual?' Peter cuts in. He looks bored.

'They were shouting at each other, near the top of the stairs. I don't know what happened, but everyone heard it. They were really loud. She was screaming, right in his face.' It was one of the few times he'd seen Will intimidated. She'd looked so impressive.

'What did you do after that?' Peter again. Eric checks the faces. They can't know anything, they would have said something by now.

'I don't know, chatted for a bit, wandered around. I know I grabbed some beers before I left, from the front room. That was a mistake!' He laughs. It isn't returned.

The page sighs as Peter turns it over. He looks from it to Eric, back again. Letting the quiet stretch out. 'And there's nothing else you can think of that would help with our enquiry?'

'Right.' Eric says. This is it, his opportunity to steer everything well away from him. To pre-empt it if someone says they saw him go into that room. 'Actually, I did go in there, into the room. I saw Will leave, then I though I should go and check she was OK. She was pretty upset.' Which had been his intention. It wouldn't have been the first girl he'd have to let down gently, disappointed after Will had got what he'd wanted then moved on. There had been enough awkward kitchen conversations when they lived together. He could talk to her, explain what a dick he was, perhaps share some hurt over his recent discovery of betrayal. That would have been it.

'And then-' Maybe he'd been angry at her, for being weak. Why did these women fall for his bullshit? She'd drunk too much, let herself get like this. She should have pushed him off, brought him back to his senses. He wasn't like that.

'I saw her, lying on the bed, passed out.' And it had all worked out. He'd made up for it by helping her, being there for her.

'Her dress was all rucked up.' He coughs. 'I'm sorry, this is difficult, because of...' He sighs. 'I mean, we're friends now, well, more than that...I don't know.' What he said on the phone. It wasn't something to make her feel better. It's true.

'It was obvious she'd had sex.' Peter's face doesn't change, but Kyle looks surprised.

'What makes you say that?' Peter asks.

'She wasn't wearing any pants, so I saw, well.' This is for the best, it will allow them to move on, together. 'There was a condom wrapper, it was empty, on the side. A couple of drinks. She was mumbling something, slurring. I put the stuff in the bin, pulled her dress down.' Finally, he can see a way out. 'She muttered something but she was too far gone, I think.'

'But you don't know what happened.' Peter isn't going to be fooled so easily.

'Well, no, but I do know what he's like. He slept with my girlfriend, we were living together at the time. And over the years, he tends to get all charming, sleep with girls, then bugger off. They get pretty angry.' His stomach clenches at what he's about to say. 'I've had to deal with them, calm them down, try to get them to leave him alone. It used to happen a lot at college. So maybe–' Eric swallows. 'Maybe they had sex and she got pissed off about it, so she's saying he raped her to get back at him.' The coffee sits sourly in his belly.

'Have you discussed this with her?' He doesn't look convinced.

'No, of course not. I couldn't.' Just one more little push. 'But she does have a bit of a temper.' The solemn faces regard him across the table, needling into his words. All he needs is a nugget of doubt, then they won't bother pursuing the case at all.

Nina

Outside, it's still light. Shadows are drooping, but she was expecting it to be the middle of the night. The sky looks tired. Holly left her with strict instructions to go straight to bed. Of course, she hadn't wanted to leave. Nina needed space. Just to exist in her flat for a while, without feeling the need to explain anything. She can talk to Holly tomorrow.

A skinny figure sits humped on the wall outside the flat, doubled over as if in pain. Nina leans forward, making sense of the features. It's Rick, reading a book. She sighs. Another person to explain things to.

She imagined the scald of the shower all the way here, buckled gently into Holly's car like a child. She doesn't want him to see her, like this. So far all she's done is walk around the living room, picking things up and putting them down again.

No, she has to say something. He's come all the way here. She shoves a hoodie on and pulls the hood up over the tails of her hair. It's colder than she thought it would be when she opens the door.

'Hi,' she says, aware of the crack in her voice.

'Are you ok?' He stands up and moves towards her, too close.

'Fine.' She can't handle more concern. 'It's been a long day. I just want a shower.'

'Of course.' He doesn't move.

'It's not that I don't appreciate it.'

'I wasn't sure you should be alone,' he says.

'I'm perfectly capable.'

'I didn't mean.' He looks so disappointed. After everything he's done for her.

'Can you let me. Be.' It sounds like a dismissal. 'Just today. I can't.'

'This is a great book.' He lifts up the arm, the pages an extension of his hand. 'And it's a sunny day.' He gestures to the dank sky and moves back to his original spot, dropping his eyes back to the page.

'I don't like the assumption,' she says. It's too much, to feel like he needs her.

'Either way. Just in case.'

Inside, she sheds her grimy clothes on the way to the bathroom, the room filling with steam. The smell of clean, scouring, scraping, erasing. She heaps far too much shower gel onto the body puff, covers herself in the soft white foam. The heat adds to her sense of lightness. She cuts the hair from her legs, underarms, the curve of her belly. Then back in the hot stream, the exfoliating mitt scouring every millimetre. The water slips it all off, draining it through the dark holes of the plug.

Nina stands in the fog of the bathroom, savouring the tightening of pink skin all over. No moisturiser, just the humanity of tension in her pores. The air is softer, more forgiving. When she prods her nose against the mirror, she realises she's smiling. Something about herself is restored.

Rummaging through her wardrobe, she finds the deep blue silk dress that comes out around the time of Christmas parties and slips into it, the fabric whispering on her body.

The flat is chaos. Food and clothing heaped in corners, books and magazines all over the sofa. She swoops round it all, shoving everything into the laundry basket, dirty or not. The plates and bowls are piled in the dishwasher, books in a cupboard and food in the bin. A proper clean can be done when she has the energy. Now to relax. She puts the lamps on and sinks onto the sofa, letting the tension sop out into the cushions.

It's dark when she wakes, the humps of furniture indistinguishable in the gloom. Little bumps sprawl over her arms. She shoves the hoodie on over the top and goes to the kitchen, setting the kettle to boil, looking for a sugary something to revive her. Holly took her stash, maybe there are biscuits somewhere. The glow of the streetlight falls on a stooped back. She blinks. It's the wheelie bin, not a figure, flicking pages. There's no sign of him.

Returning to the kettle, she goes through the motions – teabag, milk, spoon – takes it into the front room, slopping some onto her jumper as she sits down. She sits, sipping blindly, the shadows creeping up to her toes.

He doesn't live that far away. It might be polite to say thank you. He didn't have to come over. She shoves her feet into trainers and heads to the car. A draught seeps up her skirt. It's already ten. She dithers at the door, more clothes would be good but her impetus might not last if she goes back inside.

The air is chilly as she walks up the path – a coat might have been a good idea. His flat looks dark. She rings the bell anyway, hearing it echoing down the hall. There's a long silence, unbroken. The curtains are drawn, no crack of light escaping from underneath. He must be in bed. She turns and makes her way back down the path, dragging her feet. She's almost at the car when she hears a click, a wash of light falling behind her.

'You must be freezing.' He stands in the oblong of light, she can't see his face.

'It's ok,' she says, hurrying back to light and warmth.

'I'll put the kettle on.'

She follows him inside, closing the door. It's messier than she expected, stray papers and pens lying about. A pile of books on the coffee table.

'Nice place,' she says.

'Thanks.'

'Look at me,' she says, taking his hand. The skin feels thin and cool, stretched over the bones. He saw the poster. Might have looked at the contents of the memory stick. This might be the end, he won't see her the same now.

'Don't worry.' He gives her a quick smile, takes his fingers away, moving towards the kettle. They stand at opposite ends, leaning against the work surface. She glances at him but each time he's staring at the rumbling container of water, the pulsing light on the side. The rattle increases and then the final thud, a cloud of steam ballooning out underneath the kitchen cupboard. It breaks something unspoken. He busies himself, peering into cupboards to find cups, spoons, tea, milk, leaving her still, watching his nervousness.

'Nice dress,' he says.

Looking down, she spreads wide the ridiculous fabric under the University of Cambridge hoodie and offers him a curtsy. She looks ridiculous. Thick, unexploded laughter bubbles up inside her. She giggles. He looks at her, a smile starting. Then they both start laughing. They are lost in a tide of humour, a pink elephant mug hanging from his hand, her face aching from the wide and tight smile, her stomach tensing over and over. Moisture dribbles from his eyes, he goes to wipe it away and smacks himself in the head with the trunk jutting from the side of the cup. Renewed by his surprised expression, she laughs until she is gripping the side for support.

Trapped between the things he is holding, she places her cool hands on his cheeks and kisses him. He doesn't move his hands but his lips respond to hers. She moves her mouth across his cheeks, the slight fuzz of stubble, to his earlobe, the scoop of skin underneath, the hollow of his neck. Pressure in the small of her back from his hand, a sigh escaping. Back to his mouth, her hands slipping down around his waist. The clunk of porcelain, then she is encircled. Leaning in, she rests her head against his chest, hearing the increased thump caused by her.

'Thank you,' she says into his shirt.

'You don't owe me anything,' he says.

'He attacked me.' It should make up for all the things he knows about her now.

'I'm sorry.' There's emotion in his voice, almost strangled. Hopefully he won't see her differently. She isn't a used thing. Looking up, she's surprised to see moisture in his eyes. She expected revulsion, pity even, but this has none of those traits.

Nina pushes against him. He keeps his hands loosely around her waist. Reaching inside the material, he feels pale. Underneath, his heartbeat increases, the skin flushing with warmth, a tinge of sweat. She pulls back. His face remains impassive, locked in some internal question. She pulls away but the hands stay limp but locked behind her back.

He walks slowly, but quite close, behind her. At the sofa she stops, his front colliding with her back. They both giggle. Against her bum, the harder press of it. She pushes again, expectant of roaming hands, the forceful pressure, the shift into passivity. It doesn't arrive. They regard each other in the dim glow, a flickering streetlamp casting a yellow spatter on his cheek. Taking his hands, she guides him to the sofa, sits him down. He obediently leaves his arms raised while she pulls his T-shirt over his head. The bones are clear lines. She traces her fingers over them, pleased with the judder her fingers draw. His hands reach up and touch her face, stroke the curve of her neck. She pulls the jumper off, leading his hands to the silk on her body. Once more she leans in, waiting to be overtaken. His hands stop.

She slips the straps off and lets the dress fall to the floor, a chill painting her skin. She steps towards him, placing her nipple in his mouth. He waits until her hands grip his hair, then responds. She brings his hands up, cupping her bottom. Navigating between his arms, she touches herself, surprised at the level of response. Caught between his hands, hers, and his mouth, she feels no need to rush. They stay there, swaying, her movement increasing, until the breath leaves her in a bark, her legs shuddering. He presses the side of his face against her tummy and holds her while she floats back. She pushes him onto the sofa, pulling the tangle of trousers and pants off in one. He doesn't move when she places her hands on it, explores, wanders over all of him, familiarising herself with the dips and curves, the sticky fuzz under his armpits and the thicker weight of his thighs.

She lies down, his arms wrapping around her. Syllables of air squash between them, the shock of complete softness, all friction removed. Skin slipping and brushing, his foot tucked around the back of her calf. It feels insistent, a solid lump digging into the softness of her thigh. They fall into a rhythm, pressing and releasing. Her fingers find the dip in the centre of his back and draw a line down it. She squeezes her hand down between the two of them, angles it up, the tip just against her edges. They resume, neither acknowledging the incremental movement, each time advancing a little. The warm, pressing out between her legs. Another push — it's too far to be ignored. She jerks her body away, jumps up, the sudden removal leaving her cold.

'We shouldn't,' she says.

'You don't have to.' He tries to curl himself away.

'Do you have anything?' She gestures to it. 'You know.'

'Oh, right.' He scrambles up, pulls his pants on. 'Be right back.' He walks to the bathroom.

She looks down, her tummy folded over itself like a sausage. If she leans back a bit, maybe angles to the side, that's better. Waiting for his return, she keeps her body posed, bumps rising on her skin.

He comes back with the crinkled packet in his hand, sits next to her. She takes it from him. He doesn't move. This passivity gives her an urgency that's unfamiliar. Pushing him back down, she tears at the foil, slips out the squishy contents, rolls her fingers around the edge to check it's the right way round. He sits up, the erection diminishing under his tummy.

'Can we talk?' He looks nervous.

'I wasn't really in the mood for a chat.' She sits astride him again, her free hand reaching down. He stops her.

'I don't need it,' he says.

'Maybe I do.' She's unpinned all her frustrations.

'To get it over with?'

'Is that what you think?' Nina cups the side of his face.

'I don't understand,' he says.

'It's not about that.'

'Then why?'

'Just the usual reasons.' She keeps eye contact,

allowing the moment to build again. He returns her smile.

He releases her, slides back down, letting her smother him again. It's less awkward now. She savours the kissing and the proximity, not rushing, waiting until the insistent pressure has built on her hip again. She stretches it over, rolling the length of it down, a little squeeze to expel the air in the end. The need to complete this action has made her impatient. She slides forward, her knees either side of his waist. Once the tip is in, she moves her hand to his face, covered in the plastic scent. She pushes down, all in one movement this time, it sticks a little, catches, she feels pressed apart. This is the first time. Since.

She closes her eyes, the sensations returning, the feel of pressure. Forcing her eyes open, he's frozen beneath her, his face somewhere between fear and hope.

She breathes out, slowly, letting the breath unclench her. It's different. There is nothing of that horror here. Nina leans down and brushes his face, pleasure reasserting itself, the thick line of control and panic she has drawn for herself dissipating at each movement. It is safe to let go.

Increasing now, she adjusts the angle a little so she's sliding onto his pelvis, the friction jolting up through her. Mouth dropping open, sharp points of sweat standing out on her back, everything reduced to this tiny centre, the force to continue. Her legs feel tired, a slight twinge in the left calf — it all fades beneath the need, the urge, the pressure.

Afterwards he shifts over to the right so they can both lie along the sofa. She laughs a little, suddenly awkward by her nakedness, her recent exuberance. A sudden doubt pinches at her.

'Did you?'

'Oh yes.'

'Good.' She places the flat of her palm on his chest. 'I

wasn't sure, I couldn't tell. Was it?'

'You're so sexy.' His hands touch the side of her arm, drawing lines up and down it. She sags back down, the urge for conversation leaving her.

Nina

Now

'Are you OK?' Will's voice comes from far away, high up.

'What?' She's back on the sofa again. He's sat opposite her on the coffee table.

'You started making funny noises so I carried you to the sofa.' He looks worried. 'I'm sorry.'

'No you're not.' She sits up, gathers together recent events. Will turned up at Eric's flat, threatening her.

'I want you to stop, but I didn't mean to scare you,' he says. 'Water?'

'Yes please.' Nina pulls the blanket around her. 'I don't think grabbing people is the best way to reason with them.' Now she's alone with him. She looks around for her phone.

'I know, I know.' He stands up, starts walking up and down. 'It's not like you've exactly been reasonable. My car is a fucking write-off and my mum's neighbours think I'm a rapist.' He laughs. 'What a mess.'

'The water?' At least he seems calmer.

'Do you have any idea how upset those kids were when they found out I didn't have a kitten?' He walks to the kitchen, finds glasses in the first cupboard he opens. He's been here before. They're much better friends than she thought. 'Their poor mum.' Did they talk about her, in this room where she's felt so comfortable all day? 'Here.' He puts a glass in front of her.

'If we're comparing horror stories, I think I win.' There it is, under the blanket. She picks it up, jabs the corner three times.

'I don't think so.' He flicks it out of her hand before she can finish.

'He'll be home soon.' There it is again. She needs someone to protect her.

'That's why I need to talk to you.' He sits on the coffee table. 'Look, how did you guys meet?'

'I crashed my car. He was one of the witnesses. He helped me out.' Right from the start he's been there for her.

'Where did it happen? When?' It feels like she's being interrogated.

'Just outside. I was on my way to work.' What a mess she'd been.

'He doesn't live near here. It's not on his way to school. Why was he outside your house?'

'I don't know. Coincidence.' There'd been people watching, Rick was one of them.

'You think?' He stops pacing. 'I want you to know I'm risking a lot here. Your little boyfriend threatened all sorts of crap if I didn't leave you alone, forget about all that mental shit you did to me.'

'I didn't realise you were such a thoughtful rapist. Is that what you told the police?' She'd been hoping the next time she saw him would be in the newspaper.

'I'm here, aren't I? They let me go. I wasn't even there when it happened.' He raises his hands, exasperated.

'You would say that.'

'There are witnesses, people that were with me,

302

CCTV from the club. I've come from the police station now.' He shows her an ink-black finger.

'I don't understand. You got so angry, when I said no.' The way he'd casually taken a condom out, before they were fully in the room.

'Excuse me for making assumptions when a girl agrees to go upstairs with me. I don't think it was much of a leap.'

'I can withdraw consent whenever I want.' She holds the blanket closer.

'Yeah, I get it. I left, didn't I?' He stills, looks at her. 'But *he* didn't.'

'You mean Rick? He's already made a statement.'

'Ah yes, *Rick*.' He leans back, hands on hips. 'He always wanted me to call him that.'

'He said you didn't know him that well. You bullied him at school.' It had been so much fun, to have an ally. That first day when they made such a mess.

'Of course he did.' He stands up, turns away. 'I hate to break this to you but we've been best mates since school.'

'So why was he helping me? He showed me where you lived. He bought the flour.'

'I have him to thank for that little stunt?' He moves to the chair in the corner. 'I suppose he was pissed off with me shagging his chubby girlfriend.'

'What?' None of this makes sense.

'Yes, not my finest hour.' He drinks from his glass, looks out of the window.

'So what has all of this got to do with me?' She can't piece it together.

'Nina, think about it.' He leans closer. 'You know he was at that party. Why is he so desperate to get me away from it? I suggested we round people up, try and figure out who attacked you. That's when he threatened me.

You might want to be more careful around him.' So now he's interested in her welfare.

'That doesn't make any sense.' Will's trying to shift the blame. Get himself off the hook. 'He's been helping me.'

'I don't understand how you don't know who it was.'

'I don't know. It was dark. I was wasted. Lying on my front.' Back over this again.

'Nothing about his hands, anything like that?'

'You're not exactly the person I want to be talking to about this.' She scoured her memory. What had the hands felt like? The image of it wouldn't stick. Had they been thick and forceful, like she thought they had? Or were they slim, like Rick's? Surely it couldn't have been him. She looks up at Will, searching for something to say.

'I think you need to have a little chat with Eric. And for god's sake take that shit off the Internet about me.' He stands up. It seems his little investigation is over.

'You're just upset you're not getting it with my mate anymore.' She was feeling good until he turned up.

'Hey.' His voice changes. 'She's the first girl I've cared about since-' a hand over his face '-let's just say it's been a while.' He actually sounds upset.

'You need to give me some time to think about this.' She thinks back to the bruises, the hair. Surely he wasn't capable of something like that.

'Well, don't take too long.' He looks around. 'Maybe you shouldn't be here when he gets back. Do you want a lift home?'

'I've got my car.' She stands up, alert. What if he's right? Rick's hands on her last night, what they did, how many times was it? Oh, God.

'Hurry up.' He's standing at the door.

'Right.' No time for that now. She goes back to the bedroom, takes the bottoms off, then remembers all she has is the silk dress. She puts them back on, picks her phone up and goes back outside.

'That's what you're wearing?'

'I want your number.' She's spent this long working things out, a bit more won't hurt.

'Excuse me?' Will looks horrified.

'Look, if you're right, I need someone to back me up here. He might be dangerous.' It doesn't seem possible. But, just in case.

'What the fuck have I got myself into?' He looks exasperated but takes her phone. 'Bloody Eric.'

'Is that what you call him?' She takes the phone back. 'It makes him sound geeky.'

'You've met him, right?' He laughs.

They walk down the hall, outside. She's full of new urgency, another thing to be solved.

'When are you going to talk to him?' He stops by the gate.

'I don't know.' She dithers on the pavement. 'Will you be there when I do it?'

'What's it going to be, an intervention?'

'I haven't had time to think about it. We need to get him to confess.' All the times she's been alone with him. His hands on her.

'Now it's *we*? Jesus.' He probably wishes he'd never come here.

'You want to impress Holly? She'd definitely want you to help me.'

'Just let me know what the plan is, Sherlock.' He shakes his head and turns away from her.

'Whatever.' She walks towards her car, head humming. Recycling each time she saw him, what he said. Had she missed something this huge, all along? She stops, remembers herself.

'Hey,' she calls to his retreating back.

'Yeah?' He turns.

'Thanks.' A little wave.

She gets into her car and sits, waiting for her breaths to slow down. Before she pulls away she looks back at the front window. Just an hour ago she'd been sat there, wallowing in her own happiness.

Eric

Eric stands outside the window of Ernest Jones. Not as tacky as H.Samuel, but he can't afford the fancy boutique place up on Osborne Road. He's stuck between a chunky square pendant on white gold (way over budget) and a teardrop one on yellow gold. Does she even like emeralds? It's the stone of Venus, that's why he got the bracelet for Bea.

His breath is making a pale circle on the glass. Unless it's too early for this. She's only spent one night at his. It feels more advanced than that, after everything they've been through. He wants to do something, show her how happy he is.

Scanning the rest of the display for something less romantic, all he can see is a crystal hedgehog or a porcelain book with "Congratulations" on it. Hardly the sentiment he was going for. But maybe this isn't the time for grand gestures. She's still vulnerable. Can't forget they were both in the police station yesterday.

There'll be other opportunities for things like this. He goes inside and gets the hedgehog, asking the woman to gift wrap it. He's leaning on the counter, justifying all the reasons why this is a better choice, when a thought jolts him. What would their anniversary be? He thinks back to the first time they met. How it's tainted with what she thinks of him. It's still hard, to frame it the way she does.

'What can I write on the card?' she smiles.

'Right.' Happy First Sleepover? On Our First Sexual Encounter? It's all too weird. 'It's OK, I'll do it.' He pays, takes the tiny bag and heads back towards the car. He could hide it in the bathroom cabinet for her to find. Put it on the pillow so she sees it when they go to bed tonight. It's going to be great, being able to do all these things again.

'Eric?' The voice is behind him. He turns, sees Bea standing there with her excessively tall boyfriend.

'Oh, hi.' He stops, lets her walk towards him.

'You look well.' Her head-tilt smile. 'This is Leo.'

'Nice to finally meet you.' Bloody hell, it's that kid from the year above them in school who had a moped when he was fifteen. Trust Bea.

'Likewise.' Eric shakes his hand.

'Someone's been buying jewellery.' Bea points at the bag. 'Something special for a lady?'

'It's a hedgehog.' Idiot. 'I mean, yes, it's a present for a girl. Well, my girlfriend. I think.' He never manages to sound cool.

'How did you meet?' Why is this guy so interested in his love life? Maybe Bea told him about his visit, all the stuff he did to try and make things up.

'Oh, you know, mutual friend.' That's one way of putting it.

'I'm so pleased.' Bea's grin is huge. 'Good for you.' What is he, useless?

'Well, I'd better be off.' He waves the bag. 'She's an engineer.' What does that have to do with anything? 'Need to be punctual.' He turns away before Bea finishes her smile.

There's laughter behind his back. He can ignore it.

He doesn't need her approval anymore.

On the way home he pictures a repeat of the scene in his head but with Nina there. She'd say smart things, make him look good. He's different when she's around. More sure of himself. He's humming when he pulls up outside the flat.

It's dark. Maybe she's asleep. She must be exhausted after the ordeal yesterday. He didn't even message her, ask if she needed anything. The element of surprise was too important.

Eric pulls the box out as he opens the door. If she's asleep he could leave it on the pillow next to her. Write a message on a post-it. Passing from one dark room to another, his mood sinks. She's gone. He slumps onto the sofa, dropping the bag on the table.

There's a message on his phone, must have been while he was driving.

So tired, need my bed. Talk tomorrow?

There isn't even a kiss at the end. So much for having a girlfriend. All the old doubts surface. Why did she come here yesterday? Maybe he was right, it was just a way of moving on, getting over the stuff she's been obsessed with all this time. So much for a cosy evening in together.

He zaps a Lasagne for one in the microwave and eats it in front of the TV. The hedgehog sits on the table, the flickering light bouncing off its crystal spikes.

Nina

Only a couple of days since she was here. Last time she was parked by the curb, waiting for Dev to arrive and staring at her phone. Now she's sat at one of the tables, worrying a custard tart into crumbs.

She checks her phone again. Another message from Holly.

We're right here, don't worry xxxx

Her and Will are secreted around the corner in his courtesy car. He's still grumbling about the damage, saying he shouldn't be expected to help until Nina's cleared his name. No doubt Holly is to thank for his presence. It's annoying that a male body feels safer. When Nina left, Holly was giggling and wearing sunglasses. It's an odd reversal. This time she's the one being watched.

She brought the bags with her. The photos are still on her phone. If only she could be absolutely sure, before she accused him. Despite Will's posturing, she can't line up his version of events with what happened, with who Rick is.

'Hey.' She looks up and there he is. All smiles. Before

she can say anything he leans over and kisses her. 'I was getting worried.' He looks tired in the half-light. It would have been warmer inside but she felt safer out here.

'We need to talk.' No point in a pre-amble. There's too much she wants to say.

'OK, but before that.' He reaches around, takes his backpack off. 'Here.' It's a green bag with Ernest Jones written on it.

'I don't know what to say.' She looks down at the bag, back to him.

'No, it's OK.' He picks it up again, pulls a box out. 'It's not a big thing. I just wanted to…I don't know.' He opens it. There's a crystal hedgehog nestled on a blue silk cushion. 'Say thank you. It's been so lovely.'

'That's so sweet.' It can't be him.

'If you need some space, I totally understand.' He leans in, eager. 'But I thought we could go away together in the Easter holidays. Maybe even do some jungle exploring?' He puts his hand on hers.

'I don't know.' His fingers are warm. 'Look.' She has to know. It might have been those fingerprints that were on her neck. 'I want to talk about what really happened that night. At the party.'

'What?' He moves his hand away.

'I know it wasn't Will.'

'Has he been bothering you? Look, you don't have to be afraid of him.'

'We spoke.' He half stands. 'No, it's fine. Just let me get this out.' He sits back down. She can feel the table vibrate. He's jiggling one of his legs. 'It just doesn't add up. What you said, what he said, and I just wanted to check.' She takes a big breath. 'Was it you? Did you go into that room and find me there?' She can't look at him. It sounds ridiculous, out loud.

'You have to be fucking kidding me.' His leg stops

shaking.

'Can I get you anything?' The waitress hovers at a distance, looking between them.

'I think we're fine.' Nina smiles, willing her to leave. 'I just wanted to ask.' She looks back at her hands. 'Will came to your house yesterday, and said all this stuff. He said you threatened him. I started thinking about how we met, and how it was weird that you were just outside my house, and how you didn't tell me how close you were to him, and you didn't tell me that you were at the party too.' She runs out of words. Shrugs. 'I just had to ask.'

'Well this is nice.' He leans back, shaking his head. 'All the support I've given you. I barely know you and I've basically been helping you with an illegal vendetta against my mate.' His hands. Gripping the bag.

'I'm sorry. I just need to get things straight. I'm confused.' She shakes her head.

'I trusted you. I believed you. But apparently that's not good enough.' His voice is getting louder.

'People will hear.' She hisses it across the table.

'Oh I'm sorry, am I embarrassing you?' He looks around, as if there's a huge audience, not the two awkward-looking women at the next table. 'This coming from the girl who invited me to sit outside someone's house and spy on them. Who smashed up a car.' He's still holding the bag. His hands start to squeeze, release.

'Why are you so angry?' That's what she felt on her neck. On her thighs.

'Who screwed up her job, who spread lies all over Twitter.' He's shaking with it. They squeeze. Again, again. Faster. 'Who got so pissed she couldn't remember who fucked her while she was lying in the spare room with her dress rucked up.'

He stops. His breath is coming in gasps. That anger, that fury. She's felt that before.

'Oh my god.' She brings her arms around herself, covers her mouth. 'It was you.'

'No, hang on.' He reaches for her hand. 'I'm sorry, I didn't mean to be like that.' His cheeks are flushed, his words stuttering.

'It was you.' He kissed her. Just a minute ago.

'Look, I just wasn't expecting this.' His breath comes out in a rush. 'You have a right to be suspicious. I lied. About the Will thing. Maybe I thought it was weird. But I should have told you. I'm sorry.'

'Eric,' she says. 'I know.' A clench in her stomach at what they did. What she did with him. Willingly.

'What are you talking about?' He puts the bag down. Lets go of her hand.

'No more lies.' It's weirdly calming. To know.

'OK, OK.' He raises his hands. This is it. 'I'll tell you what happened.' Now everything will come out. 'I did go in. It's not the first time I've had to check on a girl once Will's done with them.'

'Right.' She clasps her hands in her lap. Breathes.

'And you were there. A bit of a state.' Little smile. 'And yes, I admit. When you were with Will earlier I'd looked at you, thought you were pretty.'

'Is that your excuse?'

'I'm sorry, I know it might seem creepy. I swear I only did it because I liked you so much.' He's still smiling. Is there something wrong with him?

'That's not a reason to attack someone.' Surely he isn't that deluded.

'No, hang on.' He rubs his face, looks embarrassed. 'I looked in your bag. Took a picture of your driving licence.'

'That's how you knew where I live.' It's even worse than she thought.

'It was just that one time, I swear. I'd been thinking

313

about you, then when I saw what happened to your car.' He shrugs. 'I figured it must be fate.'

'So you raped me and then stalked me.' This guy is seriously fucked up.

'Why do you keep saying that?' He shakes his head. 'That's what I'm telling you. I went in your bag. Then I left.'

'No.' He looks so sincere. 'I know. It was you.' How can he still be lying about this?

'You know what? I've been thinking.' He fiddles with the hedgehog, turns it round. 'There's this thing I read. About how, when it's under stress, the brain can create memories that aren't real.'

'So I made it all up?' She's told him everything.

'I don't think it works like that. There are just things about what you said, they don't really fit.'

'What are you talking about?' He wants her to think she's crazy.

'I don't know.' He looks at her. Frowns. 'Someone tries to do stuff to you and you just lie there? That doesn't sound like you at all.'

'I was fucking terrified. I wake up and find hands on me. I didn't know what to do.' She'd thought it was weird too. That she hadn't moved. Is he right?

'And I'm pretty sure you would have known who did it. Something like that. Maybe it was just a really intense nightmare.' A little laugh.

'That's your theory?' He's trying to protect himself.

'Maybe.' So light. Like it's nothing.

She spills the contents of her bag onto the table. 'Look.' It's all there. The dress, the bag, the cocktail sticks encrusted with mouldy bits of dirt.

'What is this?' He pokes at the one with her dress in.

'Evidence.' If he's faced with what he did, maybe he'll own up. 'I wanted to go to the police but I thought it was

314

stupid. I'd kissed the guy who'd done it.' She flicks through her phone. 'Or so I thought.'

'You've already been to the police.' He doesn't even look worried.

'Here.' She turns her phone around, scrolls through the pictures of the bruises, the scratch, the mark on her neck she had to cover up with a scarf. 'This is what you did to me. Does that look like a bad dream?'

He scrolls through the images. 'Oh, Nina.' Surely now he will admit it. Now he can see what he did. 'I'm so sorry this happened to you.' He looks right at her. 'But it wasn't me.' He leans in. 'I made it better, didn't I? Look at what happened afterwards. You're OK now.'

'Oh yeah, everything's great.' She snatches the phone back and thinks about all the pieces of her life, scattered around her.

'You can get your job back, your arm's better, you've stopped the crazy online thing-'

'Tell me.' She sweeps the stuff back into the bag. 'Please.'

'Nina. Everything's going to be fine.' He reaches for her hand.

'You're sick.' She pulls away. To think she'd trusted him. What a coward.

'I'm not like that.' He holds out his hands. And he's right, in a way. He looks nothing like the huge, grumbling man that she's feared on dark nights all these years. But that doesn't change what he is.

'I wanted to kill you.' She says it quietly so the women won't hear. 'I'd have these fantasies where I'd hold a pillow over your face while you were sleeping. Or I'd push you off some really tall building.' Her hands start to shake. 'Or I'd get you in my car and just drive off a cliff.' She's crying, she can't help it. 'Because then at least it would all be over.'

'But Nina.' He's shaking his head. 'It was this tiny bit of your life. Why is it so important?'

'It's not my life anymore.' She shakes her head. 'I don't know whose it is but it's not mine.'

'You can choose. Make it different.'

'Can I?' A drink would be good. 'I thought that's what I was doing. But it was just-' she waves a hand. 'All about him. About you. What does that leave me with?' Some wine, no, whisky.

'It doesn't have to change who you are.'

'It already has.' She manages to stand. A hand in hers.

'You OK?' It's Holly.

'No.' She's so tired. It rises up and covers her. 'I want to go home.'

'We can do that.'

'Nina. Come on. This is crazy. I can't believe you really think-'

'Eric.' Nina spits the unfamiliar name out. He stops, looks at her. 'I can't believe I let you touch me.' The thought of it makes her skin flinch.

'I'm right here.' Holly squeezes her hand.

'The next time you hear from me, it will be the knock of the police on your door.' She steps between Holly and Will, lets herself look at him. 'I trusted you.' He was supposed to be one of the good ones.

'This is ridiculous.' Rick's voice is behind her, she's already turned away. 'You're going to throw away what we have for some delusion?' She keeps walking.

'Seriously, just leave it.' Will puts his arm around her and she leans against him. Nina lets herself be taken away, his protests fading as they walk around the corner.

Eric

He leans over the screen, scrolling through the adverts. There's a mug of tea on a coaster next to him. He can practically feel Mum fluttering in the kitchen.

'You sure you don't want anything else?' Her voice comes through the door. He told her she wasn't allowed to come into the room after all the fuss she made.

'Fine, thanks.' There's not as many as he would have hoped. That's the problem with looking for a job somewhere like Cornwall. Not many people leave. He imagines cobbled streets and screaming gulls. A proper seaside town, not like this place with its clunky docks. He could take up surfing.

Here's one that looks interesting. Bosvigo school in Truro. He Googles it to see where it is. Really far down. It would take hours to get there. He weighs it – the stretch of miles between here and there. It feels good. An escape is definitely what is needed. It says it's a city but less than 20,000 people live there. Ah well, it will be nice. Get to know your neighbours, that sort of thing. Imagine how pleased Olivia will be when he tells them he's leaving. She can have the stupid promotion.

'I just thought you might like a snack.' She plonks a plate of crackers on the table – cheese thins and the poppy seed ones he likes.

'Thanks,' he says. Maybe if he doesn't turn round she'll leave him alone.

'Did you want to talk about anything?' No such luck. 'It just seems sudden. With your new promotion, the girlfriend.' She leaves it hanging. He's not going to help her out with a response. 'I don't know. Was it something your dad said?'

There's another one in a place called Camborne. Doesn't look quite as nice in the image search. As long as he's got a car, he could always live somewhere nice and commute in. What's the rent like down there?

'What's all this about moving to the sticks then?' Lil walks in the door, dropping her bag on the floor. She's in full work getup – she looks so grown up.

'Mum.' He turns round.

'Well, you wouldn't talk to me.' She retreats to the kitchen. He hears the kettle snap on.

'Come on, big brother. What are you upsetting Mum for? She's been whispering down the phone to me from the toilet.'

'Give me a break. I can make a decision. I'm a grown up, remember?'

'Could have fooled me.' She sits down next to him, crams three cheese thins in her mouth. 'Since when do you like the seaside?'

'It's what everyone wants. Change of pace, lovely walks. You should see the geocaching network they've got down there.'

'Look.' She lowers her voice. 'Mum was really upset. Why would you just come here and drop this on her? Don't you have Wifi at home?'

'I thought it would be good to tell her.' He could have done this at home. But then he'd end up thinking about Nina, all the stuff she said to him. He's watched

The Girl with the Dragon Tattoo, The Kite Runner, even Thelma and Louise. Every time he imagined that it was him, doing those things. It didn't feel the same. He hadn't meant to hurt her, not in the way all those characters had.

'Honestly, almost gave me a heart attack, turning up here with all this talk of moving to the other side of the world.' She's brought a tray this time. A full pot of tea and biscuits. There's even pink wafers.

'It's not that far.' He smiles, shakes his head. Can always count on Mum to look after him.

'I reckon it's this woman.' Lil swirls a spoon in her tea. 'She's got some opportunity and all of a sudden Ricky's running off after her.'

'Don't be silly. I'm not seeing her anymore.' This is the kind of thing he needs to get away from.

'A dare from Will? Come on, it must be *something*.' Lil nudges him with her teaspoon.

'We're not mates anymore.' Why can't they leave him alone?

'Finally.' Lil smiles.

'Oh dear, you're not talking about all that fuss with the posters, are you?' Mum shakes her head. 'I saw Jocelyn at the Co-op the other day. She was ever so upset. Some crazy woman put up all these pictures of William on her street. With this horrible word on. Terrible, to do something like that.'

'What?' His fingers pause in their search.

'I don't get it – what horrible word?' Lil asks.

'You know, the R-word.' Mum dunks a biscuit in her tea. 'When you haven't been given permission.'

Lil screws her face up. 'You mean rape, Mum?'

'Lilly! You don't have to say it.' Half the digestive falls in the cup.

'When was this?' Lil asks.

'Oh, it was this thing, it's over now,' he says.

'You knew about this?' Lil sits forward.

'Well, it was just.' More explaining. 'We were at this party, and there was this girl who says she was attacked, and she reckoned Will did it. She didn't see his face, so she didn't know who it was. But, anyway, he wasn't even there. So it's all a big misunderstanding.' He shrugs, like it's nothing. 'She's fine now.'

'So you know the woman. And she was raped.'

'Lilly, you don't have to keep saying it.' Mum scoops some biscuit sludge out of her cup.

'Well, sort of. I mean, it was a while ago.' He's sick of talking about this.

'Is she OK? What happened?' Lil's right next to him.

'I don't know, do I?' He squirms in his seat. 'I didn't see anything.'

'You were there?' Lil asks.

'Is this some sort of investigation? Yes I was there.' Honestly. He just wants to forget all about it.

'Have they caught the guy that did it?' She won't let it go.

'I don't know. I mean, it's not really certain that's what it was. Apparently she was really drunk.'

'So?' Lil draws the word out.

'Well, you know.'

'No.' She pushes her chair back. 'I don't.'

'Apparently she was all over William that night,' Mum says, leaning in. She's got her gossip face on. 'Honestly, what young women get up to these days. He had to go to the police station and everything.'

'Mum. It doesn't matter what she was doing. If she didn't want to have sex with him then it's still rape.' She stops mid-tirade. Her hand goes to her mouth. 'Oh my god.' Lil stands up, clattering her mug onto the table. 'It's her, isn't it?' She clutches her hands together. 'You said you had this dirty night, that she was with Will before.'

'What on earth?' Mum looks between the two of them.

'Lilly. Stop.' He shouldn't have told her anything.

'You said it was silent.' She shakes her head, her face changing. 'What did you do?'

'No. You've got the wrong idea. It wasn't like that.' Defending himself, over and over.

'Why don't you tell me what happened.' Lil sits again. Watches him.

'I'm not discussing this with Mum here.' It's too much for one day.

'She was drunk, right? So she was asking for it.' She sounds disgusted.

'That wasn't why. I mean, yes she was, but it wasn't just that. I could tell, OK?' It was ridiculous. He didn't attack her or anything.

'Enthusiastic, ongoing, mutual consent.' Lil ticks them off on her fingers.

'What does that even mean? It's not like that and you know it.' It's sex, not a maths exam.

'What did you do?' Lil's voice goes quiet.

'I told you already. A one-night thing. It's not what she says it was.'

'Come on now, this is all getting out of hand. Jocelyn said it was all fine now. William's helping her find out who did it. Nina something. And he's got a lovely new girlfriend. A nurse.' Mum opens the teapot lid and swooshes the teabags. 'A top-up while it's fresh?'

'This is the woman you went to the museum with, isn't it?' Lil grips the table. 'So what, you attacked her and then asked her out?'

'It wasn't like that.' He closes the laptop. 'I just, I told you. It felt like we had this connection. So I wanted to see her again. We got chatting, one thing led to another.

321

You know how it is.'

'No, I don't.'

'Hang on, hang on. What are you talking about?'
Mum's still holding the teapot, hovering over his mug.

'Mum. It was Eric. He's the one who attacked the
woman. Nina.' Lil sounds so sure of herself.

'Don't be silly,' Mum says.

'Exactly. It wasn't like that.' He takes the pot from
her, pours another cup. 'I didn't attack her.'

'But you slept with her?' Lil won't let it go.

'Right.'

'You said she didn't see your face.' She's worse than
the police.

'Well, like I said, she was drunk.'

'And?'

'Well, she was lying there, and then stuff started
happening, and, you know.' It's embarrassing, with Mum
here.

'Was she even conscious?' She makes it sound
terrible.

'Come on. Of course,' he says. She's staring at him.
'I mean, it wasn't the way it usually happens. But it wasn't
an attack. She didn't scream or fight me off or anything.'

'Right. Because that's what makes it non-consensual.'
Lil puts a hand on his shoulder. 'Eric, Jesus.'

'It sounds like there's been a misunderstanding.'
Mum keeps looking between them, fiddling with her
sleeves. Lil needs to drop it.

'You have to go to the police.' She squats down to his
level. Like she's helping him.

'What are you talking about?' he says.

'You've committed a crime. You need to turn
yourself in.' So dramatic.

'I don't know about that, Lilly.' Mum looks so
worried.

'Did you not hear him, Mum?' She stands up. 'He forced himself on an unconscious woman. That is a crime.'

'Well when you put it like that.' She makes him sound terrible.

'What, it makes perfect sense?' She stands up. 'If you don't do it, I will.'

'Lilly, you will do nothing of the sort.' Mum stands up too. Finally, someone to stick up for him.

'Why not? I don't know why you're defending him,' Lil says.

'Because it was a mistake, yes?' Mum turns to him, eyes pleading.

'Of course it was.' She understands. He didn't mean to hurt anyone.

'I'm sure he's sorry. There must be something he can do.' She looks at Lil.

'I know, he can take her on a date. Oh wait, you already did that.' Lil picks her bag up. 'I've had enough of this. I'm going to the police.'

'I've already spoken to them.' That'll shut her up.

'What?' She looks suspicious.

'Last weekend. They asked me about what I did, what I saw. I was free to go.'

'You lied then.' She shakes her head.

'There isn't any evidence. You can't prove it was me.' He shouldn't have to defend himself to his own family.

'You filthy little shit.'

'Lilly!'

'I had no idea this is what you were like. You know what, I take it back.' She puts her coat on. 'You are *exactly* like Dad. A pathetic excuse for a human who blames all his failings on that swinging thing between your legs.'

'Sis, come on.' She can be so dramatic.

'You do the right thing or we're done.' She stands

there, full of it, looking between them. 'I mean it.'

'There's nothing to do. It's over.' He made sure of that yesterday, with Nina.

'Probably best to move on.' Mum sits down.

'That is pathetic.' Lil leans against the wall. 'I can't believe you, I just can't.'

'We don't have to make a big fuss.' She starts stirring the pot again.

'It is big, Mum. It's terrible. He's a criminal.' She jabs a finger at him. 'I don't want to see you, I don't want to know you. Fuck off to Cornwall and rot there for all I care.' She slams the door as she leaves, making the rippled glass shake.

'What a big fuss.' He shakes his head and turns back to Mum. 'Can I have more tea?'

'Of course.' She's looking at him funny. Is her hand shaking as she pours? 'I'll just get some more biscuits.' The plate is still half full.

He turns back, opens the computer. Lil always goes over the top. She'll come round.

There are four jobs he can probably apply for and there might be some later in the year. A fresh start, that's what he needs. They can come and visit him.

'Hey, mum. You reckon Lil would come surfing with me?' He smiles as she deposits more pink wafers onto the plate.

'I don't know, love. She was pretty upset.' She stands there, fiddling with the tissue in her sleeve. 'Look, I'm sorry to ask, but I've got my book club coming over. Could you come back later, or tomorrow?'

'Oh. Sure.' She's never asked him to leave before. He snaps the laptop shut, puts it in the case. 'Sorry.' She doesn't say anything the whole time he puts his coat on, picks his stuff up.

On the way out he stops, gives her a hug.

'We're OK, right?' he asks into her shoulder.

'Fine. Everything's fine.' She pats his shoulder. As he walks to the car she shuts the door before he can turn and wave.

On the way back to his he turns the radio up loud. Drowns out the traffic, Lil's face, his thoughts. The way Nina looked at him at the cafe. Maybe he'd made a mistake, but he didn't deserve to go to prison for it. He did his best to make up for upsetting her, there's no need to drag it out even more.

Maybe this is what Dad felt like. A big, tangled wreck so he ran off to start something new. Well, he's not the only one that can do that. He rolls down the window and lets the salty air through as he drives across the seafront. It's tainted with the petrol from the docks, the fumes from the traffic. It's all tainted. Always has been.

Will, Dad, Bea, Nina, this place. No wonder he'd ended up in this mess. Once he's moved it will all be gone. He can find people that actually appreciate him. See him for who he really is.

Nina

The train station is draughty. Chewing-gum circles on the floor like disappointed confetti as she walks to the platform. Another fourteen minutes until it gets in. Her rucksack is stuffed with snacks, magazines, her Kindle with three new downloaded books. She probably won't look at any of it.

The last few weeks have been foggy. Food has been eaten – there have been empty plates and Holly's worried face peering over it. Sleep has been had – her bed is rumpled in the morning. It's been detached, her body performing motions without registering with her senses, her brain.

PTSD, the counsellor said. Everything she's managed to suppress with her obsessive behaviour. It's exhausting. As if this is only the start of a recovery, not the end. Her wide-open silences and tilted gaze have released it all from her like vomit. Everything she did. Not a flicker of judgement, of shock, on her face. Just that nod-nodding head.

But now what? The confessions have been parcelled up, blame apportioned. It should feel like closure.

As the train pulls in she sees him. Standing there, nonchalant. Waiting for her. He turns, hand lifting towards the back of his head. He's too far away to tell if it's a smile on his face, or something else. He starts walking towards her.

She holds her ground, starts doing the breathing exercises her counsellor recommended for when she starts feeling anxious. He's almost at the Pumpkin Cafe when she realises – it's not him. Just another indeterminate man with the same scruffy haircut.

The train's coming. She lets the sound of it cover up the moan she makes to release her breath. It seems impossible now. That he was sat opposite her. That they talked. That she let him sit there and whine on about his side of it without punching him in the face. It had all felt so confusing, so new. The kind man who had helped her and the sly pervert who'd pinned her down and fucked her without her consent. How could they possibly be the same person?

She climbs on the train, walks down the carriage, her bag catching on the edges of seats. They're all full. Finally there's an empty pair. It's near the toilet and facing backwards, but being alone is more important. Her bag goes on the seat next to her.

More messages from Holly. At least she's keeping the news of her and Will to a minimum. It's too close, a skin-width away from him, what happened, where they were. The only thing he's been able to find out is that he got some job down in Cornwall. Shared something on Twitter about sea fishing and pasties. So it's impossible to bump into him. She still sees him everywhere.

And one from Mum. Laura's going to come over tomorrow. By herself, apparently. That'll be the first time she hasn't had Simeone and the kids in tow for years. It's enough of an event for Nina to visit at all. Hopefully, they won't make too much of a fuss.

Another recommendation from the counsellor.

Reconnecting with family, restoring bonds, all that. Remind herself of all the years she's lived without this shadow over her.

The train leaves. Outside the window it blurs from grey to green, the horizon stretching out as they get to the Downs. It's there, somewhere. A box with a cowboy scarf hiding in it. Her message, scribbled in pencil. She's started to think of herself like this more. Pieces of her, scattered. It makes her wonder what's left of the skin she sits in.

Her phone signal drifts in and out as she moves up the country. An hour outside Leeds she gets a message from Holly. It takes her a good five minutes to scroll through it all. Her hands tighten over the phone as she reads.

His sister. Turned up at Will's house, asking to talk to him. Told him that Eric had confessed, told her everything. That she'd be happy to go to the police, support a conviction. Holly follows it with all these exclamation marks, joyous smileys.

She turns the phone off. Leans her head against the cold glass. She wasn't going crazy. It *was* him. The way he'd looked at her in the cafe, as if it were her who had the problem. That she was ridiculous to think he was capable of something like that. She closes her eyes. The movement of the train lulls her to sleep.

'Are you sure about this?' Dev stands on the pier, looking ridiculous in a high-vis lifejacket.

'Absolutely.' There's no way she's backing out now.

'Polar bears aren't that cute.' Holly pulls the strings on her hoodie so they tighten around her face.

'How far do you think I'm going?' The wind tugs at Nina's clothes. 'It's just to test it out.'

'Doesn't look very sturdy to me. You designed this, right?' Will looks the most out of place. He's wearing a leather jacket.

'I wouldn't criticise the design, mate.' Dev steadies himself, holding onto the rail as he climbs onto the boat. Will's got a point. It does look small now it's on the sea.

'Have fun.' Holly gives her a brief hug, then retreats to use Will as a windshield. She's never been one for cold weather.

'All aboard.' Dev reaches out a hand as Nina wobbles down the plank. There must be a more modern system for bridging the gap.

'Good morning.' The way the captain stands makes it look like the boat isn't even moving. 'We're in for a bumpy ride this morning so I need you to listen very carefully to the safety briefing.'

'Right.' She holds onto the side as he talks through ropes, lifejackets, flotation devices. Hopefully, none of this will be needed.

'So, let's get going.' He sways away from them to the cockpit, full of an array of buttons and switches.

'Are you telling me you know how all of that works?' she asks Dev.

'At least 90%.' He smiles. 'So, how's it going? Haven't seen you in the office for a while.'

'Hey, if trauma means you get to work from home all the time, it's worth it.' The anxiety kicks in too much in big groups of people.

'But you don't get to come to meetings. I'm sure Clive misses you.'

'I see more of that man's nostrils than I'm happy about.' He always angled his screen so she was looking up at him.

'Seriously, though. You still going to that support group?'

329

'Yeah, it's OK.' Sometimes she feels like she shouldn't be there, the stuff the other women have come out with. But just being able to say it, over and over again. Get angry, without needing to feel shame. It's definitely helping. Last week she went to Ikea and bought new pillows.

'Good for you.' Dev's been hovering around her whenever she goes into work. Nina's been to his house to help him and Amy perfect their sushi skills a couple of times.

'It's a start.' The week with Mum, the appeals procedure for her job. Lilly has asked a few times but she can't bring herself to go down that road. They would still stir up her past, pick apart who she was. There's been enough exposure for now.

'You're a tough one.' He turns his face away from her, out to the sea. They're almost at the mouth of the harbour. It's bumpy enough now, what will it be like out there?

'Not feeling it right now.' Her stomach is churning. She should have taken the anti-sickness pills. At the time it had felt like cheating, not experiencing it properly.

They move out into the open water and it starts rocking. Spray lashes her face as they bounce over the water. Her eyes sting. She grabs onto the side of the boat and tries to relax, let her legs shift with the motion. At a wave from the captain they move even faster, the wind stretching her mouth wide, pulling at the corners.

He said they'd have to drive roughly, really test it out. She raises a hand to her eyes, looks it over. Teeming with sensors, instruments, the more expensive couplings secure against the wind.

'I made that.' She speaks it into the wind and the words are dashed away. The boat turns and she sees the wide expanse of the sea. So much blue. She could point

330

this boat in one direction for weeks and not see another soul. A gull cries overhead and she looks up, sees wings folding in the sky. It brings something from her – a laugh. It mingles with the creature above her and they move, stuck between sky and sea, out into the wide-open space.

<u>Acknowledgements</u>

Huge thanks to all at SRL Publishing, especially Stuart, for believing in this book and seeing its potential. I'm honoured to be a part of their Breaking The Silence *collection, featuring books that speak out about important issues and amplifying voices we don't hear enough from. I hope this book will go some way to making people feel seen and in opening up important conversations about rape and sexual assault. Thanks also to Eli Allison for her time and dedication in designing a striking cover.*

This book started out as the main submission for my Masters in Creative Writing at City University. Thanks to all the lecturers for their help and support, to Lucy Caldwell, Clare Allan, and particularly Jonathan Myerson for his personal feedback and guidance on writing the novel. Thanks to Kerry Hudson for coming to a seminar and being such a visible and outspoken working-class writer. You made me feel like I could do it, too.

Thanks to all the other students on my course who gave me feedback and advice on early drafts during workshops, and particularly Van and Rebecca for continuing to believe in the possibility of this novel many years later!

This book wouldn't exist without extensive research into issues of sexual assault, it's impact, and aftermath. Thanks to all survivors who have shared their experiences. Also, thanks to Jill Meagher's husband, Tom, for sharing his story about the tragic death of his wife, which was the inspiration behind this book. As he said then, most rapists are not monsters hiding in the bushes, which is where the character of Eric began.

I was almost at the point of giving up on this book when I submitted it into the Spread The Word/Bookouture Prize in 2019. I was thrilled to receive professional editing feedback as one of six winners, and it is thanks to those lovely comments from Emily Gowers that I felt newly confident in this book to be able to start yet another round of submissions.

Along the way, many friends have helped me out either in the form of reading the book, listening to me rant about my characters, or just providing wine and conversation when I was feeling frustrated by the whole process. Special thanks to Jo for sharing the angst of trying to be creative when dealing with a small child, to Eve for always being strong and positive, and to Jenny for generally being fabulous.

Coming from a working-class background and a single-parent family, writing as a career wasn't exactly something I felt was possible. Thanks to my mum for supporting me with my writing all these years, even though it wasn't until I was in my thirties that I started to take myself seriously as a writer. Thanks to Emma and Heather, my lovely sisters, for being supportive and brilliant and always being there for me.

Thanks to my daughter, for being hilarious and loving, even if writing with no sleep has proved very tricky over the last few years. And to Jo, who listened to all of my crazy plot inventions (remember Anna?) and is always a loving and supportive presence.

And finally, thanks to you, lovely reader, for choosing to spend your time with my words. It means a lot. If you'd like to find out more about me and my work, go to _sarahtinsley.com_ or find me @sarahtinsleyuk on Twitter and Instagram.

CPSIA information can be obtained
at www.ICGtesting.com
Printed in the USA
LVHW041554281221
707360LV00001B/1

9 781838 279875